From tʰ

A NEW WORLD
A COLLECTIVE NOVEL BY ARVIN LOUDERMILK

A voyage ends.
An ecosystem threatens.
A foundation is struck.

A NEW WORLD

First published February 2013
Revised February 2016

Collective is the intellectual property of The Concentrium
Phoenix, Arizona USA
www.theconcentrium.com

ISBN: 978-1-943643-10-3
Library of Congress Control Number: 2012952603

Cover by Mike Iverson

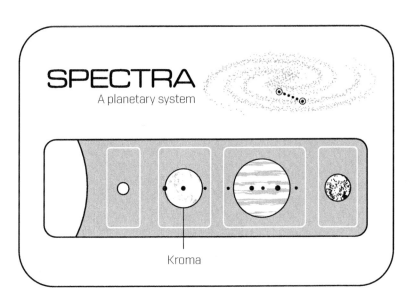

SPECTRA

A planetary system

Kroma

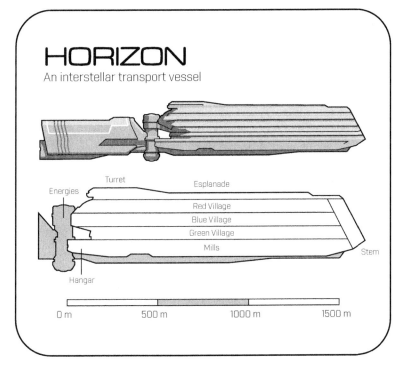

HORIZON

An interstellar transport vessel

Turret
Esplanade
Energies
Red Village
Blue Village
Green Village
Mills
Hangar
Stem

0 m   500 m   1000 m   1500 m

FOR MARY MARTINI

my mother

BEFORE

The observation screen flashed blue and white before filling itself with the blackness of open space. Dimitri Kucherov and Misha Stennikov were standing shoulder to shoulder in front of the ceiling-high image port when a female voice came online and announced the distance traveled—14.7 billion kilometers.

Dimitri shifted his weight from one leg to the other and inadvertently jabbed his elbow into Misha's arm. The embarrassed pilot took a step to the side and gave the Founder more room. Dimitri was too preoccupied to notice the gesture. The display screen held his full attention.

Minutes passed and stars glistened.

Dimitri Ivanovich Kucherov—the man who had changed the world. He was taller than most people expected, and thinner. The color of his well-tanned skin was a near match for his sienna-print suit. Atop his angular head, his hair hung thick and brown, and perfectly groomed—the gray flecks at his temples the only sign of approaching middle age.

As darkly complected as Dimitri was, Misha stood as his pasty opposite. His ligature implants—visible from any part of his body his jumpsuit did not cover—blinked in a cavalcade of colors, linking him to the innards of the ship like the living, breathing control system that he was.

"No, no. This won't do." Dimitri flipped his hand at the screen as if he were dismissing the entire universe. "Is it possible to switch to a reverse view?"

"If that's what you prefer, sir. The only reason the display is pointed forward is due to your edict that none of us should ever look back. It's what you've always spoken of, from the very earliest days. 'Looking back is wasteful.' Those are words you're famous for. And I for one have always understood the quote, and agree with its premise."

"Well, just this once, how about we ignore my little pearls of wisdom? We're about to leave the solar system. If there was ever a time to look back, this would be it." He elbowed Misha intentionally this time. "And don't tell me you don't care or think about such things. This is a monumental moment, Mr. Stennikov. This could be the last time we're able to see it with our own eyes."

Misha's cranial implants lit up, a blazing ruby red. The next instant, a dimensional representation of the planet Earth materialized inside the screen, its man-made rings ever spinning in the distance.

Dimitri stared at the blue-green wonder, muttering over and over, "My, my. My, my."

"Is there anything else I can do for you, sir?" Misha said as his implants transitioned back to an inactive gray.

"Not at the moment, no. Although I do ask that you relax. I insist upon that. I want everyone aboard to take a deep breath, and no matter what else—*find-a-way-to-relax*. Yes, our birthplace is fading into the distance. And yes, the unknown is out there beckoning. But none of that matters, not a single bit of it."

As if reminded of something, Dimitri stopped there and turned.

"Listen to me ramble on. You were correct to quote me, Mr. Stennikov. Looking back is anathema, the ultimate distraction. What we are embarking upon here will require fortitude of the highest order. The past is irrelevant. The distance forward, out of our control. From now on out, all we can realistically do is live our lives—which I remind you, is precisely what we would've been doing on Earth. And now, as we inch our way across the galaxy, it's what we have to do here. Perspective is paramount. A purposeful existence, that's what truly lies ahead."

Seventy-Eight Years Later

1

Mary Muran returned to her seat.

The other five individuals on the circular couch sipped at their glasses of wine. A miniature statue of the expedition's ship, the interstellar transport *Horizon*—a token offering presented at the beginning of Mary's remarks—was positioned at an angle on the coffee table that rested between them.

Mary whispered to her husband Camden, asking how she'd done. Camden shrugged. Mary glared back at him, and then looked away. Camden responded in kind and caught a disapproving scowl from his father, Randall Muran. Dana Muran, Camden's mother, threw a tepid slap at Randall's forearm. Mary's own father, a now elderly Dimitri Kucherov, was oblivious to all the back and forth, and on the verge of a nap. A dozen more beats of sustained silence ticked by before Kimberly Akana, the last of the group, blew out a frustrated sigh and lifted herself off the couch.

"Yuck, yuck," she said. "*Yuck, yuck.*"

Dimitri, Mary, and everyone else snapped to attention.

"What's wrong?" Randall asked Kimberly. "Is it the arthritis again?"

"No, it is *not* the arthritis again."

"Then what the devil is your problem?"

Kimberly swiveled around and bore down on the man. "What do you *think* my problem is?"

With that, she took off, limping around the backside of the couch, her fingers tracing indifferently across the subtle blue stitch work.

"It's the end of the line and none of this feels like it's really happening. We've been traveling for so long, training for even longer. How does one react to the end of a lifetime of waiting?"

"You don't," Dimitri said. "The inevitable has been accomplished. We're on the precipice of arrival. The three of us, we were lucky enough to have survived. In the end, that's all we've done. We did nothing more than survive."

Hearing this, Mary shook her head. "You know what, Dad—that might actually be the most ridiculous thing you have ever said."

"I speak the truth, young lady. And speaking the truth can never be ridiculous." Dimitri's voice was rumbling from the back of his throat. "When this expedition left Earth—and only Kimmie and Randall have the *right* to contradict me—we understood that we would be taking a massively long voyage to colonize another world. But none of us ever thought we'd get to see this place for ourselves. We hoped to survive, of course. But anyone with a lick of sense knew our chances would be slim. We left Earth assuming it would be our children who would finish this quest for us. The true discovery, and the subsequent colonization, that would be on the backs of the young, while we would serve our purpose as genetic conduits, nudging humanity forward for the chance at a better life. So, as I said, *all* we did was survive."

Camden crossed and uncrossed his legs. "Well, I for one am proud to be doing the finishing now that we have arrived. There's no two ways about that."

"We haven't arrived anywhere. Not yet." Randall held his empty wine glass out as he reached for the open bottle on the table. When his arms wouldn't extend far enough, he dropped back into the couch cushions.

"This party tonight," he huffed. "It's just pomp and nonsense for the masses, a senseless distraction. That's all any of these celebrations have been. They've gotten everyone so worked up and sentimental."

"Well, I'm sorry if this upsets you," Camden said. "But I'm feeling every emotion in the book right now—and I don't care if that makes me sentimental."

Randall rechecked his glass. It was still empty. "Bully for you. Cling to that sentimentality why don't you."

Kimberly was working on her fifth lap around the couch as she circled past Randall and grazed his shoulder. "Lighten up, for goodness' sake. Allow the boy to express himself. We've shot past Tono. We're days away from Verdan. Now is the perfect time to allow the children to show some pride."

"Sorry, but I don't think that it is," Randall said. "This is *our* moment, dammit. After all these years on this ship, this is the survivors' moment to show some pride."

"But it's not," Dimitri said. "The moment is theirs, certainly more than it was ever meant to be ours. The Camdens and the Marys of the world are here to finish the voyage for those of us who are too ancient to conquer any new frontier, let alone a whole new planet."

Mary groaned. "You three. I am getting *so* annoyed by all this negativity. You have done so much more than survive. And I don't care if you feel grumpy or melancholy about that—or even about getting older. Three of the original Trustees are here to see us reach Verdan. That accomplishment sends chills up my spine. My father and his friends did the bravest thing any human beings have ever attempted—and that's an indisputable fact. I'm as proud as Camden. Prouder even."

With that, the tension in the room seemed to lift.

Randall tilted his glass at Mary. "Now there—that's what she should have said in her toast. That last bit was heartfelt and unforced."

"She's always been better off the cuff," Kimberly said.

Dimitri nodded. "She's never been comfortable with formality. I've been working with her on it for years, but she never seems to improve."

Mary offered up no rebuttal, and before too long the critiquing tapered off.

"Alrighty then." Randall set down his glass. "I believe we all have a faux celebration to attend."

"And we're already late," Mary said.

"Then let's get our butts in gear and pretend to celebrate."

Randall struggled to extricate himself from the couch. Dana flashed Mary a knowing smirk and helped him up. Kimberly capped off her final lap around the couch and connected up with the departing Murans, stepping between them as they plodded toward the door.

Mary stared silently at Camden until he got the hint and bounded after his parents.

Dimitri leaned toward Mary, who was half a cushion away.

"Were you able to have a conversation with your brother?"

"I was. I told him the original Trustees were having a get-together—you, Kimberly, and Randall. I stressed the fact that all three of you wanted him to stop by."

"And still he refused?"

"You didn't actually think he'd come, did you? He hasn't participated in anything family related since last year. My asking wasn't going to change his mind."

"I understand," Dimitri said. "I appreciate the attempt."

"He did say he was coming to the celebration on the Esplanade." Mary widened her eyes. "There's that at least."

Dimitri responded by pointing down at a scuff on her shoe. Mary ignored the unsightly blemish and checked the time on the wall clock instead. The numbers read: 6:22. Mary stood up and offered her hands to her hundred-and-twenty-year-old father. Dimitri normally resisted offers of physical assistance, but Mary stood in front of him such insistence, such an unwillingness to relent.

"Don't give me that look," she said. "It's too long of a walk. Whether you like it or not, you need to get in your chair."

"Fine," Dimitri said as he took hold of her hands. "As long as the corridors remain clear, I'm at your mercy."

2

"Your presence has been requested onstage. This is not optional, it's an order, one which comes straight from the Directorate."

Florin Holt pulled at Jason Epelle's shirtsleeve for the second time in less than a minute. This most recent flare-up in their ongoing battle of wills was occurring atop a small stone bridge, smack dab in the center of the Esplanade, the *Horizon*'s multi-deck Earth preserve. Fellow partygoers were paying little attention to the standoff and kept brushing past the scene in a herd-like procession.

Florin restated her demands. Jason rolled his eyes and dove right back in to the conversation he'd been domineering with his brother-in-law, the ever-amiable Mikhail Kucherov.

With a grin, Florin tugged again at Jason's billowing sleeve.

"Stop that," he said, his tone sharp. "I'm on my way. I've told you that a bunch of times already."

"Yet, here you are, still standing in place like a lummox."

Jason motioned back at her with a jab of his thumb. "She insults me?"

"With somewhat good reason," Mikhail said.

Florin pulled his sleeve for a fourth, fifth, and sixth time—in quick succession. Jason's shoulders hunched up and he spun backward in an exaggerated snit.

"Look, I don't need a pain-in-the-butt lackey to—"

His thought process halted in mid-insult. He gazed down at the pair of pale legs curving out of Florin's thigh-cut silk shorts.

"My goodness," Jason muttered. "You really should have approached from the front. I'd have been a *lot* more reasonable if I'd seen those beautiful things coming my way. Wow and *wow*. Keep dressing like this, and I'll follow you anywhere you want to go. You're a shapely young woman, that's something I didn't know about you. You wear long pants a lot. It's been hard to get a sense of those legs."

Florin propped her hands on her hips as Jason continued to leer.

"Did you actually think inappropriate compliments would distract me?"

He chuckled. "It was worth a try. You never know."

"Jay, just go where they need you to go," Mikhail said before peering out across the clearing on the far side of the bridge. Swathes of attendees were beginning to mingle toward a growing gathering at the front of the stage. No announcement had been made yet, but anyone who had been to one of these events before could tell, the evening's presentations were about to begin.

"Personally," Florin said to Jason, "I could care less if you ever do what you're supposed to do. But the Directorate, for some purpose that's never really been reasonably explained to me, seems to require your presence."

Jason curtsied. "I'm indispensable."

Before he could get himself upright again, Florin flailed out with a lightning strike, thumping both of her hands into the center of his chest, a move that sent the man teetering backwards. Jason had to snag the arm of a passerby to keep himself from toppling all the way over. Florin refused to let up, landing another, less powerful shove.

"Move it," she barked as Jason disappeared down the slope of the bridge.

Mikhail smiled at Florin. "You do look especially nice today." He smiled again and strolled away in the opposite direction.

Florin stood there stupefied. "Thanks," she said once he'd gotten too far away for her acknowledgment to be heard. She glanced down at her stylish new outfit and smoothed an upturned hem. Behind her, a loud and familiar voice exploded above the party chatter.

"*Florin!* I *need* you, Florin."

Without delay, she galloped off to make her escape. At the foot of the bridge, her forward progress became impeded by the portly frame of a bearded senior citizen chatting among a throng of five toddlers. The call for her attention grew louder.

"Florin…*wait!*"

The voice was now close by, maybe just a meter or two behind her. Florin grimaced with defeat and trailed back up the bridge. Bodies parted and she soon found herself chest to chest with Vladimir Rossonov. The handsome young man's mouth was hanging open, ready to bellow out her name again and again.

"You got me," Florin said. "Now, what's so damn important?"

"Nothing's important. I just wanted to say hello."

"Vlad, I'm working. You know that I'm working."

Vladimir whirled around like a pinwheel, gesturing out at the thousand or more citizens milling about the park. "This is a party…a celebration. This is no time for work."

"Actually, it's the exact time for work—*my* work. Can you even comprehend how many people we've jammed inside here? Somebody has to manage this monstrosity."

Vladimir nodded. "I get you. And you're doing a superb job."

Florin kicked her head back and stared up at the artificial sky. "Frankly, I have *way* too many things going on right now. I don't have time for your nonsense."

Her head dropped back down as fast as it had risen and she walked away.

Vladimir charged after her. "Before you go, did you think any more about my big question?" He reached downward, struggling to take hold of her swaying hand.

"I've already told you no," she said.

"But you've had some time to think about it since then."

"You don't listen to me at all, do you?"

Vladimir got in front of her and dropped to one knee. "I love you and I want to marry you. A question like that demands a more considered answer."

"You are such an annoying goof." Florin gave him a shove and left with even more urgency this time. "You cannot do this to me while I'm working."

"One last thing," Vlad said. "Are we still getting together with everyone tomorrow?"

Florin whipped back around. "Yes. I never said that we weren't. Now please, leave me alone. Go find someone else to humiliate."

3

Walter Stoddard planted his boot on the bottom step of the stairwell as Trustee Laken Merriweather delivered another one of her rousing speeches from the Esplanade podium.

Behind Walter, shifting in and out of the dark, Rebecca Patterson paced in an imprecise rectangular pattern. The thick-bodied brunette had been shuddering and grumbling after every politically tinged utterance from the stage. The situation finally reached its boiling point when Laken made her annual call for a holiday celebrating the birthday of Dimitri Kucherov. Rebecca heard this and let loose with a blood-piercing shriek. Walter turned and shushed her.

"I have every right to express my opinion," Rebecca said.

"Not backstage you don't. People can hear you."

"I don't care if people can hear me. And you shouldn't care either."

"But I do. So I beg of you, try being polite for once."

"You just go along to get along, don't you? I find this new you so disheartening sometimes."

Walter shut his eyes. "Go ahead and say it. Whatever it is that's on your mind. Just say it."

"Don't mind if I do." Rebecca's voice deepened. "You should be speaking last, not *him*. That man should never speak before you. Not ever. It's undemocratic."

Walter ground his heel on the edge of the step. "And yet, for longer than either of us have been alive, this voyage has been 'that man's' life's work. Not mine. His. That means Dimitri speaks whenever he wants to speak."

"But you're Magistrate now." Rebecca crept over to the spot where Walter was standing and flicked the back of his salt and pepper hairline. "Who's really in charge around here, you or him?"

"In this context, does it really matter? What you're fussing about here is an issue of protocol. Founder of the Collective trumps everything else, including the office of Magistrate, understand?"

"I don't like Dimitri," Rebecca said.

"That fact has been well established."

"He only cares about himself."

"A point you've made on a near constant basis. Usually in public, and always as loud as humanly possible."

"You used to like it when I got loud."

Walter sighed at that and pushed away from the staircase. To dodge his sudden movement, Rebecca jumped to her left.

"I'm distracting you," she said before scurrying after him and grabbing ahold of the back of his shirt. When he stopped, they both stopped.

"Why would you just drop by like this?" Walter said. "I mean, it's always good to see you, Becca, but the timing here is strange."

Rebecca fiddled with the curl of her hair. "What can I say? I've been thinking a lot about the old days. The bad days now, I suppose. The idea of you celebrating a day like today, even practically headlining the day, it's more than a little ironic."

"You're not wrong about that," Walter said. "But you not protesting a day like today is not exactly devoid of irony either."

"Nah, all that's just not in me anymore. Those old fights are dead. I lost. You lost as well, and then won. *Really* won."

The crowd on the other side of the wall erupted in laughter over a snide reference Laken had just made about her venerated, but combative ex-husband, Trustee Jacob Holt.

"The old days have been on my mind as well," Walter said. "I think all either of us ever wanted was a little control over our lives. In the next few days, everyone on this ship will finally be given that opportunity, someplace beyond these manufactured walls and corridors. We're going to breathe fresh air. We're going to suffer the elements. We're going to build gorgeous cities and luxurious homes. The human race is planting roots on a brand new world. Now that's what I call success. That's what I call control."

Rebecca shook her finger at him. "Listen to you. Was that an excerpt from your speech?"

"Parts of it. So what?"

"For the record, the 'manufactured walls' bit gave you away. No one talks like that, not in real life." She wagged her finger a second time. "You cannot fool me."

Walter hiked up his shoulders. "Well, I hate to be rude, but Allison is going to be here any minute."

"Yikes, the wife and the first love—converging in the dark. That might prove awkward."

"Don't you have a husband and a newborn you can lecture and harangue?"

"The little one spits up when I lecture."

Onstage, Laken was wrapping up her remarks.

"Sorry, but you really should go," Walter said. "I have a speech to deliver. And Allison…you know."

"Of course." Rebecca made a move for the exit. "But just so you've been forewarned. I intend to cheer for you rather loudly. When everyone else is quiet, that'll be me you hear screeching like a madwoman."

"Hey, I'll take whatever adulation I can get. Knock yourself out."

The doorway opened for Rebecca. Light from the corridor poured backstage.

"I'm not kidding. I'm going to make a total spectacle of myself. And I'd better not catch you blushing either."

"That won't be a problem. I never blush."

"Oh, Walter. You're blushing right now."

BEFORE

Mikhail took a swipe at his eyes as he ducked back inside the hospital room. His teenage sister Mary was sitting slumped on the couch, an arm's reach away from their terminally ill mother. The patient, Maria Alvarez-Kucherov, was laid out on a gellular bed, unconscious for weeks, her lower body draped by a light green sheet. The etched wall behind her streamed with medical data, every piece of which keeping close check on Maria's fast-fading health.

"Who were you just talking to out there?" Mary asked.

Mikhail crossed over to his mother's bed. "Jocelyn."

"Are you guys boyfriend and girlfriend now, or what?" Mary looked right at him and grinned.

"Don't start in, okay? You know she's just my friend, and *only* my friend. The same way she's your friend."

Mikhail took another swipe at his eyes, which had become deeply reddened.

"You're upset," Mary said. "What exactly did Jocelyn say to you?"

"Nothing. She just wanted to make sure we were both okay. She wanted us to know that she cared about us, and would be there for us if we needed her."

"And that's making you cry?"

"It's making me feel, I guess. Lately, everything's been making me feel. And yet, for some stupid reason I seem to feel less in this room. It makes no sense. This is the last place I want to be. The last place ever."

Mary's response to that was to draw her legs all the way onto the couch.

"Have we heard any word from Dad?" Mikhail asked.

"Not since last night. He told me he had a short meeting this morning. But he promised he would be here as soon as it was over."

Mikhail glanced over at the information displays coursing above the bed. "It's now eighteen past noon."

"I know what time it is."

"He does realize she could die today, doesn't he? All the doctors say it's coming soon. Her body isn't going to last much longer."

"He knows. He has to know."

"Knowing is one thing. Acting like a human being is another."

Mary swung her feet back onto the floor and rose off the couch. "You're right. I'll go get him. You're upset, and he should be here, too."

Mikhail swung around the front of the bed and cut Mary off.

"Don't. It's fine if it's just us. It's always been just Mom and us. If he shows up on his own, then good. If he doesn't, what makes this different than any other day?"

"Momma makes it different," Mary said. "She's dying. That makes to-day crazy different."

"Yeah, but Mom's going whether he's here or not."

Mikhail took Mary by the hand and led her over to Maria. Taking turns, they caressed her long black hair. Her chest began to heave as her breath became unmistakably shallow.

Eight Years Later

4

Mary entered the monochromatic medical facility and found Mikhail sprawled out on the floor, his legs kicked out at the end of two room-long rows of mirroring stasis blocks.

Mary braced herself in the doorway for several seconds before pushing off and heading down the central walkway. Mikhail ignored or didn't notice his sister's intrusion. His gaze remained laser-locked on one of the dozens of ceramic chambers keeping various patients, for their various reasons, in deep cellular stasis.

The clicking of Mary's shoes filled the icy room with noise.

Mikhail reached out and touched the chamber in front of him, the one containing his wife and unborn child. Jocelyn Kucherov's distended belly—showing all nine months of fetal development—pressed flush against the transparent hatch of the hermetically sealed repository.

"Good morning," Mary said upon final approach.

Mikhail wrenched his hand away from the chamber, but gave no reply. That did not stop Mary.

"If there's a silver lining in this rift between you and father, at least I always know where I can find you. It may be a small thing, but I do feel better knowing where you are."

"There are no silver linings," Mikhail said. "Not with this. Never with this."

"Come on, must you always be so drab."

"And what else should I be? Do you actually think there's something good that can come out of this situation? Nothing is good with this situation. And I won't listen to your endless arguments to the contrary."

Mary bent down and embraced him from behind. Mikhail remained deathly still.

"Do me a favor…would you *please* stop biting my head off every time we see one another? It's a waste of energy, both yours and mine. There are only a few more days to go and Jocelyn will be woken back up. Then your child will be in your arms and maybe all this anger can finally be sated."

"It won't be. This anger is never going away."

Mary leaned back against a neighboring chamber. "Do you have any idea how worrisome your behavior has become? I know you act normal and in control in public, but whenever it's just you and me, all you do is fume and rage. You cannot allow a child to come into this world and experience the hatred you're projecting right now."

"I don't know what to tell you, Mary. He locked up my wife…my *pregnant* wife. How am I supposed to feel anything but anger?"

"What you feel and what you express are two different things. Once that child is born you have to find a way to push the bitterness aside. And that's not for me or for Father. It's not even for Jocelyn."

Mikhail slapped his hand down on the floor. "You're making this sound like it's my fault—when it's not. *He* was the one who did this, all because his grandchild had to be born first—the first damn child born on the new world. As usual, he could not take no for an answer. He had to pass that law. He had to fool Jocelyn into coming in for an obstetrics appointment. We'd told him over and over it was against our wishes, but still he had his henchmen order the doctors to strap her down and knock her out so she would stop fighting to get away. I've watched all the recordings from when it happened. It was ugly, and I *hate* him for it."

"I shouldn't be here when you're like this," Mary said.

"Do you agree with what he did?"

"It's not relevant what I think."

"Nuh-uh. Try again. You cannot cop out like that. This wasn't him letting us down for the umpteenth time. This was something else. This was something cruel."

"I know what it was."

"Then be straight with me. Do you think any government should be allowed to hold an innocent person against their will for any reason, let alone this one."

"Of course I don't agree with what was done, and you know it." Mary started fiddling with her bracelet, spinning it around and around her wrist. "We've been over this so many times, Mikhail."

"And yet you still haven't disowned him. You remain steadfast at his side, even though you know he's a monster."

"He's not a monster. He's our father."

"Well, as a father, he's been nothing but a monster—an uncaring old monster."

Mary hunched down and kissed the top of Mikhail's head. "I'm sorry, but I have to go. Rex has a doctor's appointment."

"Good," Mikhail said. "Leave. I came in here to be alone."

"So, you intend to keep punishing me for this as well?"

"I'm punishing Dimitri Kucherov and his cronies. Are you one of his cronies?"

"I don't know how to answer that."

"Oh, you know. You're just too ashamed to admit the truth while staring at his sleazy handiwork. But you're loyal to him, loyal in the way a child is always loyal to a parent. Loyal in a way I will never be again."

5

"Morgan Adams is pregnant, you idiot."

Jason squirmed, pinned against the conference room cabinet by his mother, the honorable yet diminutive, Elisabeth Epelle. The declaration she'd just made—with all the accusation therein—had left Jason stone-faced, his eyes devoid of even the slightest sense of guilt or recognition.

"Who did you say was pregnant again?" he asked all innocently.

"You heard me." Elisabeth yanked hard on his shirt collar, twisting the orange fabric into a big woolen wad. "Say something, damn you. Quit looking at me like a dunce and just admit it."

"What am I supposed to admit?"

"Are you kidding me? Let's start with the fact that your unsuspecting wife is six months pregnant. Add to that, you are *screwing* another woman. And now this tramp of yours is as pregnant as the woman you have pledged to share your life with. Try admitting one of those things. The very least you can do is admit something."

"Mother." Jason gave his shoulders a quick jerk and pried himself from her grasp. "Morgan and I are just friends. I'm telling you the truth. That baby cannot be mine."

"Oh please, you lie as easily as you breathe. It's like a compulsion with you. You get yourself into trouble, and all you can do is lie."

"I've already told you. I'm not lying."

"Yes, you are. Do you think I'd accuse you of something this terrible without being certain? This ship is one big recording device, Jason. How could you be so careless? You might be able to shut cameras down when you enter a private residence, but there is no way to prevent yourself from being seen coming in and out of anywhere with a public passageway. Affairs of even the smallest magnitude cannot be kept secret once an investigation is initiated."

Jason hesitated. "I'm under investigation? Me?"

"It was unavoidable, and out of my hands. The pregnancy diagnosis was passed onto the Directorate the moment Adams, a *divorcée*, refused to name a father when pressured on the issue by her physician. A routine investigation into her behavioral pattern was launched and your constant presence in her life kept popping up in the dimensionals. One clip in particular caught you both kissing as you left her house, two hours after entering it."

"Shit," Jason said as he was straightening out his shirt. "I guess I'm caught then. I never wanted this to touch you, Mother, not any of it. I swear I didn't."

Elisabeth shook her head. "Couldn't you have just been honest with me from the beginning?"

"How could I? I was embarrassed. You're my mother."

"I'm also the only one who's going to look out for you. How long have you been having sex with this woman?"

"A few months."

"Since her divorce?"

"From before her divorce."

"Son of mine." Elisabeth backed up a step and exhaled. "I don't know where to begin. You are a lunatic, an out-and-out lunatic. All the effort we've put into your career, and now you've sullied everything to have sex with someone other than your pregnant wife. My goodness, you've knocked up two women. You're unbelievable."

"I know, I know. I'm worthless."

Elisabeth got stern. "Don't you try to play me."

"I wasn't."

"I think you were."

"Okay, I was. A little bit."

"Don't you do that, with me or with anybody else. You have to face up to what you've done. And Angela, she has to be told. I'm off to speak with her as soon as I'm done with you."

"I wish you wouldn't," Jason said. "I should be the one who tells her."

"If that's what you prefer, then fine. But someone needs to let her know, because this will be getting beyond my control sooner rather than later."

"And I get that, totally. I'll tell her tonight."

"I want to be clear here," Elisabeth said. "You are going to be repri-manded, Jay. Legally, you're a wedded male impregnating someone outside a marriage contract. There are inevitable consequences. Believe me when I tell you, public shame is hurtling your way."

The entryway door opened. Joy Epelle, Elisabeth's youngest, burst in-side the conference room with Robin Hardy, the first of eighteen to arrive for the regularly scheduled morning briefing of the Transplant Operations group.

Elisabeth pointed at the door with one hand and held up two fingers with the other. Joy understood the unspoken request, snatching hold of Robin's arm and circling them both back out. The door closed behind them.

Jason took his seat at the head of the table. "I need to ask you some-thing without you snapping at me. What about Morgan?"

"What do you mean?"

"What do you think I mean? Who's going to tell her this is a prosecut-able thing now? She's a very sensitive person."

Elisabeth shut her eyes. "Jason, please don't tell me you have an emo-tional attachment to this woman."

"I've been sleeping with her for months. You should hope I have an attachment to her."

"An emotional attachment has never been a requirement for inter-course, young man."

"It's a requirement for me."

"Then you love this woman?"

"I'm not sure. Maybe." He reached over and turned on his desktop. Its ignition set his strained expression aglow. "To be absolutely honest, I'm not sure what I feel about anyone right now, okay? I'm confused. I've been confused for a long time."

"How wonderfully dramatic of you. But back here in the realm of reality, I suggest you stop being confused and start telling your wife what a despicable thing you've done. I will make sure the Ms. Adams is duly informed. She is no longer your concern, however. From this point forward, you will have nothing more to do with her. Consider that a formal dictate."

Elisabeth sat down on the bench behind Jason and waved in the crowd that was gathering on the other side of the semiopaque double doors.

Jason swiveled backward in his chair. "I'm really sorry about this, Mother. I know this won't be good for you when the next election comes along."

A familiar cadre of managers and aides filed their way into the room.

Elisabeth lowered her voice to a whisper. "I can fend for myself. You pay attention to your marriage."

"I will."

"And stay away from Morgan Adams."

"I will."

"You'd better."

6

Their mid-morning workout complete, the Rangers assembled themselves along the gymnasium wall. The men of the hour—Commander Camden Muran, Lieutenant Mikhail Kucherov, and operatives Samuel Oates, Bernard Stalt, and Koron Aw—had been directed to hold tight and await further instruction on what was now being described as their 'final training maneuvers.'

The unit passed the time by lobbing taunts and insults at one another. This went on until the woman known only as Kay emerged from her office and strutted across the practice mats, halting her procession a step behind the white and yellow out-of-bounds line. To a man, the Rangers fell silent.

"This here is what you idiots will be out searching for today." Kay produced an oversized metallic ring from the lining of her coat. "You might have passed the Directorate's piddling tests, but I still harbor doubts about each and every one of you. I expect to see a greater effort this time out."

Samuel broke position and said, "Problem solved. I found that ring-thing you're looking for. It's right there in your hand. Exam over. You impressed or what?"

Kay appeared to be decades older than her men, but she whisked over to Samuel with astonishing dexterity and speed, tapping the ring twice against the operative's dome-like skull.

"You want to play cute, do you? Go ahead. Grow some balls and try and take it from me."

"No, thank you," Samuel said.

Kay stepped back. "Then shut that fat trap of yours and take instruction like the good little flunky we all know you are."

"Just let her finish explaining, man," Camden said as he gave Samuel a kick. "What the hell is your problem?"

"His problems are irrelevant," Kay said. "The only problem any of you should be worrying about right now is uncovering the location of this ring's opposite number. Both have been fabricated from copper, an element that can be found in a few small pieces of jewelry and various other knickknacks, but is otherwise unused throughout the infrastructure of this ship. In other words, it'll stand out like a sore thumb when the sensors in your field belts come into contact with it."

"There are stacks of copper plating stowed in the Depots," Mikhail said. "Rows and rows of the stuff."

"And its presence there might confuse your sensors, Lieutenant."

Mikhail was squinting at her. "What else have you done? You wouldn't just simply hide something and send us out looking for it, not without rigging the game. You'd definitely set up obstacles."

"Any obstacles are yours to discover."

Mikhail turned to Bernard Stalt. "Is Leo on duty in Maintenance today?"

"I'm not sure. I'll check the duty schedule."

Bernard made an attempt to step away. Kay jumped out and pressed her forearm against his rib cage, catching the fleet-footed Ranger in mid-stride.

"You can check the schedule once you've left the gym. Not before. Got it?"

Camden whispered to Mikhail, "You were right. Leo, he's involved somehow."

"Think singularly at your own peril," Kay told the team. "There are agents throughout the ship attempting to impede your progress. It would be a mistake to focus too strongly on any one individual."

"Yeah, but it'd be an even bigger mistake to not concentrate on Leo at all," Camden said.

"Is there a time limit on the search?" Koron asked.

"Get it done as fast as you can. Limits are for the ladies."

Samuel cackled. "Says the great Lady Kay."

Kay lunged for him, but Samuel was ready this time. He skittered around Camden and hid behind him.

Mikhail nudged Samuel forward. "Come on, you dope. Let's move."

Kay was twirling the ring around her finger. "Your arrival drop is only two days away, boys. It'd be sad if you had to miss your historic trip to the surface all because you couldn't find one irrelevant little ring. What do you all think? Wouldn't that be a crying shame?"

In ragged formation, the five Rangers drifted toward the gymnasium door.

"We'll be back in no time," Mikhail said. "*With* the ring."

Koron threw up his fist. "Yep, all we need is five minutes or so."

"You shall have your ring soon, milady," Samuel said after he had shuffled safely through the door.

"Remember," Kay called out. "You are out and about with the public today. Whatever else happens, do not cause a panic."

Camden was the last to leave. "Us, cause a panic? Perish the thought."

7

The Directorate had been seated front row center. Chief Theorist Meyer Wells completed his opening statement and puttered over to the side of the stage. As the houselights were going down, he spoke a classified code word and a snippet of survey footage began to play in smeared fits and starts.

The Trustees looked at one another in exasperation.

Walter sunk down in his seat and groused, "The swashing and blurring are *still* all over your transmission, Meyer. I thought you told us the problem had been fixed."

"Not fixed—drastically improved. As you are all aware, the forager imaging nodes have been malfunctioning from the instant atmospheric descent begins. However, this transmission batch is different, so you need to watch. It does clear up."

Completely clears up or clears up enough to justify keeping that lofty job title of yours? Grand-chief-scientist-guy-who-cannot-get-a-simple-camera-to-work."

Walter's light jab elicited laughter from several of the more frustrated Trustees.

Meyer smiled knowingly and tipped his head at the fluctuating display. "You're about to see Verdan, Mr. Magistrate—your new home. I suggest you start paying close attention."

Almost as soon as Meyer had finished speaking, an aerial view of a green-hued coastline materialized out of the distortion, crystal clear and pristine. The astonished Trustees began to react.

"There it is," Jacob Holt said.

"Oh my," Walter exclaimed.

"Verdan." Laken Merriweather's eyes were glimmering with emotion.

"It's so green," Deborah Summers said. "Come to think about it, though, I guess it should be green."

Without warning, the footage reverted back to nothingness.

"Wait a second." Walter gestured up at the stage. "It's gone. Where did it go?"

"That's all the footage we received." Meyer spoke an additional command. "Let me play it for you again, slowed way down this time."

The image wound back to the point where the interference had dissipated. On this pass through, viewed at a different frame rate, the details became more observable—choppy emerald waters, a cratered mountainside, a spiraling thicket of a jungle-like plant life, and rain, a seemingly impenetrable downpour of rain.

"Amazing," Laken said. Everyone around her nodded in agreement.

"How did you do that?" Jacob asked Meyer. "It's been months and months of these probes with no luck whatsoever."

The transmission footage paused right before the distortion could return. When the houselights came back on, Meyer was beaming.

"How did I do this you ask? I turned off the forager's propulsion drive. It was as simple as that."

"Off?" Jonas Vickery said, his eyes still adjusting to the brightness of the room. "I'm confused."

"Yes, what do you mean when you say off?" Deborah asked.

"Off is off," Meyer said. "When the probe entered the atmosphere I ordered the *Vanguard* to kill the device's propulsion system, allowing the forager to free-fall to the surface."

"And that worked?"

"Somewhat, it seems. You all saw the footage. I'd hoped the cameras would function during the entire descent, but all we received back was that short flash of perfection."

Walter sat forward. "Why would killing the drive give us anything at all?"

"I can't answer that, not with any certainty. I killed the drive and it worked. That's the extent of what I know so far. It was an impulse decision stemming from equal parts malaise and desperation. I didn't know I was going to do it until I was actually giving the order. Call it an unplanned for impulse."

"Don't be modest now," Laken said. "Impulses of that sort have to come from somewhere."

Her ex-husband Jacob bristled at that. "Who cares what motivated him? It's irrelevant. What's required here are concrete answers, not desperate hunches. The lives of ten human beings continue to hang in the balance."

"But these pictures could be helpful on that as well." Meyer walked out in front of the frozen probe footage as it was zooming in on the northern banks of a zigzagging riverfront. "Look up along the right corner. I've circled the areas. See the crushed vegetation and the glints of metal? The supply cans landed. That means the spire carrying the Constructs could have landed as well. Probably did land as well."

"This is hope then?" Deborah said.

Meyer nodded. "I think hope is exactly what this is."

"Hope is for suckers," Jacob said. "This isn't proof the Constructs are still alive. It's wishing and dreaming, and I won't stand for it. It's been far too long since the Constructs' last broadcast. I require voice contact before I'll feel anything close to relief."

"Which is why we need to drop more probes," Meyer said. "I've been in near constant communication with the *Vanguard*'s ligate. She says they still have a dozen foragers remaining in the ship's compliment of probing mechanics. I could toss every one of them down, in the same manner, from slightly different points in the atmosphere, and we could end up with actual footage of where the Constructs landed."

"Or didn't land," two different Trustees said.

Meyer wandered back to his spot at the side of the screen. "That's right. That's a strong a possibility as anything else."

"Is this the only plan you have?" Walter said. "We are meant to invest all our efforts on these broken-down old probes?"

"The *Vanguard*'s probes are our sole option at the moment, yes. But we'll be there ourselves soon. Once in orbit, we'll be able to float scanners into the atmosphere and test the elemental make-up while still tethered to the *Horizon*. We can also drop our own probes, the designs of which have been advanced radically over the course of this voyage. I could go on. There's just so much more we can do once this ship is in orbit."

Dimitri, who had remained silent for the majority of the presentation, raised his hand. "Nonetheless, in the end, this problem will require human exploration to solve. That's where all these roads lead, correct?"

Meyer withered. "Yes, Mr. Kucherov. Boots on the ground. Without direct communication, that's the only way we're ever going to know anything for sure."

8

Mary had been waiting for the better part of fifteen minutes when the door beneath her finally slid open.

"Are you still here?" a voice cried out.

Mary glanced down as Courtney Cutler, her lifelong best friend—and the underling she had stopped by to chastise—entered the building in a flurry, arms pumping madly in an over-articulated display of all-out panic.

"I see you up there, sitting in front of my desk. You must really be stewing."

Courtney rounded the rail and scaled up the staircase. Her pace was swift. After years of near constant tardiness, Courtney had become skilled at making a show out of hustling-to-it.

"I'm so sorry I'm late," she said as she finished her ascent.

"First of all, I am not stewing," Mary said. "And secondly, it's not a problem. I needed to get out of my office for a few minutes anyway. Our fathers, both yours and mine, have been running me ragged all morning."

Courtney swept by and grazed Mary's arm with her painted finger-nails. "Doing their hatchet work, I presume?"

"What else? It's become their most cherished bloodsport of late."

Mary uncrossed her legs and placed her feet flat onto the floor.

Courtney slipped behind her desk. "I started keeping out of Dad's way during business hours. It's made my life *so* much easier."

"Unfortunately, that only passes his complaints on to me, avoiding you

41

for about as long as it takes for me to show up here, under orders to get your sorry butt in gear."

"He's asking for the pharmacological allotments, isn't he?"

"He is."

"They're mostly completed." Courtney looked down and started to clear off her cluttered desktop. "I'll finish them as soon as I've found my display screen."

She scooped up a day-old lunch plate and dropped into the trash.

"I hate to be a nag," Mary said. "But when you swap them over to him, I need them sent to me as well."

"As proof you've hurried me."

"We've been through this before, haven't we?"

"Far too many times."

The entranceway below opened and Camden and Samuel barged into the office, a blatant disregard of the social protocol to announce oneself before entering a physical space you did not occupy or supervise. The Ranger partners gazed up at the two women conferring around the elevated work area.

"Caught you both," Camden said.

"I can search down here," Samuel said before crossing out of sight.

Camden grunted his approval and raced up the stairs. He was at the top of the landing in a matter of seconds.

"What are you up to now?" Mary asked him.

Camden bounded over to the desk. "The devilish Miss Courtney was seen talking to Kay yesterday."

Mary held still for a second, and then said, "So?"

"Kay sent us out to look for a ring."

Courtney deposited another pile of trash into the receptacle. "Wow, that's quite the daunting task you've been given. Is this what occupies you tough guys all day now? Games of hide-and-seek?"

Camden propped his palms on the corner of the desktop. His hulking body cast a giant shadow over the workstation.

"Tell me, Dr. Cutler. What were you doing talking to Kay yesterday?"

"That's none of your business, is it?"

"It sort of is. I need an answer to win."

"If I tell you, will you leave?"

"Right away."

"Fine. I saw Kay to get her approval of the Ranger health and fitness reports. Everyone passed but you."

Camden stood all the way up and slapped at his breastbone. "Try again, beautiful. I'm the heartiest of all Rangers. I know I passed."

"There's no trace of any copper anywhere," Samuel said from below.

Courtney peered down at the man, and then shifted her confusion back over to Camden. "I thought you were looking for a ring."

"A copper ring."

"Tricky."

Camden sidestepped over to Mary. "Love you, wifey."

"I know you do." She reached up and patted his arm. "Now go play elsewhere, dearest."

"I believe I shall." Camden posed at the top of the stairs before vaulting downward.

Mary waited. Once the door had closed, she said, "What-a-flipping-dolt."

"You married him," Courtney said.

"And had *three* children with him. What's wrong with me? What's going to be wrong with them?"

Courtney motioned down at the space she had cleared around her desktop display. "I should probably start finishing that supply thingy."

Mary got up. "And I need to go harass the next slacker on my list."

"Have fun with that. And make sure you're rougher on them than you were on me."

9

"I'll say it, since none of the rest of you appear to have the guts. I don't mind being the bad guy."

With her feet dangling out over the three hundred meter drop below, Florin thumped her backside against the lip of the container stack. Her five closest friends there were with her, surrounded by an unending array of identical storage towers. In the girders above, a portable bulb provided limited illumination in what was otherwise a pitch black and off-limits warehouse space.

"I will do it, you know," Florin said. "I will. I'm not going to wait any longer either. We all agreed to do it tonight, so someone has to get the ball rolling."

Vladimir, the boy who had embarrassed Florin at the arrival celebration, was cuddling with her from behind, his legs wrapped like a twist tie around her waist.

"Do it if you're going to," he said. "But please, for once, can you do it gently?"

"I'll do it any way I want to do it." Florin grabbed onto the meaty part of his calf and pinched it.

Joy Epelle and Matt Merriweather, the long-standing couple of the group, were lying on their backs and gazing up at the gridded ceiling.

"Actually, maybe I should be the one to do it," Joy said. The volume she was speaking at ticked up a notch. "Helen…Jance."

Jance Ling halted his oblivious stroll around the perimeter of the container stack. "What did I do?" he said.

"Not a damn thing," Florin said. "And with a beautiful, single girl so close by."

Helen Baker was sitting off by herself, as far away as she could get. When Florin said what she said, Helen put her hands to her face and keeled forward.

Florin pointed over at her. "Everyone see that reaction? Helen knows what we're about to say, doesn't she?"

Helen kept her hands up, and her face hidden. "Yeah, and I've told you before, keep out of my business."

"What's going on here?" Jance asked. "What am I being blamed for now?"

"We're blaming you because you're dense. You don't see what's right in front of you." Florin tossed her head back and yelled, "You and Helen should be together—as a couple, in love, *doing* it. *Humpy, humpy, you dummy.*"

Florin's remark echoed throughout the spooky old compartment. Jance just stood there snapping his fingers as his friends stared at him in anticipation.

Not two beats later, only millimeters from the heel of Jance's shoe, a hand slapped down on the edge of the container. Jance wheeled around and squealed. The rest of the surprised teenagers observed quietly as a muscular figure pulled himself onto their perch.

"Who are you?" Florin asked the mystery man.

"Who are you?" the man asked back.

"I'm Florin Holt. My father runs the Depot decks."

"Does your father know you're in here messing around?"

"I don't, *uh*—"

Moving on, the man made his way across the stack.

Joy sat up next to Matt and said, "Hey, I know you. You're Leonid Bratsk. You're not supposed to be in here either."

Leo doffed his non-existent cap and stepped to the right. A metallic ring hung from the back of his belt. "I won't tell if you won't tell."

"Why would we tell?" Matt said.

"Good question." Leo backed over to the far corner of the stack and climbed down, vanishing as quickly as he'd appeared.

"Forget you ever saw me, kiddies. Go back to your fun."

Jance sauntered over to Joy and Matt and sat down. "What fun is he talking about? Another round of you matchmaking idiots butting your stupid noses into my life."

"Don't act like you're the victim here," Florin said. "We all know you like Helen. It's as obvious as anything. But you're just too chicken to do anything about it. That's why we're here, to push you. To make you do what you should have been doing all along."

Helen slid closer to Vlad and Florin. "Are we all going to just ignore the large, scary man who just stomped his way through here?"

Joy shrugged. "That was only Mr. Bratsk. He's not as scary as his reputation. He's really nice when you bump into him in public."

"But you know what he did, right?" Helen said. "Who he hurt?"

"Who cares what he did...*geez*." Florin flounced about, causing the strap of her blouse to slip off her shoulder. "Don't get us wandering off on one of your tangents, Helen. You know what this is about. It's about you and the blockhead here. There will be no more avoiding, from either of you."

"Oh, please," Jance said. "Talk about avoiding. You're the one who's really avoiding. Poor Vlad has asked you to marry him and you avoid that by not being straight with him. He's also your boyfriend, and you avoid that truth *all* the time."

Florin breathed in and brought her legs back up onto the container. "I guess I need to clear a few things up. First and foremost, Vlad is *not* my boyfriend. He never has been. He's a guy I'm intimate with. He's my lover. And as to his proposal, I've already given him an answer, which was a straightforward no. Whether Mr. I'll-Love-You-Forever can accept that particular answer has no relevance to this conversation whatsoever."

"Avoider," Jance said.

"It's true." Matt nodded. "You do avoid a lot. It's hard to defend you on this one, cuz."

"It's hard for me, too," Joy said.

Vladimir nuzzled his face against Florin's hair.

"They see what you don't see," he told her. "As long as we're still sleeping together, your answer is always going to be muddied. And I will love you forever. That's not something you should be making fun of me about."

"I'm not making fun." Florin pushed Vladimir backward and kissed him with some genuine passion. "You mean a lot to me. You do."

"If that's the case, then you need to say yes. You need to say you'll marry me."

Florin kissed him again, and then pulled back. "How did this become about me? We all agreed this was supposed to be about Helen and Jance."

"Tough," Jance said. "That's what you get for interfering."

"Yes or no?" Vladimir said. "I need a final answer. Here in front of our friends, will you or will you not marry me?"

The bulb above them flickered.

Florin slid leftward and created some space between she and Vlad. "I can't. I'm being as direct with you as I can possibly be. I am never going to marry you. I will never, *ever* say yes. That's something you need to learn to accept. If that means we can't see each other anymore, then I guess we're not seeing each other anymore."

10

Jerald Epelle wriggled on his back in the playpen, laughing maniacally after knocking over a wall of blocks he'd stacked in the corner of his 'personal destruction area.'

His father Jason scrutinized the production from above, allowing his son the requisite five minutes of showing off that was insisted upon whenever grown-ups entered anywhere within the two-year-old's restricted line of sight.

"That was incredible," Jason said. "Real impressive, kiddo."

Jerald scrambled back onto all fours, in a rush to re-stack the numbered blocks. Jason held steady while the encore performance was being meticulously prepared.

All ready to go, Jerald paused for dramatic effect before kicking out at the blocks and knocking two of them completely out of his pen. Jason retrieved the upended toys—numbers one and eleven—and returned them to the enclosure. Jerald rolled end over end in exaltation as his father tiptoed his way toward the bedroom in the back.

"That one was even better," Jason said as he hastened his retreat. "I'm off to see Mommy. I'll only be gone a minute."

The overhead lights in the Epelle master bedroom were faded low. Jason's wife Angela was seated on a bench in front of the dresser mirror applying a modest coat of mauve lipstick. Her outfit for the evening was powder blue, a pantsuit that had been taken out across the midsection.

Jason trudged inward and pulled off his shirt.

"You have given birth to a demolitionist, honey. He knocked two blocks right out of the pen this time."

"He knocked one out for me earlier." Angela was watching Jason through the mirror. "Apparently, I was less impressed than you were."

"One needs to be proud of something." Jason came to a stop in front of their bed and took off his shoe. "How was your day?"

"The usual." Angela swiveled around on the bench and reached down for one of her own shoes. "Your mother buzzed me an hour or so ago."

Jason feigned his surprise. "She did?"

"Yeah. She was being her cryptic self, claiming you have this big secret you need to tell me. It's vital I hear about it supposedly. I asked her to just spill the beans herself and save me the wait, but she refused to give anything up. She said it was your job to do the telling."

"Really?" Jason had removed his pants and was back on his feet, heading for the closet dressed only in his boxers.

Angela slipped on a second shoe. "I've been worried sick since the moment she called. Her tone was kind of strange. She was not in a good mood, and she doesn't call often. Generally, she only calls when you've done something wrong."

"That's not the only reason she calls."

"It's the only reason she calls me."

Jason unhooked a black dinner jacket and slacks combo from his end of the closet. He remained where he was for the moment, safely out of sight.

"So," Angela said. "What is that she wanted you to tell me?"

"Honestly, I have no idea."

"Come on. How can you have no idea?"

Jason walked out of the closet and stripped the jacket off its hanger and flung it across the bed. "For starters, Mom has been in meetings with the Directorate all afternoon. I haven't seen her. Yeah, I had a quick run-in with her this morning, but now is the first I'm hearing of any secret."

"It was supposedly a *vital* secret."

"Whatever kind of secret it is."

Angela shook her head. "Jay, I know that you're lying to me. Your mother's call came in just a little while ago. She wasn't in any meeting."

"I can't believe you don't trust me," he said. "I'm not lying. They do allow breaks during meetings, you know. They even allow personal calls."

Angela lifted herself off the bench. "Forget it. It doesn't matter. Your mother will be at dinner. I'll just find out then."

She bent down and took a second look at herself in the mirror.

"Actually, she's not coming tonight," Jason said as he stepped into his slacks. "As I tried to tell you before, Mom's busy with the Directorate all evening. No one is going to see her until tomorrow morning at the earliest."

"Tonight or tomorrow, the truth is coming out eventually." Angela wound her way out of the room.

Jason retrieved his dinner jacket. "Tell me something I don't know."

11

"There's no sign of him."

Mikhail was crouched down low in the bushes, camouflaged amid the two-story domiciles blanketing the pseudo-exterior of the Green Village residential deck, the bottommost living area on board the *Horizon*. The surrounding streets and sidewalks bustled with local citizenry, scurrying to and fro for various public and private meals.

Mikhail completed an additional survey of the interlocking homes and repeated his appraisal. "I don't see the guy. Did you get that, Cam? I do not see him anywhere."

The hushed voice of Camden Muran came online, deep within Mikhail's ear. "I heard you. I just needed a second to think. The Core's telling us he's here at home, but we haven't seen any sign of him—and his roommate claims he's still at work."

"The roommate could be lying. He's Leo's friend. We cannot trust him."

"Or maybe we can. Travis was acting all put out when I asked if Leo was hiding inside. And I've already knocked twice. If I knock again, he'll go whine to the Sergeant."

"Does that matter right now? Leo's got to be in there somewhere. It's impossible for someone to separate themselves from their link."

"I'd be in complete agreement with you if this was anyone but Leo." Camden's breathing was becoming more and more audible. "Bernard, you still linked up? Where are you?"

"About four blocks east," a third voice said. "On the back side of the village."

"I want you to come around and cover the rear exit. Mikhail, you need to get yourself up front with me. Hustle it…both of you."

Mikhail came out of his crouch. A gray-haired woman who was strolling by at the time screamed, frightened by the sudden appearance of an unknown male hiding among the shrubbery.

Mikhail held out his hands. "My apologies, ma'am. I didn't mean to scare you."

Once she recognized who Mikhail was, the woman quieted down. Mikhail gave her a quick salute and ran off.

"Who were you talking to just then?" Camden asked.

"A lady I just scared half to death."

"Would you stop being so damned friendly and get your ass over here. I need you, Mikhail."

"I get it. I'm on my way."

Mikhail shot across lawn after lawn, dodging at least a half dozen citizens along the way. Leo Bratsk's home grew nearer, only three lots ahead. Camden was already there, standing out in the center of the roadway.

Looking up, Mikhail spotted a figure on the top of Leo's home.

"He's on the roof, Cam. Do you see?"

Camden's head jerked upward. At that same instant, from out of nowhere, Hollis Craddock, a former rugby teammate of Leo's, charged ahead and tackled the Ranger Commander. The two tumbled around together until Hollis had wrestled Camden into an unbreakable hold in the grass.

Mikhail increased his stride.

As if on cue, Leo dropped a wire-thin line and rappelled down the side of his home, hitting the front lawn a split second after he'd jumped. Camden continued to struggle with Hollis, but could not manage to pull himself free. Leo ran past them, the prized copper ring flapping tauntingly on his belt.

"Get *after* him," Camden shouted.

Neglecting years of training, Mikhail abandoned his flank and focused his full attention on Leo, allowing a tall woman in a plain brown worker's uniform to slip in on his right, a pushcart dinner tray utilized as a crude secondary disguise. The woman, Tella Webb, another apparent associate of Leo's, swung her leg out and tripped the unsuspecting Ranger. Mikhail toppled over and smacked face first into the curb.

"You're done." Tella pressed her boot against the back of Mikhail's neck. "Don't make me stomp you any harder."

Mikhail went limp as a trail of blood trickled into his mouth.

"Nice move there," he said. "I don't think we've ever met, at least not formally. I'm Mikhail Kucherov."

Tella ignored him.

"Aren't you going to introduce yourself?" Mikhail asked her.

"Why should I?" Tella was keeping a close eye on Leo as he picked up steam in the distance. "Ask around about me, if you're so interested. I believe the two of us are about to become the talk of the town. Mr. Perfect taken down by a scrawny little commoner. The gossip mill is gonna feast on this one for quite some time."

12

Standing in the doorway, Walter unbuttoned his collar. Allison Stoddard, his spouse of more than thirty years, was scrambling from kitchen cabinet to kitchen cabinet, restocking dishes and plates that had been washed and dried while Walter had been saying his extended goodbyes outside.

"Courtney and the kids just left," he said.

"I kind of figured." Allison put the last plate back into place.

"I could tell there was something in the air tonight," Walter said. "On the way out, Jimmy informed me of his intention to become an artist once his coursework is completed. It might be painting, or it could end up being sculpting, but I should expect him to do something creative with his life."

"He's worried you'll be upset with his decision."

"And why would such a thing upset me?"

"Why do you think?" Allison turned around and rinsed her hands off in the sink. "You pontificate on and on about how the Kucherov children have this blessed responsibility to pledge their lives to politics. A statement like that does not exist in a vacuum. Jimmy hears it, and thinks you expect him to be a politician, like his grandfather."

"There's a big difference between our family and the Kucherovs."

"Not to a child there isn't."

Walter placed his hand on the recently cleaned counter. He was humming. "Should I have a heart-to-heart with him? I assumed he'd know I wasn't referring to him when I made my proclamations. His mother is a physician. Clearly, I'm not too pushy about my family's career choices."

Allison backed away from the sink, her wet fingers dripping at her side. "You do realize, your own daughter works for you, the Collective's chief politician. Yes, she's a trained physician, but her career's been made more administrative than I'm sure she'd prefer."

"Point taken. I guess I manipulate even when I don't mean to manipulate. I'll speak to Jimmy. I promise to be frank and honest with him. I want the boy to live a life of his own choosing."

Allison dried her hands on a hanging dish towel. "Before we go upstairs, there's something else I need to speak to you about. I heard this strange rumor. Did Rebecca Patterson stop by to see you before your speech yesterday?"

Walter nodded. "She did, right before you arrived actually. I'm kind of surprised the two of you didn't run into each other."

Allison came right up to him and cupped his cheek. "My darling, since when are you and Rebecca Patterson on speaking terms?"

Walter took a moment. "I should have told you before now, I know. We first spoke after the birth of her daughter. I peeked in at the hospital to offer my congratulations, and perhaps an olive leaf. We got to talking, apologizing mostly."

"I see," Allison said.

"It's nothing intimate, believe me."

Allison let go of his face. "Please, I'm well aware of what she meant to you. I wasn't living in a cave back then. I saw how hot the two of you ran. Rebecca and Walter, the great rabble-rousers. Inseparable. Perfect for one another. The two of you had one of those special kind of loves."

"More like a special kind of disaster. There were good reasons why we didn't stay together."

"Agreed. And once you had finally faced those reasons, you went and married the more politically palatable alternative."

"That's not true. That's completely, absolutely untrue."

"It's more true than it's not."

"No, it isn't. I love you, Allie, and you know that. The feelings between us have never wavered."

"Oh, Walter. You do live in your own world sometimes."

He clutched onto her hip. "Listen to me, there's only one thing you need to know about Rebecca and me. That woman and I *still* can't be in the same room together without arguing. It's pathetic."

"Nice try," Allison said. "But it was never just plain-old arguing with you two, now was it? No, it was passion. It was heat. It was the kind of feeling that never goes away. I get that. I've always gotten that. I just can't compete with it. I never could."

She removed his hand from her person and stalked off.

Walter chased after her. "Allison."

"Just leave me be," she said as she headed up the stairs. "I'm begging you. Can you just leave me the hell alone?"

BEFORE

"Tell us the story," Dimitri said. "Tell us how Kay plucked you from the crowd."

Leo sat back in the padded chair and locked eyes with Mary, the beautiful young woman seated opposite him at the Kucherov family dining table.

"If you don't mind, sir," Leo said. "Could we put my story off for another minute or two? Your daughter was in the middle of talking about her etiquette lessons, and I was enjoying hearing about that. They seem way more intense than any of Kay's training sessions, and far less civilized. I didn't even know etiquette training was still a requirement these days. Nobody I know has to do it."

"You know me now," Mary said. "And etiquette lessons are a strict requirement in this house."

Leo touched the knot in his tie and smiled. "I guess we do know each other now. Before tonight, though, I only knew of you. Really, when it comes down to it, we've only just met."

"But doesn't it feel like we're already the best of friends?"

Mary winked at Leo. Everyone at the table noticed.

"Wowza, sis," Mikhail said from the far end of the table. "When did you become such a flirt?"

"I wasn't flirting. I was just being friendly. You should try it sometime." Mary leaned across the table. "Just so you're aware, Commander Bratsk, my brother is a jerk who has no respect for anyone. He can also be mean and spiteful for no reason at all. I consider this to be among his worst qualities. Keep that in mind when you're ordering the lout around."

Mikhail made a choking noise and said, "I know you're trying to be funny, sis, but humor is not your thing. And for the record, Leo's as mean and as spiteful as I am. That's the way Kay wants us to be."

Dimitri cleared his throat and the teasing ceased.

"Sir, I apologize." Leo gave the man at the head of the table a firm nod. "I should've just told you the story.

Since the moment Leo had arrived, Mary had been watching him like a hawk. Only fifteen years old, she was mature for her years, and had made a concerted effort to dress glamorously for the dinner party. The tight white skirt and revealing cream-colored blouse were uncharacteristic of her normal choices in attire, but striking enough for even her father to offer his compliments when she made her grand entrance via the stairs.

Mikhail deposited his napkin next his half-finished dinner plate. "I have a suggestion. Since Leo's our guest—and for some reason seems to enjoy listening to Mary's ramblings about forks and spoons—I say we let her keep rambling. I know you like to control things, Dad, but if you hadn't noticed, everyone seems to be enjoying themselves for once."

"I did notice that. That not withstanding, this dinner is not being held in Mary's honor, it's being held in Leonid's."

"Which is why I say we let him be the one who decides what we talk about."

"I want to thank you all for inviting me," Leo said. "It's been a pleasure to spend time here. The meal was terrific. I cannot thank everyone enough."

"Oh, I believe there are many ways you could thank us." Dimitri picked up his wine glass. "To begin with, you could the story of the first time you met Kay."

Mikhail grabbed his own glass. "Actually, come to think of it, I'd rather hear about the first time you met Kay, Dad. I know there's a story there, or so the rumors claim. Would you care to enlighten us on this top-secret subject?"

"Leonid first." Dimitri took a sip of his wine and motioned at their guest. "Any time you're ready to share with us, young man. We cannot wait to hear from you."

Mary was grinning. "Yes, Commander. We're all just prickling with excitement."

Leo breathed in. "It happened several years ago—meeting Kay that is. The rugby team I was playing for had just won the tournament championship. Kay saw something in the way we played together and wanted to reform us into some sort of military unit. I didn't know what she was talking about at the time, but she's such an unusual person, and I was curious, so I played along. Weeks of interviews followed, some even with you, sir."

Leo dipped his head at Dimitri, who nodded back.

"It took a while for me to be told what the unit's real purpose was going to be, but once I had all the facts, I was kind of bowled over by the prospect. To be a part of the Verdan landing team, it was a real vertical leap for someone like me. And now it's gone far beyond some woman's whim to reshape a rugby team. This is an opportunity to make a lasting mark on history, and I'm thrilled to be called upon."

Leo stopped speaking and glanced around the table. There was no reaction from anyone, not Dimitri, Mikhail, or even Mary, his biggest fan.

"That's all there is really," Leo added in summation. "Sorry, I guess it wasn't that interesting of a story after all."

"But it's *such* an interesting story," Dimitri said. "You just skipped over the part where Kay saw you—"

His neck twitched. A call was coming through. Dimitri held up his hand to silence the group. "Walter…good evening."

Leo looked to Mary as she she mouthed the words 'I'm sorry.'

"Dad tends to prioritize work, even at home," Mikhail said. "He doesn't mean anything by it—at least I assume he doesn't. Mary and I have sort of gotten used to being cut off and dismissed as if we weren't even there. Eventually, you'll get used to it, too."

"Excellent news," Dimitri said after he'd tapped out of the call. "Now that we've finished with dinner, Walter Stoddard and his wife are going to be dropping by to wish our new Commander well. They should be arriving any second now."

Dimitri stood up, faster than he should have. Once he'd braced himself, he said, "They're bringing Courtney as well, Mary. I'm going to meet them at the door. Anyone care to join me?"

Mikhail got up and lent his father a hand. Before they knew it, Mary and Leo were all alone at the table.

"So, the Stoddards are on their way over," Mary said. "I'll bet you can't contain yourself."

Voices could be heard entering in the other room.

Leo smiled and said, "The times he interviewed me, Magistrate Stoddard seemed like a pretty nice guy. I don't think I've ever met his wife before."

"Well, you're about to. Prepare yourself, it's going to be about as exciting as your Kay story was."

Leo cowered a little. "I know. I was dreading having to tell it. There's just nothing interesting about the way we met. I tried to stick with your etiquette class story, but your father kind of forced my hand."

"My etiquette story wasn't exactly riveting either. It was just basic small talk. You know, me finding anything I could to keep Dad from speechifying."

Leo pushed his chair back. "Me, I liked what you had to say, and the way you said it. I think you have a great sense of humor. I don't know what your brother is talking about."

"Thank you, but Mikhail's right. I'm not all that funny. Not normally, anyway."

The voices in the other room grew louder. Leo stood up.

"Maybe if you have some free time in the next few days, we could get together and talk about some incidents in our life that are a bit more interesting than etiquette and field training."

Mary stood as well, smoothing out her skirt as she rose. "That sounds really great, Leo. It honestly does. Personally, I'd love for us to hang out.

But my father, he might not approve. To be blunt, I'm pretty sure he'd outright forbid it."

Leo moved closer to her until they were just millimeters apart. "You think? He'd forbid us from having a conversation? Why's that? We're talking right now, under his own roof."

"True, but you don't know my father."

"I know him somewhat. I think he likes me."

"Oh, he does. I can tell. But if he started not to."

"Sure." Leo eased back a step. "I get what you're saying. There's no pressure. It was just a suggestion."

"Don't be like that. Talking with you is something that I—"

Leo held out his hands and stopped her there. "No reason to explain. All I wanted was for us to get to know each other better."

"And I want that, too. We just have to be careful about how we go about this."

From the living room, Dimitri called out with a firm request for anyone still at the table to come out and socialize with everyone else. Mary led the way as Leo entered to a rousing round of applause.

Five Years Later

13

Kay told Leo to hold onto the ring. She would do the same with hers. The two of them then lined up in front of the closed gymnasium doors.

"How bad was it?" she asked him.

"You mean you weren't watching live."

"I couldn't bring myself to. And I know I asked you to do this for me. But this late in the game, an ass-kicking was only going to depress me."

Leo grinned. "Boy, have you mellowed."

"Well, it doesn't take a genius to figure out you were going slaughter those dolts."

"Is that compassion I'm hearing? I must say, sir, that's sensitive and downright girlie behavior."

Kay shot him the dirtiest of looks. "You should not mock me, you know. If you keep mocking me, I'll have no choice but to smack you one."

"You should smack yourself for being so soft."

"Maybe," she said.

"There's no maybe about it. You were never this soft on me."

"Because you have a thicker hide than they do. Now please, stop mocking me and make your damn report."

Leo's grin grew wider. "The pursuit itself, I'd say it was fairly strenuous. I ran the men around the ship for a few hours, and then holed up in the Depots. That's where Sammo almost caught me, believe it or not. After that, I waited out in plain sight at my place and had Hollis and Tella take them down, pinning their ears back in public, just like you wanted."

"And they're on their way back here? You're certain of that?"

"Tella was supposed to fill them in on where you and I would be waiting, so I can only assume that they are. Tella always does what she's supposed to do."

"I'll bet," Kay said. "I hear she has some other skills as well."

"And then some. We'll have to watch the recordings after this, but she totally laid out Mikhail. I was already in flight, so I was only able to witness it out of the corner of my eye. But, man, she really flattened him."

"Good. It's exactly what they needed, all of them. I know you haven't been around the team much lately, but things have gotten far too overbearing. Not a one of these idiots are taking the next few days seriously enough. To the so-called 'Chosen Ones,' a glorious outcome has never been in doubt. You can see it written all over their faces, there's this supreme confidence they have that makes me want to strangle each and every one of them."

"Confidence isn't the worst quality this team could possess."

"To me, to is. Doubt sharpens the senses. Nobody knows what to expect on this moon. Verdan could be nothing but a big, green marshmallow—or it could be hostile as hell. I need these guys focused on that moment where everything about this potential debacle will be put to the test."

"I assume there's still no word from the Constructs."

"None that I know of. Dimitri hasn't told me if there has been. I'd assume he'd want to run any new information past me immediately."

"The radio silence," Leo said. "It's troubling."

"It is," Kay said. She held steady for a second, and then started shaking her head. "You always cut right to it, don't you? It should have been you, you know. You're the only one who can command this mission properly."

"Don't, sir. That's all in the past."

"But it's not in the past. Nothing about this can be in the past until this landing has been secured and accomplished. Not hearing from the advance team is troubling, you're right. What the hell is going on down there? I mean it. What in the holy hell is going on down there? The dangers ahead, they could be staggering. Why can't anyone see that?"

"Just have the guys tread carefully. It's all anyone can realistically do."

"No, I could do more. I could strong-arm Dimitri and *make* him put you back on the squad."

Leo re-squared his shoulders. "He wouldn't, and I wouldn't want him to. I got the punishment I deserved."

"Okay, but that's debatable. Yeah, for a split second you lost control. There's no doubt about that. But the rest of us on this ship shouldn't be made to suffer for your mistakes. It's a waste of our best resource. It's a waste of you."

"It is what it is," Leo said. "I'm sorry I let you all down."

Above the doorframe, a red warning light went off.

"They're here," Kay said. "Late as ever."

Leo furrowed his brow. "Arms forward then. Show them the rings. Let these arrogant pricks see what they can and cannot do."

The Next Afternoon

14

Helen charged into Transplant headquarters with a bouquet of sunflowers cradled in her arms. Florin, who had been noodling at her desk, abandoned the post-landing shipment schedules and stood up to greet her friend.

"Brought your stash by to brag, have you? Jance must have been out picking all morning."

"These aren't mine," Helen said as she set the flowers onto Florin's workstation. They'd been collected in a translucent, pear-shaped vase.

"Whose are they then?"

"Don't ask me. I assume they're yours, or Mary's. They were sitting outside when I came up. I think there's a message attached."

Helen spun the bouquet counterclockwise so Florin could activate the engraved notation. Once she had, a short paragraph lit up: *'For Florin. A beautiful impulse for a beautiful girl.'*

Florin rolled her eyes. "Vladimir…the sap."

"I don't think it was him," Helen said. "I just ran into Vlad a little while ago and he was pestering me about how to get you to change your mind. This was on the other side of the ship. There's no way he could have beaten me over here."

"I'm confused," Florin said. "It's such a Vlad thing to do."

"It's someone else who sent them. It has to be."

"All right, but who?"

"Maybe it's someone else you're having sex with."

"I am not having sex with anyone but Vlad."

Helen snickered. "We both know that's not true. About ten times over."

"No, not ten." Florin brushed the tips of the flowers. "Not even close to ten."

"However many it is. Do you know who it could be? You *have* to know who it could be."

"I don't." Florin sat back down. "But I know how to find out."

She tapped her desktop three times, until the Core voice requested password authorization.

"Close your ears, please."

Helen obliged halfheartedly.

"Breakaway," Florin said.

"Dimensional access secured," the Core responded.

Florin gave her friend a stern look. "That's the office's code word. I'm going to change it the second you leave."

"Spoilsport."

Florin and Helen watched as thirty-eight squares of security clips blinked one by one onto her mainframe. A quick perusal led to several images of a man in his late twenties, dark haired and slender, depositing the bouquet beside the entranceway doors.

"Derek Lucas," Florin said.

"You're sleeping with Derek Lucas?"

Florin met Helen's disbelieving gaze. "No, I've never slept with the guy. I swear, it never happened. Not even once."

15

Morgan Adams ducked behind the trunk of a blooming magnolia tree. It was a precarious hiding spot, at best. Everyone on the village patio had been watching her as she scrambled from tree to tree, including Jason and Joy Epelle, who were just finishing up a late afternoon lunch.

Joy said to her brother, "She's still there, watching you."

"Don't judge." His back to the tree, Jason sat forward. "It's not her fault."

"Damn right it isn't. It's *yours*."

"And don't judge me either. This is about as unusual as a situation can get. It makes sense how she's acting. I've been ignoring her calls, and I'm not entirely certain anyone has talked to her yet. Mom said she was gonna."

"As long as you yourself don't do the talking. Mother already wants to throttle you."

Jason said something under his breath and pushed aside what was left of his sandwich. "I didn't tell Angela last night. Mom was expecting me to, but I couldn't go through with it."

Joy just stared at him. "You're a crazy person, you know. A horn-dog crazy person."

"Stop it. It's not like that. I care about this woman."

"I'm not entirely sure which woman you are referring to at the moment, but either way you are *loco* crazy."

Jason raised his napkin and dabbed at his face. His mouth had been hanging open so long spittle had started to trail down his chin. One dab became two. A third dab came attached with a whimper.

"Oh, buck up, you big baby." Joy reached across the table and gave the top of his hand a smack. "Tell me why you chickened out with Angela."

His napkin was still up near his mouth, which garbled his words. "I was scared. I promised myself that I would tell her, but you know how I am. She asked me about it right away, too. Mom had called ahead."

"Of course she did."

He drew the napkin away. "I just couldn't hurt her. I care for her too much. When presented with the choice of lying or telling the truth, a lie is always easier on the person about to be walloped, isn't it?"

"Sometimes...*maybe*. But in this situation, the lie is easier for you. And the easier-for-you part is only temporary. There's no way Angela isn't going to find out. If Mom is true to form, she's probably already been told."

Jason's eyes widened. "You think? I haven't heard a peep from Angela all morning. Maybe that's why."

"I don't think so. Angela would never confront you over a link. She'll wait to get you in person, and *then* cut your neck."

"That's not funny."

"Yeah, you're right. There are worse places she might cut."

Jason whimpered again. "You're my sister. Aren't you supposed to be nice to me at a time like this?"

"No, I'm supposed to be tough on you at a time like this. I'm supposed to back my sister-in-law, whom I adore, at a time like this. I'm a woman, like Mother, Jay. What you have done is so fundamentally offensive."

"I didn't mean to," he said.

"Well, if you have a brain in your head, you will not use gems like 'I didn't mean to' when Angela comes at you screaming. The excuses in your admittedly limited quiver are going to need to be a bit more inspired, and much more from the heart."

"What should I say then?"

Joy was about to respond when something caught her eye over at the magnolia tree.

"Uh-oh. Don't look, but you-know-who is coming our way."

Morgan was already in full stride, holding something spherical in her closed left fist.

"She's on final approach," Joy said.

Morgan's grip fell loose, revealing a small orange clawed between her fingers. She careened past Jason and dropped the orange onto the center of the table. It bounced once before rolling toward Joy. Morgan continued forward and disappeared from view.

"An orange?" Joy nudged the piece of fruit with her knuckle. "What the heck is this? Is she out of her mind?"

"It's a signal," Jason said. "Our signal."

"An orange is your signal?"

"Yep, we've used it before. She's telling me where she wants to meet. In the hothouse, ASAP." Jason picked the orange up and set it in his lap. "She is not out of her mind, by the way."

"Maybe not. But you're out of yours if you meet her again."

"I have to," he said.

"You don't have to. You really don't."

"That's the thing, though. I think I do."

16

Walter was the first to exit, steps ahead of the oncoming stampede. The daily Civilities meeting had just broken up, and its varied personnel had come pouring out into the courtyard.

Never the most agile of men, Walter allowed himself to get caught up in the flow. Eventually, he found himself drawn over to a thin wooden bench. He appropriated the space at the same moment his daughter Courtney whisked by. She kept waving at him until she was all the way down the street.

The courtyard soon emptied and Walter gazed up at the twenty-meter high ceilings. A digital cloud mass was moving in. He gnawed on his lower lip and gave his knee an extra-hard slap. Thirty more seconds of delay elapsed before Walter finally activated his link.

"Rebecca Patterson, call."

He ran his fingers through his hair as he waited for a response.

"Walter J. Stoddard," the voice in his ear said. "Now isn't this a surprise? I feel so honored, a call from the king of the universe."

"Are you busy, Becca?"

"Not as busy as I assume you should be."

"I'm taking a break. I needed a moment to relax."

"I don't believe you. You've never been all that concerned about relaxation. What are you really up to? You're not in your office. I can hear the fake wind and bird noises. I'll bet you're in between buildings somewhere, hiding out."

"Wrong. I'm seated on a bench, where anyone with two good eyes can see me. I hide from no man, or woman."

"Shucks," Rebecca said. "I was hoping this was going to be more covert."

"I realize that you're teasing me, but please don't say that again. I'm in enough trouble as it is."

"All right, now I'm interested. Trouble. Tell me more."

"Are you alone?"

"Alone in my den. Alan's at work. No one is listening in, if that's what you're worried about."

Walter shut his eyes and said, "Allison knows that you and I have been talking."

"Oh, and is that a problem?"

"It shouldn't have been, but I hadn't talked to her about it yet. Then, some busybody tells her you stopped by to see me before my speech. To say the least, she's not thrilled that you and I are on speaking terms again."

"I'm kind of surprised it's such a big deal," Rebecca said. "Alan knows, and he doesn't appear to mind. You and I hadn't spoken in decades. He understands how much I missed you. He's happy we established some common ground. He's been his same old wonderful self about all of it."

"Unfortunately, Allison is not quite that understanding."

"Have you done anything unrelated to annoy her? Knowing you, that's always a possibility. Maybe she's actually mad about something else."

"No, she's mad about this. She and I get along well otherwise. Our marriage is sound."

"What is it that you want from me, Walter? Why are you calling?"

"To make a request. I wanted to know if you and Alan would come over to our place for dinner some evening. I think it'd be a good way to calm Allison's fears, to see that you're as happily married as she and I are."

There was a long pause on the line.

"I don't know. That sounds an awful lot like a favor to me. And I don't remember owing you any favors, Mr. Magistrate."

"How about if we call it a gesture instead? We're supposed to be friends now, correct? Shouldn't our spouses be friends as well?"

"I don't see any reason why not."

"So, you'll come?"

"Alan is busy with his designs for the new settlement, as you are no doubt well aware. But I don't see why we can't squeeze some time in for dinner."

"Thank you," Walter said.

"My pleasure. An evening of patching holes in my former beau's marriage, how could any ex-girlfriend say no to that?"

17

Mikhail had gotten up and had never come back. The injury to his mouth had been his excuse. The cuts and abrasions from his curbside fall turned out to be relatively minor, but Mikhail had milked them for all they were worth.

After ten minutes had passed, Mary went to check on her brother and tracked him down to an antique rocker in the living room. When he refused to speak to her, she used that as her own excuse to bow out.

The party, a pre-launch Ranger feast, showed the first signs of wrapping up when the children from the conglomerated families began tearing in and out of the entry room, ignoring the familiar "sad man" plopped in the corner.

The other four members of the five-man landing squad were released by their spouses and meandered out of the dining room. Koron came up on one side of Mikhail. Bernard the other. Camden and Samuel took one look at their teammates' sour expression and made a hasty retreat.

Koron said, "What's up, boyo?"

"Not much." Mikhail yawned. "Just full from dinner. I've been sitting here watching the kids run around like maniacs."

"Is everything all right? You don't seem that enthused."

"There are things on my mind, I guess."

"This isn't about what Leo's girl did to you, is it?" Bernard said.

"No. It's not about my busted lip either. It's about what you think it's about. Jocelyn and the baby. I'm sorry. I know nobody likes it when I mope."

"You're not moping," Bernard said. "Not in any way that I can tell."

"I am, though. I came out here so I wouldn't ruin anybody else's fun. I really do apologize, guys. I've worked hard to keep my struggles compartmentalized."

"You don't have to do that, not here," Koron said. "My house is your house. I want you to be yourself when you're here. The good and the bad."

Mikhail looked over at him and brought his hands together in a clap. "Nope. Enough of the pity party. I think I need to go thank your wife, Koron."

Mikhail shot up like a rocket and barreled into the kitchen. With Bernard and Koron in tow, he made his way over to the three wives. Betty Aw, Melindan Stalt, and Willow Oates were all standing together in a row, arranging plates in the dishwasher. Camden and Samuel were at a small table on the flip side of the breakfast bar with fresh bottles of beer in their grasps.

Before Mikhail could say anything, a thunderous crash emanated from the wall behind Camden.

"Kei and Karel are fighting again," Betty said. "Husband, can you?"

Koron flexed his biceps. "My pleasure. I gotta go bust some skulls. Anyone care to lend a hand?"

Bernard accepted the offer, and they were off.

Betty shouted after them, "No spanking, either one of you. Just get them to *stop* with the roughhousing."

Koron's voice had faded as he raced down the hallway. "Gotcha. No blood."

Mikhail approached Koron's wife. "Betty, I wanted to thank you for dinner. It was wonderful. I appreciate you having me." He bent down and kissed her on the cheek. "Excuse my messed up mouth. You're the best. Thanks a lot."

"You're welcome," she said. "You're always welcome."

Willow pressed her forefinger against her own cheek. "Hey, I want one as well. Betty didn't do this by herself."

"Me first," Melindan said as she stepped between Mikhail and Willow. "I did more than these two combined. And don't even think about wasting my time with a peck on the cheek. I want mine right on the lips, handsome."

With a smile, Mikhail did as he was told

BEFORE

"Don't even start. I couldn't tell you about this. I know you too well. You'd have just rejected the idea, without thinking or caring about how I actually felt."

Mary was sitting with her father on the edge of her bed. Less than an hour earlier she'd been glimpsed by an unidentified citizen who had informed Dimitri about a secluded dinner date she was having with one Leonid Bratsk. According to Mary's own admission, this was the sixth time the two of them had spent time alone together, and a serious romance had blossomed.

"I should have known I couldn't have anything for myself," Mary said.

"Do you understand why I'm so against the two of you seeing one another?" Dimitri asked.

"Of course. You like to control things."

"That is not the issue here, young lady."

"It is, Dad. It *so* is."

"Well, think again. I'm against the two of you seeing one another because of the deep familial differences. Under no circumstances will you romantically intermingle with this young man. True, Leonid is a strong and responsible person, more than equipped to lead our landing team on Verdan. But his bloodline, it is not up to Kucherov stock. His great-grandfather was never even supposed to take part in this voyage. His selection sprang from his replacement status, which to my mind is no status at all.

Do you understand what I'm telling you? Leonid would never have been on this ship if it weren't for someone else having second thoughts. The two of you don't belong together, and I will do everything in my power to keep it that way."

"Do you realize this is why I never tell you anything? You always get so superior and snobby. You can't help yourself."

"I think you didn't inform me because you understand in your heart of hearts that Leonid is wrong for you."

"Believe me, that is not what I think at all. But what would you know? It's not as if you've ever seen me as a real person. I'm just a chess piece to you. It's the same for Mikhail. We get no say in anything. You just expect us to be whatever it is that you want us to be, no questions asked."

"That particular interpretation is your brother talking."

"It's me talking also. Me, a girl who likes someone outside of her family's precious inner circle. A girl who is finally sick to death of her father trying to manage every aspect of her life."

"What is that you expect me to do then? Disregard my years of experience? To act against everything I've ever believed in?"

"Yeah, that's exactly what I expect you to do. You should forgo your stupid, arrogant prejudices and let me do what I want to do for once."

Dimitri nodded. "All right, you have a point. I can be flexible. We can try it your way."

"You're just saying that."

"I am not. If you agree to do something for me, then I will do something for you."

"What is it that you want me to do?"

"I want you to stop seeing Leonid."

Mary looked over at him and clenched her teeth. "Just stop. I'm not going to allow you to hoodwink me."

"Hear me out, Mary. This is a serious proposal I'm making here, and a fair one. If you and Leonid take a break for a while, I will consider allowing you to see one another at a later date. In the meantime, you shall begin dating a few men of my own choosing. These will be gentlemen who I see as potential husbands for you."

"I'll bet you already have a list compiled. You've probably been keeping one since I was still in diapers."

"As a matter of fact, I have been. There's one for Mikhail as well. You two are the Collective's future leaders. Who you marry is of the utmost importance. I would never leave such a thing to chance."

"You've never left anything to chance."

Dimitri puffed out his chest. "I'm pleased that you have taken notice of that fact. I take pride in my preparedness, and so should you."

"Oh, yes, it's my *favorite* thing about you."

"Your sarcasm aside, do we have a deal? Will you and Leonid take a break and give me a chance to wield my vaunted matchmaking skills?"

Mary threw her arm back and grabbed one of her pillows. "What kind of names are you talking about here? You have to give me at least one before I'll agree." She paused, pulling the pillow tight. "And don't make it someone from the Four Families either. That would be lame, and obvious, and kind of make my point for me."

"What about Kale Vickery? He's from a decent family. And he's strapping and athletic like someone else we will not mention."

"He also just got married. You need to keep that list of yours updated, Dad."

Dimitri bobbed his head. "What about Camden Muran? He's not married."

"No, but he's divorced, with *kids*. And he's a way older than me. Also, the Murans are a part of what…you can say it, the Four Families."

"There's nothing wrong with the Four Families."

"I never said that there was. But hey, why limit my already limited choices?"

"Fine, I promise to widen my parameters then, as long as we have ourselves an agreement. You and Leonid will take a break until further notice. I see this as our best way to proceed."

"I don't, but it's not like you're giving me much choice. I'll respect your wishes, for now."

"Thank you. That means a lot to me."

"But you need to be well aware that I'm never going to give up on Leo. I have feelings for him, Dad. *Real* feelings. So while you march out your sorry band of suitors, I'm going to spend all my energy convincing you what a great guy he is. And I'm going to keep doing it until I wear you down. I'm falling in love with this man. I think you should understand that. I'm only going along with this to sway you—and because there's no way you could ever find anyone better than Leo. You couldn't even find anyone better than him when you were searching for someone to command the Rangers. You looked high and low, and after all the hemming and hawing, you still had to go with everybody else's first choice. That's the way it's going to be here. There's no one better than Leo. No one anywhere."

"Daughter dear, with open eyes and a dash of reasonable thinking, a deaf, dumb, and blind person could find you a better match for you than Leonid Bratsk."

Mary smiled and let that one go.

Dimitri got up and limped over to the door. "If we're done here, I think it's about time for you to place a call. Leonid needs to be informed about our arrangement. The ground rules are simple, you are *not* to see one another."

"We are not to see one another for a *while*," Mary said as she freed one of her hands from the pillow.

"Until I agree otherwise," Dimitri insisted.

Mary pressed her ear. "Leo Bratsk, call." After a momentary wait, she said, "Hi. Sorry to be coming at you with this out of nowhere, but there's something I need to tell you. It's something bad, although maybe it could also turn into something good."

Mary listened for a second.

"Yeah, he found out. He knows everything."

She listened some more.

"I know, but maybe it's not as bad as all that. Crazily enough, he just offered us a way forward."

Five Years Later

18

Camden knelt down in the dark and nuzzled his face against the mattress. Mary stirred, but did not wake. The corner of a blue and green comforter was all that was covering her otherwise naked frame.

Snoring next to Mary was another nude woman, her head hidden among a strewn collection of floral print scarves. Camden kept still, observing the two female bodies until Mary's breathing had begun to sputter. He blew gently on her cheek and her eyes opened in a sudden, agitated snap.

"You left dinner without saying goodbye," he whispered.

Mary was still half unconscious. "This was my night, my free night."

"It was your free night *after* dinner."

"It's my free night full stop. I went to the dinner for Mikhail, remember? That's the *only* reason I went."

"Okay, and then you abandoned him. The next time any of us saw him he was sulking in that rickety old antique."

The figure on the other side of the bed twitched and said, "Shut up, you two. People are trying to snooze."

Camden took in another eye full. "I see you, Courtney. I see *all* of you."

Dr. Courtney Cutler's legs kicked out as she reached down for the covers.

"Don't be shy on my account," Camden said. "You have a gorgeous body. There's no reason to hide it away."

Courtney pulled hard on the comforter, and in the process, almost jostled Mary off the bed.

"Careful," Mary said. "I'm as exposed as you are."

Once she'd reclaimed a majority of the bedding, Courtney used it to curl up into the fetal position. "Go to sleep. Both of you."

"Sounds like a plan to me." Camden leapt up and started to remove his shirt.

"Don't even think about it," Mary said.

Camden held his hands out innocently. "What? She's the one who offered."

"Because I wanted you out of here, ya big oaf. Get outta here. *Go!*"

"There are two naked ladies in this bed, and you expect me to just leave?"

Mary chuckled. "Don't push your luck, okay? You aren't even supposed to be here. It violates the agreement."

Camden tucked his shirt back in. "I know, but I was worried." He maneuvered around the nightstand and backed up against the wall. "You took off so suddenly. I thought you and Mikhail had another one of your knock-down, drag-outs."

"We're fine. We didn't fight, at least."

"Good."

"And the kids are okay?"

"You bet. They're asleep at my place."

"Asleep?" Mary flipped over and struggled to find him again in the dark. "Are you out of your mind? The children are too young to be left on their own. You know that."

"And they're not alone. Give me some credit. I left Sammo and Willow to keep watch."

"Did you tell Sam and Willow where you were going?"

"Of course not. They think I'm out checking on some emergency with Emily and the other kids."

"They cannot know about this, Cam. No one can ever know about this."

"And they won't. No one but the three of us have any idea about the agreement, I promise. I haven't said a word. So if anyone knows anything, they haven't heard it from me."

The Next Morning

19

Jason and Morgan were alone in the port-side observation lounge, seated back to back on the end of two perpendicular viewing aisles. Outside the ship, on the other side of the reinforced glass, the pearlescent white planet of Kroma loomed ever larger, dwarfing the little green moon that was just becoming visible off the starboard bow.

"Sorry to be the bearer of such bad news," Jason said. "But I thought it'd be better if you heard it from me."

Morgan hunched forward and propped her elbows on her knees. It took her a second before she could speak. "I knew something was going on. I hadn't heard from you in days. I thought you were trying to break it off with me."

"Not a chance. I'd never break it off with you."

"You might not have any other choice now."

Jason turned around and draped himself over the back of the chair. "They have evidence of us being together, or so my mother says. I don't want you lying to protect me. I've already admitted everything. So should you. I'm sure an investigator will be coming by to interrogate you in a day or two. Tell this person everything. I think the truth is our best defense here, don't you?"

"I suppose."

"We sure did fool Joy, though." Jason smiled. "She really thinks we're meeting up in the hothouse. I'll bet her and Mom are waiting for us there right now."

Morgan popped out of her chair. "This is stupid. One of us really needs to go. I never would have suggested that we meet if I had already known we'd been found out."

Jason shot up as well. "I'll go. I just need to know something first. Do you still want us to be together? Is that still the plan here?"

"The truth is, it doesn't matter what I think."

"It matters to me."

"I realize that, Jay. But you're the one who's married to someone else—someone who's just as pregnant as I am."

"I know, and I think I know how I want this to end. I'm just having a bit of trouble saying it out loud."

"Maybe that's your subconscious telling you something. Maybe you're not as sure as you think you are. You need to really consider this. Once you have, you'll be able to make the best, most informed decision that you can."

"And I have to do this all by myself?" he said.

"Like it or not, yours is the only opinion that matters, as right or wrong as that may be."

"I'll think about it, like you said. That's probably all I'll be thinking about."

With that, Jason stepped forward and reached out for her.

"Don't," Morgan said. "Cameras, remember? No touching."

"Are you going to be on your own tonight?" he asked. "With all that's going on, I don't think you should be alone."

"I don't have much of a choice. The kids are with Derek. The house is empty."

"Make your sister come over then. You need to be with somebody. You shouldn't be alone."

Morgan made a move for the door, and then pirouetted back around. "I was worried I was never going to see you again. If nothing else, at least we got this one last chance to be alone."

20

Florin's foot was tapping indiscriminately against the stucco-covered wall.

"Huh, I wondered what that noise was," a voice said from behind the door.

Derek Lucas walked out onto the porch, trailed by his two young daughters, Kitty and Ashley. The siblings bounded ahead on opposite sides of their father, arms raised high, linked together by impenetrable holds of the hands.

"Kitty thought it might be a puppy, struggling to get inside," Derek said.

Kitty was adamant. "I still think it could be."

"Sorry." Florin drew her foot away from the wall. "I didn't realize I was doing that. I was just working up the nerve to knock."

There was a sudden awareness in Derek's eyes. "Are you here because of the—"

"The flowers, *yeah*. I wanted to thank you."

"You're welcome. It's no big thing. I tend to gather flowers when I pass them by, if they're pretty enough. It's become something of a personal tic, I fear. I'm always picking flowers. Always."

Derek brought himself and the kids to an abrupt halt in front of where Florin was standing. Ashley, the youngest, began to fidget and squirm.

"The three of us were on our way to daycare," Derek said. "Would you like to tag along?"

"Sure, why not." Florin took a single step forward.

Derek squeezed his daughters' hands. "Girls, this here is Ms. Florin Holt. She works with me at the Transplant offices."

Kitty and Ashley grunted out their acknowledgments and Florin waved back as the uneasy foursome began chugging their way down the sidewalk.

"Do you work with my Mom, too?" Ashley asked Florin.

"Sort of. I help oversee all three departments where your Mom and Dad work."

"Daddy picks flowers for Mommy, too," Kitty said.

"Oh, does he?"

Derek shook his head. "I *used* to pick flowers for their mother—a past-tense exercise."

"And a fruitless one, now that you're no longer married."

"Then you know that we've, *uh*—"

"Word tends to get around when a man ends a marriage to a woman as beautiful as Morgan Adams."

"Good. It's a relief that you know," Derek said. "I wasn't sure. I didn't know how to bring it up in casual conversation."

"Because you're shy," Florin said, "Or so I've been told."

Ashley twirled. Derek raised their mutual grip so she could continue to spin around and around.

"Daddy's shy," she sang out. *"Daddy's shy."*

"Are you three going to the festival tonight?" Florin asked while Ashley was still singing.

"The kids are," Derek said.

Kitty gave Florin a nasty glare. "Mommy is taking us."

"I'm not invited." Derek cowered and tipped his head at the tramway in the distance. "Which of the parties have you been assigned to oversee?"

"Not a darn one," Florin said. "I'm off for the night. I've done too many of these things in a row. Mary says I'm owed a break, and I'm finding it hard to disagree. I deserve a night to be on my own. You know, fancy free, unattached…all alone."

"Well, that should be fun for you," Derek said.

Ashley shook her father's arm. "She's trying to get you to ask to go with her, Dad."

Florin smiled. "I was actually."

Derek lowered his voice. "Maybe we could meet up later tonight and, *uh*, go together?"

"That sounds nice," Florin said.

As the stroll went on, Ashley kept singing, Kitty kept glowering, and Florin and Derek said very little else.

21

"Thanks for showing up," Mikhail said. "I really appreciate it."

"Hey, you couldn't have stopped me from being here."

Joy wrapped her arm around Mikhail's waist as they walked stride for stride down the hospital corridor.

"Mom wanted to come as well. I know you don't like dealing with her because of the way she voted. But she was planning to come. Things came up, though. Directorate business."

Mikhail looked up at the ceiling and laughed. "Boy, do I know that excuse."

"It wasn't an excuse. She really was busy."

"I know. I didn't say that to be disagreeable. It's just something I've heard my entire life. A true Kucherov tradition. Mary couldn't be here because she had to be there for the Directorate as well. I get the Director-ate business excuse was all I meant. It's more a part of me than my DNA."

Joy let her head rest against Mikhail's arm. "Okay—but we Epelles aren't short on excuses either. Jason was supposed to show up, and he has no good excuse whatsoever."

The double doors leading into the stasis block slid open, without command.

"I told him he didn't have to," Mikhail said as they stepped inside. "From what I hear, Jay has a lot of troubles of his own."

"Boy, does he. And Mom is all ready to strangle him over them. He's been with that other woman again, after he promised he wouldn't. He all but admitted it to me before he did it, too. Yeah, sure, he tried to fool me as to where the rendezvous was happening. But I've never bought into his bull before, so why would I start buying into it now?"

Joy sniffled as they situated themselves on opposite sides of the familiar clear-topped container.

"My beautiful sister," Joy said. "I can't believe we're going be able to talk to her again, in only a few more hours."

Mikhail ran his fingers along the length of the chamber. "There are times I can't even remember what her voice sounded like."

"Whenever that happened to me, I would just watch old dimensionals. I wish I'd known you had the same problem. I could've suggested that. The videos might've helped you to remember."

"I just came here when I wanted to remember. This is where she is, so this is where I needed to be."

"But she looks so different in there. She doesn't look like herself at all."

Mikhail shrugged. "She looks the way she looks. This is the real her, and that's all that matters to me."

"I know, but this room, it can be so gloomy. It's not a healthy place. And you were in here for hours at a time. There was no need for that. Her body might be here, but her mind is elsewhere. I was always kind of hoping you'd spend more time with us, with her family. That would've been a whole lot better than wallowing in this place."

"I wasn't always wallowing." Mikhail spread his fingers out on the glass. "When I'm able to be close to her like this, I know there's going to be an end point. I *will* be with her again. Looking at dimensionals, though, it just feels like she's dead, like it does when I look at footage of my mother."

"I never thought about it that way," Joy said. "And why would I? I've never lost anybody. Not permanently like that."

"I really do miss her," Mikhail said. "I love her so much. Maybe it wasn't all that mutual at first, but my feelings changed over time—they grew."

"I remember."

"It's embarrassing to admit, but I've been on pins and needles the last couple of days. I'm just a much better person when I'm with her. All I want is to be with her again."

"You will be," Joy said. "Soon. Sooner than you can even imagine."

BEFORE

Mary pried herself from Leo's arms. "Oh, no. Somebody's calling."

Leo drew her back to him and kissed her softly. "It could be anybody. Relax. If you don't want this person to know anything, all you have to do is remain calm. If you get online and start acting nervous, you'll give us away."

Mary's eyes narrowed as the Core voice spoke into her ear.

"It's my father."

"That's not unusual, is it? He probably just needs to speak with you. It could be about anything."

"I can't put this off much longer. He gets impatient. I've got to answer this."

"Then answer it." Leo took her by the hand. "I'm right here with you. Think calm thoughts."

Mary tapped her ear. "Hello, Dad. How are you?"

"What took you so long to respond?" Dimitri said.

"I was in the middle of something."

"I'll say. You were in the middle of kissing someone you are not supposed to be kissing."

"What do you mean?"

"Don't play stupid, young lady. You are alone with Leonid on the Esplanade, against the terms of our understanding."

"Where are you?" Mary scrambled to her feet and whipped around in a circle. "Are you lurking out there somewhere? Are you spying on me? I know there are no cameras out here, not in the meadows."

"I do not need to lurk. And I do not require visual aids."

"Someone tipped you off again, didn't they?"

"You don't get to question me. You are the one in trouble here. Deep trouble."

Mary motioned eastward and Leo went over and checked the tree line.

"Having me spied on is creepy, Dad. You do know that, right?"

"And lying is despicable. Breaking a promise is even worse."

Mary stomped her foot into the ground. "I have done *everything* you've told me to do."

"Everything except stay away from Leonid."

"That's right, but I have gone out on umpteen dates with your *applicants*. I even went out on one with Camden last night—and it was *horrible*."

"Doing only half of what you're supposed to do would be seen as a failure in anyone's eyes. How can any of these men compete if you are secretly seeing the person I do not want you to see?"

"Oh, so you finally get it. None of them *can* compete, which means that I'm done. Our understanding is over."

Leo returned, swooping in from behind to help prop her up.

"You're correct there," Dimitri said. "Our understanding is over. You deceived me and have left no room for compromise. From this moment forward, you are never to see this man again. Consider these words an official dictate."

"Good luck trying to enforce that," Mary said. "I love Leo. I won't give him up for anything."

"But of course you will. What other choice do you have? Would you rip the man's career away from him? Because if this does not stop, that is precisely what will happen. Because of your intransigence, I will be forced to remove Leonid as Ranger Commander. And the fault, it will not lie with me. In your possessiveness—in your childish desire to love this man—you will take away everything that makes him special. You will literally rip him from the history books, making him once again the nothing he was almost certainly born to be."

"Why are you always *so* cruel?" Mary said.

"Why are you always so defiant?"

"Because I'm just like you."

The line went quiet for a moment.

"I'm done arguing," Dimitri said. "The time has come for you to do the right thing. You and Leonid are not to be. That was decided the moment you chose to lie. The only question left on the table is will you continue to fight me in vain, or will you do what's best and let Leonid go. The choice is difficult, Mary, but it is one a leader must make. Whether we like it or not, even the most privileged in life do not always get what we want. Despite our position and power, each of us, we only get what we are allowed."

"But I love him, Dad."

"Love is irrelevant. It's best you learn that the hard way."

Mary spun around and buried her face in Leo's chest.

"Break it off with him," Dimitri said. "Break it off quickly. I promise you, this is the last chance either one of you is going to get."

Five Years Later

22

The Green Village maintenance crew had been deployed across the plaza, preparing the grounds for the night's final arrival celebration, to be held concurrently on all three residential decks.

Leo, the lowest ranking of the crewmen, was on all fours in the grass, depressing the top of a tubular dispenser as a fifteenth bulb was propelled skyward. The mobile lighting device rose a dozen meters into the air, locked into alignment with its mates, beeped twice, and began emanating a faint and repeating purple flicker.

Leo was just about to install bulb sixteen when he caught a glimpse of Mary stepping off the northwestern tramway. He managed to look away before she could catch him staring. He slid the lighting dispenser one spot forward.

"Hello," Mary said as she strode into speaking distance. "Not to nitpick, but that last bulb doesn't look like it's operating properly."

"It is, though," Leo replied. "Every fifth light in the chain has been set to shimmer. It hasn't been explained to me why that is, but from what I can gather, conventional wisdom believes it adds ambiance and excitement to an otherwise dull event."

"Shouldn't an event summon said excitement on its own?"

"One would think."

Leo hopped up and offered his hand in greeting. Mary just stood there, mesmerized by the red-brown penal mark that had been tattooed across his forehead. The momentary distraction caused Leo's hand to hang ignored a second too long. He yanked it back to his side. After Mary had regained her senses, she inched up to him and kissed him on the cheek instead.

"I hope I'm not hassling you or keeping you from your work. I haven't seen you in ages, and wanted to check in. Do you have a little time to talk?"

Leo gestured south. There was a bench across the lawn. They strolled toward it, side by side.

"Did you hear about Kay?" Mary asked him.

"I'm not exactly sure what you're referring to, but I did do some work for her the other day. Is that what you're asking me about?"

"No. This is something else. Kay barged into the Directorate session yesterday and demanded that you be reinstated into the Rangers. It became this big ordeal."

As they were arriving at their destination, Leo grumbled, "I never asked her to do that, you know."

"I never thought that you did." Mary bent down and brushed away a light layer of leaves that were scattered across the bench. "But Kay, as always, was quite insistent. She kept saying again and again that you're the only man for the job."

"I bet that went over well."

Mary sat down and slapped the open space to her left. "I need you to sit, too. I won't be able to concentrate if you're standing there hovering at attention."

Leo obeyed, and Mary went on.

"Kay's request was rejected in the end. But it was going your way at first. And then—"

"Deborah."

"I cannot confirm or deny, but you know how she can be."

Leo nodded. "I sort of have to be careful what I say. I don't want to take away from anything that happened. She was wronged. What I did to her was unforgivable."

"Have the two of you spoken recently?"

"I'm not permitted to speak to her. That was part of my sentence, like the tattoo and the maintenance work."

"Of course," Mary said. "I'd forgotten."

"It wouldn't matter anyway. No apology from me could change anything. And after all the bad will I built up with your father when you and I were going through our covert phase, any effort to redeem myself would come off as hollow and self-interested."

Mary flicked away a loose leaf she'd missed during her initial sweep.

"I don't know how aware you are of this," she said, "but my father's pretty ashamed about what he did to keep us apart. He'd never admit it, but he is. Your furlough sentence could have been much, much worse."

"Of that, I am well aware."

Leo retrieved his canteen from the back of his belt and offered Mary a drink, which she politely declined. He shook the canteen and said, "I married Deborah too quickly after you broke up with me. But I would have done anything to forget, so I rushed into things."

"I wasn't any better. I'd already married Camden at that point. Everything happened so fast."

Leo flipped open the canteen top. "Deb and I, we had a relationship that predated the two of us. But it was always a casual thing. The marriage was a bad idea from the start. Happiness wasn't something I wanted anymore. I didn't want anything after you."

"Neither did I," Mary said.

"I don't why I brought all this up. It's over and done with, and nothing can change it."

"Kay sure thinks she can change things."

"But she can't. She should know that."

"She believes in you," Mary said. "A lot of us believe in you."

"And too many more condemn me." Leo finally took a swig from the canteen, and then re-capped it. "I'm under no delusion. I want to be on that ship with the men more than anything, but that cannot happen. I wish Kay would stop bullying everyone on my behalf. It's unseemly, and makes my shame feel that much more perverse."

Mary put her hand on Leo's back. "I wish you wouldn't think that way. You are a dear man who made a horrific mistake. And despite everything, I still get that core, incredible person you are. I loved you so much. You must know that."

"Don't, Mary...I'm begging you."

"But I have things to say. Things that should have been said a long time ago."

"I know exactly what you have to say, and saying it will do neither of us any good."

"All right. Whatever you want." She yanked her hand away and returned it to her lap.

"If we had been together," Leo told her, "you have to know, what I did to Deborah, I could never have done that to you."

"Of course you couldn't. Because if I had stood up to my father and you and I had gotten married, there'd have been no reason for you to be so angry."

"We really shouldn't be talking about any of this," Leo said.

"I know, I know." Mary lifted herself off the bench. "I should get going, and you need to get back to work."

Leo got up as well and together they cut across the lawn. They didn't speak another word until they were all the way over to the tramway.

"Kay can go too far sometimes," Leo said. "But that doesn't mean she isn't right about a few things. The unknown, it is precarious. Make sure to tell Camden he needs to be beyond cautious when the team hits the ground. He should never stop thinking. Whisper that into his ear. Hammer it home. He needs to be on his toes at all times. Concentration is everything as far as this landing is concerned. That's his one true duty as mission commander, unflinching concentration."

Mary got back on to the tram car. "I'll make him understand. I'll relay every word."

"I appreciate it. It's always a pleasure to see you, Mary."

"Same here. We'll talk again soon."

23

Jason came waltzing through the front door. Angela was waiting there in the living room, huddled on the couch. To her right, a knickknack cabinet lay overturned, its contents shattered and splayed across the carpeted floor.

"You ready for the party, honey?"

Angela was staring up at Jason as he crossed into view. "What did you just say to me?"

"What do you think I said? I was asking about the party. Are you ready to go?"

Jason squatted down over the fallen cabinet and inspected several of the broken keepsakes. "What the heck happened to your collection?"

"I know, you piece of crap. I know everything."

Jason closed his eyes and set the porcelain clown head back where he had found it. He eased himself upward and took a wide path around the mess on the floor.

"Who told you?" he asked as he plopped down next to his wife on the black and blue sofa.

"Does it matter who told me? *You* were supposed to tell me. Why didn't you tell me? Why did you let this horror stew?"

He clicked the roof of his mouth with his tongue. "I don't know. I felt guilty."

"You are a sad and pathetic man. This cannot be a revelation to you, can it? You really do make me sick."

"Geez, what do you want? I said I felt guilty."

"Don't you dare try to turn this. I'm not going to believe a word that comes out of your mouth, so you might as well stop."

"I love you, honey. You know that I do."

"I know nothing of the sort. You impregnated another woman—*that* is what you think of me. I mean, it's bad enough that you had to stick it in her. But then, with your horrid luck and complete incompetence with everything you've ever touched, you had to amp up this mess with a baby—*another* baby. What is wrong with you? Don't you know a thing? Have you never learned to pull out? That's what you do when you're cheating, Jay. You pull the hell out."

He shook his head. "I don't know what to say."

"Start with this—you never loved me. It's obvious you never did."

"You're wrong."

"No, *you* are wrong. Mentally. Morally. Legally. You've screwed up both of our lives, not to mention our children's lives. We're all going to be pariahs."

"I know. I'm sorry." Jason attempted to slide closer to her, but the couch was long, and she just scooted farther away.

"Oh, you're sorry, all right. Sorry that you're potent. Sorry that you make babies like this mindless, horny rabbit. Was one woman not good enough for you? Were our *children* not good enough for you? Tell me, what was so important about this woman that you had to go and destroy all of our lives?"

"Do you want me to leave?" he said as he pointed over at the door. "If you want me to, I'll go right now."

Angela's mouth was hanging open. "And go live with *her*. No way. That cannot happen. You understand me? You and Morgan Adams are done. You are done with that child, and you are done with her. We'll never get past this publicly if you *ever* get caught with her again."

Jason looked at her and winced.

Angela balled up her fists. "You've seen her again, haven't you?"

"Just once. This morning…briefly. It was in public, so don't worry. She told me to think about what's happened. She wants me to think about it hard."

"Terrific. That should tell you how well she knows you. Thinking is the *last* thing that you should ever do."

"You're right. I'm an idiot."

"No more of her, I mean it. Appearances are everything from here on out, especially while the investigation is underway. Do not disregard me on this. I am in complete charge now. You will do as I say—*everything* that I say."

"Just so I'm clear," Jason said. "Are you telling me that I get to keep on living here?"

"What other choice do I have? I'm pregnant. The only way to keep you out of serious trouble, and save me eternal ridicule, is to keep up appearances."

"Then you're going with my mother's plan?"

"If you have a better idea, then now is the time."

"Thank you," he said. "I don't deserve it, but thank you anyway."

Angela lifted herself off the couch. Her rounded belly slowed her upward momentum, but did not impede it.

"I'm off to bed. You are sitting on your bed. Get your own blanket."

"So, we're *not* going to the arrival party?" Jason said.

"I think it's best if I skip that tonight. You should probably skip it as well. Who knows what kind of trouble you'd get into on your own."

"Is it okay if I say good night to Jerald?"

"He's at my parents' house," Angela said as she hobbled down the hall.

"That's probably wise." A second later, Jason was up and chasing after her. "Can you hold on a minute? I have more apologies to make. Please, stop. You *need* to hear what I have to say."

Angela planted her feet in the bedroom doorway. "The only thing I need to do is cry. The only thing you need to do is stay out of my sight."

24

Florin danced her way around Derek, who was doing everything he could to keep up with the accelerated beat. Face to face once more, Derek took Florin by the hand and she whirled, her mini-dress bobbing high before cascading back into place. The song reached its soft crescendo of an ending and Florin twirled twice more before falling into her partner's waiting arms. Derek seized the split-second lull as an opportunity to exit the parquet floor. Florin was having none of that. She clamped down on his wrist and pulled him close.

"One more time. I'm not ready to stop."

"Sorry. No more for me. I'm due a break."

"The old man needs a rest, huh?"

"Tease me all you like, but I still require a breather." Derek held his hand out at an unoccupied patio table three rows away. "After you?"

Florin was snapping her fingers as they weaved their way through the crowd. The entire population of the Red Village deck appeared to be in attendance. Lights flickered. Voices hummed. Spirits soared.

"Wait," Florin said. "We have to do something first."

"What?" Derek asked, immediately suspicious. "What are we doing now?"

"You need to meet my family."

"*Your* family?"

Florin tore off and Derek had to make an effort to catch up.

"I don't think meeting your family is appropriate. Not yet at least. You know what I'm talking about, this is our first date."

"It's too late now," Florin said. "They've seen us."

There were three people seated at the Merriweather's table. One was a young man around Florin's age. The other was a woman in her seventies. Lastly, there was Kimberly Akana, the esteemed ex-Trustee, and the eternally well-thought-of "treasures of all treasures."

"Hello, hello," Kimberly said. "You look beautiful tonight, my dear. Downright fetching."

Florin curtseyed. "Thank you."

"And who is this handsome friend of yours?"

"This is Derek Lucas, Nana. We work together in the Transplant offices. He's the Scholastics Manager. And I'm his boss. Sort of." Florin turned to make sure her date was still paying attention. "Derek, this is my great-grandmother, Kimberly Akana."

Derek approached the table and shook the elderly woman's hand. "It's a pleasure to make your acquaintance, Madam Trustee. I've admired your work for as long as I can remember. The way you shepherded the expert-specific lesson plans through the Directorate was the stuff of legends where I grew up. My parents were—are—primary-ed teachers, and what you accomplished inspired me to become a teacher as well. The idea of Einstein giving lessons on physics, and having Dickens teach creative writing—it changed the entire education system. To even consider it now, it still blows my mind. It was true original thinking. Thank you for that, and for everything else you've done for the Collective."

The young man at the table said, "Hold up there, don't go too overboard with the compliments. Kimmie will never stop talking about this stuff if you do. She loves to yammer on about lesson plans. There's nothing this woman loves more than a lesson plan."

Florin rolled her eyes. "And this spoilsport here is Tristan. He's one of my brothers."

"Hello, Tristan," Derek said.

"It's good to meet you."

The two men shook hands.

"Oh, and sis," Tristan said. "In case you were unaware, while you were dancing, your dress was flying every which way."

Florin smirked. "Was it? I guess I was unaware."

Derek played along. "I was unaware as well."

"What a polite young man," Kimberly said.

"Well, everyone else sure did notice," Tristan said. "And I do mean everyone."

The woman next to him, who'd yet to be introduced, swatted Tristan on the arm. "And I'm Laken Merriweather, grandmother to these two bickering brats."

"Nice to meet you all," Derek said.

Florin scanned the immediate area. "Where are Mom and Dad, and everyone else?"

"They're around, somewhere," Laken said. "I'm sure they'll be back in a minute or two."

"Did you need them for something specific?" Kimberly asked.

"No, not really. I just thought it'd be easier if they met Derek while we were already going through the process. It'd save us the effort later, if the need arises."

Laken removed a strewn coat from the back of an otherwise empty chair. "As I said, they shouldn't be gone long. Would you two like to sit down?"

"We'd better not," Florin said. "Derek was nervous enough just to meet you. I don't want to force him to have an extended conversation, that might induce cardiac arrest."

"How are the schedule changes proceeding?" Laken asked Florin.

"Good. I made all the cuts you were asking for."

"And did you strike yourself off the first day list?"

"Yes, but only because you and Mary ordered me to."

"It's not that you cannot go down to the moon, hon. It's that you cannot go down there right away. This is not your personal adventure hour we're running here. You being down there would be too much of a risk.

You have no training."

"I know that."

"When everything is determined to be safe," Laken said, "I'll make certain you're one of the first civilians to travel down."

"Thank you. I appreciate that." Florin snagged Derek's hand. "We should probably go find a table of our own, right?"

Derek nodded.

"You two enjoy yourselves," Kimberly said. "And I hope we get to see more of you, Derek."

Laken and Tristan offered up their own pleasantries. Derek said good-bye to all three, and he and Florin were off.

"That wasn't so bad," Florin said once they were several steps away. "Was it?"

"In reality...no. In the abstract, however, your family can be rather intimidating. All the history. All the great leaders. And your great-grandmother, still so vibrant. I was sure I was going to say something stupid."

"But you didn't."

"Because they're all so pleasant. Getting to speak with Mrs. Akana was a genuine thrill. I wasn't just blowing smoke with all my compliments. I've seen her around before, but I never would have gone up and pestered her on my own like that, not if I wasn't with you."

"Well, they all seemed to like you."

"That's a relief," he said.

"Not that you're out of the woods yet. You still have to meet my father." Florin slid into a chair at the first empty table she could find. "He likes to pretend he's some kind of a tough guy, particularly around my many suitors. The trick is to go chest-to-chest with him right off the bat."

Derek took the chair directly across from Florin. A few tables down, he noticed two teenage boys were glaring over at him.

"Do you know those young men over there?" Derek asked, his voice hushed.

Florin turned to see who he was referring to.

"I do. Unfortunately."

"Why are they giving me the evil eye?"

"Vlad is a guy I sort of date sometimes. His clodhopper cohort is his best buddy Jance."

Derek crossed his arms. "A guy you date sometimes, huh? I didn't know you were dating anyone at the moment."

"I'm not going steady with anyone, if that's what you're trying to say. I prefer to keep things casual."

Without warning, Florin leapt up and switched chairs to the one right beside Derek.

"I have to ask," he said. "What did you mean by that? You prefer to keep things casual?"

"I mean, I see several guys at the same time. Individually, that is. I don't literally see them all at the same time."

"I didn't think you were dating anyone at all," Derek said.

"Yeah, you said that before. But aren't you and I on a date now?"

"Obviously." Derek took another long look at the two glaring teenagers. "Was your relationship with this Vlad serious?"

"Serious in his mind. Not serious in reality."

"Is he in love with you?"

"Oh, desperately in love," Florin raised her voice as if she wanted Vladimir to overhear everything she said. "*Way* too intensely in love."

"And you don't feel the same way?"

"I'm sixteen. Now is not the time to be serious about anything, especially about love."

"Most girls your age are serious about exactly that. Sixteen is the age most girls get married on this ship. This is the time of life when things do tend to move beyond the casual."

"You sound just like Vladimir, which is not a compliment."

"There's no reason to get testy," Derek said. "I was married young, as young as you are now. If you find yourself in a good situation, there's nothing wrong with getting married early."

"And how well did that work out for you? It's not as if you're married anymore."

"It worked for as long as it worked. I have my daughters, and I got a good start in life. The right kind of start in life."

"Sure, but I'd rather spend my teenage years actually discovering what kind of man I want to spend the rest of my life with. If that's a problem for you, let me know now."

Derek shrugged.

"Then I consider this subject is closed." Florin gave Derek a light smack on the arm. "Get your butt up. I'm not finished dancing yet."

"I can't. I still need more of a breather." Derek motioned over at Vladimir. "Why don't you ask your friend to share a number or two. I don't mind. I didn't show up tonight with a plan to come between you and another man. It'd only be fair if you gave him a dance as well."

Florin leaned in and whispered into Derek's ear, "I don't want to dance with Vlad. I came here with you. I *only* want to dance with you. So, whenever you're ready, I will be ready. I can be patient if I have to be, believe it or not."

"You don't have to wait is what I'm trying to say. You can dance with whomever you want to dance with."

"Would you stop being so magnanimous. You're not stepping on anyone's toes here, okay?"

"Okay."

"Good. I don't want mopey 'ol Vlad scaring you away. As you can probably tell, I can be scary enough on my own."

25

"We're running out of time, and there's something I really need to discuss with you."

Camden waved Mary off. "Sorry, my sweet, no can do. My date with destiny awaits. Whatever it is that you need, we're going to have to put it off."

Unhappy, Mary slipped her hand under the table and pinched his leg.

Camden's families, both of his families, had gathered as one. A pair of circular tables had been pushed together to accommodate the ever-expanding brood. Camden sat at the head of one place setting with Mary. Their eldest son Rex, a portly toddler, lay in his mother's lap, worn out at this unusually late point in the evening. Infants Kip and Charin dozed in matching cradles that were lined up head to toe on the surface of the table.

The children from Camden's first marriage filled the secondary settings. Charles, Sarah, Vincent, and Luke were all much older than Mary's kids, and at times, could be somewhat aloof with their stepmother. Currently, the four were bunched up in quiet conversation with their own mother, Emily Corson, and the two babies from her most recent marriage.

"For your information," Mary said, "what I have to tell you cannot and will not be put off." She returned her hand to the table and bumped Charin's cradle, which stirred both of her infants. "And don't you ever treat me like I'm stupid, or can be ignored. I know what your schedule is. You have a half hour before the preflight briefing. I won't let you b.s. me into backing off. I have things to say, mission-centric things."

Camden slumped down in his chair. "I see, you intend to steal away my potential last few minutes with my children?"

Up from his seat at the other table, Charles Muran tapped his father on the shoulder.

"Did I just hear you were taking off, Dad? I'd like to say something first."

Camden turned to the anxious fifteen-year-old. "Go ahead, kiddo. What's on your mind?"

"It's nothing huge. I just wanted to wish you luck and make sure you know how proud I am of what you're doing. Having my own father leading the landing team is just about the coolest thing ever. I didn't want to let this kind of moment go by without saying I love you, and I'm lucky that you're my dad."

Charles extended his arm to seal the proclamation with a handshake. Camden jumped up and brought the boy into his arms, hugging him until he gasped.

"That's wonderful to hear, son. Particularly with these jittery nerves I've been having."

"There's no way you can be nervous," Charles said. "Not you."

Father and son separated. The other children began to chime in.

"Love you, too, Daddy," Sarah said.

"Yeah, love you," Vincent said.

"And be careful," Luke added. "Real careful."

Camden moved around and embraced each of the children, one by one. Emotion was getting the better of the gregarious Ranger. Even Emily patted him on the back as he plodded by.

"Take care of yourself, you big galoot."

Charles sat back down and said to his father, "I'll be on the ground the day after tomorrow, with Mary and the Transplants. If everything goes like it's supposed to, we can meet up for chow then. Sound good to you?"

"I *cannot* wait," Camden bellowed.

Out of nowhere, Emily had started shaking her arm. "Mary—you need to take a look at the front of the stage."

Mary swiveled left and saw what had Emily so concerned. Dimitri was sneaking up behind Mikhail. Drawing Rex from her lap, Mary handed the grumbling boy to Camden.

"I have to get over there. We'll speak after the briefing, Cam. We still need to have our chat."

"If there's time."

Mary called back to the table after she was already in mid-stride. "Emily, could you keep an eye on the babies for a sec?"

"You bet."

Mary ran toward the stage and her voice grew louder. "I'm so sorry to do this to everyone, but this is a major league fire here, and I'm the only one who can put it out."

26

"Mikhail, I know you have chosen not to speak with me. You believe I have done you wrong, and I respect that. The endless choices I have made in my life have not always been palatable, even to myself. All I can say in my defense is that I have always acted in the interest of others. Fortune, personal desires—love—they have always come second to me. Family has come second as well. The priority of my life is to make certain the colonists on this voyage have everything they need to survive. And what this society needs at the moment is a win—a large win. Success tonight, literal or otherwise, will bolster what are sure to be rough transition days ahead. I did what I did because you *had* to be the first of us to set foot upon Verdan. And your daughter, she *had* to be the first child born on Verdan. These are the storybook conclusions, and they had to happen. When times passes and hurt feelings fade, I am certain you will begin to see things the way I have seen things. This last year, and its inherent darkness, was not endured on a whim. What was done was done for others, for these people here on this ship, untethered for so many years. If nothing else, I needed to take this moment to thank you for your sacrifices. I didn't want you to do what you are about to do without understanding that you do it for something greater."

Dimitri collected his hands in his lap. He was positioned directly behind Mikhail, hovering in place with the assistance of his mover chair—a device he had never utilized in such a public forum.

Throughout his father's spiel, Mikhail had remained perfectly still. Afterward, he wasn't moving much either.

Mary came racing over. Out of breath, she dropped her hands on the back of the chair, clutching onto it to keep herself from collapsing from exertion.

"What's going on here?" she asked both men.

Mikhail flipped his hand at Dimitri. "This thing in the cripple chair wants to be forgiven."

"Don't call him that," Mary said. "That's out of line."

"Approaching me here, where this living skeleton knew I couldn't overreact, that was out of line as well. But I don't hear you complaining about that."

Mary tightened her grip on the mover chair and pushed it away. "Let's go, Dad."

"Don't hurry off," Mikhail said. "I'll walk with you."

People were beginning to take notice. After so long, the great family was together again, strolling down the sidewalk.

"Go away," Mary told her brother.

"Ah, don't be that way. Let's give the old man what he wanted, the much-needed image of us as a happy little unit. The show tonight would mean nothing without that."

Mary shook her head. "This meanness will not help Jocelyn, you know."

"Who said it was meant to? I do what I do to help everyone else. I'm not self-centered and hateful. I'm like Dad. I'm a giver."

One person in the crowd cheered, and before too long everyone present was cheering. The sight of Dimitri and his children filled the party with an uncontainable joy.

Mikhail joined his sister behind the chair and saluted the crowd. "My wife and child may have been locked up against their wills and kept asleep unnaturally, but at least we have this glorious moment. The Kucherovs are reunited. The Collective is triumphant. Any and all problems will surely disintegrate away."

"Yeah, well," Mary said. "The moment has happened now. We're done.

Leave us alone."

Mikhail bared his most winning smile. "But I'm only doing what Dad wanted. He likes to boast that he sees the world three, four steps ahead. And yet there are a few things that even he hasn't considered."

Dimitri was eying the crowd as he said, "What haven't I seen, son?"

"The epilogue, of course. Yes, you get what you want, as always. I will step out and be the first. And my daughter will do her bit as well. But like all good melodramas, there will be a reckoning, a price to pay for the villains of our tale."

"*Stop* it," Mary said. "Just *stop* it."

"I wish I could, sis. But this is all out of my hands now. The die has been cast. Those responsible for the brutalization of Jocelyn and my child will *never* get to see that child. And I mean never. If I have to run away to some unknown crevice on that moon, I will make it my life's work to keep the responsible parties far away from my girl. Knowing her, loving her, *using* her, it won't happen, not ever again."

Mikhail hurled his arms up in celebration.

"Talk about your storybook endings. This one, it's going to be my all-time favorite."

27

Walter had witnessed everything. He and his family were together at their table, only twenty short meters away.

Initially, he'd gotten up when Dimitri had sped past them, on his way over to Mikhail. Exerting control, Allison had refused to allow Walter to leave, insisting that Courtney and the kids be given at least a few more minutes of together time. The events surrounding the landing would take him away soon enough. Until they did, he was theirs and theirs alone.

Allison's decree held firm for several minutes. But after the Kucherovs had separated, and the cheers had faded, Walter was on his feet again.

"I'll be right back," he said.

Allison grabbed him by the back of his belt, preventing his escape. "Don't you dare."

"I have to. You didn't see what I just saw. He needs me."

"I do not care," Allison said.

Walter thrashed around a bit, but Allison would not give in.

"Mary's with Dimitri," Courtney said. She was seated next to her husband Bailey. "She can handle whatever it is you think is going on."

Walter watched as Mary bent down and spoke to her father.

"I guess you're right," he said.

Allison released her grip on him and Walter sulked back to his seat. Following a few vague comments about Mikhail's show of family unity, the conversation deviated back to the grandchildren, and Jimmy's latest and greatest art project. It was a watercolor of Verdan, a self-described swirl of green and white. The boy called the image up on the tabletop display and they all marveled at his newfound gift with colors.

Day One

28

"When the hell are we going to be let out of here?" Mikhail said, to no one in particular.

"Two minutes, supposedly." The response came from the far end of the lineup.

The five Rangers were standing in front of a wall of curtained-off changing ports. To a man, the reconnaissance unit exuded varying degrees of anxiety and impatience. Mikhail's hips were rocking and he was repeating the number two as if he held it in unassailable contempt. Camden had removed his right glove and was tearing away at a frayed fingernail. Bernard was doing nothing but staring downward while Koron kept changing his stance. Samuel, generally the most distractible of the lot, was humming along to his favorite military march.

The launch room the Rangers had been assigned was, in actuality, a cannibalized recreations center, chosen for its size and proximity, located a single deck above of the *Horizon*'s starboard hangar bay. Following their well-rehearsed schedule to the letter, the five men had entered said area and promptly changed into their field gear, emerging one after the other, outfitted to the nines, and ready to disembark.

The base component of their customized environment suits was a light brown sheath, a skintight protective garment designed to protect from any form of weather the team might encounter on the alien surface below. Remotely monitored, and fully connected to the ship's grid architecture, the pale fabric stretched up and down the men's muscular frames, from the sides of their faces to the stockings around their feet. Loose-fitting khaki pants overlaid the sheaths from the waist down. Powering the ensemble, pouched energy packs were wrapped firmly around their waists.

"I don't know about you guys, but I am bored out of my freaking mind," Mikhail said as he jerked out of position and stomped toward the door. The reinforced metal on the soles of his boots clicked and clacked, accentuating his every step. When he ran up against a sealed doorway, and it did not open, Mikhail brought himself up to a bright red line and yelled out at anyone who might be listening in. "Let's *go* already, people."

Camden came up next to him. His boots were making an identical clacking noise. "In a minute and a half, that's precisely what we will be doing. But first, you need to back yourself up. At least for now, I take the point."

"I apologize." Mikhail swung rightward and allowed Camden to take his place at the front of the line. "I didn't mean anything by that. I just have my father's voice stuck in my head. *Always take the lead. Never equivocate.*"

Camden nodded. "What did your father want on the patio tonight?"

"To talk. To rationalize his brutality. I couldn't stomach a word he said, so I gave him what he deserved, I told him what I really think of him."

Mikhail laughed at that, a little too loudly.

"Good for you," Camden said. "But now you're gonna have to let all that go. You're acting like you could go catatonic again, and I can't have that. I know it's difficult, but I need you to push everything out of your head except this mission. Until this is over, our minds—*all* of our minds—they need to be as clear as we can make them."

"I'll be okay," Mikhail said. "I'm just feeling a little frustrated. The sooner we get going, the sooner Jocelyn will be woken up. Once that happens, I'll be as right as rain again."

Camden counted off with his fingers. "Land safely. Find the Constructs. And don't screw anything up. If we can pull those three things off, then Jocelyn is back in your arms in a matter of hours. It's all up to us now."

"The way it should be."

Mikhail's gaze was drifting, from the door, to the floor, to the ceiling. The man, clearly, was a million miles away.

Camden was about to say something else when the door behind him slid open and Kay appeared. Mikhail and Camden took a full step backward so she could enter. Almost at once, the other Rangers began hooting and howling. Much to her embarrassment, Kay was decked out in a sequined white evening gown.

"Look who's looking hot," Camden said.

"I've been telling you all," Samuel said. "Pasty skin is such a ridiculous turn on."

"This dress was not my idea." Kay yanked on the pliable fabric. "The Founder wanted me to wear it, and I'm stripping out of it first chance I get."

Samuel hopped up and down. "*Damn*, and we have to leave? I'm gonna hate to miss that party."

"Moving on." Kay adjusted her bra strap and jabbed her finger over her shoulder, drawing the men's attention to the outer hallway. "The time has arrived. We're ready to go. For those of you too slow on the uptake, the hangar entrance is just outside, a mere four doors down. Come on, follow me out."

"Which way is right again?" Samuel asked. "Do that pointy thing one more time."

His jest went ignored. Kay put her foot back down on the activation pad and the door reopened. The sound of raucous applause spilled into the room.

"It's your moment, fellas. There are a few people waiting outside to wish you luck."

"Who's out there?" Mikhail asked.

Kay backed through the doorway as the clapping grew louder. "Honestly, I think it's just about everyone."

Camden strutted out first, followed by Mikhail. The hallway was indeed packed, lined with significant figures from all walks of Collective life, including the Rangers' own families, who were standing beside the highest-ranking politicians. Samuel rushed over and hugged his wife. Koron picked up his sons. Bernard saluted the crowd. Camden blew a kiss at Mary and his children, all seven of them. Mikhail glanced over at the delegation of Directorate Trustees. Walter was in the lead, but Dimitri was nowhere to be seen.

"Best of luck, boys," somebody yelled.

Final farewells were made and the Rangers wheeled around and headed for the tubular hub in the center of the four-corridor intersection. Down each of the passageways, the crowds were crushed in tight. The noise levels increased again when the Rangers jaunted into view. Koron, Bernard, Samuel, and Mikhail all entered the tram car. Camden paused and executed a dramatic bow, to the elation of the onlookers. A group chant began.

Rangers! Rangers!

Camden stepped backward, as brazen as can be, and the tram doors closed in front of him. In an instant, the roar of the crowd was cut off.

"That was kind of fun," Samuel said.

The tram car jolted upward.

Camden snuck a quick look at Mikhail. "He wasn't there. Dimitri is always present for these sorts of things, even when he's as sick as a dog. But I looked for him all down the line, and he wasn't there. What the heck did you say to him?"

"I told him the truth," Mikhail said. "I told him how life is going to be from now on out."

29

"Has anyone seen Trustee Kucherov? Please, any help you can give me. It's important that I find him."

Walter continued to maneuver his way through the throng of late-night partygoers. Every time he stopped to question anyone, the encounter concluded in the same way—with his eyes shifting from side to side, searching for any sign or trace of his missing friend.

Annabeth Corrine eventually flagged Walter down, and with a head bob to the south, sent him off in the proper direction. He tracked Dimitri down thirty seconds later. The great man was seated in front of the stage, his mover chair abandoned beside a recently replanted fir tree.

Walter swerved into the aisle where Dimitri had situated himself. "Where the heck have you been?" he asked when he was still a meter or so away. "When you didn't show for the ceremony in the corridor, I became concerned. What on earth happened?"

Dimitri was staring ahead at the pair of dimensional columns that were projecting down on the stage. The first of the images was monitoring the Rangers and their support crew as the two teams were strapped into a ring of reinforced safety harnesses. The second cone displayed an exterior hangar bay view of the *Spear*, the spire aircraft that was serving as the primary transport for the long-awaited operation.

Walter took a seat and said, "Are you awake? Is that what's going on? Have you been dozing?"

Dimitri did not respond, although his eyes did appear to be open.

"If nothing else, can I get some feedback from you? Were you able to see the send-off in the hallway?"

Dimitri cleared his throat. "I saw it."

"Was everything working visually? What I'm asking is, was it working the way you wanted it to?"

"It was terrific. Perfect. Every base was covered. The boys looked surprised, and Camden made a semi-adorable spectacle of himself. That bow of his was inspired. I couldn't have asked for better optics."

"Unless, of course, you yourself had been there."

Dimitri scratched the side of his face. "I decided my presence wasn't appropriate this evening. I didn't want to be a distraction."

"Come on, you're just being silly."

"I am never silly, Walter. I am incapable of silliness."

"But you are overly sensitive. I understand that Mikhail lashed out at you, but I warned you about approaching him. For the moment, forgiveness from him is a long way off. You have told me before you accepted that. Your son may be malleable on certain fronts, but the Jocelyn situation will never be one of them."

Dimitri lowered his head. "I did not approach him to fish for his forgiveness. I wanted to explain my motivations. The boy has never given me the opportunity to make my case for what was done. I needed to do that, for myself."

Walter nodded. "You have to promise me you will let this go for the time being. Mikhail will come around. I know that he will. Mary knows that he will, too. She has said as much, to both of us."

"I've never been as confident about that as the two of you seem to be."

"Then trust that we are both smart people, and actually know a few things."

"Of course I trust you, Walter. Of course I do."

The Core voice popped online and announced, "Citizens of the Collective, the Verdan countdown clock has now reached fifteen minutes to launch."

30

All strapped in, Camden shouted, "What do you mean you've never actually flown this thing before? How is such a thing even possible?"

"Logic makes it possible." The scratchy voice of Tarissa Solano, the *Spear*'s lead pilot, rang down from above. "Before this morning, name a place where I could have flown this ship? While the *Horizon* was rocketing through space at gazillions of kilometers per hour? Maybe while we were jumping through a quantum fissure? Please, Commander, you cannot be this dense. Think about it. A spire is a landing vessel. With no place to land, it's impossible for me to have flown one before today. I'm sorry if this fact bothers you, but I'll have you know I've run thousands upon thousands of simulations, and they have all been severely rough. My guess is, far rougher than anything we'll encounter in the atmosphere today. You can check the meteorology reports. Visibility over the drop zone is good. In other words, relax and shut your mouth. The aerial portion of this mission is well in hand. You just worry about looking good and walking erect. As far as I can tell, that's about all that's being asked of you today."

"Hey now, that was uncalled for," Camden said, a beat or two after Tarissa had stopped speaking. "I think we're being asked to do more than walk erect. We've been issued weapons, haven't we?"

"Yeah," Mikhail said. "If only we could fire without Directorate permission."

Samuel jumped into the fray. "You can't let her get away with that, boss.

Why does she care so much if we're erect or not?"

"Solano," Camden said, reestablishing contact with the command pod. "My men and I want to lodge a complaint. These excuses of yours, they're not making any of us feel any better. We're not asking for much here. All we want is a pilot up top who knows how to fly. You know, someone with some actual experience."

"And that's precisely what you have," Tarissa said. "The most experienced pilot available. You're welcome. You can go back to shutting your mouth now."

"Best of luck from the rest of us down here," Mikhail said. "We all have total and complete confidence in you, Tarissa. Camden does as well. Don't take what he has to say too personally. He's well aware of your skill. He just likes to rile people up."

"Is that so? I guess that would explain why he's been going around calling me that crazy old bat of a pilot."

Camden shrank in his seat. "Who told you that?"

"Just about anyone who's come into contact with you."

Camden fought back a grin. "Listen, I only phrased it that way because I was so enamored by your amazing ability to soar through the air. It's like you can fly almost naturally? You know, like a bat."

"Clever boy," Tarissa said. "But how do you justify the use of the pejorative *crazy old*?"

"Oh, that was just me being dicky. Sorry."

Camden and Samuel exchanged a high five.

"Sadly," Tarissa said. "Playtime is at an end. I still have an updated flight plan to go over with you and the support crew. I'll be back with that in just one second."

Silence reigned once more. The Rangers' interests shifted to the ring of observation windows that wound all the way around them. Outside the spire, swarms of technicians were piloting repair cranes along the exterior of the giant aircraft, giving the ship its final, obligatory once over.

Koron and Bernard, the Rangers at the far ends of the circular harness chain, turned to acknowledge the four civilians on their respective left and right. Bernard nodded his head at Documentarian Jon Adello and Chief Physician William Holt. Koron eyed Chief Technician Alexander Ling, and, the most unsettled of the bunch, Chief Theorist Meyer Wells.

"Well, well," Camden said, never able to remain silent for long. "Any day now with that rundown would be nice. It's not like we're under any time constraints or anything."

Tarissa barked out a short voice command to the *Horizon*'s ligate and said, "All right, listen up, you yahoos. In one minute and forty-seven seconds, the bottom of the hangar deck will open and the clamps holding this ship to the ceiling will release. You will feel a slight jolt, and then the *Spear* will fall into open space. Our push drive engines will then be fired and move us into orbital position just above the coordinates where the Construct spire either crashed or landed. Once the proper alignments have been set, we will enter the Verdanian atmosphere. Upon said entry, the ship's hoop drive will fire up and we'll begin a controlled free fall to the surface. At seven hundred and fifty kilometers before splat, the deceleration process will level out, and I will set us down nice and softly on the ground."

Camden faked a yawn. "Is that? Please tell me that's it. I am so bored."

"That's it," Tarissa said. "We're now thirty-six seconds out. Get ready. The hangar is opening."

Mikhail checked the countdown clock on the windowpane in front of him.

Camden gave his kneecaps a smack. "I don't know about the rest of you guys, but I'm ready to go make us some history."

The other Rangers cheered and hollered. The support crew joined in as well, although at much lesser volumes.

"The day is *now*," Camden cried. "The ass-kicking explorers...*they-are-us!*"

The copilot's voice cut into the outburst. "We are at three, two, one. The hatch is clear. We have full release. The *Spear* is dropping. I repeat, the *Spear* is dropping."

31

"I can't see a damn thing," Samuel said. "Can any of you?"

Eight voices responded, a clamor of roars, grunts, and full-on complaints.

For the last several minutes, the only images on the observation windows had been the live feeds from the cameras attached to the aft end of the spire. As it turned out, the cloud cover below had been thicker than expected.

Tarissa spoke into the men's ears. "Sorry about the lack of picture, fellas. The cameras are picking up what the cameras are picking up. There's not much I can do about that. To confirm, though, we *are* in the Verdanian atmosphere. And we're hurtling toward the surface."

Meyer Wells asked, "What about the ultraviolet feeds, Tarissa? What are you seeing there?"

"I can switch on that view if you'd like."

"Switch on whatever works," Camden said. "Why would we want to keep watching a bunch of stupid clouds?"

Without another word, the camera imagery transitioned into red and black amorphous blotches, which to the human eye were barely decipherable as continents, oceans, and miscellaneous vegetation.

While everyone was reacting to the change, the spire shook briefly and the images blinked to white for ten long seconds before reestablishing themselves.

"We just lost contact with the *Horizon*, didn't we?" Meyer said.

Tarissa did not answer, nor did anyone else in the control pod.

"And it seems we just lost communication in here as well." Meyer sighed. "So, it's happened. It's done and gone."

Camden touched his ear. "*Spear* pod, call."

"You won't be able connect," Meyer said.

"Why not? Are the links dead or something?" Camden kept tapping his ear.

"Without an ongoing frequency fix to the *Horizon* they are."

Meyer sat forward and studied the streams of data coursing across the bottom half of his windowpane.

"This was always a probability. It's what occurred when the probes were dropped, and also when the Constructs' spire first entered the atmosphere. I call it the frustrating trend. It's happened time and time again. Grid systems break through the ozone layer, and then *boom*. Communication, camera feeds, they've all been severed."

Mikhail gestured at the red and black blotches. "Then this must be a replay or a recording. We're still seeing images."

"No, it's live. Look at the time code." Meyer's eyes shifted from the data stream to the grid band around his wrist. "Interesting. We're still able to see what the ship is seeing, which is good. This gives us a pile of new facts. Communications systems are off, but onboard cameras are still in operation, independently, like the entire spire appears to be. This is significant. The first probes we fired transmitted nothing back because communication with them was lost. Now, we must assume they kept operating past the demarcation point in the ozone layer. That is excellent news on the open question of whether the Constructs survived or not."

"Okay," Camden said. "What do we do now?"

"Us here? We do nothing." Meyer settled back into his flight harness, re-affixing his gaze on the pulsating ultraviolets. "Tarissa will fly us into position and put us down on the ground. The *Horizon*, they're set to execute a patch job of mine if contact with us was lost, as we expected it would be."

"Plans were in place then?" Camden said.

"Oh, yes. Every contingency was thought through."

The spire shook again, which sent a murmur through the landing team.

"Was that supposed to happen?" Koron asked.

"I don't know," Meyer said. "How could I know? Despite my tendency toward talkativeness, when it comes to this moon, I am not an authority on anything. To be blunt, I know as little as you boys do."

"That's obviously not true," Mikhail said. "Look at all the stuff you just told us."

"That was prior knowledge. From this moment forward, I proceed as if I know nothing at all. It appears, my friends, we are now free-falling in more ways than one."

32

"This is the *Horizon*. Can you hear us? I say again, this is the *Horizon*. Can anyone out there hear us? I repeat—"

33

The *Spear* trembled one last time, ever so slightly.

"Was that it?" Camden said. "Have we landed?"

Meyer was clutching the straps of his safety harness. "I believe so. The engine just stopped revolving, and the ship appears to be holding steady."

The two teams became extra-quiet as they concentrated to hear any kind of audio confirmation to the question at hand. Suddenly, the surrounding windows displays faded to black.

"That was an automated action," Meyer said. "No views outside until we've disembarked."

Koron went to pop open his restraints. Camden and Mikhail's voices boomed out to stop him in angry, two-part harmony.

"What?" Koron said, shaking his head in confusion. "We've landed, haven't we? It's obvious we're not descending anymore. The pressure and pull are all gone."

"I want everyone to listen up," Camden said. "Stop acting on assumption. We don't know what's going on out there. The *Horizon* is the only flight experience any of us have ever known, and that thing barely feels like it's moving most of the time. So let's stay put, okay? When the pilots tell us we've arrived, then we'll know we've arrived."

A door to the right of Camden slid open, delivering the thin-framed, sixty-six-year-old Tarissa onto the passenger deck.

"We've obviously landed, fellas. You can get up and move around.

There's no reason to stay harnessed up."

Koron looked over at Camden and widened his eyes.

Camden relented. "Release yourselves at will, people. The lady says we're here."

Tarissa crossed over to Meyer as the teams rose up and stretched their limbs. Mikhail saw the two older expedition members beginning to converse and came up beside them.

"Were there any problems?" Meyer asked Tarissa.

"Not after the comms died."

"Where did we land? On the camera feeds, I saw that you were improvising."

She used her palm as a makeshift map. "I touched down about a klick and a half from the spot where you think the Construct cans landed. There was an open field of some sort we weren't expecting to find. I took advantage of that, and got us closer than we intended."

"Did you see any sign of the other spire?" Mikhail asked.

"I did not. I was too concerned with getting us down in one piece."

"It was an amazing landing, by the way," Mikhail said. "The struts hit the ground and most of us barely noticed. I should have offered my compliments right off."

Camden was making his own approach, his right thumb held up in admiration of Tarissa's unquestionable prowess in the flight chair. "That goes ditto from me."

"Thank you both," Tarissa said, and let the subject drop there.

Camden turned to Meyer. "Earlier, you were bragging to us about a patch job, doc. Now that we're securely on the ground, do you care to elaborate?"

Meyer was smiling. "The *Vanguard*, the Constructs' advance ship, that will be the centerpiece of the endeavor. By the time the *Horizon* lost communications with us, the *Vanguard* had shifted into a geosynchronous orbit. A rather lengthy tether will be released from there, connected to a small relay transmitter. This transmitter will then be lowered into the atmosphere until it reaches the position where we were disconnected, which was right past the ozone layer. The hope is, in that sweet spot, a hardwired link can be established from atmosphere to transmitter, and then from the *Vanguard* to the *Horizon*."

"A transmitter on a string is going to swing wildly, isn't it?" Mikhail said.

"Not from a geosynchronous orbit. It's similar to the way the old rail system operated on Earth."

"But for this tether to reach. It would need to be thousands of kilometers long," Camden said. "We just had one that long on hand?"

"A week ago we didn't. But we do now. I had it fabricated and transferred over to the *Vanguard* this very afternoon, an hour or so after we entered orbit around Verdan."

The other three support crew chiefs came hobbling over, as did Samuel, Koron, and Bernard. Everyone on deck was now huddling up in that one isolated spot.

"When are we going to be allowed to get out of here and start searching for the Constructs?" Samuel asked. "That's the question that matters most to me right now. I'm sure it matters to the rest of you guys, too."

"We exit when communication is restored, or at zero six hundred hours," Meyer said.

Samuel groaned. "What are we supposed to do until then? Hang out and wait while there's a whole new planet on the other side of these windows? Give me a break. Can't we at least take a quick peak outside?"

"Absolutely not," Meyer said. "As I reminded you before, the Directorate ordered a complete visual blackout until the first step is taken. They want the drama of that moment to remain pure. I know that isn't the answer you were looking for, but you can always watch the ultraviolet feeds and see what you can see there. As far as I'm aware, in an emergency situation, that's not against the rules."

Samuel walked away. "How thrilling. I can't get enough of those blood-red blobs of nothing."

34

"Can anyone hear me? This is the *Horizon*. Please respond. Can anyone out there hear me?"

Acting upon continual prompting from the army of technologists clustered in around him, Walter had been repeating this handful of phrases, in varied succession, for the last three hours plus.

"One more time. Can anyone—"

Walter glanced away from the display nook to cough just as an image from inside the *Spear* flickered into view. Meyer was in the center of the frame, standing next to Tarissa. Both were waving at the camera.

"We hear you," Meyer said. "Can you stop it with that same blasted question? It's getting on everyone's nerves."

Walter had another cough in him. "If you didn't like hearing it, then you should have answered faster."

"Where's the fun in that?" Meyer locked his hands behind his back. "Operation Connect worked like a charm, I see. A positional transmitter was the solution. This proves it is something in the ozone layer that's been cutting off transmission."

"You were right," Walter said. "I was doubtful, but you had it figured out all along."

"Ah, it was nothing but a little problem solving." The volume of Meyer's voice ticked up. "Can one of my people please tell me why it took so long to get the tether operational? Before I left, we had everything timed down to thirty-seven minutes."

Walter spoke for the group. "There were technical issues. You will have ample time to parse the details later."

The Rangers, minus Mikhail, piled in behind Meyer and Tarissa.

"Can we get out of this deathtrap now?" Camden asked. "We're all getting a bit antsy."

"I hear you," Walter said. "But first things first. I've been told to check. Are your personal links working?"

Camden tapped his ear. "Walter Stoddard, call."

After an obligatory Core message, the sound of Camden's voice shifted into Walter's head. "I guess this is what you'd call working. Right, boss?"

There was a minuscule amount of delay between the link and the image feed. Otherwise, functionality appeared normal.

Camden bent down on one knee and held his hands together in prayer. "Now that that's done, I beg of you, can we please get going and do what we're supposed to do? Save some lives…take a walk."

"Keep your pants on, Commander. I still have matters to discuss with Meyer. Get lost for a moment, all of you."

The Rangers dispersed. Tarissa caught Meyer's glance.

"I'm going back up top," she said.

Meyer nodded as he watched her leave.

"Are all the men a hundred percent?" Walter asked. "Did the landing go well? You have landed, correct?"

"It's been three hours and our pilot was standing next to me when the transmitter reconnected us. You'd better hope that we landed."

Walter grinned. "What's it look like outside?"

"I'd have no idea. Nobody has peeked."

"Really? Truly?"

"This team follows orders, sir. We were told to wait, and wait is what we did."

Somebody cackled behind Meyer.

"Well, wait time is over. The exit clock is set at five minutes. Get Mikhail into position. We're going outside."

35

Mary led Dimitri to center stage. Then, under his own steam, he doddered out to the edge of the platform and raised his right arm. The familiar gesture, coupled with the firmest of expressions, signaled to all those present that extraneous conversation must now cease and Dimitri be given their undivided attention. In an almost simultaneous fashion, the crowd drew hushed, waiting to hear the important update that was sure to follow.

"My friends, I thank you for your patience during the blackout. In the last several minutes we finally received confirmation from the surface. The ship and its passengers have landed safely *and* securely."

The news set off an emotional firestorm. Cheers and applause caught wind, sweeping across the patio, snuffing out every other wisp of sound. Only whistles and screams wafted above. Where few were standing before, now everyone had risen, happy and joyous. It had worked. Hope had not failed them. The *Spear* had landed.

"I'm thrilled as well," Dimitri said, energized by the crowd's response. "And I can't wait to see what this world looks like, up close and in detail. To elaborate, I will allow my daughter to inform you about what will be coming next."

Mary stepped around her father and gestured upwards. "Visuals from the surface have also been restored."

On the stage behind her, the live dimensional feeds were slowly reconstituting themselves. The shot on the left was from a ceiling camera on the

Spear, looking down on a bubble-like breathing apparatus that had been clamped down over the skull of one of the Rangers. Also attached to the hi-tech environment suit were a variety of add-on pieces of body armor, and a small tracer pistol that had been holstered to the man's right hip.

"You can't quite see his face at the moment," Mary said, "but that is my brother Mikhail. He's about to climb out of the landing craft. When he does, the helmet camera he has on will begin transmitting. What Mikhail sees, we will also be seeing."

Mary returned to where she had previously been standing and put her arm around her father.

"I suggest everyone gets comfortable and keeps their eyes peeled," Dimitri said. "It won't be long now, and nothing will ever be the same again."

36

"The current external temperature is twenty-nine point four degrees Celsius," the Core voice said. "The oxygen level is nineteen point seven five percent. It is permissible to exit the vehicle whenever the order is given, Lieutenant Kucherov."

Mikhail's eyes were following the trail of numbers that had just been recited to him as they ticked up and down on the hatch's readout displays, never veering out of the demarcated safe areas of yellow or green.

"If everything checks out, then why am I still standing here like an idiot?" he said. "Are the cameras transmitting yet? Can people see me standing here? I certainly hope I'm doing this for the entertainment of somebody."

"There's no delay," Meyer said through their link connection. "We're right on schedule. The mobile cameras were released ninety seconds ago, and are moving into place now. They will activate automatically the moment we open the hatch."

"Lieutenant," a third voice said. "This is Walter Stoddard. I'm prepared to give the order. I suggest you take a deep breath."

"Is the audio feed live in here?" Mikhail asked. "Can any of the civilians hear me?"

"There's only a video transmission so far," Meyer said. "For the moment, you can still speak freely."

Mikhail placed his open hand on the reinforced hatch.

"While I still have the chance, Walter, I wanted to say something to you. And that something is—*fuck you*. Fuck you for what you did to Jocelyn. And *fuck you* for being my father's stooge."

"Are you done?" Walter said calmly.

"No, but I've said my piece. Just so you know, after today, the gloves are off. I won't be playing the nice guy anymore."

The front of Mikhail's breather had begun to fog up. He straightened his shoulders and removed his hand from the hatch.

"Don't let this take forever, asshole. Just give the damn order."

"Audio recording commencing," Meyer said. "We are now broadcasting live."

Walter held the silence, giving the moment the heft it deserved.

"Landing craft one. This is Directorate Magistrate Walter Stoddard. With the authority granted me by the people of the Echo Collective, I hereby order the exterior hatch opened. Lieutenant Kucherov, you may step outside at any time. A grateful government wishes you all the luck in the world."

A hiss was heard as the exit partition lit up. A split second later, the door slid upward, locking itself into the roof of the exchange.

A bright radiance swept over Mikhail and bathed the hatchway in a stark, mossy glow. Through the opening, a mountain range could be seen. The formations across its face were soft and round, without any hint of sharpness or edge. A twenty-five meter green field was all that lay between the spire and the first discernible piece of foliage—a stubby tree line that descended from the base of the mountain range like a long, blue-green lava flow.

"A single step forward," Mikhail said as he inched over to the drop-off line and braced his hand against the ventilation slats.

"For all those watching with me, I intend to keep my head lowered until I get all the way outside. I don't want to see anything else until I have a more open view."

He tilted his head downward. The field beneath him was shimmering—a hot, irradiating neon. On more detailed inspection, the ground was more of a swamp than a traditional field. Its surface jiggled and shook, the combined effect of steady local winds and the mechanized rumble of the spire.

"I'm going out," Mikhail said as he lowered his right boot and stuck it into the muck, where it sunk down to his upper calf before apparently colliding with something solid.

"It's real squishy, like I've stepped into a vat of gelatin. I think I should probably put my full weight on this foot before I drop the other."

As he did that, his boot sunk even farther, well past his calf, to the bottom of his knee.

"It's certainly softer than I would have assumed, but I'm not sinking down any lower."

He pushed again and again. His footing appeared secure.

"I suppose I should say something significant."

He closed his eyes and then reopened them.

"I step out onto this extraterrestrial world not as the first of my species, but as the eleventh. We must never forget our first and most important task today, and the rescue nature therein. Yes, we have landed after a long and arduous journey, but there were ten other souls who arrived here in advance of us, and did what I am about to do, long before I was allowed through this door. Our celebration will only begin once we know that the brave Constructs are safe in our tribe once again. Now, back to the big step…and this grand, green soil."

Mikhail brought his left leg down and planted it next to its twin. He held it there for a while, squishing in place until he decided to lift his head and take his first full look around.

A swarm of mobile cameras were flying in hover patterns around the ship. Blessed with a more peripheral view, the helmet camera could now discern that the tree line was a part of something much larger. Encircling the landing area were swooping acreages of forest, extending outward for kilometers in all four directions. The tops of the tree line were in fact strange blue cylindrical domes, strapped to the ground by vine-like lengths of dangling stalks. The dome tops floated in a drifting pattern, swaying as one.

"I guess the sky looks like I expected the sky to look," Mikhail said as he peered through a small split between the vine stalks. A nearby beach-front could be seen, and a smidgen of the horizon line.

"It's green is what I'm trying to say, with familiar white clouds and such. Everything else I'm seeing, though, it's as alien as we've all been expecting. It has a basic Earth-like make-up—water, ground, mountains, sky—but it's so scrambled up and weird. This goo in particular, it's loose and slimy. I feel like I'd be sucked all the way down if I moved too fast."

"Mikhail, oxygen levels remain a go," Meyer said. "If you wish, you may remove your helmet. The cameras will switch to externals the second you detach."

"Don't mind if I do." Mikhail depressed a button on the underside of his breather. Following that, he pushed an identical button on his chest plate. A locking mechanism was released. Mikhail clutched hold of the helmet on both sides and removed it from his person. An instant later, his lungs were breathing in natural air for the first time in his life. The act appeared to unsteady him, far more than any of the sights and sounds had.

"I don't appear to be dying," he said. "Which is good." He placed the breather at his feet, leaving it to float freely atop the muck.

William Holt, the support team physician, had a question. "How do you feel, Lieutenant? Is there any dizziness? Any sense of unease?"

"Nope. I'm fine. I don't feel much different at all."

"Be sure to keep us updated. If you feel anything unusual, speak up immediately."

"Will do."

Something big flew over Mikhail, catching his eye and casting a scatter shot of interconnected shadows across the wetness.

"Did the cameras pick that up? There was some sort of flock flying above me. It was traveling fast, and it's moving westward. Please tell me we got a picture of that."

"We did," Meyer said. "And we're analyzing it as we speak. We'll get back to you with an update as soon as we have something concrete to share. Right now, we want you to take a couple of steps around the ship. Can you manage that? Take as much time as you need. Go slow."

Mikhail pushed off. "Slow it is."

With one cautious step after another, Mikhail trudged his way around the circular base of the spire, his boots splashing and squashing as he went. At eight steps forward he ducked beneath a landing strut and was given his initial view to the south. What could be seen on this side of the aircraft was much like what could be seen outside the hatch. The floating forest stood wide and dominant. There was a set of mountains in this direction as well, but less rotund than the ones to the north, and more distant.

Mikhail set off again, using the strut as leverage at the same moment something cawed behind him. Mikhail spun to react, but with the exception of the colorful vegetation, there was nothing there that hadn't been there before.

"How important is it that I go all the way around?" he asked after his left boot appeared to get stuck in the goo. "I'm at about the halfway mark now, and my footing is degenerating a bit. The muck around this section is extremely thick."

"Hold where you are one minute, Lieutenant," someone said to him. "We're discussing another matter at the moment."

Two mobile cameras zipped past him as Mikhail managed to free his boot. Several seconds went by and the wind began to kick up, far harder than any simulated breeze on the *Horizon*. Mikhail crept backwards, pinning himself against the hull of the big, beige ship.

"All right, Lieutenant," Meyer said. There was a franticness to his voice. "The cameras have picked up a ground-based object moving to the north-northeast. We want this investigated, which you cannot do on your own."

"Yes, sir." Mikhail gave the ship a slap. "Send out the boys. We'll go take a look for you."

37

"So, how do you feel?"

"Overwhelmed," Dimitri said. "Out of my own body. In a daze, like I've dreamt the entire event."

Mary nodded and patted her father on the arm. The two of them were backstage, taking a short break while they waited for the rest of the Rangers to disembark.

"You wouldn't have believed the look on your face," Mary said. "When Mikhail removed his helmet, I turned away because I couldn't actually be looking if something bad happened. Then I saw you. You were holding your breath as you watched. Did you realize you were doing that?"

"I did not realize that." Dimitri rubbed at his eyes.

Mary stepped closer to him. "You can say it, you know. You can admit that you're proud of him."

"I am proud, without a doubt. I am proud of so many things. As a civilization, what we have achieved here is dumbfounding, and hard to get my head around, even after all these years. We've traversed the galaxy, and we are about to colonize another world. I don't think I ever truly believed it would happen, not deep down. That's what's gotten me so out of sorts, I think. I've always assumed I was a true believer, but judging by my response, maybe I wasn't. Perhaps that is why I was holding my breath. What I was seeing was so real, yet at the same time, so utterly impossible."

"I get all of that," Mary said. "But no matter what else, you need to be proud of him, and him alone. Mikhail took the world on his shoulders just now. He ignored his anger and did his duty. And although it would have been easy for him to do so, he didn't do one thing to embarrass you. And this is despite some truly dark circumstances. That's what you've been preaching to us since were little children. 'We must set aside our own needs and desires.' And about five minutes ago, right before your eyes, your son did all that and more. So please, be proud of him, Dad. In your heart, this cannot be about anyone else."

Dimitri looked away. "If I tell you I'm proud, then I'm proud. And you're correct—your brother did everything that was asked of him. But, if you recall, he did make a point of saying he wasn't the first to set foot. He held the Constructs up as higher than his own achievement. And while noble to do so, I believe this comment was meant as a strike against me. He was making a point when he declared he wasn't the first, when clearly to us here, he *was*."

Mary shook her head. "I'll say this for you, you never cease to amaze. And you wonder why Mikhail hates you so much. It's a miracle the rest of us don't hate you as well."

38

The Rangers ventured out in two groupings. The first trekked northeast, led by Camden, with able-bodied assistance from both Samuel and Koron. This was the alpha team, charged with investigating the unknown mass sweeping its way toward them. The beta team, consisting of Mikhail and Bernard, had been ordered to continue on with the initial exploration process.

"Are you sure you don't need more than one of us to escort you?" Camden asked Mikhail from the other side of the clearing. "I can give you Koron if the ground is going to be too thick for your weak widdle legs."

Mikhail gritted his teeth and kept slogging through the muck. "Everything is well in hand, smart ass. The sludge, it's actually gotten thinner the more we've moved away from the ship."

Something wet splattered across Mikhail's face. He wiped at it and glanced down at his hand. It was more of the sludge, smeared across his fingers. During the time he'd spent outside, Mikhail's clothing had become inundated with the luminous green goop.

"We made it," Bernard said once he and Mikhail had reached the outer boundary of the tree line.

The two men craned up at the undulating growth above them. The stalks holding the dome tops to the ground were dark green in color, with flecks of red dotting the serrated-edged tips of what might otherwise be called leaves.

"They're like these stout, fat mushroom stools," Bernard said, "floating in the breeze."

A camera propelled upward and documented the largest of the dome tops.

"I see purplish orbs descending from the underbelly," Meyer said from his observation post on the *Spear*. "There's not much light under there, so I can't get an unadulterated view. But the orbs could be fruits or seedlings of some kind."

"Try smacking one of them with the camera," Mikhail suggested. "That might shake something loose. I can catch it if it falls."

"An action like that would be considered a breach in protocol, Lieutenant. For now, it's observation only for us. Sample taking will come later, and done with more expert hands than your own."

"Hey, my hands aren't too shabby. I know I can catch a piece of falling fruit easily enough."

"I have no doubt about your physical prowess. It was your lack of scientific training I was calling into question. A fully accredited biologist will be required for any sample retrieval that's undertaken, generally one with about ten to twelve years of virtual expertise."

"Well, *la-di-dah*," Mikhail said as he adjusted his footing in the muck.

"You done feeling left out yet?" Meyer said. "If you are, I need you both to get on your hands and knees. I have work for you."

Mikhail and Bernard looked at one another before they got down on all fours. While they waited for what came next, Meyer began talking to someone who asked about the possibility of intelligent life forms, and then the line went silent.

"What the hell is going on over there?" Mikhail said. "Sounds like little green men might have been discovered, or at least that had better be the case. I don't appreciate being left here in such an awkward position."

Meyer came back online. "Sorry. I keep doing that to you, don't I? There's an issue with the other Ranger team. The powers that be up on the *Horizon* have concerns."

"We can still hike over there if the need arises," Mikhail said.

"Thanks, but no thanks. Camden and company can handle the situation on their own. You and Bernard have other duties. I put you on your hands and knees for a reason. I need you to start feeling around down there and see if you can find any roots. And once we're finished with that glamorous task, I'm going to need you to stand back up and walk inside that forest. You get to be the first to accomplish that task as well. It's another milestone, Mikhail. And I promise you, far more exciting than anything Commander Muran is up to at the moment."

39

"There's no need to be concerned. I assure you, I'm friendly." The voice, which sounded male, was originating from behind a dense patch of the dome stalks. "I'm going to step on through now. I promise to take things as slowly as I can."

A bearded humanoid in a filth-covered jumpsuit slipped through the overgrowth, his arms held above his head in a show of surrender.

"I'm one of the construction crewmen from the *Vanguard*," the red-headed man said. "My name is Adam. My friends and I have been down here on the surface for more than a year now. All this time we've been on our own, with no communication, and no idea what's been happening above."

"You're Adam Ballard," Camden said. Like his two colleagues on either side of him, his tracer gun was in hand, aimed and ready to fire. "You *are* one of the Constructs. I recognize you from your last health snapshot."

"I don't know how that could even be possible, looking the way I look, but I'm pleased we won't have too much of a disagreement on the subject. Could I get your names as well, and maybe some information about where you're from? I assume it's the *Horizon*, but you never know. I learned to stop jumping to conclusions about sixteen months ago."

Camden lowered his weapon. "I can only imagine. We've been outside our spire less than ten minutes, and I'm still not sure my senses are working properly." He gave Adam a smile. "My name's Camden. This man on my left is Koron. The other fellow is Sam. Yes, we're from the *Horizon*, and yes, we're here to rescue you. We appreciate you making it so easy for us."

"Not a problem." Adam nodded at the other two Rangers. All three tracers had now been re-holstered. In turn, Adam lowered his arms.

"Where's the rest of your group?" Samuel asked. "The other Constructs. Where are they?"

"Not too far away."

Adam reached backward and removed a signal flare from one of the pockets on the leg of his pants. He lit the little orange stick and raised it high, allowing the dark smoke to drift into the sky.

"After everything that's happened, we discovered it's best not to risk more than one life at a time. I drew the short straw this time out."

The blazing flare kept billowing upward.

"It might take them a while to get here. It's best to cut through the swayers as slowly as possible."

"Swayers?" Koron said. "Oh, the trees." He tipped his head at the towering plant life.

"Swayers are what we call them at least. They're not poisonous, but they can cut you up pretty badly. Also, you should never chop away at them to make a path because this place goes berserk whenever you disrupt anything, especially the greenery."

"What else should we be paying attention to?" Camden asked.

"Quite a lot, actually. The worst of it is this white stuff. It lurks and travels around in streams. It's best to avoid that stuff completely."

Samuel turned to Camden, but it was Adam he was speaking to. "Two of our guys are already out exploring. Maybe you should tell us what else they should be trying to avoid."

"Just about everything." Adam dipped the flare into the muck and snuffed it out. "You need to bring whoever that is back in. None of you knows this place well enough to be out exploring."

Camden touched his ear. "Kay, I'm sure you just heard all that. Maybe we should call the other guys in."

He paused.

"All right, I got you." Camden's eyes met Adam's. "Mikhail and Bernard are on their way back to the ship."

"Good. I think that's best for now." Adam's hands had begun to shake, which was making it difficult for him to hold on to the spent flare.

Camden whooshed over to Adam and held his hand out to help. "Just how much danger have you people been in?"

"It's been on and off, I guess. More on than off sometimes."

"I'm so sorry."

"Nothing for you to be sorry about. We're the ones who should be sorry. We were here to build, and we haven't accomplished one damn thing so far."

"Don't worry about that," Camden said. "It's no that important."

"I think that it is. But surviving, that was all we had time for. Those of us who did survive. This is what I've been dreading telling you. Not all of us made it. Very few of us, in fact."

40

Walter spoke through a live dimensional hook-up with the *Horizon*. "I want this next statement to be on the record. I am mortified by what you have been put through—both you and your lost comrades, who have now been legally designated as deceased members of the Echo Collective, and will soon be given every honor and award available to them. So will all of you. Your contribution to this undertaking is beyond my ability to successfully communicate. The bravery and tenacity you've shown is a testament to all humanity. No one will ever forget what you have sacrificed."

The Constructs nodded. They'll all been seated together on the back half of the *Spear*'s oval-shaped operations table. Meyer Wells, William Holt, and Mikhail Kucherov sat across from them, hushed and respectful. Off to the side of the table, waist-high images of Walter and Dimitri floated in place like disembodied apparitions.

"I second every sentiment Walter just shared," Dimitri said. "And I add that it is wonderful to see all of you. I remember you five from your days in the Gemini Collectives. And Adam, if you're able to recognize me, we know one another particularly well. Our days in Phoenix and the old Alpha were long ago, but you were always such a sweet-natured child." Dimitri breathed out and wobbled his head dreamily. "I look at all of you, and those familiar, unchanged faces. It's like an eerie mirror, reminding me of how old I've become."

Adam sat up in his seat. "That's crazy, sir. I recognized you right off.

You haven't changed as much as you think you have. You're still the same old Dima. As serious as a heart attack, and prone to flowery speeches."

Mikhail glanced at his father, his interest piqued. But then, the conversation moved on.

"You haven't changed much either," Dimitri said. "Quite literally so. Stasis has kept you well preserved, young man. I am envious, and am looking forward to catching up. You have other friends aboard the *Horizon* who will be equally anxious to see you. I'm certain that all of you do. Hopefully, the horror of this last year will soon be replaced by wave after wave of happy reunions."

Adam nodded.

"Now, I understand one of you has been selected as spokesperson for the group."

"That's me, sir." The Construct in the middle of the lineup held up her hand to draw attention her way. What was left of her jumpsuit was ripped at the shoulder and her black hair had been cut short in a jagged fashion, to well above her ears.

"Before we begin," Walter said. "Can I get each of your names for my own sake? I'd hate to refer to anybody in an improper manner."

"I'm Anne Dougherty," the spokesperson said. "I was voted in as leader after Captain McCann was killed. I have dual specialties. Construction technologies and structural engineering."

"And I'm Adam Ballard, which has already been established. I also handle construction technologies, but my expertise lies more in the mechanical engineering field."

Anne added, "Adam has been our lead scout from the moment we landed. Captain McCann called him a born bloodhound. So, if you need to know anything about the wheres and hows around here, Adam's your guy."

"Excellent," Dimitri said.

Next up was a sturdy-looking blonde. Like Anne, most of her hair had been chopped away, and she was bandaged across her forehead. Her ratty, long-sleeved pullover had been rolled up to her elbows.

"My name is Christina Roth, or just Christie if you prefer. I'm a voltric engineer, in charge of the power systems for that city we never got around to building."

All heads turned to the man next to Christina. He was the youngest of the group, and the most untouched in terms of visible wounds or physical impairments. His curly brown hair had traces of green in it, but was otherwise adequately maintained.

"I'm Nick Finn," he said. "I'm also a voltrics guy. It seems we voltrics people lucked out. More of us survived than anybody."

The last of the Constructs was also the most unsettling. The left arm of the man had been severed from the shoulder socket down. Fresh bandaging was wrapped around the stump while the rest of his clothing remained caked in blood dried months before. With everyone present staring at him, a smile formed on his lacerated face.

"I'm Robert Granger, and soon as we get a chance, I should probably see a doctor. I appear to be missing something."

"Robert, are you in any pain?" William asked.

"No. I told you when I came aboard, I'm feeling okay. But with all these eyes on me, I suddenly got reminded of what I don't have anymore. My friends here have gotten used to seeing me like this, so that kind of helped me to forget."

"We didn't mean to offend," Mikhail said.

"And I didn't take it that way. I was just saying. I know I'm missing an arm, and I know it's going to get replaced. *C'est la vie.*"

"Shall we begin?" The image of Walter reached forward for something and a large portion of his arm disappeared from view. "I realize there's recorded footage of much of what has happened to you—our mainframe is uploading it from your campsite as we speak. But beyond what we will obviously learn from that, I would like to hear your own personal accounts, even if it's just a general overview. So, if you can, tell us about the landing, take us through it from the minute communication was lost. That's the last we heard from you."

"Before we start in on that," Anne said. "A few of our colleagues weren't introduced. They're not here to tell you their names, so can I have another couple of moments to do that for them?"

"Of course, my dear," Dimitri said. "You may say whatever you wish."

Anne placed both hands on the table. "Calvin McCann, he was our Captain. He died three weeks in. Then there was Terry Hammond. He actually died first, before the Captain, from wounds sustained in what you were just asking about—the landing. Samantha Hill and Ryan Stevenson, they were together romantically. They'd started a relationship after a couple of weeks on the surface, and had snuck off for some alone time. They ended up lying down in the wrong spot."

Mention of this made Adam twitch. Anne kept going.

"Brandon Reece was the last of us that we lost. It was the least surprising of the deaths, but it was also the one that nearly knocked the hope right out of us. Bran was such a cheerful guy, and so positive. I wish he could have gone a little more painlessly."

Anne stopped there, and no one else said another word. Christina was beginning to sniffle when Mikhail clenched up his fist and began thumping it against his chest. He did this again and again, creating a slow and steady beat. Adam picked up on what the Ranger was up to and did the same. All the Constructs soon followed suit. Eventually, even Walter and Dimitri were pounding their chests in salute.

"Thank you for that," Anne said once the moment had passed. "The landing." She looked down. "It wasn't a landing exactly. It was more like a tumble that didn't become a crash. The Captain was behind the stick, and he did his best. But the winds down here."

She made eye contact with Mikhail.

"I'm sure you felt them while you were outside. They start off as nothing, and then can get so brutal. You can't even walk sometimes without being blown off your feet."

Mikhail nodded his acknowledgment.

"Anyway," Anne said. "Terry was hurt when we hit the ground. The Captain said he had gotten up and unstrapped himself to help locate a spot for us to land. He wasn't buckled back in when our spire got caught in one of those crazy gusts. From there, we flipped upside down and were tossed into the soup, or the muck—whatever you want to call it."

"The ground is harder than it feels underneath all that goop," Adam said. "And the ship came down side-first, which folded the hoop drive in on itself. Terry was ping-ponged all over the flight pod. When we found him, his was body was all broken and limp."

"And his skull was split open," Christina said. "But he survived somehow, for a little while."

Anne sighed. "Three days he hung on. If we'd known we were going to be down here on our own for as long as we were—with no word from the *Vanguard*—I don't know how we would have handled it. We talked about ending the pain for him, but it never came to that. We didn't know anything for certain at that time, so there was still a chance communication could be restored. When it was, we thought Gracie would fly down herself and help us."

"Gracie would not have been allowed to fly down," Meyer said. "She'd been ordered to remain with the *Vanguard*. I take full responsibility for that decision. The risk was too great. You'd already lost two ligates on the trip from Earth. The ship cannot operate without a ligate on board. And with a probable communications loss when anything mechanical hit the atmosphere, all that would've been accomplished was her being lost as well."

"We figured it was something like that," Adam said.

Nick, who had just sneezed, rubbed his nose and said, "She must feel terrible about that."

William leaned forward and offered Nick a handkerchief. "Can you tell us a little more about how the Captain was lost," he said.

It was Adam who responded. "We were setting charges for the city's foundation. We found this location we can show you later and began fencing out a perimeter. The soup wasn't as deep in this spot. It barely went down to the knuckle. So charges were laid. The Captain set off the first one. *Boom*. Then the second, that's when the fizz came."

Meyer's eyes got big. "The fizz?"

"Yeah, I mentioned the stuff to your men outside. They're these small bubbly things that travel around in streams. They're all over the place. They tend to keep clear generally, but they're always around. Every time we've tried to build or alter the landscape, they attack—in force. This is what happened when the Captain was killed. It's what the fizz does. They erupt out of nowhere, and melt you down. They can be a klick away, and then you step on the wrong twig, and they come shooting out of the ground and slither all over you."

Anne nudged Adam's shoulder. "But they don't shoot out of just anywhere. Make sure they understand that. There are places to go to avoid them."

"She's right. There is. If the fizz approaches, what you need to do is find some elevation. Climb onto a rock or scamper up a swayer."

"Are you telling us it's safe to climb one of those?" Mikhail said.

"If you have gloves on, sure. But almost anything vertical will work. There are lots of other kinds of big plants farther out, away from the lake. I'm no scientist, so I'm not sure how any of this stuff should be classified. I don't know if size has anything to do with calling something a tree. The swayers' roots are shallow, and they have no trunks, that I know for sure."

"You see?" Meyer said to Mikhail. "Root systems. Important."

Walter said, "I'm confused. How did this substance 'melt' Captain McCann?"

"The fizz is not a substance exactly," Adam said. "It's alive but...never mind. I don't know how to explain what happened to the Captain. He was just there, and then he wasn't."

"There was no trace of his body left at all," Anne said.

"Our dog was up on the platform, too," Christina said. "Her name was Stubby. She was a sheep dog. She was always right beside the Captain. She was right beside him when—"

Christina dropped the subject there. So did everyone else.

"How many times was construction attempted?" Dimitri asked the group.

"We tried to flatten out the ground only that once, for obvious reasons,"

Anne said. "Later on, we tried to build some shelter for ourselves. But whenever or wherever we made an attempt, the object or building was destroyed."

"If it wasn't the fizz, it was something else," Adam said.

"How long did these attempts go on?"

"For the first month and a half, until we realized how senseless it was. None of us has a natural sciences background. Construction of any kind seemed to be out of our control."

Meyer brought up a notepad on the tabletop. "Allow me to jot a few things down. I also have a question. If you weren't able to build shelter for yourselves, where did you live? In your spire?"

"The spire wasn't going to work," Anne said. "It ended up being destroyed. We got as much of the equipment off as we could. But whenever we came back to it, the ship had sunken deeper and deeper into the soup. Until eventually, it was gone."

"The ground was that permeable where you landed? Even beneath this so-called soup?"

"I tried to explain this before," Adam said. "The ground here is very, very hard—hence the crash. But that didn't stop the ship from sinking over time. I leave that to you to tell me why."

"Erosion of that sort would be highly unusual," Meyer said. "This soup must contain acidic base materials."

"But how could it?" Anne said. "It hasn't eaten away at any of us. And it's been fairly hard to avoid the stuff. It's everywhere I have ever been. Even in the places that change."

"Yeah, I hadn't mentioned that yet," Adam said. "That's another bit of nuttiness you need to be brought up to speed on. Things can just change down here, with no rhyme or reason. A hill will be there one day, and the next it is either smaller or gone. Tree lines shift. Water lines expand and retract. It's like the natural processes are being speeded up. We've archived it on video. You'll see the evidence in our dimensionals. It's like this field you set down in. I've hiked through this area dozens of times on my scouts, and I've never seen a clearing this wide or round. I know for a fact that this spot was not here just last week. But now it is."

Meyer typed in a few more notes.

"If you didn't live inside your spire," Walter said, "then where did you live?"

Anne shrugged. "In the storage cans."

"The containers that were dropped from the *Vanguard*?" William had a sickened expression on his face. "You lived in those boxes for the entire sixteen months?"

"There was no place else we could live," Anne said. "We needed to find shelter somewhere, and that's what the moon allowed us."

"And really, it wasn't that bad," Adam said, backing her up. "When you cleared out the supplies there was plenty of room. And we had sleeping gear from the spire. To me, it was good that we could all keep so close."

"So brave," Dimitri said. "No one should have endured what you all have endured."

"It's over now," Adam said. "Which is a relief."

Walter turned. "Meyer and William, how much more would you like to hear? Do you have enough information to make your recommendations? If you do, I'd like to bring these five up to the *Horizon* and finish our debriefing here. The Rangers need to go back out soon rather than later. To make that happen, the Directorate will have to meet and decide on some particulars for any new ventures outside. I'd like to get that process going as soon as possible. So what do you say? Have you gotten enough information for now? I believe these people have earned some rest and recuperation. Can we all agree on giving it to them?"

"Debriefing up there is fine by me," Meyer said. "I do suggest a historian is assigned immediately, to get everyone's accounts down in detail. But other than that, I have no objection to giving these people a break."

Adam shot out of his chair. "Look, everyone, I know I'm in no position, but I'm not going anywhere. I can't believe you're just going to shove us aside. If that's actually the case, I'm telling you right now, you do not have anywhere close to enough information. We've hardly told you anything. You know that the ecosystem is dangerous if you try to cut something down or build something where you're not supposed to be building something. But there is way more to this than that. This place is strange. And in our *sixteen* months here, we have all learned a lot. You cannot whisk us away and expect us to sit quietly while this man and his friends risk their lives."

Adam and Mikhail exchanged nods.

"We're still valuable," Adam continued. "We know things. We should be allowed to stay down here and help out with whatever surveying you're planning. I assume most of that is going to be scouting for construction sites. That's something I've been working on for months. If you want to waste all my hard work, then go ahead. But if you go that way, you'd be making a *huge* mistake."

"Adam," Dimitri said. "Don't you think it might be better if you did your consulting from the confines of the *Horizon*? Your colleagues are injured, as I'm certain you are as well. These injuries need to be tended to. Don't you think it's time for someone else to start taking the risks?"

Adam shook his head. "No, not really. I'd prefer to stay."

Anne stood up next to Adam and put her hand on his shoulder. "Listen to this man. You need us down here. No matter how smart and capable some of you may be, and I can see plainly that you are, this moon is not like anything you've ever studied. This place is insane. So insane it makes my brain hurt sometimes."

"If you force us to leave, then fine," Adam said. "But we won't quit on you just because we're tired."

"You got that right. We're not quitting," Nick said.

Christina stood up as well. "None of us are."

Robert's response was slow in coming, but no less adamant. "We're not going anywhere. That's final. We're here for the duration."

"Understood," Dimitri said. "Walter and I will take your requests to the rest of the Directorate. You will have new itinerary breakdowns within the hour. And I must say, you are all impressive individuals. Of that, there is no doubt."

Mikhail locked eyes with Adam and thumped his chest again. Adam's reply was two determined thumps of his own.

41

The transmission indicator switched off and the overhead office lights transitioned back to their normal, pre-broadcast brightness.

"I know one thing for certain," Walter said. "Robert Granger is not staying down there. The way his arm looks is shocking, and the sooner the replacement surgery happens, the more likely the attachment will stick first time out."

Dimitri tipped backward in his mover chair and draped his arm over his forehead. "That was never going to happen anyway, despite the man's virtuous response."

"Are you all right?" Walter asked.

"I'm fine. Just feeling a bit worn down."

"Would you like to get some rest before we debate this?"

"There's no time. It's already nine hundred hours. Let's get everything taken care of, then I'll get my beauty sleep."

Walter took a sip of his coffee. "Okay. What's your overall stance on the Constructs remaining where they are? Robert Granger is obviously out. I think Christina Roth should be out as well. There was a slurred nature to the way she spoke."

"I'm okay with two of them staying, but no more," Dimitri said.

"Then we only have to whittle it down by one. Anne and that Adam fellow seem like the most logical choices. They were the ones who wanted it the most, and they also appear to be the most knowledgeable."

"They're definitely the two who did the most talking."

"The decision makes itself then. Anne and Adam stay. The other three will be transported here as soon as the spire can fly back up. In the meantime, our priority needs to be sifting out locations for at least two separate build sites—one for a temporary base of operations, and another for a permanent settlement. The engineers tell me that the area the Constructs had pinpointed last year does not look like it's going to work for us now—the soup bed has risen. Meyer is launching cameras now to initiate a wider search. I told him to make sure the base site location was as close as he could get to the clearing. He thinks he's already found a spot, on the far edge of the forest."

"The Rangers will need to investigate," Dimitri said as he dragged his arm back down to his side.

"Let's keep their current rosters intact. Mikhail's group will proceed with the publicly viewed exploratory expedition, and Camden will concentrate on the search. The two Constructs will be split between them."

"By their own admission, Adam seems to be the most tuned-in to the moon's eccentricities, he'd be better off with Camden's unit. We need all the practical information concentrated there. What we need from Mikhail is to go find pretty things, and then show us said pretty things. The real work, the dangerous work, I want that to remain Camden's purview."

Walter nodded. "Agreed."

Dimitri yawned.

"I believe that settles things for now," Walter said as he pressed a red oval on the corner of his desktop. "I just put in a summons for the rest of the council. We should gather their votes on these matters as soon as we can."

Walter lifted himself out of his chair and hovered over Dimitri.

"I don't know why this is, but the fact that you know these Constructs kind of took me by surprise. All the months of talking and worrying about them after communication was lost, I would have assumed you'd have spoken more personally about these people."

Dimitri activated his chair and piloted himself away from the desk.

"You know me, I prefer to keep the past in the past. Adam, he lived in the first concentric community, where your great-grandfather also lived. He used to shadow me constantly. I adored the boy, and you know I have never been that fond of youngsters. But this one, he was so full of enthusiasm, and unaccountably genuine. He charmed me. He was that kind of child."

"And the others?"

"Nicholas Finn grew up in the Alpha Collective as well, and lived there for most of his life. The other three I only got to know when they became finalists to join the voyage. That's who the Constructs were, if you recall, applicants with building aptitudes who had no chance of making the cut for the *Horizon*'s final three hundred."

Dimitri zipped over to Walter's monitoring station in the far corner of the office. Activity around the *Spear* was increasing.

"I like that you know them," Walter said. "It feels right somehow, like everyone new is still connected."

"That's one way to look at it. But from my perspective, it makes me feel as if I've woken from a long slumber, and there are figments of my former life, looking no different than they did eighty years earlier. And it's not as if I don't accept that I'm a shade of the man I once was, and am on my last legs. But to see associates and friends looking exactly as they did almost a hundred years ago. I don't know how to describe the way this has affected me. I apologize for being obtuse, but I don't. I need to get my head around this before I can speak any more eloquently on the matter."

"Of course," Walter said. "I didn't mean to pry. You can consider the subject dropped."

42

Adam sloshed his way across the clearing and gave Mikhail a nudge. "I hear you're interested in seeing some wild animals."

Mikhail lowered the pair of binocs he'd been looking through. "I am. I *really* am."

"Allow me then," Adam said. "First lesson, you're looking in the wrong direction. Position yourself toward the southeast."

Mikhail spun around and repositioned the binocs against his eye sockets. The two Ranger teams, and three of the five Constructs, stopped talking among themselves and started wandering over to where Adam and Mikhail were standing.

Adam placed his hand on Mikhail's back and aligned him into the proper viewing angle. "You see that?"

"I don't see squat."

"You need to look harder. Focus on the swayers. I can see the movement with my bare eyes." Adam bit down on his lower lip and suppressed his smile. "At the very least, I'm surprised you can't *hear* them."

"Hear?" Mikhail said. "I'm not hearing anything."

Slowly, an actual sound began to permeate.

Mikhail's neck stiffened. "A whirring noise…and it's getting louder."

"Steady, you don't want to miss this."

"Damn right I don't. I don't want to miss a thing."

Above the sawyer tops, several kilometers away, a swarm of round flying objects hurtled upward. As fast as they'd appeared, the horde descended out of sight, falling back below the swayer line, their whir pitching high.

Adam backed away from Mikhail and began imitating the noise. Soon after, so did Anne and Nick. The objects popped back up, speeding headlong toward the clearing.

"What are you guys up to?" Mikhail said, a little freaked out.

"Showing you animals. You wanted to see animals."

The velocity of the flying creatures increased.

Mikhail hooked his binocs onto his belt. The other four Rangers gathered in around him as the horde soared above their heads—all twenty of the beasts skimming effortlessly around the exterior of the spire.

One of the creatures performed a mid-air somersault and lowered itself to the level of the curious onlookers. Up close, the animal was not as round as it first appeared, but more oblong in shape, and about two meters in length. Its outer covering resembled strips of cauliflower that had been blended together in a soft, gray sheen. From its hind end, a set of transparent, cloak-like wings were jetting out and flittering in the mid-morning gust.

"You can get in as close as you want," Adam told Mikhail. "They don't have mouths. They won't bite."

The whirring increased as Mikhail made his approach. "Do you have a name for these things?" he asked with his arm outstretched. "I know you must have some name. You've named everything else."

"Sows," Adam said. He was keeping close watch on Mikhail. "That's what Anne calls them. They're herbivores. They graze on the swayers."

"But you said they don't have mouths. How can they eat if they don't have mouths?"

"I'm probably going to be saying this again and again the next few days, but I'm no biologist. I've just observed some things. And what I've observed with these sows tells me that they consume trees and plants. Later you'll see them floating over a swayer bed, and the next thing you know, an entire section of the stuff will be disintegrated."

Mikhail hesitated for a second, and then lowered his hand onto the back of the animal. Nothing sudden happened, so he rubbed his palm up and down.

"You're going to love what happens next," Adam said.

The whirring changed pitch again, becoming more of a deep-bellied grumble.

"They're *purring*." Mikhail spun toward his teammates and used his free arm to motion them over. "You can touch them. They're *purring*."

The Rangers all crowded in, each of them placing their hands on the sow, feeling and experiencing the animal's friendly response.

"I can't believe they purr," Mikhail said. "How great is that?"

43

The Transplant chiefs had gathered around the conference room table. Mary, the bureau's director, was the only person present still on their feet. She circled anxiously around the room, from the table to the entryway and back again.

The meeting, a last minute check-down of the individual departments, had been on the schedule for six long years, since the earliest inception of the bureau. Jason Epelle was in attendance as the overseer of the Operations group, the 'getting-things-done' group, which managed all personnel transfers and infrastructure establishment on the surface of Verdan. Civilities and its many medical intricacies was Courtney Cutler's offshoot. Disciplines, and the science and exploration therein, was Betty Aw's domain. Florin Holt was also at the table as Mary's liaison and trusted right hand.

"It's actually happening," Mary said. "We're a go."

"Sort of figured," Jason said. "We all just watched the landing, didn't we?"

"Just figuring isn't going to cut it anymore." Mary brought herself to a stop between Jason and Courtney and grabbed the back of their chairs. "Due to events on the ground, the docket has been shuffled around somewhat. The Constructs appear to have had massive problems down there, which means we're starting from scratch."

"The delays from that," Courtney said, "they could go on for days."

"Weeks probably," Betty said.

Mary nodded. "Within the hour, the Rangers will be on the hunt for a site where we can build our settlement. But yes, as things stand now, you're both right. The delays are potentially an ongoing problem. But this is why we planned for alternative scenarios. They've drilled this possibility into our heads from the beginning."

"Then we're taking the expedited route," Jason said.

"Correct. I need the infrastructure crew to be ready at a moment's notice. They'll be going down first now, not the framers. I want everyone on call. If need be, Jason, lock these people up in your offices. Because once we're ready to go, we are ready to go."

"What about Courtney and I?" Betty asked.

"Courtney needs to be ready to bring Jocelyn out of stasis." Mary gave her friend's chair a shake. "The birth will be happening soon. It's just a matter of when my father feels the timing is right."

"The stasis team already have Jocelyn out of the blocks," Courtney said. "She's in a hospital room now, waiting to be drawn out."

"Excellent," Mary said.

"I guess this means my people are on the sidelines until construction is underway," Betty said.

Mary shrugged. "Maybe yes. Maybe no. The Directorate is still mulling over the prospect of sending science teams out with the Ranger units. As to that, when I know more, you'll know more."

"Until then," Betty said, "I can lend Jason a hand with his crews."

"Initiative. I love it." Mary released her hold on the chairs. "You're all picture perfect. It's like you don't need me here at all."

Florin rapped her knuckles on the table. "Just so everyone is aware, Mary and I will be assuming alternating shifts in the command center. One of us will be there at all times. We expect you and your deputies to be there as much and as often as you can as well, especially during the moments when your teams are on the clock."

"Anything else?" Mary asked Florin.

"That's all from me."

"Then we're dismissed."

Florin and the three chiefs gathered their various belongings before heading toward the door. Mary trailed along behind them.

"There is one thing I need to be extra clear about," Mary said. "Anything you know about the Constructs and their troubles has to remain highly classified. There's no wiggle room here. Share this information with no one, not even your subordinates."

"Is there a reason why not?" Jason asked. "It's something everyone's going to find out about eventually."

"True, but the Directorate wants to keep tight control on the rollout of information, to make certain we keep a sense of calm up here."

Together, the Transplants strolled out into the courtyard and began splitting off in separate directions. A few steps down the sidewalk, Mary pulled up and called her team back with a snap of her fingers.

"One last thing. Have fun with this the next few days. Don't get too serious or too wrapped up in any little difficulty that comes up. Your people will be taking their cues from you, make sure you remain positive and upbeat."

Florin and the chiefs waited for anything more.

"That's all," Mary said. "I want to be kept updated on an hourly basis."

And with that, the courtyard emptied.

44

"What would you like to see first?" Anne asked.

She, Mikhail, and Bernard were trekking side by side toward the swayer forest. A formation of six mobile cameras was following them from the front, with an additional six trailing from behind.

"Maybe you'd like to see some water? Some Verdanian water?"

Anne pushed the swayer stalks aside and slid between them. The three-person row became a single file line.

"I assume you're already leading us in that direction," Mikhail said.

"I am."

Bernard stepped over a patch of purple-hued flowers. "How far away are we?"

"Not very," Anne said. "Just a hop, skip, and a jump."

45

"The swayers will start thinning out soon," Adam said.

Camden, Samuel, and Koron were following behind the scraggly mechanical engineer, navigating the dense maze of almost imperceptible paths and crannies. Unlike Mikhail's foray into the unknown, there was only one lone camera along to document Camden's unit.

"The going will get easier after we clear the forest," Adam said. "I promise."

"We're doing fine," Camden said. "Although, deciding which way to move, and then which branch to move so we can initiate that move, it does takes a little getting used to. I feel like any choice I make could end up being catastrophically wrong."

Adam glanced back at him. "It doesn't have to be. Just keep an eye on me. Do what I do."

"Way ahead of you there," Camden said. "You have our full attention, sir. We're thrilled to have someone along who knows their shit, believe me."

"Tell me if I'm going too fast."

"You just do what's necessary. We can keep up. We've trained long and hard for this."

"That's good," Adam said. "Because I sure didn't."

"You've taken to it well, though," Koron said from the tail end of the pack. There was a slight trace of exertion in his voice. The natural air was taking its toll.

Adam brought his boot out of the soup and checked the heel before dropping it back down. "I've done all right, I guess. I appreciate the compliment. But you kind of just do what you have to do. You don't really think about it."

"Oh, our boss Kay is going to *love* you," Samuel said. "You have her kind of attitude, humble with guts to spare. You're going to get recruited for sure, that I can promise you."

Adam got the procession going again. "Kay, huh? Dimitri used to have a bodyguard named Kay, spelled K-A-Y. It was a super long time ago, when I was around five or six years old."

"It's the same name," Samuel said. "But our Kay's not that old. I mean, she's old, but only like seventy or eighty. She's kind of a badass, too, and scarily spry."

Adam stopped again and took hold of a dried-up hunk of foliage that had become draped between two swayer stalks. With a twist of his wrist, he yanked the detritus free and tossed it into the soup.

"It's a good idea to leave yourself a few bread crumbs," he said. "I try to use dead vegetation as my markers. Never pull anything down that's still alive. This connects back to what I told you about never chopping anything away with a machete."

Cautiously, Camden, Samuel, and Koron maneuvered around the deposited 'bread crumb.'

"These markers of yours, is there a system to how you place them?" Koron asked.

"No system. I just lay stuff down every once in a while. It's temporary thing, in case I ever got lost. I never wanted to take the wrong way home."

"The wrong way could end up being pretty wrong, I would assume." Camden said.

"Yep." Adam waved the three operatives past him. "Hustle up. We're almost there. You'll be seeing the mountain soon. Like I said, the going is about to get a whole lot easier."

46

Mikhail leapt onto the outcropping of gray-green stones and bounded forward until he had reached the water's edge.

"Maybe you shouldn't go out that far," Anne said, to no avail.

Mikhail gazed across the lake, entranced, utterly so. His follow cameras levitated behind him, careful not to stray in or out of his line of sight.

"I'm so tempted," he said, stretching out his leg and setting his boot down in the tide. "I feel like diving in for a swim."

"Don't you dare," the voice in Mikhail's ear commanded.

He grinned.

"This water's really odd looking," Bernard said from the top of the outcropping. "It's all green and sickly, but also kind of sparkly."

Glints of reflected light were popping all across the surface of the waterway. A stout cliff face backed the uppermost portion of the lake, its spiraling waterfall dumping a continuous stream of liquid into the basin below. With the exception of the stones Mikhail was standing on, a blue-budded fauna dominated every other square inch of the perimeter.

Anne took her own look across the lake. "I think all the sparkling might be a time of day thing. I've never seen this spot shimmer like this before. But I also have not spent a whole lot of time out here. We had our water recycling units from the spire. Water just wasn't a significant need."

Again, she asked Mikhail to step back. Half of the cameras had split off to document the shoreline. Reluctantly, Mikhail removed his boot from the water.

"The field we landed in sure wasn't this pretty," Bernard said. "I'm glad the cameras had the chance to catch this."

"I'm glad my *eyes* had the chance to catch this," Mikhail said as he whirled back around. "I'm telling you, I'm swooning. I was never sold on the idea of this place before, and yet I am now. This is home. The trip we made, it wasn't a waste. Everything has been worth it."

He pointed downward. "I'm going to build a house right on these rocks."

Mikhail was starting to say something else when Bernard tore his tracer pistol from its holster.

"What's that crawling toward you? Mikhail, look behind you—at your feet. Something's coming out of the water."

A trail of orbs were snaking their way upward, linked together by a pink, fleshy cord.

"You need to step down *now*," Anne told Mikhail. *"Right now.* I don't know what this is. I don't know if it's dangerous."

"You heard the woman, Lieutenant," the voice from above said. "Fall back. Get off those rocks."

"I will. Just give me a second." Mikhail squatted down as the slithering life form crept closer. More coils began to wriggle from the water.

"Holy crap," Bernard said. "Those things...they're sparkling, too. Is that what's going on out there? Is that water filled with these things?"

He swiveled toward Anne for a quick second and then returned his gaze to the approaching coils. The aim of his pistol flipped from side to side, from coil to coil.

Anne stomped her foot against the stones. *"Damn* you, Mikhail. Either get back over here, or get out your gun."

"This is Meyer Wells, Lieutenant," a new voice said. "Do as Ms. Dougherty tells you."

Mikhail removed his tracer and took two big steps toward Anne and Bernard. It no longer mattered. The number of coils had quadrupled and had closed in around him. One nipped at his boot—its mouth perfectly round, and its tiny teeth bared.

"What do I do now?" Mikhail asked. The coils were beginning to wind up his pant leg.

Anne muttered, "You waited too long. I don't know what to tell you. You only have one chance. You gotta run."

"But they're all over the place. Which way do I go?"

"Run right over the top of them," Meyer said. "Do it *now*. Just *run*."

Mikhail lunged, but was toppled over before he could complete his first step. His legs had become too wound up in the coils. His upper body took the worst of the fall and he lost his grip on his weapon. The coils kept drawing in around him. He jerked and kicked, but could not twist his way out of his predicament.

Bernard ran to his friend's side, trampling across the coils. Anne held back and called out for Mikhail to keep crawling, to keep fighting.

Bernard fired his tracer, targeting anything in sight. Anne screamed, but not a sound could be heard over the barrage of weapon fire. Mikhail regained his own pistol and shot as well. The coils being blasted were damaged severely, cracking into soft-centered shards. There was more firing, from both Mikhail and Bernard.

Out in the middle of the lake, something stirred.

Another coil, a hundred times the size of those on the shore, erupted from below and speared straight into the sky, water spitting from its innards. Bernard's random firing went unabated, and unsuccessful.

The larger coil fully extended itself and came careening down on the outcropping. There was only a nanosecond after that. Mikhail stared at Bernard as his tracer fired for the last time. The coil came down with enormous momentum, pummeling Mikhail into the stones, and clipping Bernard across the leg.

The coil lay quivering, spasming. Anne cried out as it flicked back up, its underside marred by blood, flesh, and bone.

47

"What was that? *What* did we just see?" Mary pushed herself back into the couch. "Where's Mikhail? *What just happened to Mikhail?*"

Her father had no answer for her.

Like everyone else aboard the *Horizon*, Dimitri and Mary had been watching Mikhail's jaunt with equal parts awe and inspiration. And then, it had all come crashing down.

"My dear boy," Dimitri said. "My dear, lovely boy."

Mary sobbed. "He didn't just die, did he? Did we just watch him *die?*"

Dimitri's hand fell flat on her back. "I'm so sorry, sweetheart."

The instant he touched her, Mary lunged off the couch and charged over to the dimensional nook. The terrible images on Verdan were still playing out.

The central camera was positioned high, with a sharp close-up embedded in a circle along the bottommost corner of the display. Mikhail had been pulverized. Only bare traces of him remained on the outcropping. In the intervening seconds, the coils had retreated, and the shimmering had all but ceased. Anne was shrieking for help as she attempted to tend to an injured Bernard, her hand on what was left of his bleeding limb.

Mary got as close as she could get to the image container, watching and reeling.

"Can't anybody hear her?" she said. "People need to get over there. *Dad*, someone needs to send someone over. Make a call."

"Help is irrelevant," Dimitri said. "Your brother is gone."

Mary wiped at the wetness in her eyes. She was furious. "I *know* that. I saw what *you* just saw. But Bernard—he's lying there helpless."

"The support team saw everything as well. Help is already on the way. A call from me would be superfluous, and might possibly slow things down."

Mary sank to her knees and fell back onto the carpet. "This can't be happening. This *cannot* be happening."

"Mary, my love," Dimitri said, moving as far forward as he could without falling off the couch. "For now, you can go ahead and unburden yourself as much as you like. But once people start coming around, you'll need to pull yourself together."

Mary gave the carpeting a slap. "I don't *need* to do anything. *Shut up.*"

"I will not shut up. You cannot let the public see you like this."

"I don't *care* what the public sees."

"But you need to care. The people have just lost a man they see as their future leader. That makes you their future now. They'll be looking to you. When they do, you need to be strong for them."

"What are you even talking about? Mikhail just died like two seconds ago. I don't care about being strong. Who can be strong at a time like this?"

"People die, my dear. People that we love. All we can do is push on. The only thing we can do is be strong."

Mary curled herself into a ball. "Didn't you hear me? I *don't* care. My brother just died. I don't care about *anything*. And *you* shouldn't care about anything either."

48

They laid Bernard on a gurney and ferried him onto the spire.

Anne was observing from the edge of the clearing, her clothing drenched with his blood. Adam approached with caution.

"Hey," he said. "You need to get on board, too. They'll be taking off any second."

"I can't," Anne said. "This was my fault. I can't leave when what just happened was *my* fault."

Adam tried to put his arm around her, but she had already started to tread back into the forest.

"There's no use running away," he said, elevating the volume of his voice. "One of those muscle-bound Rangers will just toss you aboard if they have to. You may be able to play all tough with me, but those boys don't mess around."

Anne stopped where she was, a half meter outside the tree line.

"They're not so tough. They die just as easily as the rest of us."

"Please." Adam crept closer to her. "I don't know what else to say. There's no real choice here. You *have* to get on board. The people on the ship are demanding it. After everything that's happened, you need to be checked out."

"Emotionally checked out, you mean."

"Yes," he said after finally being able to get his arm around her. "Because that's what you need right now. I'll be needing it too before this is all over."

Anne shrugged and gave in. In silence, they drifted across the clearing.

Anne entered the ship's hatchway, leaving Adam in the muck. After having gone all the way inside, she burst back out.

"Do *you* think it was my fault?"

"Not any more than it's my fault, or *their* fault. It's just what happened. Fault doesn't enter into it. I've told you that a million times, haven't I?"

"I just needed to hear it again."

"I'll see you soon," he said.

The hatchway closed and Adam backed up toward the swayers. In a self-propelled gust, the *Spear* lifted itself out of the soup.

49

The emergency Directorate session had not yet been called to order, but already discussion had descended into all-out panic.

Ten minutes had passed since Elisabeth Epelle had left the chambers to retrieve Dimitri from his home. The coworkers she left behind had gotten crabby in the interim. Walter attempted to maintain the peace, shooting down as many wild assumptions as he could.

Deborah Summers was instigator number one. The sandy-haired blonde was leading the charge for a complete pullback of moon resources until a safer colonization plan could be instituted. Jacob Holt and Jonas Vickery were in basic agreement with Deborah, but taking it even further, they thought it imperative to cancel the transplantation process altogether. Antoinette Beal and Laken Merriweather were also interested in slowing things down, but not to the draconian extent their colleagues were proposing. Laken, a trained psychologist, was just finishing up her appraisal of the mental health ramifications of remaining aboard the *Horizon* for the foreseeable future. As she stated it, the possibility of this was not out of the question.

Walter drummed his fingers against the lip of the table. "We are *not* going to stay aboard this ship in perpetuity. That's out of the question. Any analysis that encourages such an option, I consider suspect, if not downright asinine."

"It is not asinine," Laken said. "It's not even suspect."

"It's an extreme step, you have to admit."

"No, I don't think that it is, not with the future of this society in question."

"The future of nothing is in question," Walter said. "We've suffered a setback, and the natural thing to do is to run and hide. That's all I've really heard from any of you. In so many words, you're telling me that you want to quit—the situation is too tough. And how do I know that? Because I feel like quitting right now, too."

"So where does this leave us?" Jonas asked.

"With a do-over," Antoinette said. "We land again, except on the other moon this time, where we'll survey remotely, in advance. This is the best option left to us. That hellscape down there is not an option, not anymore."

"You could be on to something there," Deborah said. "Azur has always been a viable alternative."

"Oh, so *now* you are willing to look at alternatives?" Walter said, refusing to even look at Deborah, the woman who was seated right next to him. "Five minutes ago you were all ready to give up."

"I was not. I suggested that we pull back and proceed with caution. From the beginning I have said this, long before this debacle of a landing. There was no reason to jump in head first the instant we entered orbit. We should have taken the time to do this in scientific manner, and not a militaristic one."

"Don't even start," Walter said. "There will be no second guessing when it comes to Mikhail. Your own personal issues with the Rangers aside, Trustee Summers, we took the path we took because it was the logical one. With the status of the Constructs still an open question, we established a plan all of us agreed upon, even you. Every vote pertaining to the landing has been unanimous."

"But not always unanimous by choice. We all know there are times when it's best to just go along. I know *you* understand that, Walter. You're the undisputed master of going along."

Walter was in mid-retort when Antoinette interrupted him.

"Dimitri's outside." She was gesturing down at the surveillance feed on the table. "He's talking to people as Elisabeth pushes him toward the door. That's probably what took them so long. I'll bet he's been inundated with well-wishers along the way."

"Speaking of which," Jacob said. "How are we supposed to react when he comes inside? Do we mention it right off, or do we ease into any declarations of sympathies?"

Walter took a moment before he answered. "I suggest we let him take the lead on that. If Dimitri wants something, even sympathy, he's the type to let that be known."

The door opened and Elisabeth ushered Dimitri inside. He was in his mover chair and was wearing a black suit and tie.

"We're here," Elisabeth said, giving Dimitri control of the chair and swerving around to the far side of the table.

Dimitri parked the mover chair beside his usual seat, which was unoccupied. He did not switch over.

"We should begin as soon as possible," he said. "I want to go over my daughter-in-law's birth schedule. I think we should move ahead with that at once, in hope it might boost morale. But first, I require a private word with Magistrate Stoddard."

The council responded with assorted 'fines,' 'sures,' and 'no problems.' As these responses were trailing off, Walter walked over and knelt down next to the mover chair.

"I'd like to take over this session if that's all right," Dimitri said. "I have a task for you elsewhere. An extremely important task."

"Tell me."

Dimitri whispered a name. Walter nodded and made a beeline for the door.

Dimitri wasn't quite finished, catching Walter just before he'd left.

"I've already informed Kay of my decision. She's on her way here now."

Walter nodded again.

50

"Mr. Magistrate. Hello."

"Hello, Leonid. I apologize for popping by unannounced, but I need to speak with you for a moment."

"Of course. Come on in."

The two men shook hands as Walter marched inside.

"Thank you for being so welcoming. Normally, I'm loath to intrude."

"Really, sir, it's not a problem."

With Leo in the lead, the two men sauntered out of the foyer and stepped down into the well-kept living room. The cocoa brown walls were filled with sporting awards and service medals, some marked with the name of Travis Matas, but most had been awarded to Leo himself.

"Are we alone?" Walter asked. There was a hushed quality to his voice.

"My roommate is gone, if that's what you mean. You can speak freely."

Leo offered Walter a place on the couch, which he accepted. Leo remained standing, his hands behind his back, locked at attention.

"Do you know why I've come?"

"I have my suspicions."

"I assumed that you would. You were always the brightest of men. So sharp, so to the point. All this made your fall ever more tragic. I wish things had played out differently."

"As do I," Leo said. "Particularly now."

"Then you were watching as Mikhail, *uh*—" Walter's head was bouncing around with embarrassment. "You witnessed how the accident unfolded I guess I should say."

"I watched every second of the landing, sir. Until just now, when you arrived at the door. I turned it off. I did not want to be rude."

Walter repositioned himself on the couch and crossed his legs. "What I'm about to ask you is by no means official yet. The Directorate itself must still be wrangled with. But if it can be arranged, would you return to active service with the Rangers, to at least get us through the early stages of this tragedy?"

"Who's asking this, sir? Who has given this their approval?"

"Dimitri has. It was his suggestion. I am here at his request."

"And Deborah?"

"Trustee Summers will be asked to vote on your reinstatement if and when you agree to return. No one will mention this to her until we have your firm agreement."

Leo's head began to shake. "You should've run this by her, sir. I've always insisted she have the right of first refusal. I harmed her while we were married, you know this. I will agree to nothing until she has given her unequivocal consent."

"But she will never give her consent," Walter said. "And her consent is not necessary. We only need a majority vote."

"I don't know what to tell you then. I cannot do this if she's going to fight it."

"Let me ask you this. If Deborah says yes, would you say yes?"

"I would not hesitate to say yes. When asked, I am always at the Collective's service."

Walter brushed off his pant leg and rose. "That's all I needed to know."

"What did I just say? What else is going on here? What are you planning?"

"I'm not planning anything. I am going to attempt to reason with Deborah Summers."

"All by yourself?"

"I assume I'll have the assistance of the rest of the council, and the considerable persuasive power of the Founder himself. He is on our side here, remember?"

Leo escorted Walter out. "Deborah will never give in easily, sir."

"I know that, Leonid. And neither will any of us."

51

Jason came sprinting into the waiting room and gave his mother a hug. Once he'd finished with Elisabeth, he slid over to his sister Joy and clutched her just as hard. His father Richard was seated in a chair next to a potted plant. The two men greeted one another with a simple hello.

"I'm glad you got here so fast," Elisabeth said. "This should go quickly once the Directorate has all its ducks in a row"

"I wouldn't have missed this for anything." Jason spun off his back foot and asked, "Where are they keeping Jocelyn? I thought we were supposed to have a private room with her. When can we see her?"

Dr. Courtney Cutler appeared in the waiting room doorway, dressed in a turquoise medical smock. "You'll be able to see her soon, Jay. Her room is being cleared now."

Jason swooped over to his colleague. "I hope you and your people have a solid plan for this. My sister's life cannot be put at risk."

"It won't be," Elisabeth said, before Courtney could make her case. "Security plans are being readied. Dimitri is taking care of it all."

Courtney leaned in and told Jason, "Since I'm going to be down there as well, you can bet your ass I'll be doing everything possible to keep Jocelyn safe."

"I knew that," Jason said. "I didn't mean to come off so gruff. I'm just worried about Jocelyn and the baby."

"Of course you are." She squeezed Jason's arm and addressed everyone in the room. "Before I go check in on the patient, I wanted to say how sorry I am for your loss. I haven't a chance to speak with Mary yet, but I still wanted to express my condolences to all of you. Mikhail was the sweetest man I have ever known, and probably the most loved. The word tragedy does not begin to cover this."

The Epelles responded with equally heartfelt reciprocations, and then Courtney exited.

Elisabeth limped over to Richard and settled down on his lap.

"My beautiful girl," she said, more to herself than to him. "Jocelyn loved that man so much. The poor thing. This is going to devastate her."

Richard nodded and pulled his wife close.

BEFORE

A husky blond man accompanied Mary through the door. The round-walled room they entered looked like a traditional living space, with a bed, a desk, and a small bathroom opposite the door. In reality, the room was a holding facility, made clear by several signs of its maximum security—titanium walls, external cameras, tracking sensors in the floor, and no view out into the rest of the ship.

Mary ambled over to the foot of the bed. The guard was shadowing her closely.

"You need to sit up," she said.

The individual she had come to see was lying on his back, his size fourteen boots draped over the far left corner of the mattress. Mary and this man had been staring at each other since she'd first stepped inside the cell.

Mary tapped the guard on the arm and asked him to leave, which he did, with no attempt at argument or persuasion to the contrary.

"What are you doing here?" Leo said after the guard had gone.

"I wanted to see how you were, and to find out if you needed anything."

The door closed with a clang.

"I don't need anything. Thank you, though." Leo sat up, swung his legs around, and dropped his feet onto the floor.

"May I make myself comfortable?" Mary asked him.

"Be my guest." Leo held his arm out over the bed. His body had left a massive indentation on the checkered-print comforter. "Sorry there aren't that many places to sit. Just the bed and the desk chair. If we get desperate, I guess there's the desk itself."

Mary eased herself down onto the edge of the bed. "This will do," she said as she tucked her hands into her lap and oriented her body toward Leo. It was as close as the two of them had been in months.

"Belated congratulations, by the way," Leo said. "I heard about your pregnancy when your father made the announcement last week. I'm happy for you, and for Camden."

"That's sweet of you to say, Leo. But I did not come here to talk about myself or the baby. I came here because you are in trouble—*serious* trouble. Rumors are already flying, even though there have been no formal charges yet. Personally, I only know what my father has told me, and I refuse to trust the word of somebody who's already so against you. That's why I came. I needed to hear it from you. I want to help, if that's possible. But first, in your own words, you need to tell me what you've done."

When she was done, Leo glanced away. It was well past midnight, although the brightness of the room gave no outward sign of the time either way.

"I'm not going anywhere," Mary said after several seconds had ticked by. "You might as well hop to it."

Leo shrugged. "What's the point? Anything you've heard is more than likely the truth. I did what they've said I've done. I cannot sugarcoat it for you. Your father would never do that, and neither will I."

"At least tell me what possessed you then. Did she say something to cause this, or did you lash out for some other reason? When Dad woke me up and told me you'd been arrested, I felt sick. I couldn't believe it. Deborah is your wife, Leo. You married her. You made a commitment to her. And then you go and do *this*."

Leo closed his eyes. "Do you know how she's doing?"

"She's in the hospital, and probably will be for a month. You hurt her badly."

His eyes snapped back open. "I figured as much. I've asked about her every time someone has come in here. But no one will tell me anything."

"They're under orders not to. I probably shouldn't have told you anything either."

"I know, but I'm concerned. Despite what everyone thinks of me, I am concerned."

"I realize that, but what you feel no longer matters. They're going to prosecute you. Do you understand what I'm telling you? Deborah is insisting upon it. She's out for blood."

"And she should be," Leo said. He slid backward and propped himself up against the headboard of the bed. "I deserve everything that's coming to me."

"Enough of that," Mary said. "I need more from you than self pity right now. I need to know why."

"What if I don't know why?"

"Oh, please. You are not a man who does things with no reason."

Leo looked up at the ceiling and shook his head.

"I can wait all night, you know," Mary said.

"I don't want to talk about this with you."

"I don't care. I'm the only one who's going to look out for you."

"And I really wish you wouldn't. You need to let me go, Mary. Like you said, Deborah is out for blood. I hurt her. I did what I did and now I'm throwing myself on the Directorate's mercy. They can do with me as they will. I've already made my confession. They didn't have to send you in here to make me say it again, to you of all people."

"I'm not here for the Directorate. I'm here because I care about you. I know I'm married to Camden now, and you're married—"

"To the woman I beat."

"You're just feeling sorry for yourself," Mary said. "I won't tolerate that. Talk to me."

"I can't. You're going to hate me afterward. Don't you get that?"

"Then so be it. I'll hate you." Mary extended her arms and steadied herself on the mattress. "Tell me, dammit."

"Fine," Leo said through gritted teeth. "Deb and I, we were arguing at the dinner table. She had just told me something I didn't like, something that made me very mad. After I refused to play along with this other thing she wanted, she went berserk, throwing a glass on the floor and a plate at my head."

He touched the skin above his right brow. There was a tiny hint of discoloration.

"It struck me here."

Mary bent forward to study the mark. "I can see something, but it hardly looks like a major injury."

"It's not. And it didn't even hurt then, but boy did it piss me off. Coupled with what she had told me, I was good and pissed."

"You need to stop being so vague," Mary said. "Tell me what she said to you, whatever it was that made you so angry."

"But it's not important."

"Obviously it was. Talk to me."

Out in the corridor, a female voice screeched. Neither Mary nor Leo reacted to noise in any way.

"Deb wanted out," Leo said. "She told me our marriage was over. She wanted to marry someone else. Let me correct that, she probably *should* have married someone else. Those were her exact words."

"But the two of you have been barely married two months."

"And I told her that. But she said she had never stopped sleeping with Jack Summers. They'd been having sex from almost the moment she and I had been married."

Mary slumped forward. "I'm sorry, Leo."

"I don't know why I was so surprised. Before she and I got back together again, Deb had been hot and heavy with Jack. This was when you and I were still sneaking around. Once your father put an end to that, and then you married Camden, she and I rekindled. I proposed not too soon after. She swore up and down that it was over between her and Jack, but I guess that it wasn't."

"Is the revelation about Jack the thing that set off the plate throwing incident?"

"Sort of. She also told me she wanted to petition for an annulment, to render our marriage contract void. I wouldn't agree to that, though."

"I don't blame you," Mary said.

"I was out of my mind with anger. She didn't want to be married to me anymore, and I needed time to think about that. The unfaithfulness in particular was a hard thing for me to accept, and I told her so. But that wasn't what she wanted to hear. And the more I refused to agree to the annulment, the more crazed she got, escalating to the broken glass, and in turn, the plate cracking against my skull."

"How much of this have you told to the investigators?" Mary said.

"About the affair? None of it. It's not anyone's business."

Her voice dropped low. "Leo...you need to tell these people *everything*. There are mitigating circumstances here."

"But I hit her," he said. "Regardless of anything she might or might not have done, I did hit her."

"And you'll be punished for that, no matter what. But if you make this other information public, she will be punished as well. She violated your marriage contract. That could cause her all kinds of hell. And maybe it might alter the public perception of what you've done."

"It shouldn't. This was all my fault."

"But it doesn't sound like it was all your fault."

"Only because I haven't finished my story. I told you the why, but I didn't tell you the how. The attack was worse than you realize."

"What are you trying to say?"

"I'm trying to say that I'm a piece of shit."

"You have to stop putting this all on yourself."

"I put it on myself because I deserve to have it put on me."

"Leo, if you have something more to say, then say it. Tell me everything. It's for your own good."

Leo took a breath. "After she threw the plate, I chased her into the kitchen. She grabbed a mug off the counter and tried to hurl it, but I snatched her by the arm and stopped her. So she slapped me with her other arm. Then she told me I didn't want the annulment because it was going to be the second time I couldn't keep a woman I cared about. She told me she had never loved me, just like you had never loved me—and she slapped me again. That's when I lost it. I just clenched up my fist and punched her. She looked up at me, blood oozing from her mouth and she laughed. I've never been more enraged in my life. I hit her again and again and again. I didn't stop until she had collapsed onto the floor."

"Leo," Mary said, soft and distant.

"You need to listen to me very closely here. Mitigating circumstances are irrelevant. I am the one at fault. She had cheated on me and was scheming to cast me aside. I couldn't handle being cast aside again. I make no excuses. I lashed out, and I understand this. She hurt me and all I thought about was giving her that hurt back, harder than she could ever have given it to me."

"But there's more to that story," Mary said. "You feel guilty about the attack, so you've given up. Of course you have to accept the majority of the blame, but Deborah is not blameless either."

"Maybe. But under any circumstances, she did not deserve what I did to her. And I did do it to her, exactly as I described."

Mary tried to reach out for him, but he just scooted out of the way.

"No," he said. "No contact."

"But I want to be here for you," she said.

"You can't. You shouldn't. I'm a brute. That's what you've never really gotten about me. But your father, he recognized it right off. I'm nothing but a muscle-bound thug. I am built to hurt things. It's what I've been trained for, and it's the only thing I've ever been good at. Becoming a Ranger was just about the only way I *ever* could have strayed into your stratosphere. We met because I'm physically gifted, a man who can dole out violence. That's what Kay noticed about me. *That's* the story your father wanted me to tell that night. I once knocked three different men unconscious in one of our scrums. That's what he found so amusing. That's how Kay plucked me out of obscurity, which should make it clear to anyone—I do not belong in decent company. Seriously, that has to be the reason your father didn't want us together, and that's why Deb rejected me, too. I don't belong. I've always known it. I've never belonged anywhere."

Tears were falling down Mary's cheek. She wiped them away.

"You belonged with me, Leo. We should have been together. I should've been your wife. I loved you so much."

"Listen to yourself. I just beat my wife senseless. We *never* should have been together. It's the most obvious thing in the universe to me now. Just go. Leave me to my violent little existence. I enjoy being a Ranger. I like being brutal. I'm good at hurting things. I excel at it. Being a decent, loving husband, that's obviously not the right path for me."

Mary stared at him, blank-faced. "You don't get what's going on here, do you? Your Ranger days are over if you don't try and put some of this on a woman who undoubtedly wronged you. The Directorate won't hesitate. They'll brush you aside. Politically, you won't be allowed to serve in any capacity, not after this. You will be tattooed and cast from sight. The situation as it stands now is untenable. Serving on the Rangers is too high a position for a person who's been convicted of a violent crime."

Leo lowered his head. "I guess I should have figured as much."

"Yes, you should have. The ramifications here are more dire than you know."

"I doesn't matter now. I'm tired, Mary, and it's too late at night for you to be in here. I want to be alone. I already told you—I don't belong in good company anymore. Do me one last favor and just go."

"I won't allow you to fall into some hole. If I leave, I will be back."

"Don't. I'm begging you. If your father won't allow me to lead or even be a Ranger, then he certainly won't allow you to be seen with me."

Mary climbed off the bed. "I'm a married woman now. My father doesn't get a say in my life anymore."

Leo withheld comment, which was a comment in itself.

Mary wandered over to the door and requested to be let out. There was a slight delay while she waited for the guard to tap in the necessary code.

"I'm so sorry this happened," she said. "And I'm even sorrier that you won't stand up for yourself."

"And I'm sorry I hurt Deborah. But that *is* what I did. Sorry doesn't get anybody anywhere. We have to live with the things we've done, even you Kucherovs. Even someone from my lowly family. In the end, we all get what's coming to us."

"You will be hearing from me again. I won't let you fall forever."

"Just forget about me."

"I can't. Forgetting about you is an impossibility for me."

The cell door closed and Leo stretched out on the bed, his pupils focused in on one of the small security cameras embedded into the ceiling. The room dimmed to darkness, and the red activation lights blinked and glowed, like two great stars in the night.

Four Years Later

52

Kay brought her fist down on the table. The crack it made startled several of the more disinterested Trustees, forcing them to pay closer attention to what the Ranger guru had to say.

"What am I really asking for here? One man. To keep us all safe, all I am asking for is a single soul."

"Yes," Jonas said. "But this man you're asking us for is damaged goods, a savage who beat his own wife."

"That's my issue here," Antoinette said. "I'll most likely give Dimitri whatever he wants in the end, but Leonid Bratsk is not a man who deserves redemption."

"And who deserves anything?" Kay said as she wound her way around the octagonal table. "Forgive me, but that particular point of view loses sight of the bigger picture. The question is not whether Leo deserves another chance. The question is, did Mikhail have to die?"

All around the table there were gasps and recriminations. Before too long, everyone had turned to Dimitri at table position three, who appeared completely unaffected by what had just been said.

Kay began waving her arms. "Over here. I'm the one who was talking." The council's attention swung back to her.

"You all don't have to feign such shock. Dimitri knows what I'm talking about. Since Leo was expelled, the two of us have had this conversation on an almost weekly basis. There were reasons Leo was my one and only choice to lead the landing team. He had it all—strength, dexterity, instinct, intelligence, and yes," she said, staring across the table at a stone-faced Deborah, "a penchant for violence. These are the qualities that are necessary on a mission like this. We needed someone who could take control, someone who was not afraid of Mikhail's celebrity and could keep the boy's tendency toward absentmindedness in check. All the Rangers behaved differently when Leo was in charge. He's a born soldier, and the men responded to that. And his skill levels, they are off the chart. He has gone through all of my jungle training sessions and never made one mistake—not one. He's been perfect. None of the rest of the men had even a forty percent success rate. But Leo, he's been incapable of stumbling. As I've been trying to tell you for umpteen years now, he was and is the perfect man for this job."

"Perfect is certainly not the word I'd use for him," Deborah said. "The man made his own bed. Now, the sick disgusting abuser gets to lie in it."

"You sit there and act so high and mighty," Kay said, "as if you were an innocent in all this. I know more about what happened than you think I do."

Walter picked up his gavel and held it out at Kay, who was coming their way. "We're getting off track here. I can't tolerate vague accusations. Trustee Summers is not the issue in question at the moment."

Kay got right in Deborah's face. "But of course she is. This is *all* about her. You've had the votes for reinstatement for a while now. Time in and time out it has been seven-to one, the same result, without change. On any other issue, a result like that would have passed. But on this, you allow the hurt feelings of one woman to control the safety of this entire expedition."

"That's such a lie," Deborah said.

Kay loomed over her. "You'd know all about lies, wouldn't you, you witch?"

"*Kay,*" Dimitri said. "Find a place to sit down. You're making everyone nervous."

Kay backed away and took a seat along the dividing wall on the far side of the table.

"I think you can all at least admit one thing," she said. "I have been right about this from the start. This new home of ours is a dangerous place, possibly more dangerous than I even imagined. To be frank, I still haven't gotten my head around the ramifications. And if I can't get my head around that, how is someone like Camden Muran going to manage. I mean, he's a good and decent man, but he's just a front, an attractive figurehead held out for whatever symbolic victory you politicos were attempting to manufacture. And Mikhail, he was the same. This is all the more reason I should've fought harder. I understood the dangers, but I went along with this playacting nonsense when I should have demanded you send a legitimate team down instead. And that's what Leo is, the genuine article. The Rangers should have remained the way they began, a bona fide field team, with a flavor of showmanship, but at its core, hard-nosed and vicious. Maybe that would've changed things. Maybe if we go that way now, a team like that can set things right."

Deborah sat forward. "All right. Let's pretend I accept what you're saying. You understood what none of the rest understood. Why then did you never seek out a replacement for your pet? That monster can hardly be the only gifted soldier aboard this ship."

"His name is Leonid," Kay said. "Leo, if you're his friend."

"But I'm not his friend. And 'monster' is as good a name for him as any."

Kay stood back up and shrugged at Dimitri. "I can't do it, boss. I can't talk to her. She's more unreasonable and unpleasant than I am. And I'm a cantankerous old harpy."

"You're right about one thing," Deborah said. "You sure are old."

"You don't stop, do you?" Kay said. "I can see how someone might want to beat you to a pulp. I really can."

"*Enough*," Dimitri said. "Both of you."

"Sorry, but it's not enough," Kay said. "I realize Leo did a heinous thing, but I do not have to convince anyone at this table that this woman can push people's buttons. Leo's the born soldier. She's the born trouble-maker. You can see it, right there in her mean-spirited eyes."

"I see. I get it now," Deborah said. "You're telling everyone it was okay for me to be beaten. Since I'm such an unrepentant bitch, that gave him the right to strike a defenseless woman."

"What does being a woman have to do with this? If it's wrong to hit someone, then it's wrong to hit someone. As a woman myself, I'm offended that you hold your gender up as some sort of shield for your actions. You are a human being. And yes, it's wrong to strike another human being. That's as far as my sympathy for you goes."

"Being defenseless was my point. I made the man angry, so what? I've made a lot of people angry. No one else has ever beaten me into submission."

Kay took another step in Deborah's direction. "Well, if you'd care to step outside, I don't mind being person number two."

Several of the other Trustees grumbled.

Dimitri flicked his hand at the door. "Get *out*, Kay. Go now. I will not put up with behavior of this sort. What have I told you about you and your threats?"

Kay gave Deborah one last stare as she strutted away. "Believe me, I wouldn't have been so easy on you, princess. I sure wouldn't have stopped after a couple of blows. I'd have kept going until there was *nothing* left of your face."

The door slid open and Kay was gone.

Deborah ran her fingers down the back of her head. There was a glint of sweat on her face. "And this is the person you people bring in to convince me?"

"I brought her in to lay out the facts," Dimitri said. "Which she did. Her temper is another matter. It's something I've never been able to control."

Deborah took a sip from her water glass. "So, you expect me to take the word of someone who is more irrational than the cretin who broke my jaw? Are violent maniacs really the sort of people you want in charge down there, sir? I know I don't. I'm sorry to remain so intransigent, but my vote will not change. That monster will not be allowed to rejoin the

Rangers."

"Deborah, you do realize your vote is not required," Walter said. "We can do this without you."

"No, you can't. You said he wouldn't agree to rejoin if I didn't approve."

"How does the vote count stand?" Walter said as he glanced around the table. "Who agrees that Leonid Bratsk should return to the Rangers forthwith?"

Seven hands went up, with only Deborah refusing.

"It's never going to happen," she said. "I will *never* vote yes. And if you go around me, I will tell everyone I was against it. I will *never* stop telling people that."

Dimitri lifted his hands onto the tabletop and started to type. "That's all right. Tell people whatever you like. I sympathize with your reluctance to vote yes, Trustee Summers, but now is not the time for personal grievances."

He composed a third sentence, and then a fourth. "There's another way out of this predicament, if you so choose. For the public good, you could abstain. I see this as more than a mere face-saving maneuver. You are too close to this man, and are therefore unable to render an unbiased opinion on the matter at hand. This is what Leonid will be told. This is what you will agree to."

"I can't agree to that," Deborah said.

"I think that you can, as a favor to me. My son and heir has just been killed. Will you deny me this favor? Would you look a grieving father in the eyes and refuse him this one request? I don't believe you'd do that. The political ramifications of such a denial could become counterproductive to your re-election efforts. Consequently, when push comes to shove, I believe you will see the light and abstain. I know this because I know how strong and loyal you are. As the selfless public figure you've held yourself up as these last two years, you will push aside your own personal anger for the betterment of the Collective. All of the rest of us have done so in the past. It is your turn to do so now."

Deborah's lips had bunched up and her eyelids had narrowed. "He cannot be put into a leadership position, and his placement can only be temporary. He can do whatever is necessary down there, but he does not get to be the hero. Scum like him should never be allowed to be the hero."

Dimitri looked up from the speech he was writing. "Is that all? Are you agreeing to abstain?"

"As you so eloquently pointed out, I have no other choice."

Dimitri went back to his typing.

"Then the motion is passed, seven to zero," Walter said. "Leonid Bratsk is hereby temporarily reinstated into the Echo Rangers."

A chime went off, signifying the successful passage of a legislative order.

"Now, on to further business."

53

It was Kay who informed Leo. Equipment parcels were ready and waiting on his back patio and he was out the door in a matter of minutes.

He'd made it a block down the road when a pair of voices called out to him. Hollis Craddock and Tella Webb were jogging toward him, geared up in the same Ranger sheaths and khakis Leo was now wearing.

"This is you," he said. The link convo he and Kay had been having was ongoing. "How did you manage this?"

"With Mikhail gone and Bernard injured, we needed more bodies. And since these two just kicked the Rangers' asses recently, that shot their names to the top of my list."

Hollis and Tella caught up with Leo. Both were smiling. Leo stopped and told them he required a second on his own. They scooted a few steps down the sidewalk to give him a bit of space.

"You do approve of these two, don't you?" Kay asked him. "You've been training with them for a couple of years now, correct?"

"Yeah, but it hasn't been *that* kind of training. The three of us just worked out together to keep in shape. And every once in a while, I'd teach them a few tactics."

"Look, I get why you're concerned, Leo. But some training is better than no training, and they do work well with you. That's important. Plus, we don't have a whole lot of options at the moment. The pickings are slim."

"The thing is, these two haven't been put through even one field simulation. It wasn't permitted. I didn't have access to that level of grid-ware, not after I was convicted."

"Let's compromise," Kay said. "Until they prove themselves, we keep them partnered up with more experienced hands. Does that ease your concerns any?"

"I want to talk to them before I answer that."

Leo called his friends back over. Hollis was as big and beefy a specimen as he was. Tella was thin and athletic, with a perfectly toned musculature.

"Guys, I appreciate what you're doing here, but we all saw the feed from earlier. This could be life-threatening work. Be sure of what you're risking here. You both have children. I do not."

"Let's worry about someone else's child right now," Tella said.

Hollis was nodding along. "Let's go get the Kucherov baby born. After that, then you can try and convince us to back out."

Tella smirked. "Like that's ever going to happen."

"I assume this means we're all set," Kay said.

Leo motioned his friends onward. "Let's go. No more lollygagging. We got us a baby that needs birthing.

54

Courtney whispered into Mary's ear. "I am so worried about you, honey. I hate the idea of leaving you here alone."

Mary used Courtney's waist for leverage and slipped free of their embrace. "I'll be fine," she said.

They were the last two stragglers on the gantry, a step away from the wide-open hatchway. The giant hoop drive engine had begun its initial rotation, which was causing the surrounding infrastructure to rumble and shake.

"Everything's going to be all right down there," Courtney said. "You do know that, don't you?"

"Easy for you to say." Mary backed up until she had bumped against the railing.

"It *will* be okay," Courtney said. "I promise you. Nothing worse can possibly happen."

"I appreciate the positivity, but worse things can definitely happen, and usually do."

Mary peered down at the circular opening at the bottom of the hangar. Verdan's emerald green atmosphere swirled beneath them.

"The birth was going to happen eventually," Courtney said. "Therefore, we might as well get through it. Also, I don't think your father is wrong about the timing here. The sooner that child is born, the sooner people can feel something good again. This sort off thing could help."

"That's certainly the conventional wisdom," Mary said.

"It's more than that. It's all we have left."

"Just be careful. With everything…you, Jocelyn, and the baby."

"Don't worry, Mary." Courtney held her hand over her chest. "You'll be right here with me. You're always here with me. I love you."

"I love you, too," Mary said.

"Did you hear the news?" Courtney said. "Leo's been reinstated. You know he'll keep everyone safe."

Before Mary could respond, a buzzer rang out that reverberated across the bay.

Courtney took off toward the hatchway. "That's them hurrying me. I need to get my butt in gear. We can talk about this when I get back."

Mary blew her a kiss. "Attentiveness and diligence, my friend."

"Things I have never, ever been known for," Courtney said as she scooted on board.

55

A video close-up of Tarissa Solano was relayed throughout the *Horizon*.

"Flight number two to the surface of Verdan is set to launch, this time out, from the aircraft *Javelin*. We are a go in three, two, *one*—"

A blast of interference cut the image transmission to black. Despite this, Tarissa's audio play-by-play soared above all.

"If anyone can still hear me, we've dropped. Everything's looking great. We're on our way back down."

56

Leo emerged first, tracer pistol in hand. His boots dropped into the ooze and he made his way toward what was left of the original landing team. Kay, Hollis, and Tella came springing out behind him, following his every bob and weave.

"Well, look who it is," Camden said as he stepped away from the sway-er stalks. "My illustrious predecessor. Glad you could join us, Leo, now that all the heavy lifting has been done."

Leo moved past Camden and waded over to Adam.

"I've been told you're our resident ecosystem expert. Do I have that right?"

"You do," Adam said.

"I'm Leo, pleased to meet you. I'm going to need you to stay as close to me as you can for the next half hour or so. The plan is to get this over with quickly. I want you there beside me, tugging on my arm the instant you see anything that doesn't feel kosher."

Adam looked over at Camden, who was already bearing down on Leo.

"What do you think you're doing?" Camden said, going chest to chest with the bigger man. "I'm in charge. I was told you were only coming down to lend a hand. What the hell are you trying to pull with this ordering people around crap?"

"He's trying to keep your sister-in-law and her baby safe," Kay said as she separated the two men. "Dimitri agreed that Leo wouldn't be placed

242

into an overall command position, but that doesn't mean he won't be given organizational control over certain high-profile missions. This is one of those missions, so you're just going to have to deal with it. This comes straight from Dimitri. Until that child is born, what Leo says goes."

Kay walked off and Leo lowered his voice.

"This doesn't have to be a thing, Cam. All I need is someone near me who knows more than I do."

"Sure, I've gotten used to that sort of thing as well," Camden said. "Adam's become a real asset to me."

"That's terrific, but I'm only borrowing him for a little while. No one is here to step on your toes. We're here to keep an eye out, to prevent another catastrophe."

"What about those two?" Camden motioned over at Hollis and Tella. "They're the jerks who attacked us the other day."

Both Hollis and Tella had their backs to Leo and Camden, watching as the spire launched several dozen surveillance cameras from its hull.

Leo called out to them, "Recruits…get your asses over here."

Hollis spun around. So did Tella.

"Do either of you have anything to say to this man," Leo said.

Tella's head dipped. "Sorry?"

"Sorry about covers it," Hollis said to Camden. "We were just following orders, Commander. I tried to go easy on you with that tackle in the street. I hope I didn't hurt you too bad."

"You didn't." Camden flexed his arms and stared Hollis down. "You couldn't."

"We should talk." Leo hooked Camden by the shoulder and directed him over to an open spot a meter or so away.

"I don't want to talk to you right now," Camden said.

"Tough. What we're doing here is more important than anyone's bruised ego. That's Jocelyn over there in that ship—Mikhail's wife. She and her baby need to be kept safe. That's our one and only priority. So how about we put everyone available to work on that? Kay's got a protection pattern already drawn up. If you want, she can help you implement it."

"What if I have my own plan?"

"Go argue that out with her. If you can convince that woman otherwise, then be my guest. All I ask is that everybody stays in constant link contact. Shout out anything unusual that you see. The actual birth is supposed to happen imminently. That spire will be taking off as soon as that child is born."

Camden drifted away and started barking out orders, which Kay told everyone to ignore.

Adam returned to Leo's side just as the new arrival started scanning the swayer tops.

"I've been told it doesn't get too dark around here," Leo said.

Adam held his right arm out and drew Leo's attention over to the gargantuan white planet in the sky.

"That's right. The reflected light from Kroma keeps things in a constant twilight state. In all my time down here, it has never gotten any darker than it is now. In the mornings, it gets slightly brighter for fourteen hours or so. Then it gets like this again for another thirteen."

"Does anything strange happen during this twilight state?"

"No more than usual. Strange things happen pretty much around the clock here."

"I got you," Leo said. "Again, I'm in perpetual link with the pilot and the doctor. If you see anything out of the norm, I have the authority to give a takeoff order at a moment's notice. You will have a big say in that."

Leo rechecked the status of his weapon. "Whatever you do, don't stray too far. I'm counting on those eyes and ears of yours. This baby's welfare is in our hands. We cannot screw that up."

Adam hesitated for a second, and then nodded. Leo stepped left and took another look at the swayer tops. The surveillance cameras had formed two contiguous chains above the tree line. Every angle was covered.

"Actually," Courtney said, speaking in Leo's ear. "The baby is about to be in my hands, literally so."

"I read you loud and clear, doctor."

"Just so you're kept up to date with everything I know," Courtney said.

"I have Jocelyn on the table and I've already made a series of injections to expedite dilation. Her contractions have sped up accordingly. I can revive her at any time. Just give me the go ahead."

"I need another minute, please."

Leo counted off the position of each member of the security detail. They were all lined up in a circle around the ship, weapons drawn. Only Leo and Adam were out of formation.

"Doctor, I think we're good out here. My people are where they need to be. Whenever you're ready, do your thing."

"Okay," Courtney said. "The anitocin has been injected into her bloodstream. She should be awake in a matter of seconds."

BEFORE

Mikhail and Jocelyn were on a date, their first, arranged by the former to be a low-key occasion—dinner on the patio, followed by drinks in the park.

Mikhail took Jocelyn's hand as they walked beneath a sycamore tree. They both had gotten all dressed up for the big night. He, in his black blazer and a white shirt and tie. She, in a sleeveless yellow sundress, her dark brown hair combed down and cascading across her shoulders. A spread awaited them on the hill—a candy-stripped blanket topped by two crystal glasses, not yet filled, and a bottle of champagne on ice.

"This is very romantic," Jocelyn said as they settled down next to one another.

"Well, if we're going to do this, we might as well do it right. I've wasted too much time already."

"It hasn't been a waste," Jocelyn said. "I'll take you any way I can get you."

"I know that, but you deserve so much more. You deserve the best." Mikhail reached over and placed his hand on her knee. "I've been denying my feelings for you for so long…for as long as I've known you, really."

Jocelyn shrugged. "I'm just thrilled you finally noticed how I felt. I mean, come on, there were times when I was making it incredibly obvious."

"I'm an idiot." Mikhail slipped his free hand into his left back pocket. "And you…you are the most beautiful woman I have ever known."

Jocelyn smiled at that. "I never thought you looked at me that way. I wasn't sure you looked at me in any way."

"All I can say in my defense, things haven't been too normal since my Mom died. I've been unsure about everything, even of how I felt about you."

"And how do you feel about me?"

"Like this."

Mikhail drew his hand from behind his back and revealed a small gold ring that was resting in his palm.

"I feel like I was born to give you this, and to ask this question."

"Oh, Mikhail." Jocelyn's hands flew up to her mouth. "I can't believe this."

"I want you to marry me, Jocelyn. I've wanted this for longer than I've been able to say. If you feel the same way about me, why should we go halfway in and just date? Why the heck would we wait to *really* be together one second longer."

"For about a million reasons," Jocelyn said. "It's too soon for one."

"But I love you. No more wasting time, okay? We have so much to do with our lives, like starting our own family. I don't want to wait for that." He pulled his hand back, "But if you've got to reject me for the It's-too-soon reason—just do it. Reject me. I can take it."

Jocelyn leaned toward him, her eyes wide. "I have no intention of rejecting you. Don't be stupid. You've always been the man for me, that I'm sure of. It's the one thing I have never doubted."

"I'm not doubting it anymore either."

He squeezed her knee with one hand and held the ring back out with the other.

"I need your official answer. I'm not going to be able to breath until you've given it to me."

Jocelyn sighed. "I say yes. I say that I love you."

Mikhail slipped the ring onto her finger. And with a kiss, their engagement was sealed.

Three Years Later

57

"It was utter lunacy. The goofball actually proposed to me on our *first* date."

Jocelyn had not stopped talking since the moment she awoke. She was dazed, in a stupor, telling stories to no one in particular.

"We hear you," Courtney said from the base of the operating table, a white surgical mask adhered across her face. "Everything's going to be all right."

With that, she disappeared between her patient's legs just as the baby was beginning to crown. Blazing lamps bore down from above. A middle-aged nurse was at the front of the table, her hand held steady on the patient's arm.

"He couldn't even wait a day." Jocelyn laughed, her amusement transforming into a hacking cough, which only made her voice grow throatier. Despite everything, she kept on speaking, her mind and body functioning on diametrically opposed planes. "Maybe, possibly...I might've expected a proposal on our *second* date."

Just then, Jocelyn's chest and arms spasmed. *"What's* going on? I felt funny for a moment there."

"Your body is normalizing itself as it comes out of stasis," Courtney said, popping up for a brief instant to meet Jocelyn's gaze. "You'll be drifting in and out of lucidity for the next several hours or so. Right this second, however, I need a huge favor from you. If you can understand what I'm saying, I need you to push. I need you to push as hard as you can. Your baby is coming, your precious baby. I know how much you were looking forward to this, so I need you to push. Push, now, Jocelyn—*push*."

"Is she even listening to you?" the nurse asked.

"She's not pushing, but the baby's still coming anyway. It should only be a minute or so more."

The nurse draped a wet towel over Jocelyn's brow. "I'm not sure how much of this she's feeling. I've never seen a woman in labor behave like this."

"It's just an after effect of the stasis procedure. She's lucky. I'd have given anything to skip over the pain when I had my kids."

"I'm not exaggerating about *any* of this," Jocelyn said. "He and I didn't even make love until *after* we were married. And let me tell you, did I end up dodging a bullet there. He seemed to know what he was doing—or at least he knew more than me. I would have assumed he'd never been with anyone else, but he must have. He knew all my spots right off."

"This has now become officially embarrassing," the nurse said. "People back on the ship are listening in. The *things* she's saying."

"Ah, it's fine. It'll only make Mikhail's legend grow larger."

Jocelyn's leg jerked and Courtney said, "Here we go."

A cry filled the converted passenger space.

"Look at that face. She's so gorgeous."

Courtney lifted the wet, wriggling child upward and checked her from head to toe. Jocelyn kept bragging about Mikhail's prowess in the bedroom while Courtney wrapped the newborn in a blanket and escorted her over to her mother. For a minute or so, the baby wailed and wailed until something changed in Jocelyn's expression.

"Where am I?" she asked, suddenly coherent.

"You're on one of the spire ships, Jocelyn, on the surface of Verdan. This is your child. Your beautiful baby girl."

"This is *my* baby?" Tears were falling. Jocelyn attempted to reach up, but her body was much too stiff to cooperate.

Courtney brought the crying baby as close as she could. "She's most definitely yours. You should be proud. Have you decided on a name yet?"

"Mikhail wanted to wait until we could see her. But I already knew what her name should be. I've known for a long time."

"Tell me. Tell everyone. What are you going to call her?"

"Tana," Jocelyn said. "Tana Marie."

58

"He's been asking for you," the voice in her ear said. "You need to come see him, as soon as you can."

Mary was lying back in her bed watching the feed of her niece's birth while her own three children slept peacefully at her side. Down on Verdan, Jocelyn had faded back to unconsciousness and the baby was continuing to cry. Courtney and the nurse were doing their best to soothe her, but as one could already tell, this was quite the vociferous child.

"Are you feeling poorly?" Walter asked after Mary didn't respond. "Do you need to see someone, perhaps? For medical reasons, or even psychological ones."

"I'm not in the mood for this," Mary said. "Would you please just leave me alone."

"Not in the mood for what?"

"For you...for my father."

"Have you considered the fact that your father may be in need of you right now?"

"And have you considered the fact that I could care less?"

"Well, if you won't speak to anyone professionally, maybe you'd consider speaking with me? You know I would do anything to help you, Mary. Today's tragedy has been heart shattering. And the way you're feeling, it's completely understandable."

"I told you, Walter. I'm not in the mood."

A NEW WORLD

"Understood and accepted. I get it. You cannot come by at the moment. But would you think about swinging by later, after everything has calmed down? Or maybe I can bring your father to you. Would that be preferable? He's not one to take no for an answer, as you are well aware."

"All I want is to be left alone," Mary said. "*That's* what's preferable."

"Where are your children?"

"Right next to me, if that's any of your business."

"I was only trying to—"

"Just stop, Walter. Think about what you are doing and stop. I said I wanted to be left alone. Please honor my request. I'm hanging up now. Goodbye."

Mary gave her ear a tap and disconnected the call.

Day Two

59

A long rectangular slab thumped against the side of another long rectangular slab and locked magnetically. Piece by piece, a staging area was being formed, standing at the moment, two levels high. At its foundation, the growing edifice was hovering a mere half meter above the Verdanian soup.

"It's strange to see something actually being built around here," Adam said from a stack of construction materials on the other side of the clearing.

Dr. William Holt, who was also on the stack, tugged on Adam's arm. "Hold still."

A warbling insect flew past them. William tightened his grip around Adam's biceps and pressed a cone-shaped insertion device against the base of his ear. A yellow light flashed on the device's handle and Adam gasped out a tiny choke of pain.

"Ow," he said. "You promised that wasn't going to hurt."

"And it didn't, not really." William released his hold on the man. "After all you've been through, I'd have expected you to be tougher than that."

"Alas, I was more lucky than tough." Adam dusted off his new pair of khakis, this despite the lack of any soup or soil anywhere on his person.

At that same moment, the slab beneath them self-activated and the doctor and the construction specialist steadied themselves.

"Time to switch again," Adam said.

In unison, the two men stepped backward onto the slab below as the newly activated slab floated off toward its mates along the tree line.

"I guess I'm done here," William said as he hopped back aboard his crane, a small transportation platform he had parked near the end of the slab stack. He laid his hands on the vehicle's control pad.

"Before I go, I need you to activate your link and try it out."

Adam pressed two fingers beneath his ear. As he said his name, his head was filled with the voice of the Core, requesting further instruction. With no further instruction to give, he canceled the connection.

"I guess it works. How am I supposed to know if it's any different?"

"It's not any different audibly, but the *Horizon*'s grid network has now been merged with the *Vanguard*'s. You'll be able to connect with any citizen now, including the Rangers you'll be surveying with later."

"I see," Adam said. "Thank you."

"You're quite welcome."

The crane kicked up trace amounts of soup as it took off toward the spire.

Adam returned his gaze to the ongoing installation process. The previous slab had fastened into place, turning the topmost tier into a perfect square. The next slab underneath him snapped to life.

As he was switching from slab to slab, two skiffs came zipping around the backside of the spire. These were open-shelled vehicles, snub-nosed in shape, capable of complex degrees of maneuverability, high-altitude limits, and top-tier speeds—and they were headed Adam's way.

Approximately fifteen meters from the stack, the two skiffs decelerated and pulled up beside one another. Camden's voice burst into Adam's ear and told him to hold tight. They'd be there in a second. There was something that had to be taken care of first.

60

The two Rangers crossed to their respective ship railings so they could converse face to face.

"I feel I need to apologize for the way I showed up here yesterday," Leo said. "My presence cannot be making you feel particularly good right now. I'd like for us to talk about that, openly and honestly, like the good operatives I know we both are."

"There's not much to say." Camden bent over the railing and wiped away a soup smudge on the side of his ship. "The situation is what it is. You're back, and that's that."

"You need to understand, I'm here to help, to do anything you ask. You have my word on that. I will not stick my nose in or countermand again, no matter what the Directorate says. I follow orders. I don't give them. I'm now the low man on the totem pole."

Camden glanced back up and rolled his eyes. "You could never be the low man, Leo. Not around here. The guys trust you too much."

"Maybe. But that's because they know I won't fail you. You know that as well." Leo raised his hand and saluted. "I've said my piece. I'm awaiting your orders, Commander."

Camden held the silence a good long while, and then grazed his ear.

"Sam, where the hell are you people? Leo and I have been sitting around out here waiting for you dipshits. We're supposed to be getting something accomplished today, if you recall."

The man on the other end of the connection attempted to respond.

"I'm not interested in your excuses. Just get your sorry butts out here. And if it somehow slipped your mind, we're over at the stacks with Adam. You remember Adam, he's the only other guy around here who knows how to show up on time."

Another pause.

"Oh, yeah. Well, fuck you, too. Muran out."

Camden grinned. Leo grinned back.

"Let's go get Adam," Camden said as he charged back to his helm.

"Yes, sir," Leo said. "Whatever you say, sir."

61

"Despite of all these recent impediments," Rebecca said. "I expect you Directorate dunderheads to keep acting boldly. Being scared off by a few setbacks seems to be in direct opposition to the entire purpose of this endeavor. Aren't we supposed to be starting a new colony on another world? That's what I've always been told. And since all but three hundred of us had the misfortune to be born here, through no choice of our own, the least you people in power could do is see this mess through to the end, no matter what troubles we end up encountering. I know it's difficult, but the time has come for someone around here to show some backbone, dammit. Seriously, what's wrong with you people?"

Walter smiled. He was seated at his desk as he chatted with his friend, one eye on the video feeds from Verdan as the Rangers were flying out of the clearing.

"Did hear me when I said we haven't found any solid ground to build on?" he said. "If we cannot find that, there'll be no place to put this new colony of ours."

"My husband's a pretty clever fellow, you know. You posted him as lead architect for a reason."

"Yes, but none of this is a one-man task."

"I'll have you know, most historically significant undertakings have begun with the ingenuity of a single individual. I'll bet your mentor understands that. And here we are today, standing at a legitimate, yet agonizing crossroads. How about we put everything we have on my Alan? He's a whiz, Walter. Even if there is no solid ground down there, he'll find a way to build something, even if it's in the air or on the water."

"Not the water. *Anything* but the water. You saw those things that came out of that lake and killed Mikhail. No way. You can forget about the water."

Rebecca waited a moment and said, "But I can't be the only one who's thinking this. That boy could have saved himself by simply stepping out of the way. Instead, he stood there gawking, and that cost him his life."

Walter laid his hand down on the desk, his fingers splayed. "I *never* want to hear you saying that in public, okay?"

"I'll say whatever I want to say in public. Just you try and stop me."

Under his breath, Walter chuckled. "I tell you what, you might be wasting your life on whatever histories you're busy compiling right now. You should just stop all that at once and run for office. One thing I'm certain of, with those endless opinions of yours, you'd be perfect for the job."

"Gack. Serving on the council with Dimitri Kucherov and his know-it-all ilk, who in their right mind would ever want to do that?"

"Clearly, not you."

"Clearly. No, thank you. The mere thought of it makes me sick to my stomach."

"On that note," Walter said. "I should probably get back to it. I'd like it if we talked again, though."

"Hey, you know where to find me. We should also probably find some time for that dinner with our spouses you were so keen on before."

"We will. Once things slow down."

"Don't get all squishy on me, Walter. There's always time for socializing, even during a crisis. Learn to let your hair down, for goodness' sake. Stop and smell the roses for once in your misbegotten life."

"I will. Goodbye, Rebecca."

"Goodbye, my liege."

62

Derek had stopped by while Florin was in the shower. The Core informed her of his presence at the door just as she was lathering her hair with shampoo. Her instructions were as simple as she could make them, considering the circumstances—allow Derek in and to tell him to make himself comfortable in the living room. If he could wait, she would be down in ten to fifteen minutes. If he could not, she would, of course, understand.

Seventeen minutes later Florin came springing down the staircase in tan shorts and a pullover pink tank top. Derek stood up the instant he saw her.

"I didn't put on any make-up, so you're not seeing me at my best," Florin said as she kneaded a pair of rolled-up white socks between her thumb and forefinger. "I didn't want to make you wait any longer. I hate being *that* kind of girl."

Derek shuffled over to her and pecked her cheek. "It's not a problem. I don't mind waiting. With all that's been going on, I feel fortunate you had any time to see me at all."

They separated and retreated to two opposing pieces of furniture. Derek took a place on the couch—the same spot where he'd been sitting since he entered—while Florin selected the smaller love seat, where she immediately began to pull apart her socks.

"Have things picked up again this morning, or are they still slow?" Derek asked.

"They're still slow. Unyieldingly slow." Florin extended her left leg out and slipped one of the socks over her foot. "None of us nonessential types will be going to the surface for a while, that has been confirmed. For the time being, it's only scientists and a handful of operational people. You and I, the helper monkey and the teacher, we are officially on the sidelines." Florin yanked on the other sock and added, "It kind of sucks, too. I was really looking forward to going down there."

"I've been excited to see it for myself as well."

"I know. Who wouldn't be? The chance to see something different, that was the only reason I pushed to get placed into this dull-as-dirt bureau in the first place. The last thing in the world I wanted was to be trapped on this ship for the rest of my life."

"I don't think that's likely to happen," Derek said.

"I wouldn't be so sure. You don't know what I know."

Florin slid to the side and propped her legs on the arm of the love seat. "So Derek, was there a reason you swung by? Is there something I can do for you? Something you might be itching for?"

Derek gave her a puzzled look. "Nothing that I can think of. I just wanted check in. I know you've been cooped up in that command center for the better part of a day, and I heard you'd been released. Or at least that's the excuse I concocted in my head. Really, I just wanted to see you. I had a terrific time at the celebration last night." He paused for a second. "Or was that the night before? Time has gotten all mixed up for me. Anyway, I want us to do it again real soon, when work permits."

"What is that we did again?" Florin said. "My memory's a little fuzzy."

"We went on a date."

"Oh, yeah. That's right, the arrival celebration."

"Am I reading the signals wrong here? Did you not want to go on another date with me?"

"Frankly," Florin said. "I was kind of hoping we could skip the whole dating rigmarole and just go upstairs now."

Derek did a double take. "Wait a minute, are your parents at home?"

"I don't think that they are, but I can't say for sure."

"Would your parents *approve* of you and me going upstairs together?"

"Probably not. My father definitely would not."

"Then maybe we should respect their home," Derek said. "We've only been out together one time so far. I think we should get a couple more dinners under our belts before we take anything to the next level."

Florin stuck her tongue out at him. "Party pooper."

Derek took a deep, uncertain breath and sprang off the couch. "I'm going to let you get some sleep. Maybe we could see one another tomorrow evening?" He made his way over to where Florin was reclining. "Would that work with you schedule-wise?"

She gazed up at him blankly. "Sure. That shouldn't be a problem."

Derek crouched down, and for a second time, kissed her cheek. Before he could get too far away, Florin grabbed him by the back of his neck and hauled him over to her mouth for a longer, fuller kiss. They held together for several soft seconds before parting.

"Tomorrow," Derek said as he strolled out of the room.

Florin sang out, "There's *always* tomorrow."

63

When Jocelyn finally awoke for good, nobody noticed. She hadn't even been alone at the time. Her parents were seated beside her hospital bed and a duty nurse had just barged back in to retrieve a polka dot sweater that had been left strewn over the counter.

More than a minute went by. The nurse left, and Jocelyn attempted to lift her head off the pillow.

"Where is he?" she asked.

Elisabeth and Richard turned.

"The baby's not here," Elisabeth said. "No one expected you to wake again so soon. And the baby, she's not a he, she's a she. How much do you remember?"

"Enough." Jocelyn's head had just gotten off the pillow when her back seized up and her legs began to convulse. She cried out in agony.

Elisabeth scrambled over to her. "You cannot be moving around, sweetie. You've been in stasis for months. Your muscles are weak. You're going to need a couple of days of regenerative therapy before you can be up and moving again. The doctors say you could really hurt yourself if you're not careful. They'll have to strap you down if you attempt to move in any way. And after everything that's happened before, I wouldn't think you'd want to go through that again."

Jocelyn glared at her mother. "You have no clue what I want."

"That could very well be true, but I do have your best interest at heart."

"Sure you do. I want my husband. And I want *you* out of here."

"Before I go," Elisabeth said. "I'd like you to give me a moment to explain myself."

"Forget it. I'm not interested. I want Mikhail. I want my baby. I want *you* out of here."

Richard came over to backstop Elisabeth.

"I can't believe I have to just lie here and look at your hateful face," Jocelyn said, punching every syllable of every word.

"Please," Richard said. "Let's be civil about this."

"I can't, Daddy. It was *her* who did this to me, the unanimous final vote. I'll never forgive you for this." Down near the footboard of the bed, Jocelyn's toes twitched. "Where the hell is Mikhail?"

"That's something we need to discuss," Richard said.

"Discuss in what way?"

Elisabeth took a step back. "Perhaps explanations on that should wait until later."

Richard shook his head. "No. She needs to be told. Telling her later will only make things worse."

"Tell me what? What's going on?"

Richard put his hand on Jocelyn's arm. "There was an incident on the surface yesterday. It happened before you were taken down for Baby Tana's birth." The emotion getting the better of him, Richard had to stop for a moment. "Honey, I think we should spare you the gory details, but Mikhail…he was killed."

Jocelyn's eyelids flickered. "What did you just say?"

"It was an accident. Mikhail was taken from us, taken from you. I'm so sorry. Our hearts are breaking for you."

"He's dead?" she said, almost inaudibly.

Richard nodded. "He's gone."

Jocelyn's face had lost all its color. "I want my baby."

"Maybe now is not the best time for that," Elisabeth said from across the room.

Jocelyn shouted, *"I want my baby!"*

Elisabeth skidded to the door. "I'll go get the nurse. She'll bring in the baby. Richard, keep her calm."

"I will," he said.

Jocelyn had started to cry. "It can't be true, Daddy. It can't be. Mikhail's everything to me. Please, tell me you're lying. I love him so much. I'll *die* without him. *Please*, tell me. *Please, please, please.*"

Richard knelt down beside her. "That's the way, sweetheart. Let it out. Let it all out."

64

They sped across the treetops, leaving swirls of gossamer in their ever-lengthening wake.

The skiff deck was all full up, with Camden at the controls, Adam and Koron manning the roll bars, and Samuel holding up the rear. Due to the lack of any significant cloud cover, all four men were sweating profusely.

Adam lowered his binocs and checked the display terminal on the railing. There was a green circle on the panel marking the skiff's current location, and a second green circle to the south denoting the position of Squad Two. Leo's team had now traveled a hundred and twelve kilometers from base camp. Camden's crew had only covered half that distance.

"I'm feeling a little frustrated here," Adam said, loud enough for his voice to carry. "Even if we lucked out and accidentally flew over a piece of dry ground, we'd never be able to see it through all this vegetation. Don't you think we'd be better off doing this sort of thing on foot?"

"That's what we have cameras for," Camden said. "Slowly but surely, they're surveying every millimeter of the moon."

"Then what are we doing out here?" Adam asked.

Samuel gave the railing a slap. "Putting on a show. If we're doing something, then it looks like the Directorate is doing something."

Camden maneuvered the ship eastward, away from a riverbed that had appeared out of nowhere. The search teams had been given a handful of directives before heading out—first and foremost among these was the avoidance of bodies of water at all cost.

"A camera survey on this scale could take months," Camden said. "The thinking when it comes to us is—cast the widest net possible, and just maybe we might stumble onto something inadvertently."

"What happens if we do find a spot?"

"Then the bosses shift a few cameras in that direction, and the surveying becomes a whole lot more directed."

The skiff nosed downward as they came out across another valley of webby trees.

"You see, there's a purpose to everything," Camden said. "It may not seem that way at times, but if Dimitri is involved, someone somewhere has always got a purpose."

65

Courtney barged through the doorway and declared, "I'm coming in so we can discuss this—and I will not be taking no for an answer."

Mary backed out of the way as quickly as she could and tightened her robe. With a nod, she led Courtney into the darkened dining room.

"What you're asking me for, it wouldn't exactly make me mother of the year, now would it?"

"No one is going to judge you, Mary, not after what you've lost. And maybe knowing when not to parent is as important as parenting itself."

"I don't know what to say to that either."

"You don't have to say anything. You only have to say yes. And if you'd like, you could also pass on a terse, but well-intended thank you."

Mary led them into the kitchen and the ceiling lights flared on. An excess of illumination spilled out into the hall.

"Actually," Mary said, "I'm kind of surprised you think it's a good idea for me to be left alone. I'm really surprised about that."

Courtney followed Mary to the counter. "Oh, I think you being left alone is an atrocious idea. But I also know I'd never get you to agree to come stay with me, so I decided to offer my babysitting services instead. Call it my way of getting around your obstinance. It won't hurt you to let me do this one small thing for you."

"Sorry I'm so stubborn," Mary said.

"Point of fact, I don't think you're sorry in the least. But don't let that stop you from allowing me to take the kids for a couple of days anyway. I want to do something to help, and giving you some free time might take some of the pressure off. You're going through a lot, and I'm certain your father isn't allowing you to let up on your work."

Hearing that, Mary scowled. "I could care less what he thinks. I'll work when I want to work."

"And that's fine. But you still need to let me take the kids, at least for tonight."

"Don't you have your own work to do?"

"There's daycare, where your kids would be during the mornings and afternoons anyway." Courtney slid forward and softened her voice. "It won't be that big a deal. I'll only be taking care of them at night."

"I don't know if it's a good idea. Rex can be a handful."

"You cannot scare me off. May I go get them? Do I have your permission?"

Mary held her hand out. "Go ahead. They're in their rooms."

Courtney went to leave, and then stopped herself before she'd gotten past the refrigerator. "You do know that I want you to come with as well. That's what I really want. Bailey wants it, too. He told me so. He's your friend as much as he's my husband. He wants you with us. He wants *all* of you with us."

"That's nice to know," Mary said.

"But you still won't come."

"No."

"Then I'll take the kids and call you in the morning."

"Thank you," Mary said as she watched Courtney go.

"No need to thank me. I love you. I wish I could do more."

66

"I am not going to allow us to wallow," Walter said. "What we will do in lieu of that is redouble our efforts and push onward."

It had been one negative argument after the other. From the moment the council had taken their seats around the table—once again without Dimitri present—procrastination and delay had become the operative words of the day.

"In spirit at least, I know the six of you agree with me. The decisions being enacted today were decided upon decades ago. To cancel these plans would force the nullification of over seventy-five separate votes. I do not believe anyone here wants to start untangling that rat's mess. This moon is our new home. Get used to that. There is no other course of action to take. Any further discussion we have must be focused on Verdan, and only Verdan."

"Red tape is not going to scare anyone," Jacob said. "Some decompression time is a good thing right now. I for one could not bear anything else calamitous happening. For goodness' sake, there doesn't even appear to be any firm footing on this supposed new home of ours. What else are we supposed to do with this news like this other than allow in a dash of panic and concern?"

Antoinette raised her hand. "There's always the option I brought up yesterday."

"I forget already," Walter said. "You'll have to remind me."

"Azur. The other moon. The other potentially *habitable* moon. We could start surveying there instead. I know why Verdan was chosen for the initial settlement—it has a greater number of landmasses than Azur, which is practically all ocean. This is why it has always been seen as a secondary site, a place for future settlement. But now, perhaps it requires a closer look."

"I concur," Elisabeth said. "This other moon may be covered by water, but Verdan appears to have the same exact problem, admittedly on a shallower scale. Why aren't we looking at Azur?"

Walter eased back into his chair and folded his arms. "Because we haven't finished our surveys on Verdan yet. What percentage of the surface have we searched so far...one, two percent? Azur will always be an excellent reserve option, but don't you all think we're better served sticking to a moon where we *know* human life can survive? The Constructs survived there for sixteen months, without a hair of our resources. I think we can at least stick it out a few more days."

"But let's not forget," Deborah said. "While the Constructs were down there, they lost half their crew, and got nothing accomplished. Do I need to remind everyone of that?"

"Exactly," Antoinette said. "If nothing else, shouldn't we at least have a contingency plan for Azur in place?"

"I would assume we already have one," Walter said. "Hundreds if not thousands of potential plans have been written over the years. If one exists, it would be in the archive. I warn you, though, even if an Azur contingency is out there, it would require a lot of freshening up. Azur hasn't been considered a serious alternative for as long as I've sat on the council." He motioned over at Antoinette. "Would you like to be the one who handles the research on this? It sounds like something you might like to sink your teeth into."

"If no one disagrees, I'd love to do that."

"Excellent. Have at it then." Walter glanced down and checked his meeting summary. "Also, as a friendly reminder for everyone, early tomorrow morning, we have our first Transplant personnel transferring down to the surface. They are going to finish the staging area around the clearing where the *Spear* initially—"

Walter stopped himself there and snapped his fingers. "Shoot. With all the hand-wringing that's been going on there's something I nearly forgot."

He tapped two commands into the tabletop.

"A few minutes before we convened, another clearing was discovered between the Constructs crash site and our catch-all landing spot. The location has been marked on your displays. If you could all take a look."

En masse, the Trustees shifted their gazes downward.

"Is it dry or is it covered with goop?" Laken asked.

"Unfortunately, it's covered with goop. But it does have just enough open space to establish some hover platforms, like the landing area has. Our intention is to start constructing Echo Base on this spot, if that meets with the council's approval."

"Has Dimitri seen this?" Jacob asked.

"Not yet. I'd planned to take it to him once the seven of us had voted."

Jacob shifted in his seat. "I don't know. I'm not sure how comfortable I am voting on this without Dimitri's input."

"Are we at all surprised?" Laken said. "I don't think you're comfortable relieving yourself without Dimitri's input."

Walter gave them both a dark look. "I assure you, Jacob, there's nothing unusual going on here. The decision is not whether we will build a base or not, that plan was approved nineteen years ago. What I need right now is final approval on this particular location. We don't have a whole lot of choices here. But, if any of you actually need Dimitri's handholding, then let's get that on the record. Once that's done, we'll adjourn and run this by him when he should be given time to grieve for his son. So, if any of you want to take things in that direction, please declare yourself now."

Nobody said a word.

"All right then." Walter held his finger over a red oval in the center of his display. "Do we all agree on this location for Echo Base?"

All six said yes. After he'd finished his count, Walter said yes as well and pressed the oval.

"I have a brief question about this new clearing," Deborah said. "That's not asking too much, is it?"

"Go ahead," Walter said.

"If we're still operating on the assumption that this moon is dangerous and the vegetation should not be scarred or destroyed in any way, how will our people be able to get back and forth safely between the two sites? The map here says they're kilometers apart."

Walter smiled. "This is where it gets interesting. We're going to build a bridge."

"Is bridge building part of the plan here?" Jonas double-checked the paragraphs of information on his desktop.

"It is. It's part of the same overall plan we were supposed to reacquaint ourselves with last night. Perhaps I should rescind our votes in the affirmative so we can take some time to read it thoroughly. It's a fairly long document, but I don't mind delaying things."

"That won't be necessary," Jonas said.

"Then we remain in agreement? There's no need to micromanage the construction process?"

Six nods.

"Stupendous. The motion passes. I'll send the go-ahead to the surface."

Day Three

67

A prefabricated plank soared above the swayer plants.

A male worker was kneeling down at the front end of the construction chain, thirteen planks down the line. In his hand was a molecular binder. The follow-up section of the bridge crept toward him. An operator on a nearby crane maneuvered the piece toward the previously installed plank. The two segments connected together and the worker stretched out his arm. A glow emerged from the tip of his binder as he ran it along the new plank's outside edge. Another worker carried over a sturdy-looking guard-rail and attached it to the spot his partner had just hot fired.

Jason was over on the crane with the plank operator, there to observe. Like every other worker on-site, the man in charge wore a gray jumpsuit and a bright blue construction helmet.

The crane operator called below for an additional platform, instructing the ground crew that from now on out they did not need to wait. Once a new plank hovered above the dome tops, they were to send up the next one, unprompted.

Jason leaned in and asked, "How do you think things are going?"

"Just fine and dandy, sir."

"Is there anything I can do to speed the process up? I can call down and chastise those individuals who've been lagging."

"There's no need. We have a long way to go, almost to those peaks over there." The operator held his arm out at a hazy mountainside in the distance. "The fact is, it'd be better if the chastising came from me. I doubt you'll be here around the clock to do my chastising for me."

"Then this is going to take days not hours?" Jason said.

The operator had this exasperated look on his face. "An hour in, and you're already pushing us on the completion schedule. You're a born boss all right."

"Sorry," Jason said.

"Don't apologize. I don't mind putting up with some guff. And yeah, this is going to take a pretty long time. We're building a gargantuan bridge across an alien jungle. It's going to be difficult, and will probably get even more difficult the farther we get out. That's the reason I'm pushing the idiots below to keep the platforms coming. The lag time will get longer and longer if they don't keep up."

"I appreciate the candor," Jason said.

Another transport crane came drifting over the swayer tops. Aboard the craft was a female pilot and JC Goodwin, a member of the Transplant Operations bureau's senior staff.

"I need a word with the Chief," JC said as the two cranes met in mid-air. "We can take him back down for you."

Jason crossed over to the other crane. JC was adjusting his helmet in one hand while holding out his half-clenched fist with the other.

Jason dapped his friend on the knuckles. "What's going on? Is something the matter?"

JC cracked open his hand. He was holding a piece of paper. It had been folded eight times, into the tiniest of squares.

"No emergency or anything," JC said as he offered the piece of paper to Jason. "I was just told to come up and get you."

Jason snatched the paper from JC. Neither of the crane operators had noticed the exchange.

"Shall we?" Jason said to the pilot. "I'm just getting in the way up here."

The crane swung around and left the other crane to its work.

With JC watching, Jason began to unfold the piece of paper. It was a long note, in Morgan Adam's handwriting.

Hey, Jay. It's me. It's been a couple of days since we last talked, but I figured this might be the only safe way for us to communicate (even though before I said we shouldn't). As you know, I had been scheduled to be on the first survey mission down, but I was just informed that I would be staying on the ship due to my (I guess our) pregnancy. It's better to be safe than sorry, they say. So we still won't be seeing each other for a while. Letter writing, though—that can be a way for us to keep in touch. JC is, as you know, a good friend. He's volunteered to be the go-between for us, taking notes back and forth. I think it's a safe thing to try. You know JC would never squeal on us, so I went ahead and wrote first. If you have something to say to me, even if it's about your wife, write it down on the backside of this (and I swear, I really don't care if you do write about your wife and children, or even about the hearing and charges against you. I can handle all of it, better than you think I can). Oh, yes, in case he forgets to give it to you, I had JC bring you one of my writing pens, because I'm sure you'll be needing it (those calligraphy studies of mine aren't so useless after all). Anyway, I just wanted to touch base. I miss you so much. I want to hear from you. I hope your 'thinking' is going well. You are on my mind constantly. I thought you should know that.

Jason looked up from the note. JC was holding out a black-tipped pen for him. Jason took it. The response he wrote was short.

I'm glad you're not coming down. You and the baby mean everything to me. I could not bear it if something happened. I've been really busy so far, as you can imagine. Write back soon. I love you desperately.

The crane came in for a landing on level six of the staging area. As they were strolling back to the office, Jason refolded the letter and handed it back to JC.

68

The nurse placed Baby Tana into Jocelyn's arms. The newborn gurgled as the nurse tiptoed slowly away. Jocelyn cooed and sang, still red around the eyes after a long night of crying.

Over at the door, between baby kisses, Elisabeth took three steps inside, but came no closer.

"You two look beautiful together," she said.

Jocelyn kept her eyes on the baby. "What do you want?"

"I have a message to deliver. You're going to be released tonight. You'll need to get around in a mover chair for the time being—and you're going to require additional outpatient care—but there's no reason you have to be in the hospital for any of that. In addition, I suggest, as humbly as I'm able, that you come stay with your father and me for the time being."

"No way," Jocelyn said. "That is not going to happen."

"All right. If that's the way you feel, I'll scrounge up new living arrangements for you, with a live-in nurse. He or she can manage your physical therapy from there."

"Why can't I go back to my own home?"

"Because it's not a good idea. You shouldn't be going back there right now. The psychiatrists are all against it. The place has too many memories."

"But I want to remember." Jocelyn patted Baby Tana's head, which for some reason made the child shriek. The outburst did not faze Jocelyn one iota.

"Losing Mikhail has destroyed me, Mother—but I still want my little girl to know her father, to be inundated with the memory of him. There's nowhere better to do that than the place where we made her."

"Suit yourself," Elisabeth said, her voice drowned out by the screeching child.

"Keeping my house, that's something you can arrange for me?"

"For you, my darling, I can arrange anything."

"I guess it's time for you to be going then. You've shared your news. Our business appears complete."

"Of course. Your father and I will be by this evening to escort you home." After that was said, Elisabeth backed out of the room.

Over on the bed, the baby cried and cried.

69

Adam had called the Rangers together on the skiff dock. In the center of the clearing, the *Spear* was being fired up, its energy ring spinning into a vortex, preparing for its latest return trip into orbit.

"I've been ordered to stay behind," Adam told the group.

"We just heard," Camden said. "That's too bad. You've been a great help to us, an incredible asset. You shouldn't be cast aside like this."

Adam accepted Camden's handshake. "I guess I don't really see it as being cast aside. I'm going back to what I was sent here to do in the first place, sixteen months too late. It feels good. I'm back in my wheelhouse. I'll be building things again. I'm looking forward to it."

"Personally, I was hoping they'd make you a Ranger," Samuel said. "I think you've taken to it as naturally as any of the rest of us have."

"Thank you," Adam said. "But I have far too much construction training to be transferred at this point. And the new builders that have come down really seem to need me, which is nice."

"Doesn't surprise me that you're needed," Koron said. "You're wily and clever. That's why we need you, too."

"What kind of work will you be doing?" Tella asked him.

"I've been told, once the new cans fall, I'll be setting up a barricade fence around the base site. We'll also probably build one around this site as well, once the two positions have been bridged together."

Seven heads turned toward the construction progress. A conveyance trail of hover-powered planks was continuing to fly up and over the forest, one after the other.

"Well, good luck to you," Camden said. "We're going to miss you."

The rest of the team said their farewells and split off into the waiting skiffs. Adam had just begun to wander off when Leo called him back with a sharp whistle.

"Before you go," Leo said. "There's something you should know."

Adam trotted over to him. "Sure, what's up?"

"I intend to keep calling on you as a resource. If I have questions in the field, yours is the first name I'm going to think of. I hope you're okay with that. I know you'll be busy with your barricade fences and other pressing matters, but experience like yours, I have no intention of letting that go to waste."

"Whatever you need," Adam said. "I'll be around. Just give me a call."

Leo made his way to the skiff that Hollis and Tella were prepping. "Take care of yourself, Mr. Ballard."

"I will. You take care of yourself, too."

"Always. Measure twice, cut once, that's my motto."

Adam smiled. "Are you a builder or a soldier, Mr. Bratsk?"

"As it so happens, I come from a long line of builders. And I know one when I see one. I'm glad that you're back in your element again."

"Thanks," Adam said.

"No, thank *you*."

70

Walter went straight up the stairs and entered the first bedroom on the right.

Beneath the plaid print sheets lay a human-sized lump. Walter sidled over to the wood-carved nightstand and stared down at the unmoving figure with some visible concern in his eyes. Hesitantly, he touched the sleeping man's neck with two outstretched fingers.

Dimitri rolled over, instantly roused from his slumber.

"Why are you lurking," the great man said, his words garbled by more than a day and a half's worth of sleep.

Walter jerked his hand away as if he'd just touched something hot. "I wasn't lurking. I'm here to wake you. You told me not to let you sleep any longer than this."

"That is not what you were doing." Dimitri attempted to sit up, but his nightshirt had become tangled in the sheets. "You were seeing if I was still alive. You were checking for my pulse."

Walter tucked his hands in his pockets. "Yep, that's exactly what I was doing."

Dimitri called for the lights. Once they'd come all the way on, he pointed over at an auburn couch on the eastern wall. "Make yourself comfortable while I gather myself. You can update me on what's been happening in my absence."

Walter took the seat he'd been offered and crossed his legs. "I just finished up a meeting with Alan Patterson."

"How did that go?"

"The meeting itself, it went swimmingly. It went like meetings tend to go."

"That's good. I thought it might've been tense."

"Tense because of Rebecca?"

"Of course because of Rebecca. I know the two of you have been talking again."

"I didn't realize that you knew. Apparently, however, Alan isn't one to get all tied up into knots. He's a laid back fellow. Unlike my own wife, he understands that romantically Rebecca and I are a part of a long-dead and ancient past. Also, we're men, and we would rather not speak about such things."

"Are you telling me that in all the time the two of you have worked together, the hot-and-heavy relationship you once had with his wife has never come up?"

"Why should it have? We've concentrated on the business at hand. The work I was there to request was challenging enough, and getting more so by the minute. Now, I've tasked him with drawing up alternative settlement designs which factor in the wet, swamp-like nature of the Verdanian terrain. One possibility we mulled over is a mountain settlement, another an underground settlement. And if all else fails, Alan suggested a hovering, airborne settlement. He's off meeting with engineers now, breaking down the feasibilities of all three. I have a follow-up meeting scheduled with him this afternoon."

"Is there anything else on the docket?"

"Briefings on the construction process, a last minute run-through before the initial wave of storage cans are dropped, and right before dinner, a remote meeting with the Transplantation heads."

"Will Mary be attending that last meeting?"

"I'm not sure that she will. She's been taking a break, like you've been taking a break. Mikhail's death has been hard on her."

Dimitri's eyes got wide. "But I was only getting some extra sleep, because I'm old. The doctors *insisted* I get some extra rest. What's Mary's excuse?"

"She's upset, Dimitri."

"We all are. This entire ship is."

Dimitri dropped his legs off the side of the bed and stood up. "I want to come with you to your meetings. Is that okay with you?"

"Absolutely, whatever you want."

Walter watched as Dimitri limped toward the closet.

"The family needs to be seen as up and around at a time like this. I don't want anyone thinking we're indulging in our grief while there's work to be done."

71

"The supply drop will begin in one minute," the Core voice said as Derek pushed a borrowed food cart with dinner for two through the dual-door entranceway of the Transplant command center.

"Good. I'm not too late," Derek said, and then parked the cart next to the circular control console.

Florin peered up from the administrator's station. All around the room's interlocking display walls, various beauty shots of the *Horizon*'s hull were being spotlighted. As Derek was readying their plates, over two dozen external hatches opened themselves simultaneously on the bottom of the ship.

Florin made a short log entry with the keypad and said, "I'm not hungry. I thought I made myself clear, all I wanted was your company."

"I heard what you said. I just didn't listen to you. You can't tell me you haven't eaten in twelve hours and expect me to do nothing about that."

Derek came up behind her. "Where's everyone else? Are you alone here"

"Yeah. Mary's been taking it easy for a while. And unless there's some sort of an emergency, for something like this, even I'm not all that needed. The procedure is more or less automated once it's been enacted by the Operations Chief on the ground."

The Core voice announced, "Verdanian supply drop number one is commencing. I repeat, supply drop number one is en route."

Bursting from all twenty-four of the hatches, a shower storm of hexagonal canisters began spearing their way toward the atmosphere.

The sight of this left Derek transfixed. Florin tapped one last button on the control pad and climbed out of her chair.

"You're blocking my view," Derek said.

"Ah, shoot. Am I?" Florin squared herself in front of the man and slipped her hand under her blouse. Ever so slowly, she pushed the fabric upward.

"What are you doing?" Derek asked her.

"I'm taking my clothes off, silly." She tugged the blouse all the way over her head, revealing a light pink bra. Her hips were swaying as she crossed toward him. On the glowing displays behind her, supply can after supply can continued to rain down.

"Don't you have work to do?" he asked her.

"I just told you. I'm not all that necessary. I can do other things, if I want."

"What other things?"

"Please, you cannot be this dense."

Their lips met, but Derek wouldn't stop talking. "The doors…can anyone get inside?"

"Nope. That last tap you heard was me locking them."

They kissed again.

"So," he said. "This is going to happen. Right here, right now."

"It is." She reached backward and unfastened her bra. "I'm going to lie down on this console, and do you know what we're going to do then?"

"We're going to make love."

Florin grabbed onto his hip. "Oh, Derek…you can use a dirtier word than that."

72

"That woman, she just refuses to leave."

Jocelyn made sure the door had closed all the way and reversed her mover chair out of the foyer.

"No matter how many times I tell her I don't want her in my life anymore, it just makes her work that much harder to be underfoot every chance she gets. This is the way it's going to be, isn't it? I can either forgive her, or I will be constantly barraged by these helpful little visits."

Joy nodded broadly in the adjoining living room. Baby Tana was cradled in her arms.

"I can't tell you what to do, obviously," Joy said. "But we both know battling her is pointless. If Mom wants something, for your own sanity, you might as well give in. Mikhail eventually did. He never forgave his own father, but he gave Mom a pass. It was easier that way. He didn't want to deal with her."

Jocelyn brought the chair around in an arc, applying the brakes in front of where Joy and the baby were seated.

"Mikhail was just that way," she said. "He was always such a softy with women."

"About Mikhail," Joy said. "There are some things you need to know. I'm hesitant to say anything, however, especially with you just getting back home. You're probably already overwhelmed with emotion. I know I would be."

"I'm fine. Maybe a little confused, mostly by the way this place looks. It's spotless." Jocelyn spun the mover chair in circles as she performed another quick visual examination of the meticulously maintained quarters. "Did you or Mom have the house cleaned?"

Joy shook her head no, and the baby giggled.

"See, Tana gets it," Jocelyn said. "Her daddy was a slob. For as long as we lived here, Mikhail never picked up or put away anything. I'll bet he never picked up one thing in his entire life. The mere idea of cleaning seemed to offend him."

Joy rocked the child gently. "All of this is kind of related to what I wanted to talk to you about. While you were under, Mikhail wasn't like how you remember him. The fury he felt, it never really abated. It got stronger, and more unforgiving. Whatever feelings he had for his father before, they were gone after what he and the rest of them did to you. He was just so constantly sad and frustrated. I tried to cheer him up when I could, but it never did any good. Mary tried, too, but he started to see her as just another extension of his father. And his vitriol toward Dimitri, that got particularly ugly."

"Mikhail always had a temper," Jocelyn said. "You wouldn't see it much, not unless you'd done something wrong. But if you had, he had a tendency to lash out."

Warily, Joy asked, "Did he never lash out at you?"

"Me? No. Never. But he lashed out *because* of me." A smile eased onto her face. "It still kind of gets me going. He protected me. He lashed out in my honor."

"What are you talking about?" Joy said. "Don't just sit there grinning at me. Whatever you're referring to, I expect to hear every detail."

Jocelyn zipped the chair even closer. "It happened a few years ago. The incident involved a family member. This is why nobody is aware of it. Someone we both know was getting a little too touchy with me, and it was making me uncomfortable. It wasn't anything overtly sexual, but it was creepy, and I wanted it to stop. And as many times as I complained, this person wouldn't keep his grubby hands off me."

"Who was this?" Joy asked.

"I probably shouldn't say. It was taken care of, and it never happened again. I only really told Mikhail about it in passing. We weren't even seeing each other at the time, but the instant I told him he got all wild in the eyes and swore he would take care of it for me. And he did. Boy, did he. He brought the Rangers to this person's door and explained what was going to happen to him if he ever touched me again. I don't know what else he did or said, but I'm sure it wasn't pleasant. But this idiotic relative, he's stayed away from me altogether. And that was all because of Mikhail."

Joy tickled the baby's belly. "He was a good man."

"You bet he was."

Jocelyn's gaze drifted back across the living room. "I'm telling you, I am truly dumbfounded by this. How did this place get so clean? I sit here looking at it, and I still can't believe it."

"Maybe it was Mikhail who cleaned it," Joy said. "Maybe he did it for you."

Jocelyn went silent for a moment and then said, "Yeah, maybe."

73

Courtney went traipsing up the stairs. Mary was right behind her, wearing an ankle-length lavender skirt and a button-down blouse. The outfit, including the up-in-a-bun way she was wearing her hair, was Mary's go-to work ensemble. The sight of her friend dressed professionally again had lit a fire under Courtney, and she was hitting every step with renewed vigor. They both were.

"The last I saw of Rex he was playing with Jimmy," Courtney said as she rounded the landing.

Mary's eldest sprinted out into the hallway. "Momma!" He wrapped his arms around her legs and buried his face in the pleats of her skirt.

"How's my sweet boy?" Mary scooped him into her arms. "Mommy's missed you."

James, or Jimmy—Courtney's firstborn—poked his head out of the playroom. Once he saw that the visitor was only Mary, a semi-regular visitor to the Cutler home, he returned to the arts and crafts table behind him.

Courtney pointed forward. "The other two are in Tonya's room. My girl has designated herself head babysitter."

Just as she was about to skip over to the room in question, Courtney asked, "How about we all have dinner together tonight? I can order something in for us."

"That sounds wonderful," Mary said. "As long as we can we push it back for an hour or two. I'm sort of crunched for time. I was hoping the kids could stay here a little while longer. I really appreciate you taking them last night."

"It was my pleasure. Go do what you need to do." Courtney scrunched up her face. "What is it that you need to do?"

"Most importantly, I'm going to see Jocelyn and the baby. Then I should swing by the command center and check in. I already missed the can drop. I don't intend to miss anything else. I hate the idea of people picking up the slack for me, even you." The corners of her mouth curled up into something approximating a smile. "You all have your own lives to lead."

"Such as they are."

Mary put Rex down on the floor and rubbed the top of his head. "I'll be back in a jiffy, kiddo. You get to sleep in your own bed tonight. I just have a teensy bit of work to do first."

"He's been having fun here, haven't you?" Courtney rubbed his head a second time. "Jimmy's been teaching him how to draw."

"Be back real soon, Mommy," Rex said. "I missed you like you missed me."

Mary knelt down and met the boy's height. "Don't you worry. I'll be back before you know it."

Day Four

74

Survey Flight Thirteen was being conducted by two of the Rangers, along with two members of the Transplant surface team. Koron was the expedition's leader, while Tella served as his principal scout assistant. Jason Epelle had also volunteered, his second such attachment to the high-speed pursuit of dry land. Making his initial foray into the wilderness was Charles Muran, the Ranger Commander's teenage son. Charles was an environmental biology apprentice, and being placed onto an actual field expedition was a dream come true. When he first arrived on the surface his father had fought hard to have him remanded back to the *Horizon*, but Charles went to his mother Emily and used her influence to keep him right where he was, right where any self-respecting scientist would kill to be.

"It's all so breathtaking," Charles said.

The skiff was halfway through an extended flight over the white, chalky surface of a seaside forest thatch. A shimmering green light reflected up in halos as the brittle vegetation crumbled and shook under the ongoing barrage from the skiff's oscillating hover engines.

"It's like nothing anyone could have ever expected," Charles said. "I feel so lucky. I feel like screaming."

"Then do it," Koron said. "Let those feelings all out."

Charles grabbed hold of the roll bar above him, tossed his head back, and yelled at the top of his lungs. Once he'd worn his voice to a nub, he looked over at Jason. The Operations Chief was not having the glorious

time that Charles was. As he went about the search pattern he'd been assigned, he was fiddling with something in his hand. One second he was
holding the object tight, the next he was cupping it between his fingers.

"What have you got there?" Charles asked him, as friendly as can be.

"A pen," Jason said. "It was a gift from a frien—"

A deep, sustained boom echoed across the terrain. It had come from
Koron's quadrant, out in front of the speeding ship.

Jason spun around. "What was that?"

"Something just exploded in front of us," Koron said. "See it there?
Dust and debris are flying every which way."

The occurrence was at least a kilometer ahead of them. Pieces of the
white treetops were pillowing downward. In the center of the eruption, a
continuous stream of black was spraying skyward and spreading out in a
star formation before funneling back down the gaping hole it had sprung
through.

Koron swung his arm back. "Charlie, I need you up here. You're our
resident nature expert."

Charles jockeyed his way through the crowded skiff and positioned
himself next to Koron.

"Well, kid, what's your assessment?"

Charles used a pair of binocs to get a better look. "First off, I think it
should be made clear that I'm an apprentice who knows next to nothing—"

"Just tell me what you think."

There was another eruption, to the west, about a third of the distance
between the original incident and the skiff.

"You all saw it that time," Koron said.

"I believe this is a conglomeration of some form of animal life," Charles
said. "See the fountaining there in the center as it shoots up through the
trees. That's group behavior."

"Should I turn out of the way?"

"I would say that's highly advisable."

The skiff swerved left, its nose aimed toward the distant coastline. The
treetops beneath the ship kicked up a cloud of white dust as the skiff's

direction changed and its speed increased.

"That should do it," Koron said as he was letting up on the turn.

A third eruption struck, out in the middle of the skiff's new trajectory.

"Well, that can't be an accident," Tella said.

On top of eruption three, there were two additional flare-ups. Along with the white refuse and the streams of black, the air around the survey skiff was being engulfed by a humming noise, alternating in wild swings of high and low registers.

"What are we going to do now?" Charles asked.

Koron pushed down on the acceleration gauge. "We max out our speed and keep heading for the coast." Sweat drizzled into his mouth and he spat at the windshield. "I know we're supposed to avoid the water, but right now I think it's more important we avoid this crap."

"The coast is too far," Tella said. She had abandoned her observation point and huddled up beside Charles. Jason had also moved closer.

"Maybe we should just stop," Jason said.

"Stopping would only make us sitting ducks." Koron slid his fingers across the controls, initiating an alternative evasion attempt, a quick shake and a hard angled cut to the right.

The number of eruptions doubled, tripled, creating a dank whirlwind of black and white.

In the midst of the ongoing tumult, Charles said, "The animals…I think they might be insects."

Jason nudged Koron from behind. "You need to stop. We're obviously not going to outrun this, but maybe we can weather it. Stop and we can all lie down flat and try to weather the storm."

"I am not stopping," Koron said.

"See there, they have wings," Charles said as the creatures spiraled around the skiff. "A double-wing set."

Tella shook Koron's arm. "*Stop*, sir—just *stop*,"

With only a blinding blizzard ahead of them, Koron had no other choice. He decreased the skiff's velocity, and alongside his four fellow team members, hit the deck.

A heartbeat later, an eruption rammed into the bottom of the skiff like a torpedo strike. The ship tilted sideways, nearly capsizing until its internal gyros reset.

A second barrage struck, this time lifting the front end of the skiff into a near perfect ninety-degree angle. The ship's tail end grazed the top of the trees, causing the craft to flip. All four survey members were dumped out, falling between the foliage and the swarm of buzzing black insects.

The skiff remained lodged on the trees, wobbling precariously as the swarm flooded downward. The weight of the craft was too much for the weak, dusty branches. Like its passengers before it, the skiff fell, plunging headlong toward the ground.

75

A mayday signal was transmitted across all available channels. The skiff carrying Survey Flight Thirteen had suffered massive inertial failure and had gone down ninety-four kilometers south-southeast of Echo Base.

The news of his son's crash sent Camden into a panic. He and Leo had just returned from their own survey missions, and were on the staging docks conversing with Kay.

Breathing haggardly, Camden asked the Core for life signs in the area and the grid voice told him it would take another minute for that to be determined. He started to make his way toward one of the skiffs when Kay blocked his path and informed him he would not be part of the rescue effort. He struggled to push past her, asking her why not. When he got no response, obscenities were shouted.

Leo stepped between them. "I can go with him. Let me go with him."

"No," Kay said. "You're going by yourself."

"A *one*-man rescue team?" Camden said. "Are you kidding me? You *must* be kidding? I always suspected it about you, but you're even loonier than I thought."

Kay leveled two prone fingers at him. "Because this involves your son, you get a pass. As to why a one-man team, how about we start with the fact that the technical specs say a skiff can only handle the combined weight of four passengers. My guess is you might be able to push that to five, but any more and the ship would have trouble getting airborne again. Are you beginning to understand? Only one passenger can go on a retrieval mission if there are four people who need retrieving."

"Look at me," Leo told Camden. "If you don't believe I can bring your son back to you, then screw Kay, you should go instead of me. But if you think I can manage it—if you think I'm the person most adept to save your boy—then you've got to step aside. Time's wasting."

Camden gritted his teeth and motioned Leo on. "Go," he said.

Leo leapt aboard the skiff and fired up the burst drive.

"I'll get your boy back, Cam. I'll do whatever I have to do. Don't you doubt that for a second."

76

Jason lay broken in the muck.

The other three passengers were already back on their feet and milling around in the swampy maze of knotted-up branches. With the exception of Jason, injuries were relatively minor. Koron's face had been lacerated, from his scalp to his cheekbone, cutting at a looping angle across the bridge of his nose. Swipes and dabs from his filthy fingers had done little to stop the bleeding. Tella's ills were far less visible. She had begun to grouse about what she assumed were several broken ribs and a severe ankle sprain. Charles, however, claimed to have no injuries at all. Tella checked him over anyway, patting up and down his relevant extremities while Koron tended to Jason.

"You do appear to be all right," Tella said as she finished squeezing Charles' forearm. She grimaced, and then let the happy-go-lucky teenager go. "How did you take a drop like that and have nothing happen to you?"

"I fell and I landed. I don't know how I lucked out," Charles said. "At the moment, though, I think I'm a little more interested in where those insects flew off to. They could come flying back any time."

Twenty meters above, the rupture they had tumbled through was still allowing in a faint green light. Charles tilted his head upward, and with his extended arm, tracked the path the skiff had cut through the serpentine tree trunks.

"The ship should be thataway," he said, gesturing in a westerly direction.

"I wonder if it can still fly."

Without a concern in the world, the boy charged ahead.

Tella chased after him just as Koron squatted down beside Jason. The wounded civilian had just regained consciousness and was moaning in pain. Enveloped by the soup, all that could really be seen of Jason was his outstretched face and neck, and the knob of his right knee. Clouds of blood were swirling around him.

Koron plunged his hand into the soup and inquired, "Where does it hurt?"

"If I say everywhere, will it make me look like a wimp?"

"Under these circumstances, I wouldn't think so."

Koron began to pat Jason down, which made him scream.

"Sorry about that. Where's the most intense pain?" Koron's hands were moving around more gently now.

"Around my stomach, and probably my legs."

Koron's left hand halted as his fingers snagged on something. "I think I found where the stomach pain is coming from. Don't freak out on me, but I believe you might have one of these branches sticking through you. I need you to remain incredibly still."

Jason winced. "I knew it was something bad."

A priority summons broke into the links of three of the four survivors.

"Survey team, this is the Ranger Commander. The Core has finally been able to reestablish contact. We can now read vital signs from some of you. Can you give us a verbal update on your individual conditions?"

"We're all alive," Tella said as she and Charles marched back over to their colleagues.

"I'm a-okay, Dad," Charles said. "Don't you worry about me."

"That's a huge relief, son...*huge*." Camden's sigh was audible. "Your exploring days are at an end. You do understand this, yes?"

"I'll never give it up. Just like you'd never give it up."

"We shall see about that."

Koron held his arm up and motioned for Tella's attention. "My link isn't working. What's he telling you?"

Tella started speaking for both ends of the conversation.

"Here's our situation, Commander. Koron's link is damaged and Chief Epelle is badly injured." She looked at Koron for confirmation, who nodded in the affirmative. "When can we expect to get out of here?"

"Leo is in a skiff as we speak. We're patching him through now. Hold on."

77

Leo's skiff came swooping over the waterway.

"One of you needs to get over to the crashed ship and unload the stretcher. It'll be on the left side of the hold, bolted directly above the first aid pack."

"We'll probably need the first aid pack as well," Tella said.

"I would assume so."

"I'll go get both."

Leo angled the skiff upward, gaining a few degrees of altitude as he closed in on a driftwood coastline.

"Mr. Bratsk," Charles said. "Koron wants to know if you have a plan to get us out of here?"

"The shape of one at least. He won't like it, but the four of you are going to have to find way to move through that mess. You're not that far from the edge of the forest. I'll find someplace nearby where I can set down and pick you up."

"The only problem with that," Charles said. "There's not a whole lot of space to maneuver down here. There are trunks and branches everywhere. And it's really dark. I'm not sure we can even get out of here on foot. Having a stretcher along will only make things that much more difficult."

"There's no other choice, Charles. There are bulbs in the skiff if you need them."

"I'm pulling those out, too," Tella said.

Leo banked the skiff right. "In the meantime, how are all of you holding up? What's the mood like down there, Charles?"

"Low, I guess. Koron's worried about hacking down any vegetation. I think his concern is mostly stemming from all the warnings he got from the Constructs."

"Believe me, I have similar concerns," Leo said. "But we need to get Mr. Epelle out of there. Time is of the essence."

"I agree," Charles said. "If my opinion counts for anything."

"It does."

Leo glanced down at the schematic line being drawn across his display.

"I'll be over your position in another few seconds. I'm looking for a suitable pick-up point now. There…got one. It's to the north of you. I need all of you headed north, ASAP."

78

Jason could not keep his eyes open. He'd been strapped down on the slow-moving stretcher for the better part of an hour, a broken-off hunk of tree branch protruding from the base of his stomach. Wads of gauze bandaging had been mashed in around the wound to stop up the ongoing flow of blood.

As it was edging around a particularly sharp bend, the corner of the stretcher rammed into a low-lying limb. The device required a second or two to rebalance itself, as did its two human controllers—Tella in the rear and Charles out in front. Koron was pacing a dozen steps ahead of the party, on the lookout for the clearest and safest path forward.

Tella braced her boot against an upturned rock and bent down next to Jason's ear. "What's that in your hand, tough guy?"

The response he gave was faint. "This? It's just a pen."

"I thought I saw you playing around with something on the skiff." Tella smiled at him and eased the stretcher forward. "Were you holding onto that silly thing the whole way down? I have to say, if that's true, that was a real stupid thing to do."

"I couldn't lose it. It belongs to someone I care about. There's no way I was just going to let it go."

Koron stopped and said, "We have a major impasse coming up on the right, people."

Tella brought the stretcher to a halt.

"Mr. Bratsk...impasse ahead," Charles said.

Leo's voice snapped online. "Describe the impasse."

Charles wadded over to Koron. They both stood on branches to observe the blockage—a knotted, wall-like growth of green and white vines. Small spikes were protruding up and down its expansive length.

"It's basically a climbing plant of some sort," Charles said. "It stretches out on either side of us, and trails upward, as far as I can see. It doesn't seem to be connected to the tree trunks, not in any symbiotic way. It is quite dense, though. Even if we turned the stretcher onto its side, as we were able to do earlier, nothing skinner than a toothpick is getting through."

Koron touched one of the barbs with his gloved hand. "I think we might have just hit the end of the road."

"There's definitely no going around it," Charles said. "Any alternatives you have, Mr. Bratsk, would be greatly appreciated."

"Okay," Leo said. "Currently, I'm right on the other side of you. I can actually hear you rustling around over there. That said, I cannot see any trace of this plant you've described. I'll wander around and see if I can find another way out. You do the same on your end."

"That's a no-go," Tella said. "We're running out of time. Epelle's skin is turning gray, and his bleeding has gotten worse."

"We need to cut through then," Leo said. This was followed by a long pause.

"Tell me Koron's reaction, Charles. We haven't had to cut anything so far. Is he up for this?"

"Leo thinks we have no choice but to cut," Charles said.

Koron nodded back at him. "I don't see any other way either. We're not going to let a man die over this. And I think we can get through this stuff pretty quickly."

"It's what we need to do," Tella said. "Let's just do it."

"You heard the lady," Leo said.

Charles and Koron detached a pair of machetes that had been tacked to the side of the stretcher and began hacking away at the blockage. Within thirty seconds or so, a small opening had been created. There were a few assorted tree trunks on the other side, but other than that, plenty of space to maneuver. Leo could be seen through the largest of these gaps ripping away loose branches. Green refuse was falling into the soup. From above, particles from the chalky treetops sifted down on them like snow. The chopping ceased for a moment, and the stretcher surged through the opening, getting stuck briefly as it smacked up against an extra-thick branch. Tella laid in with a more solid shove and the stretcher came out the other side.

"Let's get this man loaded up," Leo commanded. "No dawdling."

Koron joined Tella behind the stretcher as the trudged their way toward the skiff. Ahead of them was the crest of a u-shaped waterway, not twenty meters out.

After he'd come through, Charles glanced back at the jagged hole they'd made in the vegetation. There was no sign of any attacking creatures.

Tella and Koron got Jason and the stretcher stowed on board. Leo and Charles were just about to join them when the soup exploded around their feet. A deluge of white globules spat into the air and poured down on an immobilized Charles. Leo made a move to help him up, but the stream had already become a full-on wave and washed the boy back into the branches.

Leo shook his arm at the skiff. "Get the ship in the air *now. Up! Up!*"

"We're not leaving you," Tella said as Koron took his place at the flight controls.

"Yes, you are. Someone has to go after the kid. And since I'm the unlucky idiot still on the ground, I guess I volunteer."

Tella yelled something at him, but her words, if not the sentiment, were lost as the skiff's engines ignited.

She tapped back into their communication link and said, "Don't be an idiot, Leo. You don't know where Charles went, or if he's even alive? How are you going to find him? There's nothing you can do."

"Sure there is. I can do this."

Leo unholstered his tracer pistol and began firing at the forest. A trunk split in two and the upper portion of the tree toppled into the soup. He kept firing, shredding everything in sight. White dust cracked and puffed with every shot.

"See, it's simple. All you need to do is piss these fuckers off."

"You are out of your mind," Tella said as the skiff became airborne. "That stuff is going to drag you away, too."

"That's the plan," he said, firing three more shots and emptying the tracer's projectile chamber.

The soup was rippling as the globules made their return. This time, the intensity of the onslaught was exponential. An enormous deluge flooded across the beachfront. Leo was knocked over in an instant. As he was being trawled off, his head was bobbing up and down.

"We'll be back for you," Tella promised.

"Don't worry about me." Leo was fighting to keep his nose and mouth above the barrage. "I can fend for myself."

Another white wave struck and pulled Leo under. In the blink of an eye, he was gone.

79

Adam was waiting on the dock with several anxious Rangers as the skiff roared back into the clearing.

Dr. William Holt hurried over to the stretcher and got his first up-close look at Jason. The spire's engine was already in full spin, ready to deliver the patient to the Red Village hospital—the *Horizon*'s state-of-the-art medical facility. Jason, the stretcher, and William were loaded onto a secondary hover platform and delivered into the belly of the ship. The hatchway closed, and the *Spear* lifted off without delay. The extreme thrust turned the clearing into a momentary tsunami of silt and soup.

While everyone else was distracted, Camden commandeered the still idling skiff. "I'm going back out," he said.

There was no argument from Kay, or from anyone else.

Adam leapt on board as well, cutting in front of both Samuel and Hollis. "I'm going with you," he told the Commander.

Camden slapped down on the accelerator. A millisecond later, the skiff was a dot in the sky.

80

When Leo regained consciousness, it was dark.

"Scary, scary," he said as he floated about, engulfed from the neck down in a thick, unknown liquid. He dug around in his field belt until he found a hand-sized illumination bulb in a padded rear pouch. With a hard click to its base, the device sprang to life and flew from his grasp. The light emitted was powerful enough for the Ranger to now observe everything around him.

He'd found himself in a tube of some sort. The white globule substance from the beach was everywhere—above him, beneath him, swirling and pulsating around the spherical chamber at intense, almost breakneck speeds. Leo, in miraculous fashion, was remaining stationary, lodged in a pocket of relative calm.

He touched his ear. "Emergency assistance required. Echo Base, call."

The Core had no pleasant response for him. Instead, it routed his summons straight through to the scientist in charge.

Meyer Wells said, "*Leonid.* Unbelievable. You're alive." His voice trailed off as he spoke to someone close by. "He's alive. He *just* called in."

"I'd personally describe my surviving as more surprising than unbelievable. But since you're the resident big brain, Dr. Wells, I should probably leave the formal categorizations to you."

"Do you know where you are? Do you know what abducted you? Are you injured?" Meyer's questions were rapid fire.

"I believe I'm fine. The stuff I'm drifting around in is what abducted me—although it was much, much hotter when it swept me up. Now, it feels kind of cool. As to where I am, I have absolutely no clue."

Leo turned himself all the way around.

"I'm inside someplace without outside light, surrounded by a three-sixty flow of the white stuff. That's about all I can relay so far."

A female voice was nipping at Meyer in the background. Trying to ignore it, he said, "The only signal we currently have from your link is the call you just put through. We have no way of triangulating your location. We've been trying to restore communication with you since the team you rescued left the abduction point."

"Did they get back okay?"

"They did."

"And Chief Epelle. How's he doing?"

"He's currently on the *Horizon* receiving treatment. That's all I know."

Leo reached out and dragged his finger through a trail of what looked to be blood floating out among the globules. He raised his left arm. The sheath he was wearing had been ripped and there was a large gash across his elbow.

"Exactly how long was I out?" he asked Meyer.

"You and the Commander's son were taken six hours ago. Is there any sign of Charles near you?"

"None that I can see. That was the first thing I looked for."

"I will *not*," Meyer said. The anger had come exploding out of him. "Just leave me be." The voice in the background continued to chide him.

"Hey, doc," Leo said. "There's this really subtle rumbling sound in here, so I can't tell who that is you're speaking to. I'm assuming it's Kay. Just tell her to put a sock in it for a second. I'm in a real bind here, and I need your full attention."

"And you have it. For the record, the person talking is your associate Tella. She wants to speak with you."

"Tell Tella she can put a sock in it, too. I know she wants to chastise me for being irresponsible, but that can wait."

"He says you should shut up." Meyer's voice got louder, and a bit more frightened. "She's not shutting up, Leonid."

"I prefer Leo. Just ignore her as best you can. Is there still no fix on my position?"

"No. Wherever you are, your tracking signal is being blocked. I would presume in some sort of natural, geological phenomena."

"Okay. Well, I'm evidently somewhere. Once I've tracked Charles down, I'm sure I can scrounge a way outta here."

"Camden is out looking for you both now."

"I figured somebody was."

Leo made a sudden attempt to swim out into the vortex that was swirling around him. The current was too strong, and tossed him right back.

"Tell Camden I'm on the trail of his son, so he needs to remain calm, which I know would be difficult for anybody. But tell him I said so anyway."

Leo dunked himself under the white and his boot struck bottom. He resurfaced.

"Just so you know what I'm up to, I'm stuck in this one particular spot, but if I can gain a little leverage, I think I can get pulled out into the stronger flow."

"Stronger flow?" Meyer said. "What stronger flow? Hold on. Whatever it is you're attempting, I'm not sure that it's wise."

"What's not wise about looking for Charles?"

"For starters, we believe this substance is intelligent, Leo. The Constructs called it the fizz. Let's think long and hard before we aggravate it again. It's obviously dangerous, and unmistakably moody."

"I'm well aware of all of this. It's me it got pissed at, remember?"

"I do remember, which is the reason I want you to start making more considered choices. I'm not telling you you cannot act, I am telling you to think before you do act. Please, any action taken should be a mutual decision between the two of us, you understand me? Brains and brawn. We don't want another Mikhail situation here."

"I am not Mikhail. I think fast, and I act faster."

"We are all well aware of your aptitudes."

"Then we agree. I'm off to find Charles."

Leo dropped back down and pushed off. On his first attempt, he almost made it out. With a second, more concentrated push, he was drawn outward.

"Now that it's too late for any recriminations, I'm free and being dragged downstream. Don't be shocked if I have some trouble conversing for a while."

Day Five

81

It took over three hours for Mary to be informed that contact had been reestablished with Leo. She was awakened at four twenty-one in the morning, given a handful of the relevant details, and ordered to Transplant Command to await further instruction.

When Mary arrived, Florin—the duty officer on overnight watch— was chatting with Walter and Dimitri. The two men were dressed in gray suits and looking shockingly ready to face the day. Mary, on the other hand, was still wearing her sleeping attire, black stretch pants and an old sleeveless top.

"Dad…Walter," she said in greeting. "Isn't this a tad early for the two of you?"

"The current situation requires our immediate attention," Dimitri said.

Mary leaned back against one of the display arches. "How's Jay doing? The Core couldn't, or wouldn't, elaborate."

It was Walter who responded. "Jason is doing well, quite well. Elisabeth and his family are with him now. The branch he was impaled upon has been successfully removed and the tears in his stomach and intestines have been repaired. His broken bones will be set later this afternoon. We are told he will be back on his feet in a week at the latest."

"Then he's lucky," Mary said. "Luckier than some."

Dimitri acted as if he hadn't heard that and walked around to the flip side of the control center. Walter prompted Mary to follow him with a flick of his hand. Father and daughter were sitting down together as Walter led Florin out of the room.

Dimitri got right to it. "Mary, Leonid has begun to cause problems. I would like for you to speak with him, to convince him to listen to reason."

"What sort of problems is he causing?"

"He's been acting rashly, and has taken unnecessary risks. He says he's attempting to ascertain Charles' location. But at this point, in my opinion, his escapades could be causing a lot more harm than the loss of that boy."

"Is there anything more harmful than another death?" Mary glared at him. "This is my stepson you're talking about. I won't allow him to be sacrificed for *any* reason."

"I am not suggesting we sacrifice anybody. And there are always worse outcomes than death. There's the loss of this moon, and the inability for us to ever build a permanent colony here. Until we better understand the behavior of these creatures, we must act with restraint and keep provocations to a minimum."

Mary shook her head. "Can you even hear yourself when you speak? What could Leo possibly be doing? He's out looking for a missing child and you are concerned about diplomatic relations with alien goo. These are animals, Dad. They cannot possibly know any more about us than we know about them. They're just doing whatever's necessary to protect their habitat. There's no reasoning involved here, apparently on either side."

"So then, you're refusing to talk to him?"

"Oh, I'll talk to him. I *want* to talk to him." Mary swiveled around in her chair and activated the communications channel with Echo Base. "Meyer, can you hear me?"

"I hear you, Mary." The older man's voice filled the room.

"Can you patch Leo in with me?"

"I'm already on line," Leo said.

Mary closed her eyes and smiled. "Hello, you. I hear you've been causing quite the fuss down there. What in the world do you think you're doing?"

"Uh, looking for Charles. What else would I be doing? I've floated through a couple dozen passageways so far, but still no luck. I'll keep chugging on, though. I'm not one to give up easily."

"You do realize you're stressing everyone out up here. They seem to think you're putting more than yourself at risk."

"I don't know how to respond to that. They are all ninnies, worrying about the ethereal. Charles is missing. That is not ethereal, that's reality. A problem needs to be solved, and I'm going to solve it."

"Yes, but I need you to be extremely careful doing so. You cannot antagonize these things any more than we already have."

"Wow, that's eerie," Leo said. "Was that you or your father who just said that? Are his lips still moving?"

"Funny boy."

Mary looked over at one of the live transmissions from below. Construction had been temporarily shut down while the crew teams slept.

"Okay," she said. "You'll be allowed to continue to look for Charles, but you need to be good and listen to Meyer's advice. Never forget, he's much smarter than you."

"You're smarter than me, too."

"Then listen to me as well."

"I've always tried to."

"I know that you have." Mary's voice sweetened. "Come back alive. Do you hear me? I refuse to lose you. I've lost too much already. No horsing around. Be safe."

"I'll do my best. And since you wish it, I'll listen to Meyer more closely."

"Thank you. I'll check back in later."

"Looking forward to it," Leo said. "Talk to you soon."

Mary pressed the red cancel button and terminated the connection. She glanced at her father, who looked quite pleased.

"I'm eternally grateful," he said.

"Just so we understand each other, I didn't do this for *you*." Mary got up and walked away. "I'm not doing anything for you *ever* again."

82

Early on, the line of well-wishers cycling through Jason's hospital room had appeared never-ending. Nearly everyone Jason interacted with on a day-to-day basis had dropped by to see how he was doing. The list of visitors included all eight members of the Directorate, and each of the village supervisors. At the very least, the political flybys were short and to the point. Thank you for your service. We're pleased that you're all right. It was the visits with his extended family that tended to drag on too long. From his cousins to his in-laws, they all bore similar expressions, a smile masking the unstated, yet horrified reaction of seeing someone they cared about lying mangled on a gellular bed.

The lone family member who could not make it by was his sister Jocelyn. She was still recovering from her own maladies. But she did call to speak with him, assuring her big brother that she and her newborn would introduce and reintroduce themselves as soon as they were all feeling up to it.

Throughout the lengthy procession, there was one constant—Angela. Initially, Jason's wife had been sitting quietly in the corner with their son Jerald. But the boy soon grew tired and Joy took him home. From then on out, Angela performed the duties of traffic coordinator, hurrying people politely when they were being too slow, and then when their visit had concluded, escorting the next guest in.

Around midday, they were down to only one extraneous visitor.

"I should probably get going," Jason's mother said, right before she scampered off.

Angela followed her to the door, and then went back to Jason's bed. "How are you feeling? Would you like to get some sleep? I can make sure no one else comes in."

"I am pretty sleepy," he said. "I've already been in and out a bit. Don't tell anyone, but sometimes when people were fawning, I took a cat nap."

"Well, I'd say it's about time for a big boy's nap, a nice long one."

Angela was digging around in her pants pocket, fishing for something. It didn't take her long to find it. What she pulled out made Jason shudder. The pen. Morgan's pen.

"The surgeon wanted me to give this to you. You were clutching onto it when they brought you in. They said it had blood all over it so one of the nurses cleaned and disinfected it for you."

She laid it down on the nightstand.

"Is it yours? I've never seen you with a pen before. Come to think of it, I've never seen you write anything down physically. Not ever."

Jason's face betrayed nothing. "Actually, I took that stupid thing off one of the Constructs. I wanted a closer look at it. He said it was a keepsake he'd brought with him from Earth. I had an urge to touch something old, but then I forgot to give it back to him. I felt responsible for the thing. When the skiff went down, I tried to keep it safe. I didn't want to lose it in all that soup stuff on the surface, so I held it tight. I'd have felt horrible if I had been the one responsible for losing something precious."

Angela rested the back of her hand against his forehead. "It's just a thing, Jay. I'm sure this person would've understood."

"You're probably right."

Angela pulled her hand away. "I'll tell the nurses you are not to be disturbed for the next few hours, that way you can sleep through your osteopathic surgery. Will that be okay?"

"Sounds like a plan."

She bent down and kissed him on the lips. "Feel better."

"I will," he said as the lights faded low. "I'll feel much better tomorrow."

83

"You were right about one thing," Florin said. "I'm exhausted, and definitely in the mood for some attention."

"I had a feeling you might be."

Derek slipped his arm around her waist and led them through the windowed partition. Four short steps later they were out of the office park and into the Red Village proper, not all that far from their final destination—165 Cinnamon Road.

Florin mumbled something and then hit the brakes. "You know what, I've changed my mind. I don't want to go this way."

Derek's arm peeled off her as he continued down the sidewalk. Florin reached out for him and snatched hold of the back of his shirt, preventing him from getting too far way.

"But your house is this way," Derek said as he came to a stop himself.

"I know. I don't want to go to my house."

"Where do you want to go?"

"To your house."

Derek hesitated for a second. "Maybe we shouldn't. You've been on monitor duty for sixteen straight hours. I was only escorting you home so you could get some sleep."

"Sleep can wait. We should go to your house first. You can give me what I really need at your house."

Florin moved closer to him and pressed her leg against his inseam.

Derek stared back at her as if he was some sort of disapproving parent—ultra concerned, with a twinge of adamant superiority.

"This is why I didn't come by to see you while you were working last night," he said. "I'm beginning to think you have a one-track mind. We were bound to do something in that room again. And this time, we could've gotten caught."

"We were not going to get caught. No one ever stops by the command center without warning. They always call first."

"We *could* have been caught, that's my point."

Florin exhaled and put her hands on her hips. "This is unbelievable." She pivoted left and created some distance between them. "I've never had to fight so hard to get into a guy's pants before."

Derek's face was growing ever more stern. "Don't you turn this on me. I want and desire all the same things that you want and desire—but I am also developing real feelings for you. I know that you like men, especially in that way. But I hope whatever this is between us becomes something more significant than that. I want you to like me in every way. I'm happy to have sex with you as much and as often as you like, but I expect more than that, too. I'm not going to be toyed with like the other men in your life."

"Toyed with?" Florin said, sounding more surprised than shocked. "Listen, I like you a lot, but I told you before I'm not serious about relationships, not at the moment at least. If that's what you're looking for here, maybe it's best if you look someplace else. I hate to be so direct with you, but these are the facts. It's what I tell all the men that I see. I want what I want. If you want that as well, then great. If not, well, best of luck to you."

Derek made an attempt to cut the distance between them, but Florin took two steps backward.

"I hate that you see other men," Derek said. "I'm not someone who shares well. I'll do whatever you want whenever you want, but you have to only be seeing me."

Florin nodded. "Yeah, you know what, I think you might've been onto something before. I *am* tired. I should go home and get some sleep."

"Don't be that way," he said. "I didn't mean to chase you away. I honestly didn't. If I screwed up in some—"

"You didn't screw up." Florin gave him a wide berth as she circled around him. "You didn't."

"When can we see each together again?"

She hummed for a second and said, "I have another double shift in twelve hours, so give me a call in a day or two. Maybe we can talk then. Maybe."

84

Mother and daughter were together on the bed, one wailing while the other one sobbed.

The clock in the living room chimed three and Baby Tana's cries grew louder. Jocelyn brought her into an embrace. Mommy's touch comforted the newborn, so Jocelyn held her even closer. Then, her nose began to crinkle. She sat up and inspected the baby's diaper, which needed changing.

Still struggling to walk, Jocelyn limped her way into the bathroom where she cleaned the child up and put on a fresh diaper. Tana lay there on the counter, staring up distantly at her. Jocelyn, disheveled and grieving, came face to face with her reflection in the mirror. With a sigh, she activated her link.

"It's me," she said. "I'm calling to take you up on your offer."

"I was hoping that you would," Mary said.

"Can we do it soon? I just need to change clothes and make myself up a bit. I'll be ready whenever you can get over."

"Of course. I can be there in twenty minutes. Will that work?"

"Works for me," Jocelyn said as she looked away from the mirror.

"You don't sound so good," Mary said.

"I don't look so good either. But both of those things can be remedied."

"Do you want me to wrap things up a little quicker?"

"No, that's okay. Twenty minutes will be fine."

Jocelyn double tapped her ear, picked up the baby, and hobbled her way back into the bedroom.

85

The skiff pulled alongside the docking clamps and Adam stepped off. Camden was already shouting orders at the technician stationed on deck, telling him to recharge the progelant canisters, he was going back out.

Adam shared a nod with his frustrated compatriot, and took his leave. Samuel passed him by as he tromped down the platform. A bevy of supplies were slung over the Ranger's shoulder in two separate utility packs.

"Well, look who it is," a female voice said.

Adam spun to the left.

"I spy Crewman Ballard," Anne Dougherty said, her spirits high. "Unsurprisingly, you're looking even more scruffy than the last time I saw you."

Anne was standing beside a pile of emptied storage cases with two of the other Constructs—Christina Roth and Nick Finn. They had been scrubbed up since the last time they'd been on the surface, and all their scratches and wounds had been attended to. All three were outfitted in the same gray jumpsuits the other surface workers were wearing, including Adam, who hopped over to his friends and hugged each of them, as if he hadn't been in their presence in years.

"We're back," Christina said. "As you can see."

"And ready to work." Nick was the last of the three to be received. Adam clutched the side of his head, his dirty fingers mussing Nick's newly trimmed locks.

"I'm so glad you guys are here," Adam said. "I wasn't sure if they were going to let you back down."

Anne pretended to cower. "I know. After the doctors checked us out medically, we were inundated with psych evaluations. I guess we passed enough of them, though."

One eye on Adam, Nick banked his head toward the sky. "Did you know you're famous up there now? The bravest of the brave who stayed behind to help with your vast knowledge of this terrifying new world. The doctors and nurses think you're some sort of frontiersman or something, way more distinguished than any of their Rangers."

Adam looked back at the skiff at the end of the dock. "And yet, my contribution has added up to jack squat. When I went out on the skiff today I was just tagging along."

Anne came up behind him. "Tagging along? Tagging along with what?"

"We were out searching for the Commander's missing son, and one of the other Rangers."

"You're talking about the criminal Ranger, right?" Christina said.

"I don't know what he is. I do know that the man impressed me. He was so determined. That's why I volunteered to help with the search. I was already back doing construction work, but there was something about this guy. Not that I ended up being any help. We were out searching for the better part of the day, totally in vain."

Adam took a last look at Camden and Samuel. The recharge was being finalized.

"You're exhausted," Anne said.

"The father of the missing kid is exhausted as well, but he's going out again. I just couldn't do it. My eyes were strained and my legs were buckling. A replacement could do a lot more, so I bowed out."

"Well, your legs were probably buckling because you're hungry," Christina said. "Wanna go get something to eat with us?"

Anne and Christina took Adam by the arms and led him away.

As they were descending to level five, Adam asked, "How's Robert doing? He's not here, I assume?"

Nick shook his head. "No. He had his replacement arm attached yesterday, and I don't think he'll be coming back down anytime soon. We don't know more than that. Actually, we were all kept pretty sequestered. Most of the time, we didn't see anybody but the same doctors and nurses, again and again."

Christina whispered to Adam, "Nick thinks they don't want us down here at all, and they only released us because it's better than us being around regular citizens. You know, because we might tell them what it's really been like down here."

"Nick's not the only one thinking that," Anne said. "I'm thinking it, too. I tried to talk about what happened with Mikhail, but I was told discussion of that was best left unspoken. In other words, I should shut my fat mouth."

"I can't believe what I'm hearing," Adam said, looking at all three of them. "We can't get paranoid."

"That's the thing," Nick said. "I don't think that we are. The way they treated us was so strange."

"Were you treated badly?"

"Not exactly. They treated us like all of this was *our* fault."

86

"If you're truly asking for my opinion," Rebecca said. "I think you should hold a vigil. You should get everybody together on the village decks and remember the man he was."

Walter put his elbows on his desk. "I don't know. Vigils have religious connotations, don't they?"

"Not necessarily."

"But that's what you're suggesting, some sort of spiritually-tinged memorial service."

"I'm not suggesting anything really. My friend called and asked for my opinion, and that's what I've given him."

"Yes, but what you said was a bit more than just an opinion. You were flat-out suggesting something religious, and a religious ceremony is never going to fly. This was Dimitri Kucherov's son, who you know is not religious. Now is not the time to be taunting the man."

"Nobody said that it was. You're reading into things. All I was doing was suggesting you hold a public memorial service for the boy. It should not be one of Dimitri's typical button-down affairs. Whatever else you decide to do, this event, it must have a spark to it. The populace is broken-hearted. You cannot allow that to fester. Make it an all-day, all-night event. That's what a vigil actually is, it's a time of staying awake, out of respect. Let people do that as a group. And then, after they're done, you can hold a more somber memorial for the family."

"I get it now. I thought you were—" Walter stopped there.

"I know precisely what you were thinking. You all but said what you thought I was trying to do. Oh, what you must think of me."

"Everything I think of you is based on countless incidents from the past. You do realize this?"

"I do, but you need to forget about all that. My protesting impulses have atrophied, as I have consistently stated. And despite my virulent dislike for the politics and decision-making abilities of your beloved mentor, I would never use the death of his son as an opportunity to bludgeon. I just want whatever it is you people are doing to be more inclusive."

"And this is why I sought your opinion out in the first place. You've always had this innate feel for the mood of people. It's uncanny to me."

"Please, I'm no soothsayer. I am a theological historian. I understand *why* people do what they do. That's all."

"It's more than that, whether you recognize it or not."

"There's no need to lather me up, Walter. Even you must know the mood out there isn't good. It's not difficult to put two and two together. All the sullen faces. All the teary eyes. People are grief-stricken."

"Which is why we're going to do something open and friendly, just as you are suggesting. Mikhail needs to be honored in a way that no one has ever been honored before. The gesture needs to be grand and long-lasting. It might even be bigger than one funeral."

"You're going to go overboard, aren't you?"

"I don't think so. That wasn't my intention anyway. Dimitri would put up a fight if I did too much. He has this thing about memorials."

"Let's stop talking about Dimitri, okay?"

"Okay."

"How's the situation with the missus going? I don't know if you're aware, but she called me yesterday to schedule a dinner party for the four of us. She was very, very pleasant, and seemed thrilled to be throwing it."

"She seemed that way to me, too."

"Have you told her that you've been calling me almost every day?"

"I have not. The subject hasn't come up."

"Walter, my friend, you are playing with fire."
"Of that, Rebecca, I am well aware."

87

Mary and Jocelyn had been asked to wait outside. Doing as instructed, they lined up against the wall while Baby Tana snored sound asleep in the carrier between them.

"The doctor will be out in just another minute," a nurse said as she exited hospital room sixty-one with a wastebasket hooked between her fingers. "We had an accident. A bathroom accident." Her voice went extra quiet. "Someone *went* all over the place."

Mary and Jocelyn looked at one another. The nurse scampered off and opened up a utility closet, two doors down.

"Did we need to know any of that?" Mary said.

Jocelyn chuckled. "It appears that we did."

The doctor stepped out, sooner than they had been told. He was drying his hands with a paper towel and informed the two women they could go on inside.

The hospital room interior showed no outward sign of the accident the nurse had just referenced. There were just various pieces of portable medical equipment, and the patient in his bed.

"Jocelyn," Bernard Stalt said. The injured Ranger sat up and ran his fingers through his hair. "It's so good to see you. How are you feeling?"

Jocelyn pushed the carrier toward the bed. "I'm feeling fine, thank you."

"So, have there been any after-effects with the stasis?" Bernard rapped his knuckles against the side of his head. "That was a stupid question.

There must not have been much, not if you're up and around."

Jocelyn bent over him and kissed his forehead, which made the man flinch.

"I brought somebody by to see you." Jocelyn reached into the carrier and lifted out her daughter. Tana was dressed in bright red pajamas, and remained completely unconscious. Jocelyn brought her toward the bed and Bernard lit up.

"Oh my, she's so beautiful," he said.

Jocelyn held the baby out. "Go ahead. Take her. She wants to say hello."

Bernard accepted the sleeping child and cradled her in his arms. He stared at her until his eyes began to blink faster and faster.

"What did you name her?" he asked.

"Tana Marie."

"Tana Marie Kucherov," he said as if the name itself were a formal proclamation. "This might be the most beautiful baby in recorded history."

Mary swooped around to the other side of the bed. "I tend to think most children are fairly gorgeous, but this little girl, she sure is a looker."

"You and Mary came together, huh?" Bernard lugged the baby away from his chest and offered her back to her mother.

"We wanted to visit," Jocelyn said as she took Tana back. "We wanted to know how you're doing."

Bernard nodded his head several times, too many times, and then went still. "I don't know if you heard yet, but I got the official news earlier. I'm not going to be blamed."

"Blamed for what?" Mary asked.

"For what happened to Mikhail. I thought for sure I was going to be, because I didn't do enough."

"Don't be silly," Mary said. "We all saw what happened. You tried to free him. You raced straight into danger. You shot the thing that was attacking him. You did more than anyone else."

Jocelyn cringed as she returned Tana to her carrier. "Can we please not dredge any of this up? Not now, at least."

Jocelyn stood back up and placed her hand on top of the sheet that'd been drawn over Bernard's legs. "Mary said you had to have reconstructive surgery. Does it still hurt? How long are you going to be stuck here?"

"They haven't told me," Bernard said. "And no, it doesn't hurt at all."

A sudden stream of tears came tricking down Jocelyn's face.

"Well then." Mary hustled over to Jocelyn's side. "You about ready, sister-in-law? We should probably get going."

"Yeah." Jocelyn wiped at her cheeks.

Bernard's gaze shifted from woman to woman. "I'm so sorry this happened. I'm so sorry that you both have had to suffer."

"And I'm sorry, too. Sorry you got hurt." Jocelyn touched the bed one last time. "Thank you for fighting for my husband. I'll be indebted to you forever."

Bernard started over-nodding again. "Your daughter...she's beyond gorgeous. And Mikhail, he loved you so much. He talked about you all the time you were asleep. You were on his mind constantly."

"That's nice to know."

Mary extended her own arm over the hospital bed. "We should probably be off, but it was good to see you, Bernard." They exchanged a handshake. "We'll be back to see you soon."

Jocelyn offered up a quick wave as the tears continued to flow. "Talk to you later, Bernard."

"You bet. You two take care of yourselves, okay?"

88

Leo fell tail first into the open chasm. Individual fizz globules were raining down around him as he landed with a thud in yet another layer of the white.

Thirty seconds went by, then a minute. Leo jostled his head and grumbled. In his ear, Meyer insisted on knowing how he was—had he been hurt. Leo propped himself up with his hands and assured Meyer that everything was just fine.

At almost that same instant, the illumination bulb found its way through the opening above. It floated downward and spilled out its light. As if in response, the fizz around Leo began to part, exposing a smooth, stone surface. The bubbling animals retreated three meters on each side of Leo, and hung back.

Leo spit a trace of blood from his mouth. "Doctor, I believe I've stumbled into someplace different."

"Different in what way?" Meyer asked.

"It's a lot less tube-like, for one. I'd describe it as big and cavernous. And there are these circular openings all over the place. There are even a few near my feet. Each of these holes are different sizes, some large and some small. The one I came through was more on the large size."

"Anything else?"

"Well, there's a lot less of the fizz stuff in here, and it doesn't whip around like a river the way it has everywhere else."

Leo stood up, all the way up.

"As well as being shallow, the fizz in here moves out of my way when I walk, which I have to say is rather polite of the stuff."

Leo's gaze shifted to the other side of the cavern.

"Hold up, Doc. There's something else in here. Something beyond myself and my pasty shadows."

"Describe this something."

Leo approached the objects he'd been referring to.

"They appear to be sacks, rounded and hanging off what I'd hesitate to call tendrils. There are bits of fizz crawling all over them."

Leo placed his face centimeters from the rightmost sack. He touched its pulsating membrane.

"Whatever this material is, it's pliable. I think there may be something solid inside the sack I'm standing in front of. The surrounding matter is translucent, so I can see that something is in there. It's too cloudy for me to be any more certain than that."

"How many of these sacks are there? Can you estimate?"

"One, two, three, four," Leo said. "I just counted them off for you. That's all there is."

"Okay. From your initial description, I had assumed there might have been more."

"Nope, only four. I probably would have noticed them immediately if there were any more. These were out of my line of sight."

Leo called the bulb down from the top of the cavern so it could emit more light.

"I'm not certain, but the sack I was pushing on might contain something woolly."

Leo retouched the membrane and the sack next to it shook.

"Hello. In sack two, I'm certain I just saw a hand move. I believe there may be a body inside as well."

Leo ordered the bulb even closer.

"Yep," he said once the light had increased. "It's a body. This could be Charles. The skin coloring is dark like his. What should I do?"

"What do you mean what should you do?" Meyer said.

"Should I cut this thing down to make sure?"

Meyer spoke quietly to someone next to him before responding. "How is the fizz behaving?"

"Indifferently, but also aware of every step I take, if that makes any sense."

"Unsheathe one of your knives and take a slight poke at this sack and watch how the fizz reacts. That will tell us a lot."

Leo removed his back-up knife from his right boot and flipped it open. He brought its tip of the serrated blade toward the membrane, but did not pierce it.

All round the cavern, the fizz had no discernible change in their behavior.

"Looking good so far," he told Meyer. "The knife is in place. Should I go ahead and cut?"

"You need to consider that you're putting your life at risk if you do this."

"Obviously, I am well aware of that."

"I was only trying to say that I am fine if you are fine. The decision is in your hands."

"As is the knife."

Starting off, the blade made a pinprick-sized incision. There was still no reaction from the fizz, so Leo pushed the blade deeper. The knife went a quarter of the way in and dragged downward, cutting a long vertical gash that allowed Leo to see what was inside.

"It's Charles. We've found him. Tell Camden. Have somebody call him.'"

Leo touched the boy's mucus-covered neck.

"And he's breathing. He's alive, but KO'd. Make sure you tell Camden right away."

"I have someone doing that right now," Meyer said.

With one eye on the fizz, Leo kept slicing. The sack tore open at the bottom and Charles jarred loose. Leo dropped the blade and lifted the youngster into his arms.

"He's out of the sack. I have him. And the fizz is still keeping its cool."

Meyer started to say "excellent work" when a tremor beneath Leo's feet nearly toppled him over.

"The place is starting to shake," he informed HQ. "I'm slinging Charles over my shoulder."

The second that had been accomplished more fizz came blasting through every hole in the cavern wall. Leo was swept up with his charge and trawled through the quickening current.

"We're being sucked toward one of the openings. I've got a tight grip on Charles. There's no way I'm letting go."

And then, just as before, man and boy were washed away.

89

Vladimir stood there motionless, a silhouette in the bedroom doorway.

"I'm here, as requested."

"Great. Now what are you waiting for?" Florin said from beneath the covers. "Get your scrawny butt over here."

Vladimir refused to budge, an act of defiance that caused Florin to kick out at the bedding.

"Come on. Stop wasting my time. I'm naked under here. I got naked just for you."

"I doubt that," Vladimir said. "I've never been your first choice for anything."

"You don't see anyone else under here, do you?"

"What about that guy you were on a date with the other day—the teacher. Isn't he the one warming your bed these days?"

"Not tonight, he isn't."

Vladimir shifted his weight onto his other foot and pinched up his face. "I don't get you at all, Florin. I haven't heard from you in days, and now this? If I mean so little to you, then why do you keep pulling me back into your life?"

"Because I like you, just not in a forever-and-ever way. Also, you're somewhat handsome, and you know your way around my body. These are all positives to me."

Vladimir glanced back down the hallway. "Where are your parents and

Tristan tonight?"

"I can't say for sure. Probably at my grandmother's. That's where they usually are."

"I see." He drummed his finger against the doorframe.

"Vlad, you already know what you're going to do, so stop futzing around and do it. We don't have all night."

He dropped his arm and crossed into the room. First, he removed his shirt, followed by his slacks, pulling them straight over his dress shoes. The sexless striptease had Florin's full attention.

"Just so you're aware. I'm only doing this because I'm horny," Vladimir said as he sat down on the bed. "I'm not doing it because I care about you anymore, because I don't. I know you'll never love me, so I've officially stopped loving you."

"Glad to hear it. It's about time you wised up. You'll be much happier this way."

Florin crawled on top of the covers and snaked her arms around him.

"Despite your sudden lack of love for me," she said. "Is it all right if I kiss you."

"I never said that you couldn't."

She buried her face against his neck. "Lie back, okay? We need to make this quick."

Day Six

90

Leo used his hand to shield his eyes from the sun, having just come to on an upturned bed of mud. At his feet, reclining on his side, was Charles. The two of them—one half-awake, the other unconscious—were out in the open air, surrounded by a gigantic plain of gelatinous soup. Kilometers in the distance, a jagged stretch of forest was being obstructed by a light, pea-green haze. The only other object of any significance in sight was the volcano-like formation behind them, the apparent source of their expulsion from below.

Leo stretched himself out on the mud. Someone was speaking inside his ear. They were off in the background, marshaling resources of some import.

Above him, a skiff was coming into view, growing ever larger as it slanted toward the ground.

"You do realize," Camden said as he was backing the skiff up to the mud trail. "The two of you ended up on a whole other continent. When I show you how far away this is on a map, your minds are going to be blown."

Camden brought the craft to a jarring halt and high-stepped to its rear end. Leo had already grabbed Charles by the legs and was waiting for Camden to take him by the shoulders.

"How's he doing?" Camden asked while they were lifting his son on board. The mere sight of the boy was making him smile.

Leo tightened his grip on Charles. "As far as I can tell, he's okay. He's breathing, and he has a pulse. That's the best assessment I'm going to be able to give you."

They placed Charles on a medical stretcher, the same type that had been used for Jason Epelle. Leo came out of his crouch and locked eyes with Camden.

"You're bleeding," Camden said. "It's a head wound."

A trickle of blood was running down the center of Leo's barcode tattoo. He used the already mangled left sleeve of his sheath to try and clean his face and scalp.

"I wondered what that was. I thought it was just sweat."

Camden held their gaze, and then took a knee next to his son. "What you've done here, I don't know what to say."

"Then don't say anything. Your son's back, like I told you he would be. That's all that matters to me."

"I can't just let it go at that. I owe you. We both know that I do."

"I don't know anything of the sort. I got lucky. I found the kid."

"You did a hell of a lot more than that. Thank you."

"You're welcome."

Together, they made sure Charles was securely affixed to the stretcher.

"I guess we're ready," Camden said.

While his commander's back was turned, Leo had stomped over to the footlocker and was digging through its contents.

"What are you up to over there?" Camden asked him.

"I'm putting together some supplies. I'm also going to need your backpack."

"But we're going back to base. Why would you need my backpack?"

Leo kept rummaging. "You're going back, I am not."

So far, Leo's growing pile of supplies was just an accumulation of freeze-dried meals, a pair of binocs, and a previously unused field shelter.

"Explain yourself," Camden said.

Leo stopped. "If we really are on a different continent, I want to have a look around before the bosses put a limit on what we can do." He threw his arm out. "Your pack. Like I said, I'm going to need it."

"Like hell you are." Camden made a mad dash for the flight controls.

"You can't stop me," Leo said. "I'll just jump out of this ship before you even get her airborne."

Leo tried to clean the mess off his face again, this time with his hand, but the bleeding had only gotten worse.

"You can't expect me to leave you like this," Camden said. "I've spent the past day and a half out looking for you."

"I realize what I'm doing seems counterintuitive. But we need to know what's out there, and I'm in a position to go take an unfettered look. I don't want to hear any arguments to the contrary. What needs to be done needs to be done, right? And, didn't you just say you owed me one?"

"I did and I do." Camden slipped off his pack and tossed it to Leo. "Before I abandon you here, will you at least let me bandage up that wound?"

"I'll take care of it once you're gone. I promise."

Leo emptied the pack and picked through Camden's various belongings. The canteen was the only item he retained. After checking if it was full, he piled in all the items from the footlocker, including a big fistful of first aid supplies.

"What am I supposed to tell the Directorate?" Camden asked. "What are you planning to do out there? This moon is huge. On foot, how much ground can you really cover?"

Leo got himself upright again and swung the pack over his shoulder. There was another item in his left hand, which he was holding behind his back.

"Take a look around here and tell me what you see? I know what I see, open space. We haven't encountered much of that, have we? Accordingly, while you take your son back to base, I'm gonna go on a quick scout."

"The Rangers can come back and do that with you, you know. We are a team."

"I know, and you will. But I've been wanting to get a feel for this place since I first came down, and that's been difficult to do on these skiffs. Down in the tunnels, I was doing actual reconnaissance. That's what we should be doing up here as well."

"The Directorate is going to have my head for leaving you," Camden said. "They're going to throw this huge hissy fit."

"Initially, sure. But secretly, they'll all be thrilled. You know Meyer will be back in my ear the second he's told. He'll be overjoyed to be borrowing my eyes—not to mention these eyes as well."

Leo flung an oval-shaped disc into the air. This was the object he'd been holding behind his back—a mobile camera. The device was on its way back down to the skiff deck when it self-activated and soared out of sight.

"What about Mary?" Camden asked. "What do I tell her?"

"I would suggest you avoid her at all cost."

"She still cares about you…you know that she does."

"Cam, none of that stuff is relevant anymore. You can't let it worry you."

Leo leapt of the skiff and reestablished his footing in the soup. "Whatever else, promise that you'll let me get as far away as you can before you call this in. They'll ask you to come back if you're still anywhere close."

"Which way are you headed?" Camden asked.

Leo pointed north. "Toward that tree line over there. I'll be easy to spot since there doesn't look to be anything else around."

Camden went to the front of the ship and initiated the skiff controls. After a moment's hesitation, he yelled out, "Don't get yourself killed, okay? Whatever else you do, please don't get yourself killed."

Leo put his hand up in acknowledgement and splashed ahead. Behind him, the skiff gained ten meters of elevation, spun counterclockwise, and jetted off toward the continent across the sea.

91

Two men in suits led Adam into a room with a single chair in it. One of these escorts was blond, the other an overweight elderly gentleman. Judging by their primped and clean business attire, both were relative newcomers to the surface.

Adam took a seat and asked, "Do either of you know what this is about?"

"We do not, sir," the blond man said as he and his cohort hung back in the doorway. "But the one-on-one video conference is channeling through now."

The wall to the left of the door began to glow, molding into a framed image of Dimitri Kucherov and Walter Stoddard behind the same desk they'd been sitting at the last time Adam had spoken with them. Both men were grinning in the most artificial of ways.

"Mr. Ballard," Walter said. "It's good to see you again."

"It's good to see you as well, sirs."

Dimitri tilted his head at the camera. "We don't have much time to chat, Adam, but we wanted to let you know that we have chosen a new leader for the Constructs unit."

"That's good to hear. We need somebody in charge down here. Everyone's been looking to me in the interval."

Dimitri nodded. "Yes, we noticed that as well, which only made our choice that much easier."

"You mean?" Adam brought his hand to his chest. "Me? I'm the new boss?"

"You are," Walter said. "Adam Ballard, after your exemplary service and able assistance in the field, the Directorate has unanimously selected you to serve as the new Captain of the Constructs. I don't want to hear any equivocation or false modesty. I simply want an answer. Do you accept the position or not?"

"I accept. Of course, I accept it. I'm honored to be selected."

A woman came into the frame and spoke into Walter's ear. He shook his head no and returned to the issue at hand.

"Dimitri has agreed to be your direct supervisor. The plan is to put you to work right away. Currently, however, the Directorate's schedule is being consumed by some Ranger trouble. Later in the day, we hope, you will be transported up to the *Horizon* for your first briefing. Do you have any questions before we leave you?"

"None that I can think of," Adam said. "But I would like to personally pass on my condolences on the loss of Mikhail. I got to know him a little down here. He was quite the man, sir."

"Thank you," Dimitri said. "Coming from you, that means so much. We'll speak more once you've come aboard."

The transmission faded and the two administrative types at the door congratulated Adam with an exuberant round of applause.

92

Florin groaned when she saw Derek waiting on the street corner. She walked outside anyway, and headed straight toward him.

"Hi," she said, her hand flipping above her waist in a disinterested half wave. "How are you?"

"I had a visitor this morning," Derek said. There was a surprising amount of anger in his voice.

"What's wrong?" Florin asked him. "Who stopped by?"

"Vladimir. I don't know what his last name is."

Florin almost laughed, but managed to compose herself. "You mean *my* Vlad?"

"Of course, *your* Vlad. He woke up my children."

"What did he want?"

Derek looked around to be sure there was no one else in the vicinity. "He told me the two of you had sex again last night, and I was to stay away from you from now on. The two of you, you had gotten back together."

"And you believed him? He and I are most definitely not back together. I thought we were actually in agreement on that for once."

"Be honest with me. Did you two have sex last night?"

"Yes. We had sex. We slept together. But that doesn't mean we're together in the way that he means we're together, you know?"

Derek's eyes narrowed. It took him a second to respond. "When I last saw you, you said you wanted to be alone."

"That's right. Then I changed my mind. Sorry."

"You're sorry?"

"Yeah, I'm sorry."

"Florin, you were so set on going back to my place last night. But because I didn't think we should be together like that while you were so exhausted, you shooed me away."

"That was not why I shooed you away."

"Then why did you?"

"Because I changed my mind about you. I don't want to see you anymore. The realization kind of just struck me. I knew you were never going to be able to handle my lifestyle, let alone my needs, so I backed out of our rendezvous and took the next best thing available. Like I said, I'm sorry."

"This is how you tell me that we're done?"

"I guess it is. It's not like I owe you anything. Sure, I've enjoyed what time we've spent together, but I refuse to put up with your silly jealousies, and your back and forth about when or if we're going to have sex. There's too much else going on in my life right now. I have to stay focused. Sooner or later, they *are* going to let me off this damn ship."

"Look," Derek said. "I get that you're frustrated. These are frustrating times. I just don't think I can handle a relationship that's so casual. I have my own needs, too."

"I know that you do. And to be blunt, I think what you're looking for is another marriage. As I stated right from the start, that's the last thing I'm looking for. This is why it's probably best if we just end things now before feelings get any stronger."

"And they could get stronger," he said. "At least they could on my end."

"Just so you know," Florin said, "I intend to murder Vlad. He should never have bothered you with his insane delusions. I cannot apologize enough. His behavior, it was way out of line."

"Forget it. It's water under the bridge."

"Not to me, it isn't. I want to throttle the guy."

"Is that where you're going now, to throttle him?"

"I wish, but I have to get to work. I won't be able to throttle the moron" until tomorrow—which is only going to make me angrier."

A lone pedestrian came strolling by, and the conversation fell silent.

"I suppose this is it then?" Derek said once the woman was out of earshot.

"We'll still see each other around. Down on Verdan, maybe?"

Florin grabbed his hand and kissed it. They shared an extended hug before Derek went one way, and Florin went the other.

93

Angela cleared out of the way as a three-man team of orderlies lifted Jason off the gurney and deposited him onto the bed. Angela thanked them all for their efforts and walked them out. When she returned, she found her husband with his eyes closed, apparently off in dreamland. She disappeared into the master bath and left Jason to his rest.

A few minutes later, Jason was calling out for her. "Where've you *gone?* Come back. *Come back.*"

Angela's hands were still wet when she stepped out of the bathroom. "What is it? What do you need?"

"I don't need anything. I was just wondering what you're going to be doing for the rest of the day. Are you going to leave me alone? Are you going back to work?"

"I wasn't planning to do either one. And I'm not scheduled to go back to work until after your Directorate hearing. Why are you asking?"

"No reason. I just wanted to thank you for taking such good care of me. I appreciate it. Especially after everything I've done."

"Let's not get into any of that," Angela said. "Not now at least."

She combed her hair back with her fingers and reentered the bathroom, her voice carrying. "My preference would be to play it nice for a few days, all right? We'll never be able to do that if we keep talking about you, me, and *her.*"

94

"Looks like I was wrong," Leo said as he was completing his advance on the sky-high impediment. "There are branches and vegetation mixed up inside there, but this sure isn't any forest."

"How would you describe it then?" Meyer asked.

"Are we back to this again? You can see the thing for yourself. That's why I brought a second set of eyes with me this time. I was getting tired of my own endless commentary."

The triadulation camera—that second set of eyes—was now traveling a few paces ahead of Leo. Then, just as it was about to collide with the ob-struction, the device began to rise upward. In addition to its dimensional capture, the camera was snapping off close-up stills of the pieces of refuse that hardened among the soup and dirt. The remains of dozens of different species of botanical growth protruded out in all manner of jagged forms and angles.

"I appreciate the attempt at forethought," Meyer said. "And although I can now see what you see, I still expect audio reporting from you. We have plenty of probe and reconnaissance footage. What we don't have a lot of is human accounting. This is why you need to keep speaking up. It's the only reason you've been allowed to remain out there. After all the mischief you've been making lately, you're lucky you haven't been transferred back to maintenance duty."

"Just so you're aware, doc, threats don't really work on—" At the bottom of the soup, Leo's boot landed awkwardly on an unseen rise of the plain and he stumbled.

"Careful," Meyer said. "As close as you are to that obstruction, you're probably not on flat soil any longer."

"Thanks…what would I do without you?"

Leo put his hand against the obstruction, steadying himself in its shadow.

"Shit. I really hate to second-guess myself, but I might've set out in the wrong direction. I'm not sure where to go anymore. I don't see a way through this thing, and to go around it could take hours, if not days."

Leo shifted his head to the west. The obstruction curved outward until it faded off into a distant speck. The view to the east was almost identical, like the flip side of an irregular crescent.

"Do you have an aerial view of how for this stretches out in either direction?" Leo asked.

"I'll have an answer for you in a moment. Your camera is at four hundred meters, about to reach the top. Hold on."

Leo removed his right glove and dragged the tip of his index finger over an extruded piece of foliage. There was a smooth, honey-colored coating over the branch, over all the branches.

"Okay," Meyer said as Leo kept poking and prodding the obstruction. "The mass in front of you is approximately a kilometer thick. From above, it appears to be a concoction of loose sediment and refuse that's been washed down from the mountains."

"Are you telling me there are mountains on the other side of this?"

"Correct. The range begins as a hill, most likely a continuation of the mudslide. But things grows taller a bit farther to the north."

"Have you been able to find away around this mess for me? Whichever direction I need to go. It doesn't matter to me."

"There's a coastline to the west. I can see it in the orbital reconnaissance. This valley you're investigating is part of a larger river network. You are in the lower portion of that, near a large inland cove that snakes out into the southern ocean. The mountain range to the north is the majority of the detail I can see. It also looks to have the highest vantage point. Cloud cover is blotting out most everything else."

"What's my quickest path to this mountain?"

"Up and over the mudslide. If you remain patient, I can have a skiff there for you in a couple of hours."

"Don't bother. I'm perfectly capable of climbing."

Leo grabbed onto the strongest looking branch and started scaling up the formation.

"Strength-wise, are you sure you're up for this?" Meyer asked. "No one wants to see you fall."

"I know a couple of people who just might. But if I do end up falling, it'll be something coming loose that does me in. It sure as heck won't be my ability to climb a piece of moon trash."

95

"I'm here," Mary said. "What is it that you want? Thanks to you, I'm a busy woman."

Dimitri smiled at that and motioned her over to the dining room table where he was seated. There was an a place setting in front of him, and another set up to his right. The crockware set in the center of the table had been filled with some sort of specially prepared meal.

"I was hoping we could have dinner," Dimitri said. "I miss you, and I don't like how we left things."

Mary just stood there like a statue in the entryway.

"Aren't you going to say anything?"

"What do you want me to say, Dad?"

"Honestly, Mary, I don't care what you say. I just want to spend time with you. You're all I have left now."

"But that's the thing, you are not all that I have. There are plenty of people in my life. So sorry, I've already made dinner plans, and they don't include you."

Dimitri shook out his napkin. "There is no need to be rude to me. What is wrong with you?"

"There's nothing wrong with me, and there was nothing wrong with Mikhail. Now who does that leave as the party who has been wronging others?"

"Are you referring to me?"

"Yes, Father, I'm referring to you. It's always about you, making your children feel subordinate, as if we had no say or control over our lives. And don't deny it either, it's the truth. You're doing it even now as you try to trick me into having dinner with you. Just because you gave up your entire life for this overgrown playpen you've created, that has somehow morphed into your family giving their lives up as well. I have to tell you, what that did to Mikhail enrages me. It makes me hate you more than I ever thought it was possible to hate another person. You are a bully, and your personal desire to manhandle every nuance of the expedition has gotten your son killed. These are the facts. I'm supposing nothing. Mikhail was only down in that twisted place because *you* demanded he be. It wasn't because he had any aptitude for it. It was because you wanted it. And if I hadn't been such a physical weakling, I'd have been right down there beside him. Then you would've had two dead children, and you still wouldn't have cared."

Dimitri laid his hands on the edge of the table. "Think what you will of me, but I am just as affected by Mikhail's death as you are. I loved that boy beyond my ability to communicate.

"Is that so? You sure didn't love him enough to not throw Jocelyn into stasis. I think the worst of you because you've done the worst. In the last days of his life you tortured your son psychologically, all on account of the supposed importance of one child's birth. And then you send him down into an unknown alien ecosystem, putting him at enormous risk. If that's caring about a loved one, then I must despise my own children."

"Mary…Mikhail's death was a matter of happenstance. A sad accident, a stroke of terrible luck."

"I'm not so sure that it was, Dad. The truth, I think, had far more to do with his state of mind—a state of mind you put him in. Before he left, he was not all there, as you well know. He was sad and depressed, and thinking about things he should not have been thinking about."

"Point taken. And I am more than willing to listen to whatever you have to say, but can you please be sitting down while you do it?" Dimitri used his forefinger to draw her over. "Stop hovering there. Come sit at the table."

Mary shook her head. "I can talk just fine from here."

"Yes, my dear, but I can only strain my neck looking up at you for so long. I am a hundred and twenty years old. If I'm going to be chastised and accused, the least the outraged party can do is to sit and share a meal with me."

Reluctantly, Mary made her way over to the table and slipped into one of the seats with no place setting in front of it.

"I'm not hungry," she said. "And you can't make me eat. You can't make me do anything I don't want to do anymore."

"That should be obvious to all." Dimitri reached across his plate and removed the cover from the mashed potato pot. "You don't have to eat, but you will listen to what I have to say."

He dished up his potatoes and sliced turkey. Mary was bristling as he took his sweet time. Eventually, once his plate was full up, he spoke.

"Mikhail's death has been like a cudgel to my brain. I have felt everything you have accused me of and more. I did manipulate his prominence in the Rangers so he could be the first person out of the ship. I am to blame. And for whatever time I have left to live, I must find a way to deal with my guilt. But what I cannot tolerate is that you are blaming yourself as well as me. Do not deny it. This is why you are so angry with me. And this is why you walled yourself up after his death. In your own way, you sided with me on the issue of Jocelyn, and you and Mikhail never made up over that, or at least this is how I understand the situation. I put you in an awkward position, and I robbed you of your last year with your brother. Therefore, as long as you wish for this divide between us to continue, I will absorb any wrath you wish to hurl. I can take it, Mary. As you've said, and as I have now acknowledged, I am at fault. If not when Mikhail was selected to be a Ranger, then it stretches back to the moment I maneuvered to have myself put on this voyage, against the wishes of every person that I knew. One way or another, I am to blame. Nothing you say or accuse me of is ever going to change the way I feel about you. Mikhail said worse, and I still loved him. Even now, as I look at you holding me in such low esteem, I have never loved you more." He scooped up a bite of potatoes, and held it in front of his mouth. "So have at me. Do your worst...tear me to shreds."

Dimitri was swallowing his first bite when Mary shot up from the table, rattling the dinnerware and nearly tipping over the empty wine glass to her right.

"You do this to me every time," she said. "You keep talking and filibustering until I don't even know what I'm mad about anymore."

"You are mad because of Mikhail's death, my bullying, and I suppose our old struggle with Leonid may have something to do with it as well. This is the way I see things, from your perspective. This is why I would be angry at myself."

Mary's head dropped. "I can't do this right now. I will not let you calm me down. I refuse to be manipulated again."

"No one is trying to manipulate you."

"Like hell you aren't."

Mary marched out of the dining room. A second later, the front door closed behind her.

Dimitri took a second bite, and then a third, remaining right where he was until his plate had been cleared.

Day Seven

96

Meyer came back online and said, "Your twenty-seven hours have been extended. Word just came down from the higher-ups. You're going to be left on your own for a little while longer. Which means, once you're feeling refreshed and rejuvenated, you're safe to push onward again."

"Well, that was awfully kind of them to grant me an extension. On the other hand, they wouldn't have been able to find me either way. I promise you, right now, I'm well out of reach."

Leo's voice was echoing as he scaled up the last few meters of a spiked mountaintop—out of breath and sweating, careful with every handhold and foothold that he made.

"Where exactly are you?" Meyer asked. "The camera is still out on a forward scout. I can't see much from orbit either."

"I find that surprising, actually. I thought I'd be pretty easy to see from up there. Look again. I'm at the top of the tallest peak. The next time a cloud moves by, I'll wave."

It took a few seconds before Meyer responded. "You slimy, duplicitous lout."

Leo laughed. "What was that, doc? I couldn't hear you."

"I thought you sounded winded. You were supposed to be resting—*that* is what we agreed to. You would find a nice piece of shade and go to sleep under it. That was the only reason I slept myself. What happened to the plan?"

"I ignored it. I saw this rather svelte-looking mountain beckoning me and thought, why not? Can you blame me? I believed I was running out of time and should get as high as possible as soon as possible. I didn't know my twenty-seven hours were about to be extended. Thank you for that, by the way."

"You do realize that your body is going to break down if you keep trekking on with no rest. Have you at least eaten?"

"Three hours ago. I wolfed down two packs of freeze-dried protein mush. My tummy is good and full. Your concern is appreciated."

Leo secured his hand on a rock formation and gazed below. A spoon-shaped body of water lay at the base of an outlying hilltop. North of the waterway was a succession of similarly spikey peaks, like giant stone droplets treading downward. From there, the base of the mountain range opened out into a small stretch of land, a kilometer in diameter at its narrowest, and positioned aside a still green coastline. Even from such an elevated viewpoint, there was no soup in sight.

"Camera, descend," Leo said. "Direction, east."

Six klicks away, the camera made a sharp nosedive in the direction of the cove.

"What did you see?" Meyer asked him.

"I'm not entirely sure, but it might be dry land."

97

Dimitri and Walter were settling in to their assigned seats, the first two Trustees to arrive for a morning meeting on the discovery of a potential build site.

"I think I've figured it out," Walter said. "I know what we need to do. It just hit me like a damned lightning bolt. I know how we can honor Mikhail. It couldn't be any more perfect."

Dimitri turned to him. "You have my attention…tell me."

"It's this council. We need to establish a permanent seat at this table where a member of your family will always have a public voice. We can call it the Kucherov seat. Interesting, isn't it? One of your offspring permanently embedded as a part of this council, without the endless hassle of alphanumeric election zones."

"Where did this idea come from?" Dimitri asked. "I'd like to know. Is it related in any way to Mary's intransigence?"

"Actually, I'm not sure where it originates. I was conversing with Rebecca the other day, and we discussed the importance of Mikhail's loss, and what we should be doing about it. So I don't believe it has anything to do with Mary. Although, taking this idea to its logical conclusion, it would lock her into service and stop whatever drifting away she's doing at the moment. But is it directly connected to her tantrum? I don't think so. This is larger than that. For years you've been concerned about your kids not living up to your compact with this government. This could be an insurance policy toward that, a method to make certain your legacy, your bloodline, it never leaves this room."

Dimitri leaned back in his chair. "You're right. 'Interesting' is the right word for it. The only difficulty being, with Mikhail's death, my family's lineage has become severely thinned."

"Thinned maybe, but not decimated. There's still Mary and her children—and Mikhail's little girl. As it stands, hope can feel like a distant memory, but I say it still lies with your family, like it has since the beginning."

"I won't be here forever, that is true."

"None of us will be. That's the painful truth we've had to relearn these last few days. There is no permanence, there is only the law. 'It is within the law where we find hard, solid rules to live our lives by.' You said that, not me."

"You do realize, that's the umpteenth time you've thrown that quote in my face."

"And I promise to do it umpteen more. Stop making me stew, should I move ahead with this or not?"

Dimitri nodded. "The concept has merit. Put something more formalized together for me, and I'll take a closer look at it."

"I'll get right on it," Walter said.

"Whatever else you do, don't call it the Kucherov seat. That has a tacky sound to it. The naming of something is the first lap in its race to success. Solve that problem, and I'll give you my full support. How could I not?"

98

Florin came storming onto the plaza. "You have interfered in my life for the last damn time."

Vladimir was on the grass with Jance, kicking around an old, beat-up volleyball.

"Pay attention to me, idiot—I'm *talking* to *you!*"

Florin's voice had gotten so loud windows were lightening all along the adjacent housing units.

Vladimir booted the ball to an amused Jance before taking the steps necessary to meet Florin halfway.

"Ream me out all you want," Vladimir said, "but could you please stop with all the shouting."

Florin stomped her foot on the lawn. "I will speak in whatever manner I wish, and you know you can't stop me."

"No one wants to stop you. We'd just prefer it if you used your inside voice when doing so."

"Volume is *irrelevant*," she said, much louder than before.

Jance was drifting closer to the argument, the ball spinning in his hand.

"I already know what you're pissed about," Vladimir said. "You're mad I confronted your teacher friend yesterday. I'm sorry about that, but it needed to be done. There were things about the two of us that had to be made clear."

Florin got right in his face. "*Nothing* needed to be made clear. You and

I are *done*. And now, he and I are done as well. We are *all* done. Do you grasp that? Are you capable of grasping anything that I say?"

"I grasp actions, not words. And despite what you always say, you keep coming back to me. You can't even go a week without climbing into bed with me. Admit it, you want me as much as I want you."

"Not anymore, I don't. Our 'fun time' is over, you twit. Stay out of my life or suffer the consequences. We are no longer friends. We are no longer *anything*."

Jance came up beside Vladimir and tossed him the ball.

Florin glowered at them both, and then headed back the way she had come, her voice still booming. "I don't want to talk to you *ever* again, you got that? And no sleeping together again either. It's not going to happen—not ever, *ever* again.

99

Cheers rang out as the call came through ordering workers to cease all construction activity around Echo Base. A potential settlement spot had been located, and the process to confirm its viability was underway. Until further notice, no more effort was to be made to complete the base camp, or its sister site, the original spire landing field.

In a crane high above the control tower framework, Adam was working alongside his newly assigned liaison, the youthful and frizzy-haired Natalya Hardy.

"I should probably say something, shouldn't I?" Adam pressed beneath his ear. "This is Captain Ballard. You all just heard what the good people in the sky had to say. Everyone can now officially relax until tomorrow morning at the earliest. I'll get back to you on the possibility of furlough trips to the *Horizon*, but I doubt that's something that's going to be approved. Also, whatever else you do, please do not wander outside the demarcated safety zones. And for good measure, remain on a platform at all times. It's good practice from now on out. We don't want anyone else getting hurt. In other words, I beg of you, please behave."

He double tapped his ear and brought the crane in for a landing.

"All this work. It's sort of disappointing," Natalya said. "But I guess a delay is better than continuing to build something we will never use. Besides, the downtime will give you an opportunity to enjoy your surprise."

"What surprise?" Adam set the crane down atop the bright yellow bullseye engraved in the center of the landing pad. The craft kicked slightly as the thrusters were dialed back to zero.

"Don't ignore me," he said. "What surprise? You can't just leave me hanging like that."

Natalya crouched down and retrieved her knapsack from the forward storage compartment. "I screwed up. I wasn't supposed to tell you about any of this. But since I accidentally did so, I will let you know there was a special someone waiting for you while you were being briefed on the *Horizon* yesterday. There wasn't enough time for you to see this person then, but I do know they were quite anxious to catch up. You knew this person on Earth, apparently, and a reunion is imminent. How imminent, I do not know."

Adam slumped back against the flight controls. "Aren't you at least going to give me a name? Who is this person?"

"Sorry. I can't divulge. I've been sworn to secrecy." Natalya swung her knapsack ahead of her and strolled off the crane. "You'll find out for yourself soon enough anyway. It's someone important to you, though, I think."

Adam called out, "Leave me hanging, why don't you?"

100

"After all that, you just walked out on him?"

Mary handed Courtney the glass of apple juice she'd requested. Courtney mouthed the words 'thank you' and Mary shuffled to the right with the wine she had poured for herself, joining her friend on the family room sofa. Their children, all five of them, were upstairs napping.

"I think I should probably backtrack a smidge," Mary said as she straightened the front of her untucked blouse. "I did walk out, but only after I had let him have his say. And that, as ever, is what set me off."

Courtney took a sip of her juice and said, "He was swaying you to his side again, wasn't he?"

"Yes, and I didn't even see it happening. One minute I'm lobbing the truth at him, and the next I'm sympathizing with the jerk. I had to get out of there right away. If I didn't, it would have been the same old thing that always happens between us, I forgive him and let things go back to normal until the next time he does something cold-hearted and insensitive. After what happened to Mikhail, I've vowed to never go through that again."

"I see," Courtney said. "Terrific. Do what you need to do."

Mary's head cocked. "Oh my goodness, that tone in your voice. You disagree with me. You do, don't you?"

"What do you mean?"

"You're not looking at me, Courtney. What did I say that was so wrong?"

"You didn't say anything wrong."

"But."

"There is no but."

"I don't believe you. And because of that, let me be clear—these last couple of days, something has changed in me. The man may be my father, but I cannot stand the sight of him. I understand now that I should've separated myself from him a long time ago. Definitely when he locked up Jocelyn, but maybe even when he broke Leo and me up, or any other time he's tried to control me. This decision that I've come to, it hasn't even been that difficult. My father is a now a past-tense part of my life, and that's that."

Courtney broke eye contact with Mary and set her glass down on the coffee table.

"Just say it, Courtney. Whatever's on your mind, just say it."

"Oh, believe me, I intend to." Courtney settled back into the seat cushions "First of all, I want you to do whatever makes you happiest. That said, you also need to think things through before you do or say something you cannot take back. Tell me, why do you think you've never allowed a separation like this to happen before?"

"Because I'm weak. Because he could die at any second."

"That's it," Courtney said. "That's exactly why you capitulate."

"Because I'm weak?"

"No. Because you realize that he's old, and he's not going to be with us much longer. And because of that, you've put up with his nonsense, far longer than you should have."

Mary nodded. "I think about it all the time. It's going to happen sooner rather than later. He doesn't let people see how sick he's become. He's not doing well at all. I'm surprised he's lasted this long."

Courtney put her hand on Mary's thigh and a pop of static electricity caused them both to jump.

"Sorry about that," Courtney said. For a second or two, she was struggling not to laugh. "Listen to me, I love that you're finally standing your ground, but I also think you've done the right thing over the years. And you certainly have not been weak about it. At Dimitri's age, death is always going to be right around the corner. If I have any disagreements with you at all at the moment, maybe it has to do with the fact that now might not be the right time to punish him for what I admit are his many, many sins. And this isn't a suggestion to make him feel better either. After all the horror stories you've told me over the years, I can never look at the man and worship him the way my father does. But it's you I'm concerned about here, not Dimitri. You're the one who has to live on after he has gone. Maybe it would behoove you to let the anger go and be the well-meaning daughter again. I'll worry about you if you don't. Neither of us liked what became of Mikhail after he locked your father out. And right now, I'm seeing the same thing happening to you, and it concerns me. You're not an angry person, Mary, but you're becoming one. I don't want that to be your permanent state."

"I don't want that either," she said.

"Then drop it. Rail against him with Jocelyn and me, and to anyone else. But with him, I think you need to let it go—because you're not going to change him, but he *could* change you."

Mary slid closer to her and kissed her. With the children in the house, this was not something they usually dared.

"You're right," Mary said once they'd parted. "Next time I see him I'll be pleasant with him, and I'll be doing it for myself."

They kissed again.

Courtney smiled. "Do you want to hear something funny? Speaking of fathers, mine paid me a visit this afternoon. He was inquiring semi-politely on the health of Jocelyn and the baby. He wanted to be assured that all is well—*blah, blah*. But just as the conversation was ending, he sprung his true intention on me. Not very subtly, he brought up the intriguing little fact that nobody has brought Baby Tana by to see Dimitri yet. He did his best to act like it was no serious matter, but I got the hint, he wanted me to pass the suggestion on to Jocelyn."

Mary finished off her wine in one long gulp. "Why can't either one of those men make a request without being underhanded? Maybe they wouldn't annoy us so much if they did."

"Believe me, sister, you're preaching to the choir. I could not agree more."

"So what did you end up telling him?"

"Nothing. I acted like I didn't hear him. I may think it's in your best interest to forgive your father, but I don't see it that way for Jocelyn. That is a decision she needs to make on her own."

"The night he died," Mary said. "Mikhail told Dad he never wanted him to see the baby. He said he would make it his life's work to keep the child far away from him or anyone else involved in Jocelyn's imprisonment. The way he said it, it came out with such venom."

"Then Jocelyn should know that. Tell her what he said, and also tell her what Dimitri wants."

"I will." Mary balanced her glass on her knee, tilting it toward Courtney. "Are you sure you wouldn't like something stronger? You've barely had any of your juice."

"I can't." Courtney's eyes were twinkling. "I hate springing stuff like this on you, but I've been waiting for the right moment to tell you." She popped her lips. "Alcohol's out of the question. I'm pregnant, about four weeks along. I kept it to myself because of everything that's been going on. I also had to tell Bailey first, which I did, the night of the landing."

"Is he as happy as you seem to be?"

"Oh, yeah. He and my father are already conspiring on baby names. It's a boy, if I didn't say so earlier."

"You didn't. What names do they like?"

"You're not going to believe it."

"Well, the way you just said that, my first thought would be Mikhail."

"That wasn't it, but I like that. That's a very good idea."

"What names do they like?"

Courtney cringed. "Both Dad and Bailey, they think we should call him Dimitri."

101

The sediment came apart in gooey clumps.

"There's definitely some dampness here," Leo said as he dug his fingers deep into the ground. "It feels solid enough, though."

His field partner, the camera, was flying ahead of him, skimming above the yellow-leaved forest that lined the location's semi-circle perimeter, from the coastline to the west to the mountainside in the north.

Leo stood up and brushed the traces of dark brown dirt from his gloves.

"The mini-delta here might pose a problem. It's a part of that larger river network you were describing back at the mudslide. I was following this particular branch when I was making my way down the mountain. This is where it ends. The run-off dumps straight into the cove."

Leo set off and walked along these shallow streams, none of which could be classified as anything more than a brook.

"If we continue to hold firm on the idea of not damaging the landscape, I assume we can always build around these things."

He cut left and stepped into one of the streams, and then back onto the soil.

"This entire area," Meyer said. "It doesn't make a lick of sense. I've been going over the aerial footage—most of which was shot a day and a half ago—and I can see the river drainage, but there is no trace of any open glade. There's just forest and muck, like everywhere else on the moon. This whole cove, it looked nothing like it does now."

Leo increased his stride as he moved out across the flatland.

"I hear what you're saying, Meyer, but this place is way too perfect. There's no give anywhere, no matter where I walk—and I've strolled quite a ways away from the shore. The size is about right, too. The tree line to the east is at least two klicks away. Despite your quite valid concerns, I think we've found what we've been looking for."

"It seems that way to me as well, and I'm thrilled. But this footage I was referring to, what does it say about this area? What does it say about the permanence of this whole world?"

"I'm the wrong person to ask, I guess. But this is without a doubt a location where we can begin construction, no hover platforms required. I'm not sure unanswered questions are going to matter all that much to the Directorate, not while they're still so desperate to find someplace to settle."

"You're right," Meyer said. "And what do I know? I'm only a deliberate man of science."

Leo was approaching the center of the clearing when he stopped suddenly and plopped down in the mud. "Sorry to push you, my friend, but I'd say the time has come for you to make the call. Tell them that everything checks out, at least on a cursory basis."

"I will," Meyer said. "Once the cove has been dragged. We can't take a chance there's anything in there like that creature that killed Mikhail. The soil has to be tested as well. The surrounding foliage, that also needs to be analyzed."

"Well, while you're busy organizing that mess, I think I'm going to get some rest." Leo angled his body toward the tranquil waterway and stretched out his legs. "I'm officially passing out now."

"A skiff is on its way. It should be there within the hour."

"No hurry," Leo said, his eyelids drooping. "I'm fine where I am."

Four Days Later

102

The Echograd fabrication quad had just enough space in it for one small meeting room. As he had done every other morning since construction on the miracle site began, Adam Ballard had called together his seven division supervisors to share the progress each group had made over the course of the previous day. The second-to-last person he called upon was Christina Roth, his fellow *Vanguard* Construct. Christina was in charge of equipment operation and maintenance. She had nothing but high marks for the new pieces of hardware that had been shipped down from the *Horizon*. They were far more advanced than the tools the Constructs had brought with them, which everyone present agreed, made perfect sense. The *Horizon*'s big-rig devices had only recently been manufactured, while the Constructs' equipment was now almost a century old.

Christina completed her short presentation and Adam went to one of his other landing companions, Robert Granger. Robert had been back at work for two full days, but his replaced right arm was still bonding in a green stimulus sling.

"The barricades are now fully installed," Robert reported to the group. "They run around the perimeter of the site in a circle, extending well out into the cove."

"How deep were you able to get into the water?" Adam asked.

"All the way. The charge lines were nested directly into the silt. The system is super extensive. And according to all our tests, utterly impenetrable."

"Okay, so that'll keep us safe from whatever's in the water," Christina said. "But what about the air? What about anything that comes up from underground?"

"The naturalists are working with their technology counterparts on the underground possibilities. With the animal flyovers, one of the biologists has come up with a clever deterrent. It still has to be engineered and built, but when it's done, charged voltric particles will shoot into the sky whenever a foreign object approaches. Like the fencing, the charge is low-grade. The smarter people among us seem to believe it'll act as a rather insistent repellent."

"If only we had a couple of these smart people along when we first landed on this rock," Adam said.

Christina whistled out her agreement.

Everyone laughed except for a shy gentleman seated at the corner of the table. Adam looked over at him.

"Lest I forget, we have a newcomer to our little soirée. My friends, this here is Vladimir Rossonov. He's *uh*—what's your official title, Vlad?"

"It doesn't matter," the young man said. "I'm an apprentice to Alan Patterson, the city architect. He had a long-standing engagement on the *Horizon* tonight, so I'm here in his place."

"Do you have anything to update us on?"

"I do. Alan wanted me to tell you that the framing for the capitol building is ready to go up. After the temporary housing units are installed on the outskirts, he suggests we get a leg up on some of the larger pieces of infrastructure."

Adam made a note on his deskpad. "So much good news."

"So much I'm not even certain we're on Verdan anymore," Robert said. "Assure me, everyone. We are still on Verdan, correct?"

Adam grinned and made an additional note about the framing. "All right, if nothing else is pressing, how about we move on? Breakfast is being served in the mess. Last one there gets saddled with cleanup duty."

The supervisors sprang from their chairs and scattered. Soon, only Vladimir and Adam were left in the room.

Adam gestured at the door. "Better get a move on, kid. I walk slow, but not that slow. I don't care about being last, but I'm not going to make it easy for you either."

103

To keep himself upright, Dimitri had chosen to speak to his colleagues from behind a podium. It had been a last minute decision, and unusual sight in the normally table-dominated arena of the Directorate's conference room.

"I am presenting this amendment to you myself," Dimitri said. "But for transparency's sake, all creative credit for this proposal belongs to the man at my right. What Walter has come up with here is a wonder of original thinking."

Dimitri held his hand out at Walter, shifting the room's attention to the humbled Magistrate.

"As you all must now be aware, this matter pertains to my family, and to my family's future place in this government."

Dimitri cleared his throat, and began the written portion of his presentation.

"The amendment, if so passed, will hereby establish a new seat on the Directorate—a Ninth Seat. This seat shall not be elected, but inherited, held in perpetuity by the firstborn member of the Kucherov family. This individual shall be compelled to take office upon their twenty-first birthday, holding said position until their death, or until the next heir reaches the age of ascension."

Dimitri stopped there and went off script. "I freely admit, I have my reservations about this amendment. The idea of rooting a monarchy inside a government designed to be run by the will of the people concerns me. But Walter, he insists that this Ninth Seat is not in and of itself monarchical. It is merely an opportunity for the Kucherov voice to remain forever in account. An individual vote does not equate a crown, he has told me. And for the most part, I concur. Our charter was structured so no one person could ever lord over us. Because of early and sound legal underpinning, it would be impossible to do so. One vote will always remain one vote. And this is all the Ninth Seat holder will be given. This is why I insisted that the bearer of this gift of birth may only become Magistrate by his or her own election. This ironclad provision is the only reason I could feel comfortable making this proposal to you. I want to go into my good night knowing the Collective will have no kings nor queens, although it might have my blood. I have to be completely honest with you, the idea of that touches me."

He paused for a moment, and then released his grip on the podium.

"I present to you the Ninth Seat Amendment. I myself will of course defer. I suggest the seven of you vote your conscience, although I would expect nothing less. You and all the others who have served before you have made my life eternally proud."

Dimitri backed slowly away from the podium as Walter slipped in front of him.

"I open the floor to arguments," the Magistrate said.

Jonas Vickery was the first to hold up his hand.

"Jonas," Walter said. "What do you have to say on the matter?"

"Nothing. I have no argument. I held up my arm to vote, a big passionate yes. A vote for Mikhail."

Other arms went up, all around the table, each in support of the amendment, and for Dimitri's martyred son.

Walter held up his own hand and glanced over at Dimitri, who remained as stoic as ever.

Pounding his gavel, Walter made it official. "With no arguments or contentions to the country, and by unanimous vote, the Ninth Seat amendment is hereby passed. Long live the Kucherovs."

The entire Directorate repeated the cheer. *"Long live the Kucherovs."*

104

"We need to talk," Tristan said.

Florin finished rinsing off her plate and deposited it into the sink. A second later, without warning, she shoved her pajama-wearing brother aside and tore out of the kitchen.

"Don't you run from me," Tristan said, already in hot pursuit.

They darted through the living room and vaulted up the stairs. Florin only hit the brakes once she'd reached her bedroom door.

"You can't come in here, remember? Mom and Dad said you're supposed to stay out, you loser."

Florin took a careful step backward and the door behind her opened. She held out her arms to bar the entrance as best she could.

"You have no idea how ridiculous you're being," Tristan said between labored breaths. The chase had winded him. "Mom and Dad...they're the ones who told me to talk to you. Someone heard about what you've been up to, and the whole family has freaked out."

Florin's eyes widened. "What did they hear?"

"Stuff about men, lots and lots of men. Apparently, you've been sleeping with that teacher guy while you were also sleeping with Vladimir Rossonov. There are rumors about other guys as well. I've been told to tell you that there are too many men in your life. You need to pick one and be done with it. You're getting a reputation, whether you realize it or not."

"How dare any of you?" Florin dropped her arms to her side. "I'm mortified."

"Don't get all dramatic. We're worried about you. We don't want you to embarrass yourself, or the family."

"Mor-*ti*-fied," Florin said enunciating each and every syllable as she whirled around and stomped into her room.

Tristan was left standing in the doorway. "Do I have your permission to enter? It's going be difficult to talk to you from all the way out here."

"Then come inside. Don't be stupid."

Florin had sat down on the wooden hope chest that was positioned in front of her bed. Tristan took the sliver of space beside her.

"I'm warning you," Florin said. "This is my private life. I don't care what *any* of you think."

"Well, you should probably care what the public at large thinks. If you don't, your political career is going to be over before it ever even started. We've heard more rumors about you in the last few days than you could possibly imagine. That's not good. You don't want people thinking of you like that if you're planning on asking them for their vote one day."

Florin brought her knees together and huffed. "Be straight with me then. Who is saying what to whom? If you're going to meddle in my life, I demand you be specific about it."

"It all started with Grandma Laken and Kimberly. That should tell you how far afield this has gone."

Florin buried her face in her hands.

"Now you're getting it," Tristan said.

"This is so unfair. It's nobody's business."

"Rightly or wrongly, it's now become everyone's business. Grandma and Kimberly got word of it from one of their friends. You know how gossipy those old biddies are. They said you were in the plaza a couple of days ago yelling at Vladimir Rossonov under Gracie Bingham's window. She heard what you said to him, and then what he said to his friend after you had gone. What came out on both ends was not flattering to either one of you."

"I'm never going to be able to look any of you in the eyes again," Florin said, her face still hidden. "Vlad could have said anything."

"He said you've been having sex with multiple partners. He spouted off a fairly long list, too. He was cursing every name."

"I hate him so much. He's such a wormy little cretin."

"For my part, sis, when it comes to your sex life, I could care less about what or who you do. I don't think anyone would care, at least not anyone inside the family. But if you're going to do something that's so out of the norm, then you need to do it discreetly. If you don't want to be with just one man, no one will care as long as you're smart enough not to flaunt it. You know how the world works. People don't want to be faced with things like this. If a certain kind of behavior stays hidden, then fine and dandy. If it doesn't, then our parents come to me and the two of us need to have a stupid, embarrassing talk." He slipped his arm around her shoulder. "In other words, I don't ever want to have to do this again."

Florin drew her hands from her face. "Like I do?"

Tristan gave her a squeeze. "I hope you know that we can talk about anything. Yeah, we fight a lot, but if something in your life has become a problem, you have to know I'll be there for you."

Florin shook her head. "It's nothing that I need to talk about. It's just been a crazy few months. Vlad has been driving me nuts. He wants us to get married, and the more I refuse him, the more *he* refuses to listen. He thinks we're meant to be together or something."

"Then he's as stupid as he is wrong. The kid's a dweeb. He's in no way the right man for someone like you. You have Holt and Merriweather blood running through you. You have potential. He does not."

"Well, thankfully, I never stated that in quite such an obnoxious way, but I have let him know that I have no intention of marrying him. He even leaves me be sometimes. But then he and I—"

"You and he what?"

"The two of us, we click. That's probably the best way to say it. We're extremely compatible, in *that* way."

"I see. Is being compatible important to you?"

"I don't know. Isn't it important with you and Beth?"

"We're not talking about me and Beth. And least we're not supposed to be talking about me and Beth."

Florin peered up at him. "It's no fun when someone pries into your love life, is it?"

Tristan dragged his arm away and said, "Moving on, if you were serious about what you were saying, you don't like Vladimir, except for the compatibility part. What about these other men you're seeing? What about that teacher guy? You seemed sort of entranced with him at the arrival party. What's happening there?"

"Nothing. It started and it's over. He was looking for a wife and the last thing I'm looking for is a husband."

"That's okay," Tristan said. "You have time."

"Yeah, but what if I never want to get married? Is that *really* going to be okay? I'm not sure that it is. Everyone I know is so gung-ho about that stuff. It's like they can't wait to lock their lives into place."

"I suppose one's attitude on the subject depends on what one wants out of life. You go around telling everyone who will listen you want a political career. If that path continues, you *will* to have to get married sometime. There's no real choice in the matter. It's just part of the deal. Marriage and politics go hand in hand."

Florin buried her face again. "Can we please stop talking about this? *All* of this?"

"Sure, as long as you promise to keep your escapades to a minimum. None of us wants to see anything bad happen to you. Look at what's going on with Jason Epelle. He's going to lose his job because he's been sleeping around."

"That's because the idiot is married. His problems are legal. Me, I'm just your run-of-the-mill slut."

"Don't talk that way."

"Hey, you just called me everything but that, big guy. I just cut the chase and said what you and everyone else have been thinking. Oh, and make sure you tell Mom and Dad I got the message loud and clear. It's too bad they were too cowardly to talk to me about this themselves."

"You know how they are." Tristan said.

"Yeah, gutless." Florin put her hand on the corner of the chest and launched herself toward the vanity. "You need to leave now. I have to get ready for work."

Tristan stood up. "There's one other thing. Kimberly wanted me to remind you about the trip to the surface she's planning for the thirteenth. She wants all of us to be there for her. It's this colossal, emotional thing for her. We all need to make an effort. You, in particular, need to make an effort."

"I already told her I didn't want to go," Florin said as she squared herself in front of the mirror.

"Why would you do such a thing?" Tristan said. "What's the problem?"

"It's going to be the first time I'm going to be allowed down to the surface. It's not how I planned things. It'll be anti-climactic. I don't get to go down there to be in charge, I get to go down there because my family has a lot of pull. It's not at all what I was hoping for."

"What were you hoping for?"

"I don't know, something exciting?"

"You, the girl with far too many boyfriends, you're looking for excitement on a construction site? I hate to tell you, sis, you were bound to be disappointed. Or then again, maybe not."

Florin started combing her hair. "You're a pig. Leave now."

"I'm going, but you *are* planning on being there for Kimmie, right?"

"It's not like I have any other choice. This is too important to her."

Florin met Tristan's eyes in the mirror.

"What are you doing still standing there? Get out of here, weirdo. I need to get dressed."

105

There was a single empty seat on the Directorate side of the adjudication table. On the public half, just across the center split, sat Jason Trevitt Epelle, the day's accused. To his left were his sisters Jocelyn and Joy, and his father, Richard Epelle. To Jason's right was the missing Trustee, and the session's designated defender, Elisabeth Epelle. On the other side of Elisabeth sat the wife of the accused, Angela Gabrielle Rosso, legal victim of his crimes.

"The evidence has now been read and inserted into the record," Walter said. "We shall now turn to the defense. Trustee Epelle, you have the floor."

Elisabeth rose. Unlike her colleagues on the council, she was not dressed in her formal white and green robes. In lieu of that, she wore a pantsuit, colored dark gray and cut short on the hips. Jason, again able to walk under his own power, was wearing a black suit and tie. Those present in support of his cause had come outfitted in similar fineries.

"If it pleases the Directorate," Elisabeth said. "The defendant has chosen to accept the facts as entered and wishes to address the council to show penance for his actions. Is this path forward acceptable?"

Walter eyed the row of Trustees on either side of him. All were nodding.

"It is," he told Elisabeth.

"Then I will let my son speak." Elisabeth sat down as Jason stood up.

The defendant pressed his suit jacket closed, smoothed it, and began his remarks. "I wronged my wife. Before I say anything else, I want to state this as emphatically as I can. In doing what I did, I also broke important Collective laws. But the law breaking is not what has shamed me to my core. It's what I have done to my family, *that* is what makes me a true criminal. Angela has been nothing but good to me, and in a moment of weakness—"

Elisabeth whispered something to him.

"My mother is correct... *moments.* In moments of weakness, I betrayed someone I care deeply about, and that is what I think is the real issue at hand. Accordingly, acting upon that indignity, I wish to accept all punishments coming to me. In turn, I humbly request that this matter be kept from becoming any more public than it already has. I do not ask this for myself, I ask it for my wife and my children, both born and unborn, to spare them any additional undo embarrassment. I beg you to consider my plea, and my absolute shame. I do not deserve the clemency I'm asking for, but I ask for it anyway. In the future, I will do everything possible to make myself a better man."

Jason bowed, and returned to his seat.

"All right," Walter said, looking directly at Elisabeth. "Does the defense have anything else to present?"

"We do not."

"Then we can take this matter to a vote."

Before anything else could be said or done, an arm was raised.

"Am I allowed to make a statement?" Angela asked.

"Of course," Walter said. "If you wish to."

"Punish Jason all you want. I don't care. And if you choose not to make this public, I would be okay with that as we'll. But really, I don't care about any of that either. Enough people know already, and I've survived. And my son, he is young and will forget, as will everyone else. But what I am asking of you now is something my husband has no idea about. I never brought it up with him because I'm no longer interested in what he thinks. He cheated on me with impunity, so why would he deserve any say in our marriage?"

"What is it that you want from us, Mrs. Epelle?"

"I want this marriage dissolved. I want it over, effective immediately. I don't want to be Mrs. Jason Epelle anymore—and I don't want to him living under my roof. He should have visitation rights to Jerald and the unborn son inside me, but I don't want him to be my partner any longer, and I don't care who knows."

Elisabeth took her daughter-in-law by the hand.

Walter asked, "Does the defense have any reason to argue against this request?"

"It does not," Elisabeth said.

Jason whimpered. "Mother."

Elisabeth ignored him. "We in the defense are in *complete* agreement with the wishes of the injured party."

"*Is* the defense in agreement?" Dimitri asked Jason.

He shrugged. "I guess I am."

"Very well," Walter said, and then spoke directly to his fellow Trustees. "Shall we adjourn for discussion or do we go ahead and vote?"

The word 'vote' was repeated several times.

Walter lifted his gavel. "On the first issue, punishment for Mr. Epelle's now admitted crimes of adultery and impregnation while within the bounds of a legal marriage, a prearranged plea deal has been submitted in writing. Said deal agrees to the immediate dismissal of this defendant from his current posting as Chief of Operations of the Verdanian Transplantation bureau. This deal also precludes any elected governmental service by the defendant for a period of five years. Could I have a show of hands on this punishment?"

Five hands went up, with Jonas Vickery and Deborah Summers voting in the negative.

The gavel struck. "The plea agreement passes. Now, to the matter of sealing this conviction and related incidents from the public record. How do you vote?"

Again, the vote was the same. Five for. Two against.

Walter's gavel cracked a second time. "The details surrounding this conviction are now officially sealed. Any public mention of this by anyone present will be punishable by the full force of the law. You have been warned."

"Thank you for that," Jason said. "I'm indebted, to all of you."

"We are not done with you yet," Walter said. "The issue of the dissolution of the Epelle marriage must also be decided. Both parties are in agreement with the contract's termination. And taking in account the intricacies of the prior case and its conviction, I present this question to my six colleagues. Should the marriage of Angela and Jason Epelle be terminated? Once more, I call for a show of hands."

Seven hands. Seven votes for dissolution.

"The marriage contract between Jason Epelle and Angela Rosso is hereby dissolved. Neither of these two individuals may marry again for the length of the original contract. All details pertaining to living arrangements and belongings will be left to the individual parties. This hearing is now dismissed."

The gavel came down again. As everyone in attendance was beginning to stand, Walter added, "Trustee Epelle, I look forward to you being back on this side of the table."

Elisabeth gave her colleague a knowing nod.

Jason turned to his mother. "So, that's it?"

"That's it. It's over. You're free as a bird."

106

"I can't thank you enough for doing this," Mary said.

"No worries. I'm happy to oblige."

Leo held his fingers on the control panel as the skiff he was piloting soared across the valley. Mary, his hush-hush passenger, had her own hand perched on his arm as her ponytail flapped wildly in the slipstream.

"If we get caught, and someone attempts to make a fuss," she said, "I intend to take all the blame."

Leo kept looking straight ahead. "We're not going to get caught. And even if we were, I'm no fool. I know how this works. Your father would forgive you any sin. Me, not so much. Ergo, if anyone finds out, I will be strung up for desertion, grand theft, and reckless endangerment. You'll get off with a 'be better next time' pep talk."

"After what you just accomplished," Mary said. "I think you're in a far safer position than you realize. Maybe even safer than me. Dad couldn't do anything to you even if he wanted to, which I doubt he would. What you found, and the fact that you did it all on your own, that's still fresh in everybody's mind. The Collective is in a forgiving mood, especially when it comes to you."

"I'm quite positive that not everyone feels that way."

"Maybe Deborah's in a forgiving mood as well. You never know."

Leo adjusted their course to the right as they bore down on a glimmering lakefront. The skiff dropped a hundred meters, keeping plenty of height between the bottom of the ship and the surface of the water. The trip across the waterway took no longer than thirty seconds. Leo edged along the coastline until the skiff arrived at the crest of a familiar outcropping.

There was a somberness to Mary's voice. "This is it?"

"Yes. This is where he died."

Leo led Mary over to the starboard side of the skiff and together they examined the stones beneath them. The tide was lapping up and there was no trace of the creature that had killed Mary's brother on this very spot, ten short days before.

"At least there's no blood," she said. "I was afraid there'd still be blood."

"You shouldn't have worried about that."

Mary breathed in. "If girlie emotion embarrasses you, I suggest you avert your eyes."

Leo backed up. "Do whatever you need to do. Pretend like I'm not even here."

"Wait, I don't want you to go." Mary held her arm out at him. "Come here. I want you beside me, to hold me up."

Leo slipped his arms around her and her eyes shut tight.

"It's so hard to let him go," she said.

"Of course it is."

"I wouldn't have been strong enough to do this without you, you know. Most of the time, I feel so alone."

"That can't be true. You have Camden. You have Courtney. You have your father."

"But none of them are you. I'm sorry about everything, Leo. I truly am. I'm sorry I wasn't strong enough to stand up for myself. That's what I'd do today, but I just wasn't capable of that back then."

"Not this again, Mary. We have to find a way to put the past behind us. You're married now. You have beautiful children. I have long since understood. Things are as things are. Wishing has never changed anything, as sad as that is to say."

"And yet, at moments like this, you're the one I want to be with.

Knowing that, it drives me a little insane."

"Then I'm the one who's sorry."

A gust of wind blew in, bending the surrounding plant life to its roots.

Mary took in a deep breath, and said, "Goodbye, Mikhail. I hate that you're gone, but I am so proud that you were my brother."

After an appropriate amount of time had passed, Leo let her go. With a quick, short step he had returned to the flight controls. Mary gripped her hands around the guard railing.

"All done?" Leo asked her.

"All done. I've seen it now. I'm ready to go home."

107

Rebecca was talking before the door was even all the way open. "I can't stay. I came by to tell you that, face to face."

"Oh no, but you have to," Allison said, standing beside Walter in the doorway. "I've been looking forward to this all week."

"Sorry, but I can't. I apologize, to you particularly, Allison. But your husband knows why it's impossible for me to even pretend to be friendly right now."

"I know no such thing," Walter said.

Rebecca adjusted her footing on the paving and scowled at the man. "Don't tell me you didn't think it was going to get out."

"What would get out?" Allison's glance flipped back and forth between them. "What's going on?"

Walter was fiddling with his tie. "Well, if I were to hazard a guess, I would say this is about a Directorate matter that has not been made public yet. We were saving the announcement for Mikhail Kucherov's memorial service. I have no earthly idea how Rebecca found out about it, but I assume that is what has her so worked up."

Rebecca shook her finger at him. "A *monarchy?* How could you?"

"What we set up is not a monarchy."

"Like hell it isn't."

Allison slapped her hands against her side. "What are you two talking about?"

417

"Tell her," Rebecca said.

Walter looked over at his wife. "This morning, to honor Mikhail and the Kucherovs, the Directorate approved an amendment to the charter establishing an additional ninth seat on the council. This seat will be a permanent Kucherov holding, assigned to their firstborn heir."

"And this is bad?" Allison asked.

"Not to rational adults, it isn't."

Rebecca shook her finger even harder. "Don't you dare try to make me look like the deranged one here. You're the one who's deranged—giving away the future to one family. *That's* lunacy. What happened to earning what you get? Isn't that Dimitri's all-time favorite parable, the rich boy going on and on about all those swell, underprivileged people who helped form this Collective—each and every one of them, undying saints who pulled themselves up by their bootstraps. Give me a break. It's all crap. It has always been crap. And you stand there smiling because you just got your fondest wish. Your favorite family will be royalty forever, and it's all because of *you*."

"Once again, Rebecca. We must agree to disagree. The motion did pass unanimously."

"That's another thing. There was *no* public discussion about any of this. You just shoved it on through, in secret. This is what's wrong with you and your council of sycophants. It's eight deciding for four thousand. It's uneven proportionment. I *hate* it. I've *always* hated it."

"I'm sorry you feel that way," Walter said.

Rebecca pivoted to Allison, as polite as can be. "Thank you so much for the invitation, but perhaps you understand why I must bow out tonight. Alan sends his regards."

She began to back away, and then stopped. "Walter, I tell you this with the clearest mind possible—stay out of my life. Thirty years of silence was not enough."

Allison's eyes narrowed as she watched Rebecca lumber down the front pathway. "She's crazy, obsessed. Pathologically so."

"Obsessed with me?"

"No. Maybe she never has been. She's obsessed with the Kucherovs." Allison left Walter at the door. "You both are."

108

Jason picked up the last of his bags and strolled inside his former bedroom. Angela was sitting cross-legged in the center of the made bed, listening to a blaring classical music concerto in the dark.

Jason raised his voice and swung his hands about in the air. "Angela... I'm taking off."

It took her another moment to notice him, but once she had, she called out for the volume to be muted, and the room fell silent.

"Did you say goodbye to Jerald?" she asked.

"I just did. He was asleep, so I gave him a kiss I knew you wouldn't want me waking him." He patted the top of his leather satchel. "I think I have everything, though."

Angela stared at him, glassy-eyed. "Where are you planning to stay?"

"With my parents. Mom promises to find me my own place soon, but she says there are not a lot of free homes at the moment. I know that's bull, of course, because everyone's about to be moving down to the surface, including her. I think she's just trying to keep me under her roof, so I can be closely monitored."

"You can't blame her there."

"I suppose not."

Angela's blouse had begun to ride up in the front. She grabbed hold of the fabric and stretched it back across her baby bulge.

"Well," she said.

"Yep, I should be going." He shuffled his feet, and then hesitated in mid-movement. "Is it all right if I ask you something first?"

"I don't see why not."

"Did you know you were going to ask for the dissolution? What I mean is, how long have you known you were done with me?"

Angela took quite a bit of time before responding.

"I wasn't completely sure until I said it. But I knew I wasn't in love with you anymore. I've known that since before you were hurt—and yet again maybe that's only because I realized you didn't love me anymore either. I can't see you straying if you did."

"That's giving me a whole lot of credit, you know."

"I don't think so, not really. You're not the cheating type. You did what you did for a reason. And I did what I did for a reason."

"Fair enough." Jason was fingering one of the buckles on his satchel strap. "I really should go."

"Do you love her?" Angela asked as he was walking out the door. "You must. It's Morgan Adams. She's so beautiful."

Jason rested his hip against the doorframe. "I don't think I should be talking to you about this. Do you actually want to know?"

"Probably not."

"Are you going to be okay on your own?"

"I'll be fine. I have Jerald and the dancing football here." She palmed her rounded belly.

"I'll see you then. Call if you need anything. I'm not that far away."

Angela waved him on, remaining right where she was until long after he was gone.

Three Days Later

109

A serious young woman escorted Leo into the office and seated him in one of two chairs in front of the crescent-shaped desk. The woman then asked if he would like a beverage or something to eat. Leo politely declined both, and the woman exited.

Eight and a half minutes later, the door reopened behind him. Leo wheeled around to greet the person, and almost immediately had to pull back. It was his ex-wife Deborah who had come in, and she was smiling at him.

"Thank you for flying up to meet with me," she said as she hustled over to her desk. "A decision has been made, and I wanted to be the one who informed you."

"A decision?" Leo said. "What decision?"

Deborah took a seat in the armless chair. "A rather important one. One made by your betters."

"Would it be possible to share that decision with me?"

"Oh, I'd love to. But I've been asked to wait for a witness to be present. It shouldn't be too much longer. My second guest is supposed be arriving any second now." Deborah rubbed the tip of her finger against her manicured nail. "You might as well relax. We can sit here civilly for a few minutes, can't we?"

As they waited, they stared at one another. Then, an announcement came over the office's speaker system. "Mary Muran has arrived, madam."

"Send her in," Deborah said.

Mary swept into the office, stopping in her tracks the instant she saw Leo.

Deborah was smirking. "I have something to tell my former husband, Director Muran. Normally, I'd have conducted this business on my own, but my colleagues insisted someone unbiased be here when the news was delivered. You are most certainly not that, but you'll do, for my purposes at least. Sit."

Mary sat.

"This morning the Directorate met and debated a formal pardon for my abuser here." When Deborah spoke, she spoke to Mary. "Many thought his discovery of the Echograd site was reason enough to forgive his past sins. I felt differently about this, as you might suspect, so the debate continued. The matter on the table would have removed his penal tattoo and restored him to full command status, displacing your husband. I'm sure this would displease you as it displeased me, Director, but that's another issue. I was not going to allow this pardon to happen. This man brutalized me. What other choice did I have? I put all my cards on the table, promising to hold up votes, to never support anyone, and to always go against the grain. Now, some might say I already do that, but what I'd sworn to do would have taken my intransigence to a whole new level. Votes in his affirmative were soon reversed, and suddenly, I was not the only one against this pardon. It took cashing in every chip I'd managed to collect, but I was soon able to trim the vote to three to five. Which means, I win—he loses."

"So, he has to go back to maintenance work?" Mary said. "After all this man has done, he has to be *wasted* on that?"

"No. He stays with the Rangers, as a grunt. This was the final deal. Everyone wanted to take advantage of his *skills*, therefore I had to agree with his remaining on the surface. Although, upon further consideration, I no longer mind that concession so much. There are endless dangers down there, and most likely on the other two moons as well. Accidents are bound to happen. Why shouldn't one happen to him?"

Mary shot out of her chair and snatched Leo by the arm. "Come on. You don't have to put up with this."

"And you probably didn't have to either," Deborah said. "But for some odd reason, I wanted you to be the first to know."

As Mary led him out, Leo gave Deborah a salute. "I'm sorry that I beat you. I'm glad I finally got the chance to say that to you. What I did was monstrous. People are judged by the worst things they do, not the best. And you're right, I don't deserve to be pardoned. I'll never deserve it."

Mary pushed him out the door. After a brief pause, she came barreling back inside.

"What you did just now was unnecessary. You can be sure I'll be an excellent witness. My father will hear about this."

"Oh, I'm sure he will." Deborah powered up her workstation. "Don't let me stop you. Go do what you're best at. Go run to daddy."

110

An elderly woman in a hard hat tapped Adam on the shoulder. When she did this, Adam was down on one knee next to a poorly installed piece of framing, pointing out the spot where a twenty-degree bend was occurring. His voice remained friendly and even-keeled as he explained to the operator about the potential dangers of faulty foundation settings. Perfection might never be possible, but that was no reason it couldn't be strived for. After the woman tapped a second time, Adam held up his forefinger to ward her off. Once he had finished his explanation to the operator, he stood back up and offered the woman his hand

"Hello. Is there something I can do for you?"

The elderly woman replied, "No…nothing in particular. I just wanted to see you. It's been a while, and I've been hearing tales of your many exploits."

A grin in the corner of Adam's mouth grew into cheek-to-cheek smile. "Oh my goodness. I didn't recognize you at first. Those eyes. It's *you*."

Former Trustee Kimberly Akana was standing before Adam in a frilly white sundress, attended by forty-five of her children, grandchildren, and great-grandchildren—all of whom were funneling out behind her, outfitted in the same protective headgear she was.

"Give me a hug," Kimberly said as she opened up her arms. "You should have given me one the second you recognized me. And so you know, for my taste, the recognizing part took far too long."

The two old friends embraced and kissed.

Kimberly kept her hand on Adam's arm as she shimmied around to speak to her entourage. "Everyone, this is Adam J. Ballard. We grew up together, way back when in the very first Collective. I don't remember a second of my youth when the two of us weren't spending nearly all our time together. This is how long we have known one another, since we were infants."

The ninety-eight-year-old took another long look at the man. "I am older than he is, but only by five months." This made her laugh. She reached up and pinched his cheek. "Not that you could tell that now. Check out this youthful face. I adore this face, and all this bright red hair."

"I don't want to hear anything about how youthful I look," Adam said. "I don't feel all that youthful right now."

Kimberly was just starting to argue that point when her eldest daughter Laken—the Trustee who had arranged this early trip to the surface—pushed her way to the front of the line and told Adam how terrific it was to finally meet him. She'd been hearing stories about him her whole life, and it was well past time she had a face to go with the name. The other family members came up as well, including Florin and Tristan, and their parents, Amanda and Kenneth. The Holts and the Merriweathers—young and old—Adam was introduced to them all.

Eventually, the familial herd migrated apart. Laken singled out Florin and instructed the group to stick to approved areas only, all of which had been clearly marked with green beacon lights on the ground. Soon, Kimberly and Adam had been left on their own.

"It's such a thrill to see you again," Adam said. "I didn't know if you'd be—"

"Alive," Kimberly gasped.

Adam rested his elbow against the faulty piece of framing. "If you had given me more than a split second to finish that thought, I might've found a better way to phrase it than that, but yes. The chances of us ever seeing each other again were rather improbable."

Kimberly held her chin out. "How different do I look to you?"

"Older, but still you. The way you tuck your hair behind your ears when you talk is the same. You've always done it that way, with two fingers. I watched you doing it when I was meeting one of your grandchildren. Seeing that sent me right back to the Alpha, sitting on North Mountain above the compound. Those were such great times, Kimberly. I hope you know that. I was too young and stupid to express it then, but I want you to know that now."

Kimberly nodded and began to shake. Adam drew her into his arms and held her close. She sobbed into his chest, her nose and mouth mashing against his tool vest. He attempted to change the subject to something less emotional, but she kept telling him to shush up. She was fine. She just missed him was all. She was so thrilled to have him back in her life again, however long that life may be.

111

Jason and Morgan were walking hand in hand, for the whole world to see.

"I still don't get why they had to do that to us," Jason said as they were turning onto Vermilion Way, the Red Village's centermost thoroughfare. "And at the last second, too. Now, because of some kind of vindictive decision, I'm not allowed to marry the woman I love. And you just know it was meant as a kick to my you-know-whats, because it's certainly not the way these things are normally done. I know a ton of other people who didn't have to wait to get married again when their marriages were dissolved. Why should we have to wait?"

"It's called a punishment for a reason," Morgan said. "Every situation is different, so the punishment rulings were bound to be different as well. You need to stop taking stuff so personally. You got off lucky. We both got off lucky."

"I know, but—"

Morgan swung their joined arms out and jostled Jason forward.

"Can we please stop talking about punishments? We both deserved worse than we got, and yet somehow we can still be together. Count yourself fortunate. I know I do."

"So do I," Jason said. "I was just venting. You're all that matters to me, too."

He leaned in and nuzzled her neck. "And despite the prolonged delay that's going to be required, I do have every intention of marrying you.

The first chance we get three years from now, it's going to be this massive ceremony. Our baby is going to be there, and it'll be beautiful. Then, everything will be perfect."

"Everything is already perfect, Jay. I've been married before, and I don't care about any of that ceremonial nonsense. All I care about is you. And I have you now. How about we both take a breath and just enjoy that?"

For another hour, they kept on with their stroll, pausing frequently to kiss—and when chance permitted—greet every friendly face they could find.

112

"Are you telling me to let him see her, or are you telling me to keep her away from him? Because I'm not sure which way you're leading me here. Sometimes you sound like you despise the man, and sometimes you sound like you're siding with him. It's all coming off as a tad schizophrenic to me."

"I've been having trouble keeping things straight myself."

Jocelyn and Mary left the nursery and headed for the staircase.

"I don't mind if you want to lobby on your father's behalf," Jocelyn said. "I really don't. All of the arguments for and against him seeing Tana are already pretty clear in my mind. I just haven't made a final decision yet."

"I wasn't sure if you'd thought about this at all," Mary said as she followed Jocelyn down the stairs.

"What can I say? I knew a request like this would be coming. I know your father."

They completed the last of the steps and scooted out into the living room. Mary took a seat in a nearby recliner while Jocelyn chose to employ an open spot on the floor. With a practiced breath, Jocelyn folded her legs into the lotus position. Mary fell back against the headrest.

"As best as I can," she said, "I've been trying to let my issues with him go. Dad thinks I already have. And who knows? Maybe that's true. The rage inside has certainly faded to a degree. Even though sometimes, I feel bad about allowing it to."

"I'm like the worst hostess ever," Jocelyn blurted. "Would you like something to drink?"

"No, thank you. I'm fine."

Jocelyn wiggled her toes. "I hear what you're saying, Mary, but there's nothing wrong with letting things go. You certainly don't have to make excuses to me."

"I wasn't. My point was, my issues with my father are my own, and not relevant to the ones that you have with him. Yours are hard and real, and not the nebulous complaints of a neglected child. He wronged you in such a way that I'm not sure you should let him see Tana under any circumstances. It would serve him right."

"That's the way I thought I'd feel," Jocelyn said. "I probably *should* feel that way. And yet, I don't. What Dimitri did was awful, but it also seems irrelevant now that Mikhail is gone. At my brother's hearing I spent the entire time I was there staring at each of them, all the evil Trustees who voted to imprison me. The reality was, I could barely summon up any hatred. I showed them some hatred, of course. But most of the glaring and gnashing of teeth was for show, because I don't feel much of anything at the moment except love for Tana and grief for Mikhail. That's where I'm at. What good is me working myself up in vengeance going to do? It accomplishes nothing. Like you said, this is about our own well-being."

"What about your mother? Have you let it go with her as well?"

Jocelyn lifted up her hands and then dropped them back down into her lap. "Ever since Tana was born, she has bent over backward to make it up to me. She's just always there, waiting to be helpful. It's been kind of nice actually, her feeling guilty and behaving humbly for the first time in her miserable existence."

"That's funny," Mary said.

"It's also the truth. Elisabeth Epelle is a control freak. I don't care who knows it."

"And Dimitri Kucherov isn't?"

Jocelyn's head tilted to the left. "Okay. You have me beat there. Dimitri is far, far worse."

They shared a few hiccups of laughter. And yet, it didn't take long for the amusement to fade.

"You plan to let him see the baby then?" Mary said, tacking on the qualifier, "Eventually."

"I don't see why I shouldn't."

"Just so you have all the information available to you, I don't think Mikhail wanted him to see her. In fact, I know that he didn't. It was the last thing he said to Dad and me."

"Yeah, I heard he had a rough time of it," Jocelyn said. "But then again, Mikhail's not here anymore, and I have to make the best decision I can, on my own. And how I understand the world, a granddaughter should know her grandfather, no matter what I personally think of the man. That's just what my head is telling me. I'm not going to block any opportunities this child is going to have in life. I refuse to be Dimitri. That's the last thing I would ever want to be."

"Would you like me to set something up?" Mary asked. "A brief visit maybe? I can take care of it, so you never have to see him."

"When the time comes, sure. And it will probably be sooner rather than later."

"Just let me know."

"I will. Trust me, Mary, you'll be the first to know."

113

Walter stared straight into the camera and said, "My fellow citizens, hello. I come to you this evening with momentous news. At nine o'clock tomorrow morning, the Verdanian transplantation process will officially begin. In the first wave of relocations we in the Directorate will be taking residence in the nascent city of Echograd. Also in these initial wave of transfers will be select members of the Transplant bureau, along with one hundred lottery-chosen citizens who will also be traveling down to aid the construction operation as it presses on."

He stopped to smile. "After so many long years in transit, the true beginning is now upon us, with our own piece of solid ground to call our own. I welcome all of you to tune in for the live coverage in the morning as we make this all-important transition for our society. And please, remember, these are only the first steps. Soon, within months most likely, every single one of us will be living below, in a place where I'd like to believe we were all born to live."

Walter clenched up his fist and struck it against his chest in the now famous salute—Mikhail's salute.

"Additionally," he said. "The Directorate has voted to fast-track a landing on the sister moon of Azur. This is not to say that the search for more settlement sites on Verdan will not continue, because it will. But with today's decision, those searches will be extending out a little farther than we'd originally expected, to our neighboring celestial body. I tell you this so you will know there will always be plenty of room for us to grow—for our children, and for our children's children. The future remains limitless when we have a tomorrow. And we are a fortunate bunch to have so many tomorrows ahead of us. This is Magistrate Walter Stoddard signing off. I wish you all well, and a peaceful good night."

Five Days Later

114

Dimitri hit the accelerator and hovered away. Mary took off after him, chasing him around the tiny, two-room structure.

It was the inherent speed of the mover chair that gave Dimitri the upper hand. He zipped from place to place, straightening an end table in one corner of the living area, and then placing a disused storage carton on his lap in the other. At each stop, Mary would race over to him and plead her case for him to begin taking it easy. If his new quarters needed any sprucing up done, then all he needed to do was ask her, and she would do it herself, gladly, and with much less strain on her body. But Dimitri was Dimitri, and chose instead to do as he pleased.

Anxiously, he sped off again, this time striking out for the window on the right side of the reinforced front door. He pressed his nose against the glass. The window pane was round, about a third of a meter in circumference, and fifteen centimeters thick. Out near the beachfront, at the tip of the nascent city, forming gels were being sprayed over the latticework of what would soon be the Collective's capitol building.

"Have you finished running me ragged yet?" Mary asked her father as she came up from the rear. "You're worse than my kids. Can you stay in one place for more than two seconds? I'm begging you, go easy on me."

Dimitri furrowed his brow, never taking his eyes off the muddy road running between the temporary housing units.

"I know I can be a handful," he said. "But I had to make certain everything was in its place."

"I know, but we're still not expecting her for another hour. The spire hasn't even left orbit yet. Remember, you can hear it when the ship comes down. It's loud, and you've been griping about it all week."

Dimitri shrugged. "I thought she might arrive early. It's always best to plan for every possibility."

"Most of the time…yes." Mary retrieved the empty carton from her father's lap. "But Jocelyn's arriving by spire. There's no other way for her to get here. So, until you hear that atrocious noise, I really need you to calm down. It's for your own good. You know how you get, especially since you've been living down here. The gravity may be only imperceptibly different from that of the *Horizon*'s, but it still hasn't exactly helped you out much in the leg-strength department, now has it?"

Mary carried the carton over to the trash receptacle in the wall and jammed it through the automated hatch.

"This visit," Dimitri said. "It's extremely important. Important in an historical sense."

"Dad…this is just a simple get-to-know-you visit with your grand-daughter. Don't read too much into it—and do not put any extra pressure on Jocelyn. Just meet the child, and whatever you do, don't start behaving all imperially. Not everyone can stomach the proclamations from on high. I know for a fact that Jocelyn has no use for them at the moment."

Dimitri spun his chair around a hundred and eighty degrees. Mary was standing right beside him and had to jump back to avoid a painful collision with her legs.

"If Jocelyn doesn't want to hear it," he said, "I won't force it on her. But you, you and I need to be on the same wavelength here. Tana—this child— she is of supreme significance. She could be something this Collective has been in need of for a long time now. Imagine a combination of Mikhail's intelligence and Jocelyn's warmth. We may have something quite different than the normal stunted member of our family with this girl. That is a possibility we must treasure and nurture. You and I—and even Mikhail—we are not the most social of creatures. But if that youngster is raised right, and Jocelyn will most certainly do that, we could have a prodigy on our hands." His eyes met Mary's. "That is something we all need to be responsible for encouraging."

"And you may very well be right about all of this. But you cannot say a word of it to Jocelyn. Just tell her the baby is beautiful, and she looks like Mikhail. That's all she needs to hear from you. She doesn't need to be told that her child is the Second Coming. It's bad enough that everyone else is already whispering things like that. If you start in, she might just walk out."

"The people," Dimitri said. "They whisper what they whisper because they can sense the child is special."

"All children are special. At least most of them are. We respond to them in a primal and personal ways. I know you thought Mikhail was special. Perhaps you even felt that way about me as well. Maybe not as special as Mikhail was, but you held me above others, and I never liked that. It's not something I believe in. And outside of your own family, I don't think it's something you believe in either."

Dimitri reached up and grazed Mary's cheek. "You were just as special to me as your brother. You are just so loyal and never needed the coaxing that he did." He smiled. "And now, you'll be twenty-one on your birthday. Your stint as the Ninth Seat holder will begin. I am so glad I resigned my elected position and assumed the post last week. I'm thrilled to be your seat warmer. A few more months and you come of age, and I can retire for good."

"Is this really something we should be talking about?" Mary said.

"Is there any reason we shouldn't?" Dimitri rotated back around to the window and checked the streets anew. "Despite one or two of its drawbacks, I believe this Ninth Seat amendment can be a positive force. The influx of youth in particular. I think that's a wonderful thing, and not too different from the old formative days back on Earth. Twenty-year-olds started this beautiful mess, and forever more, they shall rule over it. That's a good thing. Sometimes, believe it or not, a person can stay in power for too long."

Mary grinned at him. After a moment, he grinned right back.

"What?" he said. "I understand that I've overstayed my welcome. We can both admit that. We will tell no lies, I am well past my expiration date."

Mary placed her hand on his shoulder. "There's still some juice left in you, Dad. You've sure had me running in circles all morning."

Dimitri shut his eyes. "It's odd. I don't know why I stayed on the council for so long. Arrogance, perhaps? I'm not sure. I'd like to think I would have retired long ago if we weren't getting closer and closer to these moons. But maybe not. I like to work. I've always had trouble picturing myself as a retiree."

"You'll never really retire, not completely. You'll still be poking your nose into everything, I'm sure of it. It's who you are. You're the man in charge."

Dimitri added, "If I do stay involved, it will only be as an advising citizen. That's the beauty of this amendment. It's no longer up to me. One way or the other, my better will be taking my place, and I could not be more delighted."

Mary looked away. "You're just yapping like a crazy person, aren't you? You've totally worn me out." She gestured at the other side of the room and yawned. "I think I'm going to stretch out on the couch and take a nap before Jocelyn gets here. Would you like me to take you to your bedroom so you can catch a few winks yourself?"

He shook his head. "No, thank you. But feel free to do so yourself. I want to stay where I am. I'm enjoying myself. I like staring out the window. There's so much out there to see."

115

Florin and Helen were at the tail end of the passenger line, their luggage in tow—six small pieces between them, meeting the maximum allotment for residential transfers to the moon's surface. Two of the items were carry-on bags. The four other pieces were hard-shelled footlockers that had been parked in a haphazard arrangement to the young women's immediate left.

Florin had just started to complain about the ever-lengthening wait when a gravelly voice called out from the top of the boarding center stairs.

"There you are." Jance Ling was galloping downward. "I thought you might already be gone. Lucky I didn't miss you."

"Yeah, lucky us," Florin said.

"Ah, poor, sad Florin," Jance said as he came to a stop beside them. "You know your heart would've been broken if I hadn't been here in time to see you off. You don't have to be afraid to admit it."

"Whatever," Florin said. "Keep deluding yourself, peabrain."

Jance moved closer to Helen and brushed her arm. The two exchanged cordial glances.

After that, Jance brought his hand down on the top of their luggage train. "Seeing you here is so depressing. You really are ready to go. I don't know what to say. Everyone's leaving. Vlad's been down on the ground for a week already. The gang feels like it's breaking up."

"It only feels that way cause you're the last of us left behind," Helen said. "You'll be down with us soon, though. Everyone will."

Jance waited a moment. "Well, I'm sorry if I'm being such a sap. But I'm going to miss you, both of you."

He took Helen into his arms and they held each other for several seconds before he pulled back and placed a clumsy kiss on her lips. With that done, he slid over to Florin. Their hug was even more awkward. Just as they were separating, Florin put her hand flat on his chest.

"What? No kiss for me?"

"Did you want one?" Jance said, a little unsure.

"She's kidding," Helen said.

"I don't have to be." Florin puckered up her lips.

Jance gave her a light peck before pulling her in close for another embrace. As he did so, he whispered into her ear. "A new place to live isn't going to change you. We all know what you are. You aren't fooling anyone."

He walked away, up the incline of the outer aisle. "You two take care of yourselves. Call soon, okay? And tell Vlad I said hello."

Helen waved. "See you."

Florin stood there motionless.

"He wants you, you know," Helen said. "Like every other man who was supposed to like me, he wants you more."

"Boy, do you have that wrong," Florin said. "You should have heard what he just said to me. He hates me."

"No, he doesn't. He talks about you constantly. Ever since you set the two of us up in the Depots, all he does when we're together is bitch about you." Helen's voice became jeering. "*Florin* does *this*. Florin does *that*."

"Of course he bitches about me. Like I just said, he hates me, probably because I've been using his friend as my personal sex toy." Florin eyes widened. "It makes sense that he wouldn't like me."

"It's more than that, although I'll never be able to convince you. But mark my words, you're going to have to deal with him sooner or later. If I know you, you'll probably be *doing* him sooner rather than later."

"*Hey*," Florin said, her voice growing soft. "You like him. I would *never* be with him. Not if *you* liked him."

"But I don't really like him. And I'm quite sure he doesn't like me. He makes that clearer than even he realizes."

"Still, I wouldn't do that. You mean so much to me. You're my best friend."

"I know." Helen put her back against the wall. "Forget I mentioned it. Adventure awaits. That's all that really matters, right?"

At the side entranceway, Jocelyn Kucherov entered the boarding center with Baby Tana swaddled in her arms. Florin and Helen's conversation immediately ceased, replaced by a pair of happy expressions that greeted their fellow passenger as she joined them at the back of the line.

"Well, hello," Florin said. "Long time no see."

Jocelyn tightened her grip on the baby as she looked Florin up and down. "I can't believe what I'm seeing. You were just a stick the last time I saw you. You go away for a year and sweet little girls start sprouting curves. You're very beautiful, Florin. You must be beating them off with a stick."

Helen reached out and tickled the baby's nose. Jocelyn smiled.

Florin asked Jocelyn, "What are you going down to the city for?"

"Tana needs to meet her grandfather. Today's the big day."

"Oh," Florin said.

Jocelyn shivered with embarrassment. "Yes, I know. I've taken a long time to get around to it. But it probably shouldn't wait forever."

"Probably not."

The spire pilot's voice came over the loudspeakers and the line ahead of them showed movement. "Passenger boarding onto the *Javelin* aircraft may now begin. Mechanized luggage should be placed inside a cargo tram upon entrance, to be stowed in the holds until the descent and landing processes have been completed. I apologize in advance for any weather difficulties we might encounter. There's a storm front moving in over Echograd. I'll be down to strap you all in before we drop, including our infant VIP. Phelps out."

Florin took a sweeping step to the side, holding her arm out at the widening space in front of her.

"After you," she said to Jocelyn.

Helen and Florin held back, allowing Jocelyn to gain a few steps on them. Once she had, they set off together, taking their first long steps toward home.

116

"I've called to give you fair warning," Rebecca said. "I'm not going to take any of this lying down."

Walter closed out the memo he'd been composing on his desktop. "I'm glad you changed your mind about speaking to me. Although really, who in their right mind would think you'd take anything lying down? What I expected you to be was apoplectic. And I can only assume the protests will begin again any minute now."

"There will be no protests. I've told you that a million times already, my protesting days are over."

"Then what is it that you plan to do?"

"For starters, I plan to repeal and dismantle this ridiculous Ninth Seat amendment. Many people don't like it. *You* should not like it."

Walter grinned. "Even though it was my idea. Why would I not like my own idea?"

"Because you're smarter than this."

"Obviously, that's not true, or you wouldn't be so angry."

"But that's the thing about you, Walter, you tend to hide how you truly feel. You've been doing it for years, haven't you?"

He braced his hand against the desk. "I'm a busy man, Rebecca. What is it that you're calling about? What do you really want to say?"

"I told you. I called to give you fair warning."

"Fair warning about what?"

"About my intention to stand for election—Directorate election. I'm going to win myself one of those godforsaken seats so I can be right there next to you, questioning every decision you make. One thing I'm sure of, you won't be able to get away with your back-room double-dealing anymore."

"If you win, that is."

"Oh, I'll win. And I'm going to make your life miserable."

With that, Walter broke out in applause. "Excellent, and about damn time. You should have run for office years ago. What took you so long?"

"Don't you be happy about this."

"Why not?"

"Because I don't want you to be."

"All right," he said. "But now that you've committed yourself as a candidate, the next time you call, make sure you schedule an appointment first."

Walter double tapped his ear and ended the conversation right then and there.

Two decks below and approximately four hundred meters to the west, Rebecca Patterson glanced up at the ceiling in her den and smiled.

117

Jocelyn handed Tana to Mary.

"Are you sure you don't want to come inside?"

Jocelyn was shaking her head no. "I agreed to let him see the baby, but I still don't think I can stand to be in the same room with the man. I'm afraid I might murder him on the spot."

"I hear you," Mary said as she brought the baby to her chest. "Well, you know where we are. This shouldn't take too long. He doesn't have the stamina to do much of anything anymore. He can barely get in and out of his chair under his own steam."

"There's no time limit. I'll be around." Jocelyn flipped her arms out. "You know, taking in the various sights."

Mary went back inside the hosting unit as Jocelyn stepped away from the door, her sandaled feet sinking between the loose, gravel stones.

Over near the interconnected housing domes, a loud clang was heard. A second after that, there was a short smattering of screams, followed by a shout of anger. Jocelyn perked up and headed off in that direction. The metal planks that made up the temporary walkway were filthy, and barely discernible from the rocks and mud.

The source of the disturbance was easy to locate. A hook and pulley system had dropped a support beam onto a small, bean-shaped structure, flattening it through its center. Workers were scurrying about, calling out to each other to see if anybody had been hurt.

On one of the administrative balconies above Jocelyn, a tall, lanky red-headed man stormed outside and began issuing orders to the floundering crew. He scolded the pulley operator, declaring him a clumsy, brain-dead maroon—which made Jocelyn snicker. The redhead noticed her presence on the muddy planks and stared down at her for an instant before returning to his tirade. Once that had been completed, he ambled over to the edge of the balcony.

"Sorry for the commotion," he said Jocelyn. "Accidents around here have become far too common for my liking."

"There's no need to apologize. I'm enjoying myself. It's kind of thrilling to see so much activity. Life can be kind of docile on the *Horizon*. Messy is a nice change of pace."

"I'm Adam Ballard, by the way," the man said with a nod. "And you are?"

"Jocelyn Kucherov. It's a pleasure to meet you, Mr. Ballard."

Hearing her name, Adam's face had gone stark white. He pushed away from the railing. "You need to stay right where you are. I need to talk to you properly. I'm begging you, just stay there. I'll be right down."

He raced over to the rooftop door and disappeared inside the building. Not long after that he came bursting out on the ground floor and jogged over to where Jocelyn was standing.

"I didn't mean to startle you," he said. "But I wasn't expecting to run into you like this. I was hoping to eventually, but just not so soon."

Jocelyn looked confused. "Why would you be hoping to run into me at all? Do I know you?"

"You don't, but I spent some time with your husband before he, *uh*—"

She said it for him. "Before he died."

"Yes, before that."

"If it means anything," Adam said, "I wanted you to know how much I liked the guy. He was enthusiastic and considerate, a real gentleman. He talked our ears off about you, too. He was excited about his baby's birth. He told all of us about that. And the other Rangers have talked about it since. You and your child were on his mind day and night, of that there can be no doubt. Actually, that's how I will always think of him. This brave, strapping guy who just wanted to be back with his wife and child."

Jocelyn sniffled and ran her finger under her nose. "Thank you," she said. "That's a sweet thing to share."

"Your husband, he made quite the impression on me. That's all I really wanted you to know." Adam slid his hands into his pockets. "I was also curious about what kind of woman he was married to." His stare intensified. "You are almost *exactly* what I pictured."

She curtsied. "I'm glad to hear it. Glad to hear all of it."

Adam attempted to imitate her curtsy, but his long limbs refused to cooperate.

Jocelyn smiled. They were both smiling.

Then, Adam snapped his fingers. "Hey, I've got an idea. Would you like a tour? I can make a little time and show you around."

"Oh, that's not necessary. I should probably stay close by. I'm only down here so my daughter can see her grandfather. It's the first time they've met, so I gave them some alone time. My plan was to veg out in a nice quiet corner somewhere, but the crash a minute ago sort of lured me from my doldrums."

"I see," Adam said. "So that's what was going on. There was a call a few minutes ago about a public address by Dimitri. Everyone on-site was told to gather outside his housing unit. He had a few remarks to make."

Jocelyn grumbled at that and said, "I should have known."

All of a sudden, she was charging back up the street. Adam chased after her until they rounded Dimitri's corner and ran smack dab into fifty or more people milling around by the door.

Jocelyn hung back, just across the street. Dimitri emerged seconds later with the baby in his arms and Mary at his side. He was standing under his own power—only his own power. The sight of the fragile old man holding her child made Jocelyn wince. Mary could see Jocelyn through an open space in the crowd. She hiked up her shoulders. Jocelyn frowned and tipped her head at Dimitri. Mary stepped closer to her father and cupped her hand beneath the baby's rear.

"For all those who are not aware," Dimitri said. "This is my grand-daughter...Tana Marie. Tana is the only child of my dear departed son Mikhail, and my truly wondrous daughter-in-law Jocelyn. I could not be prouder to hold this little lady, particularly here in this city." He touched the baby's face. "I stand before you today to say that it is only youth that matters. Our progeny, they are our greatest gift. This child in particular, with her spectacular parentage." He kissed the baby on the head. "She could very well become the greatest of us all. I see something special in her eyes. It's indescribable to me. So fresh, so full of promise—the living embodiment of our future. I weep to be holding her in my arms. Such a lovely, beautiful child."

Dimitri's arms started to droop. Mary called his caregiver over and took the baby away from him. The nurse led Dimitri back inside while Mary escorted Tana over to her mother. The crowd parted as she crossed the street.

"I swear, I didn't know he was going to do that," Mary said. "I'd have stopped him if I had known."

Tana was passed from aunt to mother.

"It's fine." Jocelyn made sure the baby's blanket was snug. "He was right. Everything he said was right. Somehow, some way, that sneaky old bastard, he's always right."

Three Weeks Later

118

Leo was strapped into passenger harness number three.

"I hate to burst your bubble, Cam, but I just don't think this is such a good idea. They're not going to look kindly on you if you pull this kind of stunt."

"I don't care," Camden said.

The two men were seated side by side with their fellow Rangers as the spire they were in descended through the purple skies of Azur—Kroma's only other inhabitable moon.

"You *should* care," Leo said. "You really should. They could take away your command. What you're asking me to do completely disregards an order from a superior."

"That's the thing," Camden said. "I don't think there is anyone superior to me on that council. No one besides Dimitri, anyway."

"Let's say I agree with you. Orders are still orders, even when they come from such obvious inferiors."

Camden clacked his teeth. "If you're so into obeying orders now, then start by following mine. When this bucket sets down, I want you going out first. This is my decision, superseding the faulty decision-making procedure the morons on the Directorate took."

Camden grabbed hold of his knee and yelled out, "*Oww!* Did you all see that? I'm hurt. I'm not going to be able to walk."

"What's wrong?" Samuel asked from two seats down.

"I'm pretending to injure my knee, ya dope. Go back to sleep."

Leo exhaled. "Faking an injury is not going to fool anyone. And even if you weren't able to go, they'd still send out anyone else before they'd send me. That includes one of the newbies."

"I'm done arguing," Camden said as she shut his eyes. "You're going. That's final. I'll push you out if I have to."

"With that injured knee, I'd like to see you try."

Camden got serious. "I owe you, Leo. You rescued my son. And then you went and found us a construction site when no else could. We *all* owe you. And despite what one person on that asinine council thinks, you deserve all the credit for these last few weeks. For that reason, in my infinite wisdom, I'm going to give that to you. Mikhail was first on Verdan. You will be first on Azur. It's the way it should be." He raised his hands high. "So proclaims the mighty Camden Muran."

"Fine," Leo said. "But it's your neck that's going on the chopping block."

The voice of the pilot interrupted, informing the squad they were thirty seconds from touchdown. The ship began to steady.

"A little anarchy can be a good thing," Camden said. "Trust me on that."

"On philosophical matters, you're the last person I'd ever trust. But I will get out first."

"Good." Camden pushed himself back into his harness and attempted to wiggle himself to comfort. "Can you imagine what the reaction's going to be? Man, oh man, I wish I could be up there to watch. Heads are going to explode."

One Month Later

119

Mary placed her hand on her father's chest. He did not stir.

In one quick movement she knelt down near the nightstand and turned his head toward her. Dimitri's eyelids were open, and his mouth hung agape. In addition, there was a dank gray bile that had been expelled down his chin and beard. A full minute went by before Mary reached for her ear.

"Walter Stoddard, call," she said, and then gave the man the news.

Once their conversation had been disconnected, she stood back up and glanced out the window. Construction was commencing across the burgeoning city. Her face bore no grief, no trace of emotion. There was only the emptiness of the room, and the quiet reality of one man's passing.

Also by Arvin Loudermilk
IN A FLASH
VIGIL

For more info visit
arvinloudermilk.com

Printed in Great Britain
by Amazon

20943050R00275